CHERISHING YOU, CHERISHING ME

Tylor Paige

This book is dedicated to all my fellow PCOS Divas. It's okay to not be okay.

Chapter One

BEST I CAN DO

My husband decided that Blue's first birthday was the perfect day to talk to Cleo. He spent the entire morning excited and eager to get to the Andrews' home. His good mood didn't last long, and I watched my husband freaking out the entire party. He was practically sweating. He avoided being alone with Cleo every chance he got. When she came near, I watched him look around, panicking and flat out walking away towards someone else. He looked how I felt.

He was the one who even brought it up in the first place. It was the evening after we had found out that I couldn't carry a child. I had spent most of the day in bed, wallowing in self-pity. I locked the door, not even letting the dogs in. I needed to be alone. This was my problem, not his.

To give him credit, Mark did leave me alone for most of the day. I think he was just as devastated by the news as I was, if not more so. It had been him that had brought up having kids first and I was more or less just along for the ride. However, the longer it took to conceive the more anxious and excited I grew about the idea of a little Mark Junior or mini me.

Now I was unable to give my husband, the man who had and would do anything for me, the only thing he desired. He only wanted one thing from me, and I was unable to deliver. The diagnosis was earth crushing.

He understood I needed time to accept this on my own. When he finally did come into the bedroom, he sat down on the bed next to me and pushed my hair out of my face.

"Baby, talk to me," he said in a soothing voice. I ignored him. He stayed with me in the dark room, not saying another word until I looked up.

"How are you okay with this? This was it. We've tried everything, Mark. It's over. It's not going to happen!" I choked and he pulled me up. I started to sob into his chest.

"We haven't tried everything," he said. I stopped and looked up at him curiously. He gulped and looked away; his eyes guilty.

"What are you talking about?"

He then explained his grand idea. We spent the next month discussing it at length whenever we could. It was kind of hard when Derek was practically living with us now. I wasn't too keen on the idea at first, but the more he talked about it, the more the idea grew on me. It wasn't a terrible plan.

Finally, the day came where we decided we would just go for it. Baby Blue's birthday. I wanted to do it together, but Mark wanted to talk to Cleo in private. We had argued about that, but finally I relented. He had his reasons, and I accepted that. Everything was always different when it came to her.

It wasn't just me that was mildly jealous of her relationship with my spouse. I knew that Chase had fought with Adrian at least once about it, and Dita struggled with it as well when she dated Adrian before Chase. However, Cleo was so over the moon in love with Ethan I didn't worry. She wasn't taking Mark from me any time soon. That adorable goof was only mine.

Blue's birthday came and went. Mark told me that this was the day he wanted to talk to her, but then he used Rocky, Adrian and Chase's son as an excuse not to go too far. Chase couldn't make it to the party today because he had radiation for his brain tumor. Adrian wasn't used to taking Rocky by himself just yet. He was barely two months old.

It was kind of crazy to think back to this time last year. Our little band family was growing so fast. The only ones that had children were Cleo and Ethan, and Mark and I were the only married couple. Now Derek was the only single one here, and we were the only childless couple. I watched Adrian take Rocky from Mark to go change him. I never would have imagined Mr. fast and loose would settle down and become a father.

Earlier this year, Adrian met Chase Wilson. They fell hard and fast for each other. Chase told Adrian he was dying from cancer pretty quickly into their relationship. Adrian, being well- Adrian decided that he was going to make the rest of his time here memorable.

We spent the rest of the year traveling the country, doing all sorts of fun things that we had all wanted to do before we die. Chase was so kind and such a giver. He didn't want the spotlight ever on him. That was how we got our dogs, Beau and Bonnie. It was great. Adrian was happy, Cleo and Ethan weren't fighting anymore. Mark and I were in a good place and Derek was doing Derek. The only dark spot in our lives was the fact that one day Chase would be gone.

However, everything changed when Duchess, Ethan's ex-girlfriend decided to try to kill Chase. I guess in her defense I don't think she was in the neighborhood looking for Chase, but she spotted one of the group and went for it. He was crossing the street and she floored her bright yellow Jaguar; but she missed her target.

Derek had been walking to Chase and Adrian's apartment. He saw the car and jumped into the street, shoving Chase and

Chester, their dog, out of the way. Chase was okay, but Derek had a punctured lung and both of his legs were broken.

According to Adrian, that near-death experience made Chase change his mind about not getting treatment for his tumor. That and the fact that he unknowingly fathered a child and the biological mother was dead.

The whole situation was confusing at first, but when things settled down, they were able to get more information and then explain things to us. Apparently a very successful lawyer had decided she was ready to be a parent. However, she couldn't carry a baby and had no man in her life to father the child. She went to a sperm bank and decided Chase's number was the winner. She hired a surrogate and everything was going as planned until the biological mother passed away suddenly.

The sperm bank decided to release the information to the surrogate in hopes that perhaps Chase would be interested in taking him so he wouldn't be thrown in foster care. Of course, Chase wanted him. That was the kind of man Chase was. They brought him home the day after he was born and that's how little Rocky Wilson came to join our family, and how we got the idea for what we wanted to do.

I think it was really overwhelming at first for them, under-standably. Going from two laid back guys to raising a newborn was definitely a hard transition. They had to learn how to change diapers, prepare bottles, and everything else that came with raising a child. I think Adrian struggled more than Chase did though.

"I have to work with two different pooping schedules now. Between feeding Chester and Rocky, I don't have time to feed myself," he joked, but the bags under his eyes told us that he missed those mid-day naps.

They had help though. Cleo and I were more than happy to help furnish little Rocky's room and have babysat once or twice to give them a break. I certainly didn't mind, that little boy was an angel. I would babysit more, but Cleo kind of claimed dibs on him. She was so excited for a friend of hers to have a baby. When she wasn't holding her own baby, she had Rocky in her arms.

Sometimes when they didn't know I was watching I saw how Mark watched her with all of the children. Wonder, awe, and adoration filled his eyes. If all of the other men in her life didn't do the same, I'd be worried or jealous, but I could never be. Much like on stage, Cleo stole the spotlight wherever she went. I don't think she could help it, that's just how things were. That wasn't going to change.

Not that I wanted it to. One of the first things Mark told me when we first started dating was how close him and his bandmates were. I think his exact words were, "We're all really close. Cleo lives in Michigan, but she's still a big part of my life. I'm going to tell you right now, if you can't handle that then this isn't going to work."

I'm not gonna lie, I didn't really know how to process what he had said. I didn't really understand at first. Like, what was he trying to tell me? I still didn't fully understand until he brought me to visit her and his family right before we got married.

When he called her to schedule a dinner with us, she was hesitant. Mark was so excited to see her. We had spent an afternoon with his parents, but he had marked out an entire weekend to see her and the twins.

She came to dinner without Chris, her husband at the time. She was mousy and didn't talk much about her current life. It was that night that I realized what Mark had meant. The conversation, despite Cleo trying to include me as much as she could, always turned into the two of them sharing inside jokes and reliving memories from their time on the road. I thought if anything I would be offended by how Cleo acted around Mark, but it was actually the other way around.

When Mark, or any of the other guys, saw Cleo their eyes would light up and their energy around them would change. They all became kids again and I swear if she asked them to carry her room to room and feed her grapes while she sunbathed, they would. The good thing was that Cleo was such a kind soul, she never used their affection to her advantage. Cleo helped me get over my hang ups about Cleo.

She was there for them just as much as they were there for her. They all would drop everything for each other. When Cleo's ex husband beat her to a pulp, Adrian called Mark and that night him and Derek took a red eye flight out. We were having dinner and he literally left me sitting at the table to finish eating alone.

But then when Chase and Derek's accident happened, she was the first one in the car to the hospital. She was there for them every step of the way. She took Rocky when they needed it or ordered dinner for them if they were too tired to cook. When Derek was ready to leave the hospital, she was the one to go get him. Despite her tiny size, she helped get him in the car and put his wheelchair in the back. That was no easy feat considering both of Derek's legs are in casts.

Our constantly growing group sat in the Andrews' backyard having some drinks and talking about the days event's. Cleo reached for Ethan's hand. He looked over at her with such love in his eyes.

"I can't believe we have a one year old. It feels like just yesterday I was going into labor with him," she mused. He chuckled.

"You think that's nuts. Try showing up one day and discovering you have two five-year-old twins," he said in a joking tone, but Cleo immediately glared at him. He put his hands up and tried playing it off, but then apologized quickly. Despite it all working out in the end, I know Cleo would always feel guilty for hiding the truth about the twins from him for so long.

There was an uncomfortable pause before Mark slammed a hand on the glass table.

"Now that your paternity leave is up and Derek's getting his casts off next week, when are we getting back to work?" Cleo pursed her lips in thought.

"Mmm. I guess I'm ready whenever you guys are. Sam said the shows went well, so I think he's ready for us to get back in the game."

They really were dedicated. Right before the accident they had scheduled a few shows to see the reception they'd get. Luckily, they were close enough to home that they could be home either that same night or the next day.

They talked about canceling the gigs at first. Adrian didn't want to leave Chase alone with the baby, and Derek was in a wheelchair. Chase however, insisted that he could do it and Derek was more than happy to figure out how to play sitting down. I think it actually helped their reputation. Nothing was going to keep them down, and the fans saw it.

"Can I still sit down to play? I've grown accustomed to a certain way of life," Derek joked. Everyone shot him dirty looks. Despite him having brownie points for saving Chase's life, he was still annoying.

"Keep it up and I'm going to make you play with me singing on your shoulders the whole set," Cleo teased. Derek raised his eyebrows and opened his mouth to say something dirty but the death glare he got from Cleo's husband made him shut it quickly.

The party ended when Blue fell asleep in his grandmother's arms after eating his cake. Cleo and Ethan thanked everyone for coming and insisted they didn't need anymore help cleaning up, so we took our leave.

On the way home Mark apologized to me for not saying anything.

"Mark, it's fine. It can wait. It was a good day. We didn't need to ruin it with our problems."

"Don't say it like that. You say problem like its this big, bad thing," he grumbled.

"What would you call it?"

"I don't know, issue? I don't like to think of it as a negative thing. We have to think positive. It's all going to work out."

I didn't say anything. He was too positive that this would pan out. We had to consider the fact that she might say no. It was a huge thing to ask and we couldn't hold it against her if she didn't want to do it. I didn't bother telling him this though, he had heard it a thousand times over the last month. He was just refusing to believe that she would say no.

I took the dogs out and then headed to bed early. It had been a long day. Right when I was walking upstairs to our room, I heard the front door open and knew that Derek was probably here. Adrian must have dropped him off. I figured he wouldn't be here tonight, but he was so erratic with his life that who really knew anymore what he was doing. That wheelchair didn't slow him down one bit.

I heard him and Mark talking. As I reached the landing my husband shouted up.

"I'm gonna chill down here for awhile. Derek brought over Adrian's console. We're gonna play some games." I paused and looked over the railing. My handsome husband was looking up at me with a half smile.

"Alright, but I'm starting that movie whether you're in here or not." He chuckled and blew me a quick kiss. I blew one back and followed the dogs into my bedroom.

That night I went to sleep exhausted, thinking about everything missing from my life. It was insane a little to think about. When I had first met Mark, I was still traveling with my theatre troupe. I wasn't interested in marriage, kids, or staying in one place even. I was living the life I wanted and had nothing grounding me to one place.

Now, barely three years later I was a totally different person. Besides the Rocky Horror Picture Show, I hadn't performed in years. I missed dressing up in costumes and wigs and going out on stage to play a goofy character for a few hours. I missed it, yet if I had the opportunity, I wouldn't do it again.

I wasn't a great actor. It was mostly for fun. I had never been in an arena like my husband had played. We never traveled on a fancy, luxury tour bus, or played sold out venues. There weren't any strict rules or big executives and agents breathing down our backs to do this or that. We were free.

We did what we wanted, when we wanted. Most of our traveling happened in large, renovated vans. Our only contracts we signed were for no longer than a month's time. We came and went and never looked back. Sure, we were poor, but we were happy. I tried explaining that to Mark once but he just simply didn't understand. Money wasn't everything.

I woke up the next morning to only Beau and Bonnie sharing my bed. I rolled my eyes, knowing that most likely I would go downstairs and find Mark and Derek slumped in recliners, dead asleep with controllers in their hands and headsets still on their heads. Sure enough, when I stepped into the den I was right.

Not feeling the need to disturb them I went about my morning. I fed the dogs, ate some yogurt and went for a walk. Despite my pound puppies being an older couple, they still loved taking walks. It was a nice, quiet morning. I cherished it, knowing that these came too far and few in between.

By the time I got home Mark had stirred. I found him in the kitchen, scrounging for something to eat. He didn't cook much. He had been learning to grill and enjoyed that. He was so used to quick, easy tour bus cooking that if it wasn't ramen or canned ravioli, he was clueless about how to make it, as were his bandmates.

"Hey babe, did you already eat? I could go for some oatmeal. Maybe with the cinnamon stuff you put in it?" He said, opening and shutting cupboards.

"I already ate, sorry." I leaned over and kissed his cheek before hurrying out to find something else to do. Now that the band would be back to the grind, I had to start getting used to doing things solo again. It was so nice having him home but having him rehearse nonstop meant that a tour was coming and then I'd be completely on my lonesome again.

Well not completely alone. Ethan and Chase would be home with the kids. I didn't have much in common with them, but I could always spend time with Dallas, Jimmy, Blue, and Rocky.

The twins had shown some interest in theatre after seeing the old movies from when the band did musicals. I had taken them to one of the local theaters I had performed with once or twice. They found a place for them in their production and had seemed to enjoy it. Maybe I should see if they wanted to do it again.

I went to the den and saw that Derek had moved to the couch and was curled up in a little ball trying to get back to sleep. With a sigh I went to the closet and grabbed a blanket to throw over him. He snuggled up in it and was back out in minutes.

Mark came out of the kitchen munching on a piece of toast. He tipped it at me and gave me a half-hearted smile. He was trying to guilt trip me, but it wasn't happening.

"You're a big boy, you can learn to make oatmeal," I teased. He pouted, giving me puppy dog eyes and a big pouty lip.

"Yeah but you make it so much better than I ever could," he whined, coming to kiss me. I kissed him back quickly but didn't budge.

"What's the plan for today?" he asked me, following me around the house. I went upstairs and back into our bedroom. We had a master bath connected to our room. I went straight to the bathroom and turned on the shower. Lifting my shirt up, I grabbed a towel. I glanced at him and saw him eyeing me intently. He raised an eyebrow at me and grinned wildly.

"I could go for a rinse," he said stepping forward. I smirked and shook my head.

"I'm taking a quick shower and then maybe heading over to see if the twins want to check out the theatre again."

"I could be quick," he pleaded, wrapping his arms around me and kissing my neck. His beard scratched my skin in the most arousing way. I groaned and pushed him away gently.

"Not this time. I'm still feeling a little stiff from sleeping," I said. He wiggled his eyebrows at me.

"I'm a little stiff too," we laughed, and he plopped himself down on the counter while I showered.

"I could do it today. Derek's probably sleeping in. Its our day off so Adrian won't even answer his phone let alone stop by."

"You could. Have you figured out how you want to do it? Maybe you could take her out for lunch, have a little one on one time before you just blurt it out."

"Why not? I don't think it will make it any easier. Hey Cleo, do you want some dessert and to host our unborn child in your stomach for a few months?"

I stepped out of the shower and wrapped a towel around myself. Scowling I turned to him. He flinched and looked away.

"Don't you dare say it like that. I'll kill you!" I laughed. He gave me that cheesy grin that I fell in love with and my stomach relaxed.

"You know I won't," he leapt off the counter and came to

hug me. I leaned into his chest and he kissed the top of my wet head.

"I'm sure I'll figure it out when I get there. I'll make it so she can't say no." I looked up at him and he laughed.

"I'll quit the band."

I smacked his chest and he burst into laughter. We both knew that wouldn't happen. The band was his life. His everything. Plus, you could replace the drummer.

We drove over to the giant house together. Mark was nervous. His leg was shaking wildly, and he was drumming his hands on his lap. He tried to play it off, but I could tell he was beginning to freak out.

"Mark, we don't have to do this. This was what you wanted, and I'll be okay if you decide you don't want to anymore," I said gently. I took his hand while I drove, and he stopped drumming.

"I know. I love you," he said. "I want more than anything to be a parent with you. I would give up everything to make that happen. You keep saying it's my choice but it's really not. You will be an amazing mom, and I have to make that happen."

"And what happens if she says no? I don't feel comfortable looking for a stranger to do it."

"She's not going to say no, I'm telling you," he told me again with a finality that ended the conversation. We pulled into the gates and parked the car. Tabatha, the kids' nanny, opened the door holding Blue. She told us that both Ethan and Cleo were in Ethan's home office.

"Where are the twins?" I asked her.

"They are actually with their Uncle Eric. He took them for ice cream and lunch. He's leaving tomorrow and wanted to see them before he left." I frowned. Well, now what do I do? I glanced at Mark. His face was pale. He was almost shaking. This was a mistake. If he was that worried about it then he shouldn't even ask. We both knew it was too big a thing to ask someone. I didn't know why he kept pushing it so much.

Before I could say or do anything, he grabbed my hand and pulled me down the hallway to Ethan's office. I tried to pull away, but he held me tight. He threw open the door and without hesitating he belted it out.

"Renee and I want you to have our baby!"

I had never been more embarrassed in my life. It was like all the air had been ripped out of the room. No one was speaking. Everyone was staring with our eyes wide and mouths open at Mark. Ethan was the first one to speak.

"What?"

Mark's breathing was shallow, his chest rising and falling heavily. I heard him gulp when he moved further into the room. I groaned inwardly as I followed him inside. Ethan sat at the desk while Cleo stood next to him. We sat in front of them like school children being reprimanded by the principal.

"We can't have-" Mark started and I put my hand up and then on his thigh to calm him and stop him from talking.

"I can't carry a child. My uterus is all sorts of messed up. We have tried everything we could to get pregnant. I will never be able to do it. The only way for us to become parents is to get a surrogate to carry it. Mark and I wanted to see if you, Cleo, would do it."

Cleo and Ethan both answered at the same time, but with two different answers.

"Yes!" Cleo exclaimed.

"No." Ethan said.

Once again silence filled the room. Mark began squeezing my hand. I squeezed it right back. This was it. There was no going back.

Cleo looked at her husband blankly.

"Why no? It's not your choice."

Ethan stood up. "Yeah, but I would have to deal with it the

whole time. That and we couldn't have-," he glanced at us and I urged my husband to stand up.

"We'll just give you the room," I said, feeling the heat rising to my face. We practically ran out.

Sitting in the living room we could hear them shouting at each other. We sat in cold, awkward silence on the couch.

"They could still have sex, can't they?" Mark asked suddenly.

"I don't see why not. Probably not until she is for sure pregnant. But once we know it took there really is no reason her and Ethan couldn't."

A moment later we heard the door open and Cleo came into the living room. Her face was blank.

"Could we see you guys in the office again?" We stood up and followed her back. Ethan's arms were crossed and he looked furious. I tried not to make eye contact with him, but I got the feeling it wasn't me he was mad at.

We sat back in our original chairs while Ethan leaned against the wall. Cleo sat down on the front edge of the desk. Her short legs swung back and forth. This was it. My heart was pounding in my chest. These two people determined whether we could have a child or not.

"So, there is no other way for you to have a baby," Cleo clarified. I shook my head.

"What about adoption. There's plenty of kids wanting homes," Ethan snarled. I turned to look at him.

"We have been thinking about that. If you don't want to, then that will probably be our last resort," I said rather matter of factly. He snorted.

"Are you gonna be the one taking her to all of her appointments? Who's gonna get up in the middle of the night because she wants those little chocolate oranges that you can only get at Christmas, but there is a holiday store an hour away that if you go right now you can get some before they close?" Ethan kicked off the wall and moved closer to us.

"Her being pregnant means she'll be nauseous and not fit to work like she planned, and what happens if something happens with one of our kids and she can't get to them in time because she's waddling and carrying an extra fifty pounds? We're just getting a routine down and now you want to throw a wrench in the kink just because you want a baby?" Ethan shouted at us, but he wasn't looking at me. He was shouting straight at Mark.

Mark was shrinking into his seat. He was usually a hot head and snapped whenever someone looked at him wrong, but today he was a small child. He couldn't argue with Ethan.

Cleo grabbed her husband's shirt collar and forced him to turn to her. His cold blue eyes were glaring daggers at her, but her hard brown ones were enough to kill. He softened, crossed his arms, and shut his mouth. Cleo turned back to us.

"What if we gave you fifty thousand dollars?" Mark blurted. I whipped my head around to stare at him. Did he just offer her money? Oh my God! This was mortifying. I put my head in my hands. This was a disaster.

"Do you really think money is the issue?" Ethan smirked.

"Well if she can't work," Mark said meekly.

"Mark. I don't want your money," Cleo said softly. She looked at me with such pity. I needed to leave the room. I stood up and excused myself, shutting the door quietly.

Walking down the hall I saw Tabatha. I raised my arms for her to hand me little baby Blue. She seemed very grateful for the break. I took him to the living room and bounced him lightly on my lap.

He was so adorable. I didn't know the twins when they were babies, but I assumed they were just as gorgeous as he was. He was of course, named after his bright eyes. The eyes partnered with his pale skin, jet black hair, and of course his parent's perfect genes made for one attractive child. He was going to be a heartbreaker when he was older. Much like his older siblings.

They were still young, only seven, but they were the full package. Attractive, smart, and talented. I could only imagine what this little one would grow up to be.

Blue coo'd and giggled at me while I made silly faces at him. I felt the tears beginning to well up in my eyes, but I forced myself to keep them there. I couldn't let it get to me. This was Mark's idea. I hadn't wanted it in the first place. I told him she would probably say no. It wasn't fair of us to ask her to halt her life in order for us to start ours. I can't believe we really asked.

I realized that they were no longer shouting in the office. I couldn't decide if that was a good thing or a bad thing. I shouldn't have gotten my hopes up. It just wasn't in the cards. We could adopt.

Just then the front doors burst open and the twins came running into the house. They came into the living room and shouted at me excitedly. I chuckled. Jimmy was wearing a dark pink princess dress and long cone shaped hat with the long tulle cascading down, while her twin brother Dallas had his face painted to look like a skeleton. I wondered for a moment if he had done it or had someone help him. If he hadn't, then it was pretty impressive.

I asked him and he beamed. "Tabatha helped a little today, but I did a lot of it by myself. Do you like it?"

"I love it. Maybe you can do my makeup sometime?" I asked and his face turned serious.

"Maybe. I don't really do girl makeup," he said.

"I wouldn't mind looking like a skeleton," I told him, and he lit up.

"Dal, we need to put our stuff away and go practice. We are

way behind on our sight reading," Jimmy whined. He rolled his eyes and turned back to her.

"Fine. Let's go." He started out of the room and then turned back to look at me.

"If you're still here after dinner I can do your face. We don't have to practice or do schoolwork after dinner," he explained. I nodded, not bothering to explain that we probably wouldn't be here for dinner. Hell, we might not be around for the next few weeks. Coming back after today would be so mortifying. I can't believe he just shouted it out like that. It was like my worst nightmare come to life.

They had been in that office for well over an hour. Finally, I heard the door click open and the shuffle of a number of people. They weren't talking, so it was safe to assume that was their answer. They had decided, and that was that. We couldn't force them into it. Honestly it was wrong for us to have even asked.

The three of them entered the room and stood in front of the door. Setting the baby down, I looked up at all of them. Cleo's face held no emotion whatsoever. Ethan's arms were crossed and in a permanent scowl. And then I looked into my husbands face and discovered a new kind of hope. He was smiling. He spoke first.

"Cleo is going to be our surrogate. Under one condition," he was hesitant at that last part. I stood up and ran to her. Picking her tiny frame up I squeezed her tight and thanked her over and over and over. She laughed and asked me to put her down. When I had a moment to process the news, I looked back at them.

"What's the condition?" Mark looked away guiltily, and I quickly looked towards Cleo. She was grinning ear to ear.

"I get to name it."

Chapter Two

WE'LL BE A DREAM

IT TOOK me a moment to process everything. I had to sit down. Cleo came and plopped down next to me and took my hands. I looked at her and she was grinning ear to ear.

"Renee, I can't tell you how honored I am that you would consider me for something so important. I can't wait to help you start a family. It's going to be so much fun!" She said.

"Fun? You think being pregnant is fun?" I asked skeptically. She rolled her eyes and sighed deeply.

"No, and I don't even want to think about going through labor again, but that's just a tiny detail. What's gonna be fun is the gender reveal party, the baby shower, and everything in between! You get to make a nursery and we are going to go shopping for everything. I am going to make sure you don't miss out on any of the great things that comes with expecting a baby."

I hugged her tightly again and despite me trying to hold it in, I began crying. "Oh! Don't start crying, you'll make me cry!" She sniffled, making me chuckle and of course, making me cry harder. I pulled away and she began rubbing my back to try calm me down.

"Thank you so much Cleo," was all I could muster.

"Babe, you wanna go? We probably gotta go make some calls. Get some appointments scheduled," Mark said from the doorway. I looked up to see him standing there uncomfortably. I glanced at Ethan who, although not happy, he wasn't furious anymore. Cleo's mind was made up. I stood up and after giving her another giant hug, followed Mark out.

Once we were in the car, I began bombarding him with questions. "What happened in there? How badly did Ethan flip out? Was it a negotiation of some sort?" Mark chuckled and took my hand.

"Sort of. Ethan was pissed. He was still yelling at me, but eventually Cleo put him in his place. She told him that she was doing it whether he wanted to be here for it or not. He sat down and turned his seat around to pout for awhile.

When he stopped yelling, we were able to actually talk. She asked what exactly was going on. I told her about your medical diagnosis and that we've already tried all the medicines, and nothing has worked. She thought about it for a minute and then said she'd do it again. Ethan then whipped around and started complaining again.

I assured him that we'd be paying all of her medical bills and anything else she needed we'd be there. Midnight food runs, foot massages, buying her maternity clothes. Anything she needs we'll get.

Then she got the genius idea of naming the baby. That's what took so long. We argued for a bit, but I didn't really have a leg to stand on."

I gulped. That was an issue. We had names picked out years ago before we realized getting pregnant wasn't an option.

"I guess that means no Pearl," I sighed.

"Or Oliver."

There was a pause while we let that sink in. I couldn't even begin to imagine what she'd come up with. Her own kid's names weren't exactly normal.

"They aren't that bad," Mark argued.

"Yeah, but they aren't something you can get a day job with. Those kids are destined to be musicians. I don't want to force something on my child."

"She'll pick something normal," he said hesitantly. We both knew that he couldn't know that for sure.

Walking into the house we saw Derek was just waking up. He was sitting in his boxers, smoking a cigarette and petting Duchess. He glanced up from the TV when we came in.

"What's up, losers?"

I rolled my eyes and went upstairs to nap. I couldn't deal with Derek's idiocy right now. A few hours later I dragged my feet downstairs. I went to sit with the guys when my phone started ringing. I answered it and was surprised to hear Jimmy's little voice on the other line.

"Aunt Renee?"

"Hey Jimmy, what are you up to?" I asked.

"Nothing, we just had dinner."

"Oh, that's nice. Is there something you called for?"

"Oh yeah! My friend at school Arielle told me that the theatre is doing Peter Pan. Can you take me and Dallas to audition?"

"Of course! I'd love to. That sounds like so much fun, Jimmy. When are they?"

"Tomorrow after school."

"Alright, I'll come and get you and take you. I can't wait. I gotta go, I'll see you tomorrow okay?"

"Thank you so much Aunt Renee! Okay, I gotta go tell Dallas. Bye." She hung up and I explained to the guys what the phone call was about. They were a few cans into a case of beer and didn't take their eyes off their video game. I sighed and decided to take the dogs and relax in my room for the rest of the night.

The next day Mark called and made us an appointment with the fertility specialist. Cleo would have to do a check up and they still need to take my eggs and Mark's sperm. I was still in shock at how quickly she agreed to do it. The doctor made it sound like as long as everything was fine with Cleo, everything would go fairly quick.

In the afternoon I stopped over to grab the twins for their audition. I stopped by the Andrews' home studio slash rehearsal room. They took a small smoke break. Mark wiped the sweat off his brow and tried to wipe it on me.

"Gross! Where's your shirt?" I pulled away from his hug. He laughed and grabbed his t-shirt to wipe himself off.

"Sorry babe. You here to grab the twins?" I nodded and, before I could add more, they came running in, backpacks still on. They stared up at me with their bright electric blue eyes and then realization hit them. They started jumping up and down excitedly. Jimmy grabbed me by the hand and pulled me out of the room.

"Bye mom. Bye everyone. We're going to go audition for Peter Pan," she called. They wished them good luck. I think I even heard Adrian shout for them to break a leg.

"What parts are you interested in?" I asked them as I drove.

"I liked being a fish last time," Dallas commented.

"Me too, and painting. That was fun." Jimmy added. I laughed. It was good that they liked small roles. You had to start from the bottom. I had to. I remembered my first role. I was a pilgrim at a thanksgiving play. I was in the sixth grade. It was small, but it sparked a fire in me. I loved the theatre. I smiled, realizing that our child would have art in their bones. He or she would be born with a love for the stage.

When we got to the theater, memories of the last show I performed in swept quickly over me. The Rocky Horror Picture

Show. It was so much fun being back with some of my old cast mates. I was surprised when they came back into town and had decided to set up a semi permanent residence here. They offered me a spot in their first show without hesitation. I always had a home with these people.

Oddly enough we were greeted by the very person who had greeted me way back when. Janice Richards. She was an older woman, even older now. She was just as I had remembered, short, giant glasses, and fire red hair. Only now, there were quite a few grays mixed in.

"Renee! It's been too long! Come in, come in," she ushered us inside. She directed the twins towards all the other excited, giggling children. I stayed back to chat with my old friend.

"How have you been Janice?" She smiled wide and hugged me.

"I've been good, joints are a little stiffer than they used to be, but it's nice to be staying in one place now."

"I know, I was surprised when I heard the news. I never thought any of you would grow roots."

She shrugged.

"Well, when it's time it's time. Plus, when Penny passed away, she left all of her money to the group. We voted and decided to buy a home base. We got one hell of a deal on this place," she explained. I frowned. Penny was the oldest member of our troupe, even ten years ago. She had retired, her husband was gone and the kids were out of the house, so she joined the theatre and spent the rest of her life traveling the country.

"That was so sweet of her. Well, I'm glad you settled in L.A. Are you helping with the show? My niece and nephew are so excited to audition."

"I'm directing this show." She was grinning ear to ear.

"Oh? I hadn't realized you started directing."

"I started a few years back. This will be my eighth production as director," she turned towards the children, nodding at the two I brought with me.

"How old are they?" She asked.

"Seven," I told her. She raised an eyebrow.

"Both of them? Twins?" I nodded.

"Well, I think we've found their roles."

Sure enough, the twins called me right after school on Friday to shout at me that they had been chosen to play the twins in Peter's lost boys tribe.

"That is awesome guys! You want to go get some ice cream?" Their shouts turned into screams and I had to pull the phone away from my face. Cleo's voice came through the phone.

"Hey Cleo, I'm gonna swing over and take the kids out for ice cream," I told her.

When I got there the twins were waiting for me at the door. The entire trip they talked non-stop.

"Do you want to come with us to our first rehearsal Aunt Renee?" Dallas asked as we sat down at a picnic table to eat our cold treat.

"I don't think Uncle Mark and I are doing anything. Sure, I can do that."

"It's going to be so much fun! I'm the only girl in the lost boys," Jimmy bragged. I smiled; she was so proud to be one of the boys. I wondered if she'd still feel that way in ten years. When we returned Cleo stopped me. I smiled but she didn't return it.

"The doctor's appointment is next week."

I gulped, wondering where this was going.

"I'm not gonna lie, I'm a little nervous." She crossed her arms.

"Are you having second thoughts?" I asked her and she shook her head furiously.

"No, no its not that. It's just weird that I'm going to go into a doctor's office and coming out pregnant. It's a bizarre concept I guess."

"Well this is just the first appointment, we're not quite to that part yet," I reminded her. "You're amazing for doing this for us," I added. She grinned ear to ear.

"I know," she giggled, then grew serious again. "It will be so worth it in the end to see you two become parents." I hugged her tightly and went home to find my husband and Derek brushing and putting bows in their pets' hair.

"What are you doing to poor Beau?" I ran and picked up my dog. Mark shrugged and grabbed Bonnie to start grooming her instead. I don't know what happened at that pet shelter, but something about that cat brought something out in Derek. He took that huge fluffy cat out of that place and has treated her like she really was a member of royalty. Duchess, much like the celebrity with the same name, was spoiled rotten.

"Big D needed new bows, so I thought our dogs would like them too," Mark shrugged. I rolled my eyes and left them to it.

The next week the three of us went to the doctors. Mark stayed in the lobby while I went in with her. I hadn't planned on going in with her, but at the last minute she asked me to.

The doctor assessed her quickly and within the hour determined that she was a perfect fit for surrogacy. I think we both squealed excitedly when she came back into the room all smiles.

"Our next step is to put Cleo on fertility medication, just to boost the chances. We'll keep you on that for about a month," she turned from Cleo to face me. "During that time, we'll retrieve your eggs and collect your husband's sperm and then, after the month is up, we'll do the insemination," she explained. Cleo reached for my hand and squeezed.

"Then what? I'll be pregnant?"

The doctor gave us a tight smile.

"Fingers crossed. Based on your health, there isn't really any reason it shouldn't, but there is always a chance it won't work. Just stay positive."

She left us so Cleo could get dressed. When we left the doctors office we went straight to the pharmacy and got her prescription. By the time we got back to her place it was time to take the twins to rehearsal.

As soon as we were parked, they leapt out to join their new friends. I walked into the building at a much slower pace. I stopped in the lobby to grab a cup of coffee from the little pot they keep on for the parents and other adult volunteers. I chatted with a few of my old friends, Erin and Stacie. Stacie was doing costumes and Erin was on props.

Way back when, the three of us were all young and stupid and always together. We didn't go anywhere without each other. It was a shame I hadn't kept in touch with them. It made me sad, but it felt like I hadn't missed a beat when I saw them now.

"So, after this production we are going to be doing some adult shows. Are you gonna join us?" Erin asked excitedly. I thought about it. Being here with all of my old friends was nice. Sometimes I didn't feel completely in on the jokes and stories with Mark's friends. They always tried to include me, Ethan, and now Chase, but no one could really fully be a part of the group. It would be nice to have my own friends again.

"Maybe. My schedule can be pretty heavy sometimes," I said lamely. Stacie frowned and then gave Erin an eye roll.

"Yeah, following your rock star husband across the country?" She smirked.

"Actually, I don't go with him when he tours."

"So, you should have nothing but time! Come on Renee, we've missed you. You know you miss us too," she teased. They bumped their heads together and gave me puppy dog eyes and pouty lips. I sighed and then relented.

"Okay, maybe one show. What are you guys doing this season?"

Stacie hurried behind the counter I was leaning against and began rummaging through some drawers. After a moment she produced a piece of paper with the list of shows. She handed it to me, and I began reading the list. Jeez, they really didn't slow down.

"Is that," I pointed to the next production after this one. "like the movie? With Parker Posey?" I asked. They both had matching sly smiles on their faces.

"That was the one I submitted when we were selecting this season. 'The House of Yes'," Stacie laughed. I rolled my eyes. Of course it was her.

"You should go out for it! I'll cast you. I'm directing it," she said. Erin gave her a playful smack on the shoulder.

"That's not fair, I'm auditioning for that," Erin whined. Stacie winked at me and then gave her best friend a reassuring pat.

"Okay, I won't pick people yet. But seriously, if you don't get an acting part you should totally be my assistant. It'll be the three amigos all over again. Like old times." Remembering how fun it used to be sold me on the idea.

"Okay, fine. I'll do it. Assistant could be fun," I relented.

After I finished my coffee, I went into the theater to see how the twins were doing. I leaned against the wall and my eyes went from them to the stage periodically. Those kids were destined for success. Everything they did they put their all in it. Their instruments, their sight reading, and now this. With genes like theirs though, how could they not be musical prodigies?

When I finally made it home that night, I mentioned the idea of doing another show to Mark. It was just the two of us today. Derek had gone over to Adrian's.

"That's great baby. I hate the idea of you being stuck here

while I'm with the band. You should have something you like doing too," he told me. He took a huge bite of his chicken parm and reached for my hand over the table.

"I can't wait to see you on stage again. Although, maybe a little less dry humping my friends this time?" I burst out in laughter.

During 'Rocky Horror' I had the pleasure of grabbing Chase out of the audience and taking his 'Rocky virginity'.

"I promise I'll refrain from humping any of your friends," I said, holding out my pinky to him to promise. I took a bite of my food and then I almost choked on my food when I remembered what play Stacie had picked. If it was anything like the movie, then it would definitely have some heat between the leads.

"Speaking of dry humping, you wouldn't believe what play Stacie is directing," I started and then explained what I knew about the show and how I volunteered to be the assistant. Mark laughed with me.

"Man, that's a name I haven't heard in a while. Is Erin still there too?"

I nodded and he shook his head. "They are nuts, but it sounds exactly like something she'd pick." He lifted his beer and we toasted to it. "Good luck with that one."

The following month flew by. Between taking the twins to rehearsal and making time to spend with Cleo and Mark separately, I barely had time for myself.

I didn't mind it though. It was kind of nice that Cleo was trying to make sure we went to dinner or lunch alone once a week.

"I feel like I barely know you sometimes. That needs to change," she told me once.

"Well your schedule is so full I understand it can be hard sometimes."

"Yeah, but it would be nice to have some girl friends.

When Adrian was dating Dita you guys got close and I was so jealous. It's hard though when I spend most of my time with your guys' spouses."

I frowned thinking about Dita. I loved spending time with her, but after she cheated on Adrian it would be kind of awkward to continue being friends. We didn't talk after that.

"I miss her sometimes," I mused, and Cleo's eyes hardened. She was very defensive of Adrian.

"I liked her too, but she crushed Adrian. He really liked her. I hope whoever he caught her with was worth it. Chase is so much better for him."

I nodded, understanding her harshness.

"So, the big day is next week. How are you feeling?" I asked, changing subjects. She shrugged.

"Okay. Ethan's finally calmed down and accepted it. For the most part. He's still upset that we'll have to abstain from sex for awhile. That and he says it's going to be weird if it moves when we do pick it back up," she rolled her eyes.

"Do you have a room for the nursery picked out yet?" She asked after we stopped laughing. I shook my head.

"No, we don't want to do anything baby related or tell anyone until we know for sure it took," I explained. She considered it for a minute and then nodded.

"Yeah, that makes sense. But we can't think negatively. It will take," she said fiercely.

The big day came too soon for me. Despite wanting to hold my own baby in my arms, it was still scary to think about what we were doing. They had retrieved my eggs a few days before. While I was in the room getting it done, Mark was across the hall taking care of his part.

He told me later that he was so embarrassed when he came out carrying the cup.

"I felt like everyone was staring at me," he said on the car ride home.

Cleo was the only one who needed to show up on the big day, but she asked me to go with her. Mark offered to join us, but I told him he didn't have to. He seemed relieved. When I made a joke about it, he agreed with me.

"I'm already pretty close to Cleo. I don't need to be that close," he smirked. I looked at him blankly.

"You realize you wouldn't be the one down - there, right?"

He blushed furiously and then glared at me.

"I knew that," he lied.

Despite still having some cramping from my own procedure I drove Cleo to her appointment. The appointment itself went pretty quick. She squeezed my hand for dear life the whole time, but it didn't take long for the doctor to sit up straight and announce that she was finished.

I took Cleo home and asked her if she wanted anything before I let her be. She had been quiet the whole ride home. She told me no and that she wanted to take a nap.

"I'm sorry, I just kind of want to rest," she said before I left.

I told Mark this when I got home and he furrowed his brow.

"I'm sure she's fine. It's probably just sinking in. I'll call her later."

Thankfully, Tabatha offered to take the twins to rehearsal today. I wasn't up for mindless chatter with the girls. I was too nervous. Of course, it would take a few weeks to see if she did get pregnant, but just the thought that it was official made my stomach spin.

That night Mark tried to cuddle up to me and I turned him down.

"Oh, come on, Renee. You're not in the mood?" He groaned. I turned around to look at him.

"I'm sorry, I just can't stop thinking about her."

"Whatever does it for you babe," he said, and he tried kissing my neck. I moved away.

"She regrets it."

He sighed and sat up. Turning the light on, he looked down at me. I sat up too.

"She does not regret it. I talked to her just a few hours ago. She's fine. You're stressing over nothing." I wanted to be reassured but I couldn't squash the uneasy feeling. With a deep sigh he turned the TV on and we watched TV until we fell asleep.

Halfway through the night I woke up to pee. Just as I was climbing back into bed, I saw my phone on the side table. A tiny blue light was flashing. It was a text message. Grounding the sleep from my eyes I grabbed it. The message was from Cleo.

Can you talk?

I looked at the time it was sent. It was barely an hour ago. I stepped out of the room and called her.

"Hey, do you want me to come over?" I asked when she answered. She answered in a quiet voice. It was as if she was whispering. I grabbed my keys and jumped in the car, still in my pj's. When I got to her house, she was sitting in her living room, her knees bunched up to her chin. The only light came from the TV. I sat down next to her and waited for her to speak.

"What are you gonna do if I don't get pregnant?" She asked me suddenly, not looking at me. She was staring blindly at the TV. A late night talk show was playing.

"I don't know. Probably think about adoption. Or you know, maybe this is our sign. Maybe children isn't in the cards," I said, trying to be gentle.

"I feel like your future is completely in my hands. I don't want to be the reason you don't get to be a mother. You'll be an amazing mom and I don't want to feel like I took that away from you," she said, finally looking at me. Her eyes were shiny.

I grabbed her and squeezed her tight. She sniffled. "Cleo, if you don't get pregnant, I will be fine. You have done everything you could. It wouldn't be your fault even a little. I would never hold that against you."

I rocked her while she cried softly. I felt guilty for putting all this pressure on her. After awhile she calmed down and pulled away. She wiped her eyes and forced a smile.

"I am going to will my body to make this work," she said, straightening. "Hell or high water, you are getting a baby," she declared. I chuckled and hugged her again.

"Sorry for asking you to come out," she said. I waved her off.

"Eh, it's no big deal. Why don't we have that girl time you're always asking about and have a sleepover?" She brightened. I looked at the clock, it was just after midnight.

"Do you have any popcorn? We can find some chick flicks on TV and eat snacks." She leapt up and hurried into the kitchen, returning a few minutes later with popcorn, cookies, and some pop. I laughed and she shrugged as she plopped down next to me. She opened the package of Oreos and popped one in her mouth. With a mouthful of cookie, she gave me a completely adorable, innocent look and spoke.

"What? I'm pregnant, I can eat what I want for the next nine months."

The following afternoon was filled with running errands and then taking the kids to rehearsal. On the way out Stacey stopped me and asked if I could help with painting the backdrops. I mentioned it to Mark and Derek when I finally got home.

"It will be fun. Afterwards we usually have a party," I added, trying to entice them. They both gave me looks telling me they'd rather swallow knives.

"None of that sounds fun," Derek said. "I'm busy this weekend anyways."

I smirked. "Doing what? Sitting on my couch, eating my food and sleeping til noon?" He glared at me. Picking up his beer he took a large gulp and then smirked.

"No. I'm going to be sitting on Adrian's couch, eating Adrian's food, and yes sleeping til noon. Thank you very much."

"That actually doesn't sound like such a bad plan," Mark teased me. When he saw I wasn't as amused as his partner in crime his face grew serious.

"If you want me to go I will. I'm sure it won't be as bad as it sounds." He reached for my hand across the table, stroking my knuckles. I smiled at him and softened. He winked at me, which caused Derek to groan loudly.

"Ugh, so now that you aren't trying to get pregnant are you guys going to stop with the constant PDA? You don't always have to be ready to go," he complained.

"Shut up," Mark said.

"We are not that bad. Cleo and Ethan are way worse," I defended. Derek nodded and grimaced.

"You're not lying there. Still, you two. I swear your sex noises have become my white noise. I can't sleep soundly anymore without hearing the distant sound of you two bumping uglies."

I tossed a french fry at him.

"You are disgusting."

"Why do you think I stay here more than I'm at Adrian's?"

"Because you don't want to hear him and Chase going at it?" Derek shook his head and rolled his eyes.

"Nah. I don't think they ever do it when I'm there. They are both secure in their sexuality, but I think they are still shy when it comes to that stuff. If they do anything, I never hear a peep."

I reached for my beer and giggled.

"Would you really want to though?"

Derek grimaced.

"Great, now that's an image I really didn't want in my head. Can we talk about something else? Anything else, please."

"Are you excited about getting your casts off next week?" I asked him and he gave me a shrug.

"Yes and no. I can't wait to really scratch these bad boys," he knocked on his casts. "But I will miss everyone wheeling me around and the chicks giving me that look," he wiggled his eyebrows and made a motion with his hand and mouth that made Mark clear his throat.

"So, you're going to Adrian's for the weekend or not?"

"I can. Why, what are you guys doing?"

I reached for Mark's hand again and squeezed. We looked into each other's eyes with obnoxious adoration.

"Oh nothing, just staring at each other and humping like bunnies," I said.

"My perfect weekend," Mark said.

"So how does it all work?" Derek cut back in. "Cleo's got your stuff inside her. How you gonna know if its your kid or another one of hers?"

"They aren't having sex until she knows she's pregnant. They stopped a few weeks ago," I explained. Guilt turned my stomach again.

"Oh, well that's why Ethan's been such a douche lately. I thought they were just fighting about Duchess or something."

I sat up straight.

"What did she do now? Have you heard anything yet about her trial?" Derek shook his head.

"Nothing that I know of. Of course she made bail. I don't think she can leave the country though. I'm waiting for her shave the head, attacking paparazzi meltdown. It's gotta be coming. Her book was pulled, she hit me with her freaking car, and despite that, Ethan hasn't run to her side."

Mark pulled on his shirt. "God that woman has some claws. I'm surprised my back isn't scarred from her crazy ass. Totally worth it though," he smirked.

Later in the evening Adrian came to visit. He brought Chase and tiny little Rocky. I took the baby as soon as they unbuckled him from his car seat. He was so adorable. There was no denying who his father was. He looked so much like Chase.

"Do you guys want ice cream?" I asked. Adrian said no but Chase thought about it for a moment and then nodded his head.

"I could go for some."

I had to give Rocky back to him while I got bowls and the ice cream out. Sitting two scoops of strawberry in front of him I traded Chase the ice cream for his son. It was insane how much he looked like Chase. I wondered for a moment if our child would look more like Mark or take after me.

"So, how's everything going?" I asked, shaking the thoughts away. He swallowed his bite and then smiled.

"Great actually. The doctors can already see a shrinkage in the tumor. They think another four months should do it."

"That's amazing!" He nodded and then made a weird face.

"What?"

"I- we, wanted to actually see if you could babysit on the days I go in for treatment. Now that they are going back to the studio full time Adrian can't really be there during the day with Rocky. He said that you used to nanny for Cleo."

I turned my head to look at the baby in my arms. He was smiling up at me, gently cooing. I kissed his chubby cheek and looked back at his father.

"I'd love that. He's such a sweet baby. Just give me a schedule."

That night in bed I told Mark about my babysitting Rocky and then I mentioned my musings from earlier that evening about our own baby. He chuckled and climbed into bed with me.

"Well if it's a girl I pray that she looks like you. I would not make a pretty lady."

"You think it will be a girl?" I asked. He gave me a blank look for a moment.

"Well right now its like a blueberry or something."

I snorted.

"Not even that. It's been a day. Give it a few weeks and then we can call it a blueberry." Mark's face turned serious.

"Don't mention that to her. Next thing you know we are bringing home little Blueberry Lacey."

"She wouldn't," I gasped.

"You never know with her," he chuckled.

Chapter Three

WAITING

DRIVING TO THE THEATRE SATURDAY, I found a 90's station and jammed to some boy bands and Britney. Mark never wanted to listen to pop music, so I took advantage of his absence today. I pulled in right next to Erin's car and hopped out.

It was only about 11, but when I stepped into the back where they were painting, I was handed a beer and paintbrush. I thanked Erin and saw that she wasn't going to move until I opened my drink. I grimaced but still popped the tab and took a long gulp. I had spent the night with Derek and Mark drinking and playing video games. The beer was helping the dull headache I had. The group let out a small cheer and everyone went back to business.

I looked around. There were only a handful of people here, all old friends. Erin, her husband Justin, Courtney, Brian, and Joe.

"Where's Stacie?" I asked Erin. She led me over to where they were painting what looked like the Darling's bedroom.

"Oh, she's running late. Her car stalled, so I think she's having Thomas pick her up."

"Thomas?" That name threw me off. I hadn't even thought about him in years. I had almost forgotten about him. Erin rolled her eyes and gave me a sly smile.

"Yes Thomas."

Someone turned on music and I relaxed as everyone got to work painting, building, and rigging the windows that Peter would burst through. I was directed to some paint and a blank wooden board. I zoned out easily with the simplicity of the job. About an hour later the back door opened. I turned and saw Stacie coming, lugging grocery bags.

"I got lunch, come and get it!" She shouted over the music. Erin lowered the stereo and we all stopped working. I wiped my hands on my pants and when I looked back up my heart stopped.

He looked just as I remembered him. Thomas Shane Reynolds. My first boyfriend, my first sexual partner, my first - love. I could feel my face heating up, so I turned away quickly, hoping he hadn't seen me. Of course, it wouldn't work that way for me.

"Renee? Is that your purple haired pigtails I see?" He walked over and gave me that smile I remembered all too well.

We had met when I was 16, him 17. Thomas had that easy, relaxed attractiveness. His face was chiseled, complete with chin dimple. His chestnut brown hair was longer now and looked so casually perfect. His hazel eyes were warm and genuine. Realizing I hadn't spoken yet I forced a smile and moved to hug him.

"Thomas! Wow, how have you been?" He even smelled familiar. We pulled away from each other and he brushed his hair back.

"Good. I don't ever change. How are you? Enjoying the red-carpet life?" He teased. I rolled my eyes and crossed my arms.

"Something like that. I hadn't realized you were still doing this," I commented, waving around to the the construction around us. He shrugged.

"It's in my blood." I motioned for him to come with me while we grabbed lunch with the others. It was true. Both of his parents were in the troupe.

"How are your folks?" I asked. We reached the table Stacie had put all the food on and grabbed a sandwich. She had grabbed some generic subs, little bags of chips, snack cakes, and more beer.

"Meredith and Paul are fine. Ronny got married, had a few kids. They decided to move in with them to be with the grandkids."

"Really?" I said, in shock. "I didn't think they'd ever give up the theatre." He shook his head.

"I think they still participate in a local where they're at. They live in Florida now," he shifted. "What about yourself? Any kiddos for you and your man?"

Thankfully, I was chewing, so I had time to think. Did I tell people? Was it too soon? Why was I so embarrassed? I shook my head.

"Nah, I don't think that's our thing. He travels so much," I said lamely, using the excuse I had been using for years.

"I remember once upon a time you were a traveler too," he wiggled his eyebrows suggestively. I blushed. Yeah, you were the reason I did it.

He apologized quickly. "Sorry, I don't mean to bring up old stuff. So, what brings you back?" He smiled again.

"My niece and nephew are in the show. They are playing the twins in the lost boys tribe," I boasted.

"Oh nice. Good to see kids getting into the theatre so young." We tossed our trash and started walking.

"Where do they have you at? I bet you could use some help," he winked. I rolled my eyes but still gave him a paint-brush to help me.

I picked up my own brush and started showing him what I had been doing before we took our lunch break. As I explained what they wanted, Thomas nodded his head the entire time. He raised his eyebrows and made noises to make sure I knew he was listening. He did it all with a straight face until I asked him to tell me what I said when I was done. He blinked rapidly then cracked a smile.

"I'm sorry, I wasn't listening in the slightest. We've done Peter Pan a half dozen times. The pink walls, I can figure it out."

I scowled and turned back to painting. We painted in silence for a few minutes before he sighed.

"Oh, come on now, don't do this to me. I hate having a stuck-up partner."

I gasped and turned my head.

"I am not stuck up," I glared at him. He looked skeptical.

"Really? Then why aren't you filthy like everyone else?" I glanced down at my clothes.

"I didn't have any old clothes to wear and I've been careful. There's nothing wrong with that," I defended. He smirked and pulled some of the bristles back on his brush and then let them go, flinging pink paint all over my shirt. I jumped back and swore.

"Thomas!" I squealed. He was smirking at me, his eyes watching me, tempting me to respond. I tightened my lips and grabbed my brush and slapped his cheek with it. He straightened and looked at me with bulged eyes. I tried to apologize but before I could he lifted his brush and swiped my face, from chin to forehead.

I sputtered and wiped my eyes and mouth. I knew if I tried to wipe the rest it would make it worse. I glared at him and he held his hands up.

"Can we call this even? You're not stuck up, I swear." I shot daggers at him. He stuck his tongue out, making a silly face and I softened.

"Pink suits you. Almost as well as the purple," he said in a low voice. He reached out and tugged on a curly pigtail. I pulled away from his touch. He shook his head incredulously.

"I can't believe you still keep it that color. Do you remember when I first convinced you to do it?" I smiled, thinking back on it.

"Yeah, it was right before I left home. I remember I cut my hair with kitchen scissors and you helped me dye it. Then we grabbed my bags and ditched town. I thought I was so edgy back then," I laughed. His eyes shined with amusement.

"Yeah and we had to squeeze you into our van for the next month until we got our own car. God that so embarrassing. We did not think that one through."

He had that one right. I thought when I left home to be with him it was so romantic, and we'd be free to follow our passion during the day and keep a different kind of passion going at night. But then I soon realized that every night I was crammed in a bench seat with Thomas, while his parents or brother slept around us. There was no place for privacy. There was an awkward pause and I suddenly felt weird. This trip down memory lane wasn't what I had signed up for today. Not with Thomas, anyways.

"I heard Ron got married," I said, changing subjects. He nodded.

"Yep. Nice girl named Catherine. She sold tickets at the venue we were using. He finished that show and then announced he was staying there."

"What about yourself? Did you ever get married?" I asked. I had noticed earlier that there had been no ring on his hand, but that meant little.

"Nah. I've dated. You know, the casual fling here and there. Up until recently I never wanted to settle in one place."

I frowned. I knew what he meant. Up until I met Mark, I was convinced I'd spend my entire life on the road.

"What made you change your mind?"

"Well it's not totally changed yet. The entire troupe deciding to buy this place and stay helped. More like pushed but whatever. I found a place to rent pretty quick and I enjoy the weather. Having some roots doesn't hurt, but there's nothing like the open road, sleeping under the stars," he was looking past me, perhaps imagining those stars. "Who knows, maybe I'll find another traveling troupe to join. We'll see how this goes."

We worked together laughing and making casual conversation for the rest of the afternoon. I made a point to stay away from uncomfortable topics and he was kind enough not to bring them up often. Eventually Justin came around and announced we were done for the day. I groaned as I stood up. Suddenly I felt Thomas' hands on my shoulders. He squeezed and panic shot up my spine. I moved away quickly and made an excuse about having to clean up and hurried away. After I washed my face and hair, I came back to find everyone packing up. Stacie was bringing out cases of beer out and declared that the real party was starting.

"Oh man, Renee you should have seen it. One of our last shows on the road we did this murder mystery. Thomas and Joe were in this competition the entire run of who could break who. So, we're in the last act. It's Thomas and Joe in a stand-off. They both draw guns from places they had stashed them in a previous scene. Thomas pulls out an old school pistol and Joe is looking in his drawer. He hesitates, Thomas coughs, and Joe finally reaches in and pulls out a banana," Erin told us. Everyone burst into laughter. Joe glared at Thomas.

Thomas, who was sitting next to me shrugged.

"Looks like I won."

I reached for my last beer and finished it with one large

gulp. Crushing it slightly with my grip I realized that I was more than a little tipsy.

"You're buzzed," Thomas laughed. I tried blowing it off, but it was obvious.

"I'm not that bad."

"You can't be driving," he added. I rolled my eyes but before I could protest anymore Stacie butted in.

"Why don't you drive her home? I'll have Justin and Erin take me home. You can come back for your car later tonight or something," she suggested.

"I need my car," I argued.

"Okay, well you and Thomas ride in his car, and I'll drive yours back." I knew that there was a way around this, but my mind was fuzzy from the alcohol and couldn't focus enough to figure it out. It was only when we were on the highway did I realize the answer. I smacked the dashboard excitedly.

"I could have driven with Stacey! Then she could get a ride home from you."

Thomas burst out laughing. "Wow, is being around me that bad?" He lifted his arms to take an exaggerated sniff. "I didn't miss my weekly shower," he teased. I rolled my eyes and looked over at him.

"You're not that bad. It's just weird. Seeing you after so long, with our history," I muttered.

"True. But it's not like we were together when you left. It shouldn't be weird. We're friends, always will be Renee."

"You're sure?"

"Of course. I was happy for you when you left. I wasn't pining for you or anything. We'd both moved on from that puppy love way before you bounced."

"Yeah, you're right, I guess. Sorry, I didn't mean to be so dramatic," I said.

"Eh, all good. I just chalk it up to your theatre background," he teased.

When we got to my house, I thanked him and gave him a brief hug.

"I'm glad I got to see you again. It's been too long," he told me. I nodded.

"Too long. Maybe I'll see you around the theater sometime. Stacie and Erin have been pushing me to jump back in."

Before anymore could be said my front door opened and we saw my darling husband in the door frame. Thankful for the excuse I waved goodbye and hurried inside and away from Thomas' lingering eyes.

"Morning Sleepy." My dearest husband kissed my forehead, trying to wake me. I groaned and put the pillow over my head.

"Oh come on. I've got coffee," he enticed. I inhaled deeply and sure enough the smell of coffee beans wafted into my nostrils. Opening my eyes, I sighed but sat up. I took the mug from his hands and took a long, slow sip.

"Mm, thank you," I kissed him when he leaned down.

"I know you've been pulling double duty with shuffling the kids around and helping build the sets these last few weeks. I figured you could be the one to sleep in this weekend." He kissed me again and then called the dogs to leave with him while I finished waking up.

Tonight was opening night, finally. I was so ready to be done with escorting the twins back and forth every night. Despite the time moving so fast, I was exhausted. Plus, Christmas was coming up, and I hadn't done any shopping yet. I was usually done by this time every year. Taking one last long gulp of my coffee I stood up and jumped in the shower.

By the time I made it downstairs I was running late to my hair appointment. Once my hair was refreshed, I ran home and grabbed the guys so we could get to the show early. On the I asked Mark stop at a flower shop and we each picked out a small bouquet of various flowers to give the twins at the end. "I still think we should have gotten one of those cookie bouquets or something. Dall ain't gonna want these," Derek waved his flowers around in the back. I turned my head to look back at him.

"Yeah, probably not but its the thought. Maybe for their next show I'll make something like that to bring."

We parked and when we got out of the car, we saw the rest of our crew waiting by Ethan's BMW. We went to join them. The Andrews', the Wilson's, and even Tabatha came.

"I convinced Scott, our bodyguard, to watch Blue so I could come," she explained when I greeted her.

"You bought flowers too?" Cleo asked from behind me.

"Yeah, why did you grab some?" Mark asked, he shot a glare at me. Ethan smirked.

"Yeah, we all did." He turned around and opened the back passenger door. We peered inside and counted six bouquets.

"Do you have the tickets, babe?" Cleo asked Ethan. He patted his sports coat chest pocket.

"Yep. Everyone ready?" With murmured agreements we all headed inside together. Some teenagers acting as ushers helped us to our seats. We all sat together in one line, taking up an entire row. The theatre was small, only seating about a hundred and fifty people tops. Within minutes the room was packed tight with other eager parents and family excited to see their little ones on stage.

The lights dimmed and Janice came out and introduced herself and the show. Mark reached over and took my hand, squeezing it tightly. The curtains rose and act one began. I had seen this show a million times during rehearsal, and found my mind wandering.

Cleo hadn't said much since that day she was inseminated.

We decided that it was best not to ask and stress her out more. Plus, it had barely been a month. She wouldn't even know yet.

When I forced myself to stop thinking about Cleo my mind drifted to Thomas. He had helped build and paint the sets with us the next two weekends after that. We had a lot of fun and it was so nice catching up with him. With our history he was a little too touchy-feely with me. I hadn't seen him since our last paint day, and I couldn't help but feel a little relieved. It wasn't anything other than innocent joking like I did with anyone else, but it still made me slightly uncomfortable. I shoved those thoughts out of my mind and snuggled in closer to my husband to enjoy the show.

Finally, the curtains closed and we clapped for the Darlings who had just flown off to Neverland with Peter. When intermission was over and act two began Peter and the children are finally in Neverland. When he takes them to his underground hideout all of the lost boys and Jimmy come running out to greet them. Peter quickly introduces them.

"This here is Tootles, Curly, Nibs, Slightly, and the twins," Peter boasts. Each child gets their turn to come forward and do a little dance or handshake with the Darlings. Each one was dressed in adorable animal footie pajamas. The twins came forward and spoke in perfect unison.

"It's nice to meet you!" They had put them in panda suits. With Jimmy's hair pushed back inside of her costume, the twins looked very much alike. From a stranger's point of view, they were identical twins.

Now that the twins were on stage I watched with more interest. It went by way faster than the beginning and before I knew it, they were calling them all out and bowing.

The lights went up and the audience stood up to move down to congratulate the cast and crew. I looked at our row. Everyone lifted up their bouquets and stood up together. The twins were a little shocked by all of us and all of the flowers. We hugged them and then left the theatre to get some air.

When the twins and their parents finally came out, we cheered loudly for them. Mark grabbed Jimmy and spun her around. She giggled as he put her down. "You were amazing up there, champ."

"Thanks Uncle Mark! It was a little scary at first," she said.

"As long as we don't look out into the audience it's not so bad," Dallas added. Ethan patted him on the back to urge them towards the car. He looked irritated. We turned and saw some creepy guy with a camera taking our picture. That was our cue to leave.

On the way home we talked about how great the show was.

"Other than that guy, it was great being able to do something with everyone," I commented.

"Yeah, that doesn't happen often enough. We always dreamed about hitting it big and that we wouldn't care about the lack of privacy, but now I think we all kind of hate it."

"Do you think we'll need to hire a bodyguard when we have a baby?" I asked. He was silent for a moment.

"I don't know. I think the big reason Cleo has one is because they both are easily recognizable. Being the drummer gives me a little bit of anonymity. If I'm not with Cleo, chances are unless you are a huge fan you aren't going to recognize me. Even more for you. No offense," he took his hand off the steering wheel to hold my hand. "How about we play it by ear. When he or she gets here, if things start to feel crazy and you're uncomfortable we will get one."

"Thank you," I said quietly. He chuckled.

"But it comes straight out of your hair fund," he teased me.

"In your dreams. If anything, it's coming out of your video game piggy bank," I shot back. His head fell back in laughter.

"That's fair," he decided.

The next few weeks passed quickly. Too quickly. I took the new free time I had from not taking the twins to rehearsal to christmas shop. Some people were easy. Derek got a mini fridge for the room that he shouldn't really have in my house, but I knew he'd like. Adrian got a guitar Mark told me he had been eying. We bought Ethan a new stereo and I hired someone to build a brick barbecue pit in the backyard for my gorgeous husband right after the holiday.

This was our third Christmas together in L.A, and the last two years everyone came over to our house to have Christmas Eve dinner, watch movies and eat cookies. We had plenty of rooms for everyone to stay in, and the next day we would open presents, have another dinner, and enjoy each other's company.

Right after Thanksgiving I invited the twins over to make cookies and help decorate the tree. However, I had forgotten to mention it to Mark beforehand so the tree was still put away. I made Mark dig in storage for it when they arrived. He came back into the house grumbling about spiders and how he needed to shower. I kissed his cheek and thanked him while offering him a sugar cookie from the first batch we had made. His sour mood softened, and he kissed me back.

"You're lucky I love you," he winked when I asked him to set it up as well.

"I know." I winked back. Jimmy and Dallas let out loud groans.

"Jeez, you are just like my mom and Dad," Jimmy said. We chuckled and as soon as the tree was erected and Mark stood back to admire his handiwork, I asked him if he could go find the ornaments. He shot daggers at me but went to search for them. He returned a few minutes later scowling.

"You're welcome. Box is in the living room. Next to the

tree." I walked over to him and embraced him in a hug. I rubbed my cheek against his. It was rough and stubbly.

"Thank you. You're my favorite you know," I said, kissing him.

"Yeah, yeah. Are those chocolate chip? Those are my favorite," he said heading towards the bowl on the table.

"I know, thats why we made them." I hurried towards the bowl and slapped his hand away.

"Wash your hands first, you're filthy!"

He mocked me but went to the sink. Coming back, he showed me his hands like a little boy before sticking a finger in the batter.

"I love you," he said as he finished his taste.

"When did you know you were in love?" Jimmy asked suddenly. We both turned to look at her. Her blue eyes were big and curious.

"My dad said he knew he loved my mom when he saw her sing for the first time," Dallas told us.

"Uncle Adrian said he loved Uncle Chase when he arrested him. He was going to put him in jail, but Uncle Adrian was too cute."

My mouth fell open. I can't believe he told them that. Well, I could, but still.

"So," Jimmy put her hand on her hip and looked at me expectantly. "When did you fall in love?"

"Why are you so curious all of a sudden?" Mark asked and then furrowed his brow in thought. "I knew I loved your Aunt Renee when she told me she loved my family. I told her I couldn't love someone who didn't love Uncle Derek, Uncle Adrian, and your mom. When she loved them, I loved her."

"My mom likes you too. She told me so," Jimmy said to me. The timer for the cookies went off and I hurried to take them out.

"While we wait for them to cool why don't we go decorate the tree?" I suggested.

"Can we listen to Christmas music?" Jimmy and Dallas leapt off the chairs they had been standing on. Mark ruffled Jimmy's hair and followed them out.

"We sure can. Now, who's gonna help me with the tinsel?"

After they left in the evening, I pulled out everything to start wrapping presents. Beau and Bonnie kept getting in the way and wanting to play; it was beginning to get frustrating.

"Mark, can you help?"

He came in and saw me tangled up in ribbons and tape while the dogs rolled around on the wrapping paper. He started laughing and called the dogs.

"Beau, Bonnie, get outta here!" They jumped up and quickly followed him up the stairs and into the bedroom. After we wrapped the last gift and had gotten everything put away, we went upstairs and wrapped ourselves in a blanket with the dogs at our feet. With a bowl of popcorn in between us, we settled in for a movie.

"You know, this could be the last Christmas where it's just the two of us." He said. I looked up at him.

"It could be. Remember we're not going to stress about it right now?"

He rolled his eyes.

"So what? We can think about it a little bit. I can't wait. This time next year we could have a little guy in between us."

"Or girl," I added. He smirked.

"Or girl."

I snuggled in closer.

"We just need to cherish these moments while we're here. Once we have a baby, things are going to change. It's not going to be just me and you anymore."

"That's a good thing though," he said, kissing my hair.

"I know. I just know I'll also miss it being just the two of us too."

"This is kind of a rare moment, if you think about it. Derek isn't here," he chuckled. I moved my head to look up at him.

"He's been on the go ever since they took his wheelchair. It's been nice."

"Yeah, you know he's not at Adrians or Cleo's either? They haven't heard from him in a few days. It's weird."

"Maybe he's got a girlfriend. Or at least someone else to annoy for awhile. Like you said." He wrapped his arms tighter around me. I sighed, enjoying his warmth.

"Cherish these moments."

Derek did show up on Christmas Eve right as everyone finished dinner. He came bearing bags and bags of gifts.

"Where have you been?" I asked. He rolled his eyes at me.

"Around. Do I smell hot toddies?"

"In the kitchen. Why are you being so weird?" He blinked at me but said nothing. Instead he turned to go get himself a drink.

I looked around the room and found my husband. I went to cuddle up with him. Looking up at the TV I saw that 'A Christmas Story' was playing. Holiday tradition. The 24-hour marathon must have started.

"It is getting kind of late. Why don't we take you upstairs and get you settled in." Cleo said to the twins. They followed her out of the room, excitedly talking about Santa. Not long after, the rest of us called it a night, knowing the kids would be waking us up early.

Sure enough it was about seven when our door burst open and Derek ran and jumped on our bed. I screamed for him to stop but he started screaming.

"It's Christmas! Come on get up! Santa came!"

Mark was finally able to kick him off the bed while I scrambled to sit up. He fell to the floor with an oof!

"Knock that shit out. I will kick your ass on Christmas Derek," Mark warned. Derek popped up like a damn whack a mole. He was grinning ear to ear and bouncing up and down.

"Come on! Everyone's waiting."

Sighing I reached for my purple velvet robe and tied it quickly before starting out of the room. Mark and Derek joined me a minute later.

I glanced into the living room. The kids were in there wiggling in their seats, waiting for us. I groaned.

"Can I get some coffee first?" I begged. Once we were all had our warm mugs, we returned to the living room. I looked around and realized Derek was missing. Right as I was going to ask about him he entered wearing a full Santa costume.

"Ho, Ho, Ho! Merry Christmas. Did we have two good little children this year?"

"Four, Blue and Rocky count too Santa," Jimmy said. I looked over at the babies in Cleo and Adrian's arms. Blue was enjoying the lights from the tree, while Rocky was enjoying his breakfast bottle.

"Oh, that's right. Four good little children. Are you guys ready to open some presents?" He went over to the tree and picked up a red present. "To Adrian. Ooh, I wonder what this could be?" He passed it quickly to Ethan who then passed it down until it reached its intended receiver.

Derek went through and passed out presents until we each had at least one. When we all held up our pretty wrapped boxes, he declared we could open them. The kids screamed and tore into their gifts. Mark nudged me and I looked over.

"Are you going to open your present?" The kids' excitement had made me forget about my own gift. It was a small green box. I shook it halfway into tearing it open but didn't hear anything. Pulling the box fully out of its wrapper I opened it and my breath caught in my throat.

"Oh Mark," I said as he took the box from me and pulled

the necklace out. He moved closer to me and I extended my head out so he could put it on me. He hooked the clasp and pulled away. His eyes were lit up, I'm sure they matched mine. I lunged at him, squeezing him tightly. He wrapped his arms around me.

"You like it?" He laughed. I pulled back and kissed him.

"It's gorgeous. I love it," I exclaimed.

"It's solid sterling silver and four emerald cut amethysts and its a real diamond in the center," he boasted proudly. I smirked.

"Did you memorize what the jeweler told you?"

He blushed.

"Guilty. I saw it and had to get it for you. You make it even more beautiful," he told me. I moved closer to him and he put his arm around me while we watched everyone continue opening presents.

The room quickly filled up with papers and bows everywhere. Eventually I got up and grabbed some trash bags to start picking up a little. We were running out of room.

When I sat back down with Mark, I saw he was holding two thin boxes

"Oh, we missed some?"

"Those are from me," Cleo said from across the room. I looked up and smiled. I held the box with my name while Mark opened his. It was a black shirt and when he held it up, he gasped.

"Uh, babe. I think you need to open yours."

My heart was racing, and then it stopped completely. I opened my gift and pulled the black shirt out of the box. I read the words printed on the front, and then I reread them, and reread them again. Mommy to be.

Lowering the shirt slowly, my eyes darted around the room. Everyone was grinning ear to ear at me. Finally, I made it to my husband. He was wiping his face, his eyes glistening. He pressed his lips together and with a shaky hand held up his own shirt that said Daddy to be. We stared at each other for a long moment before Derek cleared his throat loudly.

We turned back to everyone and in unison they all stood up and took off their sweaters, untied their robes and in Derek's case, slipped off his Santa coat. Underneath they were all wearing matching black shirts. Around the room we had four Uncles to be, two Cousins to be, technically four because even the babies were wearing little black onesies with the words printed on them. I had been keeping it together, despite being in shock, until I saw Cleo's shirt. She was facing away from me so I could read the back which read Aunt to be. Ethan motioned her to turn and that's when I burst into tears. The front said Just Babysitting.

Chapter Four

CARRIED AWAY

THE FIRST DOCTOR's appointment a few days later confirmed what the three home tests had told her a week ago.

"I can not tell you how hard it was not to tell you right away," she said as the three of us sat in the office as the doctor talked to us.

"I loved how you did it. It was amazing," I told her.

"Yeah, yeah. Kind of stole my thunder from my gift," Mark teased. I squeezed his hand and stood on my tiptoes to kiss his cheek. I fingered my necklace.

"It doesn't change how pretty it is," I assured him.

The doctor gave Cleo a once over and declared her examination over. "Go ahead and get dressed. Everything looks good. You've been pregnant before, so you know the drill. No alcohol, limit the seafood. I can get you the list if you want. Have you had any nausea?"

Cleo sat up and shrugged.

"Some. I've only puked once so far." The doctor nodded and pulled out her prescription pad.

"I'm going to prescribe some medicine to help in case it gets really bad. Every pregnancy is different and its better to have something to help than nothing at all." She pulled the paper off the pad and handed it to Mark. She glanced from him to me and then Cleo.

"I'll see you all in one month. If you have any sharp pain, or bleeding call us immediately. If it Is past office hours go straight to the hospital. Sound good?" We all nodded, and Mark and I left with the doctor so Cleo could get dressed.

Mark hugged me and I saw he was smiling wildly.

"So, its real, really real." I laughed.

"I guess so, Dad."

"I don't know about that. I want to be called something cool. Daddio? Pops? Padre? Or maybe I'll be more formal. Father," he tried the words out, trying to find one that worked.

"Well you have a few months to figure it out. You want to get lunch?" I asked right as Cleo came out of the room. He raised the paper in his hand.

"Let's get this first, then see about food."

An hour later we sat around Cleo's kitchen while Derek passed around various containers of Chinese.

"So, are we going to wait until the baby's born to go on tour then? People are excited about a new album, so this gives us time to work on it. No one is really pushing us right now to perform live," Derek said. I looked over at my husband, who was exchanging glances with the rest of his band. I understood the hesitation.

Cleo had gone on tour while she was pregnant with Blue. She continued performing right up until her due date. But that was her baby. She was putting her own child at risk. This one wasn't hers. Her body of course, but if something happened to the baby, we wouldn't get another chance at this.

"I want to wait. Touring while pregnant is not great. I did it once and that's enough for me. Plus, didn't we vote to make a new album instead of a revisit? We don't have anything solid for it," Cleo said. Relief flooded me. She looked at me and winked. Mark perked up and put his food down.

"Speaking of music, I have an idea," he started. Oh, I remembered him telling me about this awhile back. He had been so proud of it when he explained it.

"Okay, so the band is named after a musical. I think we should play that up." His friends gave him confused looks but urged him to continue.

"Maria Maria was from West Side Story. We used to do musicals when we were kids, why not embrace it? I think we should sample famous songs from musicals, put our own spin on them and create a whole album surrounding it. We could do music videos with like clips of when we were kids mashed together with us now. It would be an homage to the ten years, but still something fresh." He waved his hands around with enthusiasm over his idea.

Cleo straightened and looked like she was considering it. I glanced at the other two and they were deep in thought as well.

"I like it," Derek said first.

"It's genius," Adrian added.

"What songs do you have in mind?" Cleo chimed in. Mark's face lit up and he clapped his hands on the countertop. Cleo jumped up and left the room quickly. She returned with a pile of notebooks and pens. She tossed them across the counter to her bandmates and they all opened them and began discussing their future music. I finished my food silently watching them go at it. Their process was kind of fascinating to watch.

"First of all, what songs do you think we should sample? Or what musicals do you like?" Cleo asked again.

"Do I look like I watch musicals?" Derek rolled his eyes and shoved an egg roll in his mouth.

"We should definitely use the musicals we did. So, Wizard of Oz, Grease, and West Side Story," Adrian said.

"That's only three songs. What if we did each song from a different musical? There's plenty to sample from. Little Shop of Horrors, Rent, Hairspray, Oklahoma!, Chicago. Oh, that would be a fun one!" Cleo scribbled furiously on her paper.

"I like that idea. We should definitely try to get the rights for big ones that most people could identify. We'll have to call and see what ones we could get," Mark told them.

"On it," Adrian said, tapping on his phone and putting it to his ear. He smiled at the group and walked out of the room.

"Sam, hey we have an idea," he said as he left to talk to their manager.

"Mark you are a genius," Cleo exclaimed. He beamed. "I can't wait to start singing some of these. My mind is just flooding with ideas."

"Ooh, Hedwig and the Angry Inch. That could be a fun one. Should we do 'Sugar Daddy' or 'Angry Inch'?" Derek suggested, wiggling his eyebrows. Mark choked on his noodles while laughing.

"Only if you dress as Hedwig," he told him. Derek tilted his head as if considering it. Cleo gasped and we all turned.

"Oh my God. Are we going to do costumes? We've never done that before."

Mark and Derek both shook their heads furiously. I leaned against my husband and kissed his head.

"That would be cute. You guys should dress up," I teased. He glared at me to shut it before it ended up a thing. Too late, I told him with my eyes. The gears in Cleo's head were already turning.

Adrian returned a moment later smiling.

"Sam is going to look into it, but he likes the concept and thinks that we can get permission for enough to make 15 songs. Have we started picking individual songs yet?" He came back to the counter and looked at everyone's notes. Cleo shook her head.

"No, but I think our first single should be from West Side Story. I really think we should do 'Maria'." The room fell quiet for a beat.

"Makes sense," Adrian said hesitantly. "Who's gonna sing it? Could we turn it into a duet?" Cleo blushed and her eyes darted away from his and then flicked over to Derek. Adrian saw and his eyes turned hard. "No. This is bullshit."

"What if Derek did it?" All three of the men's eyes bulged and after a pause they all started talking over each other. I sighed. They were going to spend the rest of the day and at least part of the evening figuring this out. I kissed Mark's shoulder and told him that I was leaving. He frowned and apologized.

"I'm sorry babe. I know it's boring to just sit and listen. How about when I get home tonight we catch up on TV?" He kissed me quickly and as I started out of the room Adrian shouted after me.

"Hey! Are you still good to start watching Rocky this week? His first appointment is tomorrow. I nodded and blew Mark another kiss before leaving him to argue with his friends.

I went home, let the dogs out, and then plopped my butt on the couch. Man, I really needed to get a hobby or friends or something. This was ridiculous. I was my own person. I couldn't keep being just someone's wife. Beau jumped up and snuggled into my side. Bonnie followed a beat later and plopped her head on my ankles. I guess having Rocky around would be nice. He was still so little though. He'd probably just sleep most of the time. Thinking about sleep, I closed my eyes and decided a nap couldn't hurt.

I woke up to my phone ringing on the coffee table. It was on vibrate, so the rattling against the glass was noisier than if it had been turned on high. I grabbed it quickly and squinted to look at the screen. It wasn't dark out, but my vision was still blurry from sleeping.

Stacie was calling me. I answered it with a groan.

"Hello?"

"Renee? Were you sleeping?" I sat up, disturbing the dogs. They yelped at me, but I shushed them.

"Just taking a nap. What's up? What time is it?" I asked.

"Almost five. You wanna go out with a few of us old timers? Dinner, drinks, and maybe some karaoke," she teased. I considered it for a moment. Looking around, I knew that I was alone. I would have heard if someone had come in. My options were to go and have fun or sit around bored out of my mind.

"Sure, what time are you thinking?"

"In about an hour. Do you want someone to pick you up?"

"Yeah, that will work. Just call when you are on your way," I told her.

"I can't. I'm already picking up Emilie and Jordan. I'll see who has room and have them get you. I have to get showered. I'll see you soon," she hung up the phone before I could protest. Not that I had any reason to. She said old timers, so they were all my old friends.

I ran upstairs to change and refresh my hair and makeup. I had worn a yellow sundress with a white cardigan to the doctor's appointment. I couldn't wear that out for a night of drinking.

Opening up my closet I looked around. Finding a white frilled button up shirt and my favorite skinny jeans I slid those on and reached for red heels. I finished the look with matching red lipstick and applying some fresh eyeliner and mascara. I was letting the dogs out one last time when Stacie called me and said a ride was coming. I hurried to make sure they had food and water and right when I went to the hallway to wait, I saw a familiar car pull into the drive.

Thomas. I stood frozen to the spot while I watched him get out and walk up to my door. He was dressed in all black. Black dress pants, shirt and sports coat. His hair was slicked back, and he had a hint of five o clock shadow.

His knocking on the door knocked me back to earth. I shook my head and moved to answer the door. He greeted me with a charming smile.

"Hey stranger. You ready?" He said cheerily.

"Yeah, thanks for coming to get me." I said as I locked the door behind me.

"No problem. I was the only one without a full carload. It helps that I don't live as close as the rest of them do." We buckled in and moments later we were speeding off to the restaurant.

"Where are we going?" I asked, realizing we were headed into a part of town I wasn't too familiar with.

"It's called Moe's. I don't know. Erin and Justin said it was good cheap food with good cheap beer," guilt rushed over me. Since marrying Mark, I had grown accustomed to eating and shopping at more expensive places. I had almost forgotten what it was like eating at the cheapest place you could find and wearing clothes you grabbed from the free stores. Uneasiness settled over me. I didn't like the feeling of being some rich snobby millionaire's wife. That wasn't me.

We pulled into Moe's bar and grill about fifteen minutes later, just as Thomas had promised. He unbuckled himself and turned to me.

"You ready?" I nodded and stepped out with him. When we walked in and the hostess took us to our booth the group cheered and held up their beers.

I ordered a beer right away and quickly joined in the conversation with everyone. It was easy since I knew everyone. It was so nice to see my old friends.

Due to us being the last ones to show, Thomas had to sit next to me. Which wasn't too bad until Laurie, Vanna, and Michelle showed up. They had to add another table and push the rest of us even closer together. Thomas and I had taken the table at the far end, but now we were squished even tighter. He gently pushed my shoulder with his and chuckled. I smiled back, it wasn't a big deal, I argued with myself. Everyone was a sardine in here.

Erin and Stacie sat across from us. When the waitress came back around, we started looking at the menus for appetizers.

"I want nachos. This place has the best salsa," Stacie said.

"You wanna split something Renee?" Thomas asked, not taking his eyes off his menu. I opened mine and started searching through the list. Nachos, pretzels, potato skins, mozzarella sticks, pretty standard stuff.

"I like mozz sticks," I offered. "Ooh and onion rings." Thomas chuckled and shut his menu.

"How about you order one, I'll order the other, and then we share?"

"That works. Best of both worlds," I said cheerily. The waitress took our orders and we relaxed back into conversation.

"Ugh, I am so glad the kids' production is over. It's fun, but so much work keeping all the little kids on track," Erin said. We all drank to that.

"I can not wait to start the next production," Stacie added.

"Especially with the overkill budget," Justin piped in from next to Erin. I looked at him curiously.

"What happened?" The small group around me started smiling ear to ear.

"Well we went looking for sponsors like we always do for any production. We weren't having much luck because of the title. Well Lizzie," he tipped his beer in the direction of a petite blonde on the other side of the tables. "She had the idea of going into a toy store and ask. They were so excited about it they doubled what we were asking for.

"Toy store?" Everyone around me chuckled. Thomas

nudged me. I turned. He looked slightly uncomfortable. He took a long gulp of his beer.

"Uh, adult toy store, Renee."

I could feel the heat coming to my face as I mouthed an O. Once everyone stopped laughing at me, I opened my mouth again.

"That's awesome though. Who would have guessed?"

Justin beamed.

"We just need to put them in the playbill and mention them before and after each performance. So worth it." Just as many of us were finishing off our first beers the waitress returned with the appetizers and took more drink orders. I noticed that Thomas declined another beer and asked for a coke instead. He saw the look I was giving him, and he shrugged.

"I want to be able to drive my car home. No biggie," he smiled again. I grabbed an onion ring from his basket, and he took a mozzarella stick out of mine.

While we ate, we talked about past shows and life on the road.

"My favorite production was 'The Taming of the Shrew'. I hated when we did Shakespeare but that one was fun," Thomas said.

"Wasn't that your first lead role?" I rolled my eyes. He laughed.

"Yeah, and yours too if I recall." I smiled, thinking about it.

"That was so much fun because all of us got to be in it," Stacie added. "I loved playing Bianca," she sighed deeply.

"We need more shows like that. Why did you have to pick a play with such a small cast to direct?" Erin shot at Stacie who only shrugged and took a drink of her beer.

"Eh, you'll get over it. When it's your turn to direct, pick something bigger," she shot back. Erin glared but said nothing else. Stacie looked over at me.

"Are you still auditioning?"

I bit my lip. I wanted to, but with Cleo being pregnant and me watching Chase and Adrian's newborn now, I hesitated. Plus, the band was picking stuff back up. Wait, wasn't I just complaining about needing something to do?

"Yep. That's the plan. I need to start getting out of the house more," I decided. She smiled widely.

"Great. Next Tuesday and Wednesday evening. I expect to see you there." She pointed at the rest of us around the tables. "I expect all of you to be there." Everyone laughed.

"There's only five parts, and you've pretty much given one to Renee," Someone said from down the table. She scrunched up her face.

"Not true. She has to audition just like everyone else. Who knows, maybe she forgot how to act. It's been a few years," she smirked. I rolled my eyes.

"Maybe. I guess I shouldn't come try out until I brushed up some," I teased. She stuck out her tongue at me and demanded I show up. I put up my hands in surrender.

"You got it boss."

My phone buzzed in my pocket suddenly. I took it out and saw Mark texted me. He was apologizing for still not being home. He said that he'd be out late. I replied that I had went out with my friends and would be home late as well. He shot me one last XO before he said he had to get back to work.

"Husband?" Thomas asked me when I put my phone away.

"Yeah, he's working late tonight. They are working on a new album," I explained.

"Ooh. I love Maria Maria. Are they gonna tour again soon?" Justin asked.

"I don't know. I don't get too involved in his career. It's a lot to take in sometimes."

"I bet. Do you go with him when they tour?" Erin asked. I shook my head.

"No. Although I did follow them with Cleo's twins for a few weeks. I was their nanny while they were gone. Wives and girlfriends typically don't come along to stuff like that."

"That sucks. What do you do when he's gone?" I didn't say anything for a long moment. I didn't know how to answer. Nothing. I did nothing.

"Well the last time I watched the twins, but that's why I was thinking about getting back into the theatre. I need something to do while he's working."

"Well we are glad to have you back." Stacie said. Erin stood up and came around to hug me tightly.

"You have no idea how much we missed you."

After dinner the waitress cleared our tables and a voice came over the intercom and announced that karaoke would be starting in five minutes. The table started cheering and squealing with excitement.

"Who's going first?" Justin called down the tables. A few hands shot up quickly. Michelle stood up to grab the big book of songs from the bar. She returned with the sign-up sheet and the book to pass along.

By the time it got down to Thomas and I, people had already started getting on stage. We heard very drunk renditions of 'We are the Champions', 'Livin La Vida Loca', and a group of girls sang 'Mickey', the cheerleaders anthem.

"What are you gonna sing?" Thomas asked me as I leaned over him to share the book.

"Ugh, do I have to?" I groaned. Everyone around me said "Yes" in unison.

"It's tradition. You want to be a part of us again, you have to get up there."

"I hate singing," I complained. I wasn't like Cleo. Singing didn't come naturally to me. I quickly pushed those negative thoughts away. It wasn't her fault I couldn't sing.

"Why don't we go up together. You can be my back up," Thomas teased. I considered it.

"What do they have?" I looked at the book again.

"Let's do something fun," he suggested and then pointed to a song. My eyes found where he was pointing, and I laughed.

"Perfect. Sign us up."

When it was finally our turn Thomas and I scurried up on stage and he promptly grabbed a mic and declared that he wouldn't need the TV prompter. The music started and everyone started chuckling, and some even groaned. I grabbed my own mic and began walking around the stage like Thomas was.

As Thomas rapped the words to Vanilla Ice's 'Jump around', I joined in for the chorus. When it was over, we hugged each other and he took my hand to help me down off the stage. Returning to our seats Stacie gave us a look.

"You two are adorable. Time doesn't change a thing." Everyone muttered agreements to her statement. I glanced at Thomas who wasn't nodding either. Time had changed things. We weren't the teenagers that jammed out for hours to bad rap music. I cleared my throat awkwardly as we sat back down.

I didn't get back up on stage for the rest of the night. I was content watching everyone else get up there and act silly. Thomas went up one more time to sing some Frankie Valli. He had one hell of a voice.

When he returned back to his seat, we spent the rest of the evening commenting and playfully making fun of everyone else. He told me stories of things I had missed while I was gone. Who had hooked up and who broke up. Which ones fell on stage, or who forgot to put on a wig for an entire act. He had me laughing the entire night.

Last call was finally announced. I had been casually drinking all night, so I had a light buzz but nothing serious. I decided against another drink. Everyone began pulling on jackets and grabbing purses. I stood up and Thomas grabbed mine and helped me into it.

"I'm glad you came out tonight Renee," Stacie said as we were all walking out.

"Me too. I need to get out of the house more. Thanks for inviting me."

I walked with Thomas to his car. He opened my door for me and helped me inside. He slid onto his side and we were quickly on the road heading to my place.

"Thanks for the ride," I told him.

"No problem. Like I said, your place isn't far from mine." We drove in silence for a bit. I checked my phone and was disappointed to see that Mark hadn't called or sent me a message. It was late. Did he crash at Cleo's? I wouldn't be surprised if they all did, but still, a phone call would have been nice.

"Everything okay?" Thomas asked, glancing at me.

"Yeah, my husband was just working late tonight. When they get into a project, they really go full force. They don't stop until it's perfect."

"Is he gone a lot?" I shook my head.

"No, not really. When he's touring sure, but when he's not he's usually home for dinner. It's just boring sometimes waiting for him to come back."

"Well maybe getting back into the theatre will be good for you. I know everyone is excited to see you again. When you showed up for Rocky Horror it was all everyone could talk about."

I smiled. It was nice feeling wanted and welcomed. Not that the band wasn't like that. I just didn't have much in common with them. I missed being able to converse like I had tonight.

Too soon we pulled into my driveway. I frowned when I saw that there were no lights on. He must have passed out on their couch. I thanked Thomas one more time and got out of the car. I went inside and I noticed it was a few moments before he pulled out of the driveway. It confused me. I didn't want to believe it, but some tiny part of me wondered if he still had feelings for me. I had caught him more than once looking at me with emotions I couldn't place. I shook those thoughts out of my brain. I didn't want to stress about something that didn't even matter. Regardless of his feelings, I knew my own. I moved on long ago and was happy where I was. With who I was with.

Both dogs greeted me at the door. Setting my coat and purse aside I let them out in the back and called Mark.

"Hello?" He answered on the second ring. He sounded wide awake.

"Mark? Where are you?"

"I'm on my way home now babe. Sorry we ran late. We really did some heavy work today. I can't wait to see you. I miss you already," he said. My heart softened.

"I miss you too. I'll see you soon." I hung up the phone and called for the dogs to come in. After I closed the doors, I hurried up the stairs and went to my closet. Pulling my dinner clothes off I reached for a pink, lacy nightie. It was one of Mark's favorites. It had been so long since we had had time together, I couldn't even remember the last time.

Slipping that on I went into the bathroom and washed my face off but put on some mascara and light pink lipstick on. When I was satisfied with my appearance I went to lay on the bed and wait for my husband.

Minutes later I heard the front door open and shut. His heavy footsteps came up the stairs slowly. He must be exhausted, I realized. I suddenly felt self conscious and wanted to change out of these and into something more comfortable. He was going to be too tired to appreciate it.

When he opened the bedroom door and saw me, he froze in the doorway. His tired face lit up as he took me in. His eyes started at my face and slowly moved down over my chest, my hips, and finally my legs. He took a few steps into the room and sat down on the bed. His hand reached out to caress my thigh.

"Hey you, what are you doing?"

I sighed heavily, looking up at him with hooded eyes. I batted my eyelashes and fell onto the bed.

"Oh nothing. I was just thinking of going to bed. How was work?" He ignored my question. His fingers started trailing up my leg.

"Weird, I was tired, but suddenly I got a little extra burst of energy. I can't figure out why." His hands reached the edge of my nightie and he began playing with the lace.

"This is my favorite one," he murmured.

I sat up and pushed his chest gently. He fell onto the bed and I swung my legs over his body to climb on top of him. I leaned down and kissed his lips, then his jaw, then his neck. He groaned. I felt him pulse from inside his jeans.

"I know, that's why I picked it out."

My hands started exploring his body as I trailed kisses down. I lifted his shirt and kissed his lower abs while I played with his belt. He was rock hard and pressed against my thigh.

"I'm sorry I've been working so much. I don't mean to neglect you," he moaned. I undid his belt and started slipping his pants down.

He lifted his hips to help me. When I started playing with his boxers he hissed.

"Oh, don't tease me." I smirked and adjusted the slit in his underwear and his full length sprang out to greet my mouth. I took him in and sank down all the way to the base. He gasped and reached for my hands. He squeezed them as I worked his shaft slowly, then picking up the pace.

"Oh baby, if you want any fun you are going to have to stop," he groaned. I removed my mouth from him and sat up. He leaned forward and grabbed me, pulling me down to his chest. He kissed me and quickly moved to my neck. I gasped as he nibbled gently on the tender skin.

His hands reached for my chest. He rubbed the lacy cloth covering my breasts.

"You're gorgeous. I love your body," he groaned as his hands started drifting down my nightie. He found my panties and began teasing me by tracing the lace, but not moving them aside. I was slick and ready for him. He discovered that quickly and let out a low growl. He rolled me over, climbing on top of me.

"I want you," he said, slipping a finger inside me. He moved in and out slowly, then as I let out moans of pleasure he moved faster.

"Do you want me?" He asked. I closed my eyes and nodded quickly. My body was beginning to ache with need for him.

The nod was all he needed to kick off his pants and slip off my panties. I reached for his shirt and he practically ripped it off and flung it across the room. In one swift motion he pushed my legs apart and slid inside me. I lost my breath for a moment. He leaned down and kissed me as he began thrusting. His lips moved to my ear, then my neck again. I could barely take it.

"Faster," I whispered and he did as told. I groaned as my orgasm quickly started building. I could tell Mark was not far behind me. He asked me to change positions.

Moving quickly, I pushed him onto the mattress and sank down onto his hardness.

"Oh my God," he moaned, tilting his head back. I reached

for his shoulders and began moving. I was close. I closed my eyes and just as I was reaching my climax. My orgasm came and erupted all over my body.

I couldn't focus, my vision grew hazy for a long moment as the ultimate pleasure flooded my veins. When my body calmed back down, I rested my body down on Marks and he finished a moment later. It had been way too long since our bodies connected in that way and I was overwhelmed, mentally and physically.

Mark must have felt the same way. Moments later he started snoring softly, and I turned to look at him. I leaned over to run my fingers through his hair. This man loved me so unconditionally, and I in return would do anything for him as well. He was the full package. Gorgeous, funny, smart, and most of all, he loved me for who I was.

My soft touches must have roused him. He opened his eyes a slit and smiled at me. He reached over and pulled me into him. I cuddled into his warm embrace and tried not to think about all the things that caused me stress on a daily basis. Instead I forced myself to remember all the reasons I had married this man. I fell asleep at ten; his smile.

Chapter Five

YOU AND I BOTH

MARK BARELY HAD time to eat his breakfast and enjoy his coffee before he was running out the door for rehearsal. All week he would get up, eat quickly and then leave, returning after midnight. If I hadn't been through this before I might have been irritated. I remembered this from before. When they were working on their last album, they were all like this. The only difference was last time I had more things to occupy my time.

This time around Cleo and Ethan had hired a private nanny for the kids. Sure, I could go get them to do stuff with, but my help wasn't needed. I did get to watch Rocky two to three times a week now, but he still didn't do much. Out of the four times I'd watched him, he'd been awake for maybe an hour at most. I could play with him or feed him then but most of the time he slept. He was a lazy baby. But once I dropped him off with Chase in the evening, I was left twiddling my fingers.

Today was one of my off days. Chase didn't have a doctor's appointment, so my schedule was completely empty. Plopping down on the couch with the dogs again I grabbed my phone and called Stacie. She answered on the first ring.

"Are you coming tonight?" She asked quickly before I could even say hello. Oh! I had been so worked up over the Thomas thing that I had totally forgotten about the auditions.

"Yes. I told you I would. What are you up to?"

"I am about to leave to drive four hours to San Luis Obispo for the scripts and some furniture," she sighed. "You want to come with? We can swing by and grab you," she offered. I sat up.

"Sure, I've got nothing else better to do. We?" I asked.

"Thomas. Justin was called in to work last minute. Something about some big head honchos coming and they needed to get some things fixed super quick. Thomas was the only one available to come. I need someone strong to load it all up. Be ready, we're on our way now." She hung up before I could protest. Not that I really had any reason to. It was either go or sit around the house bored out of my mind.

They picked me up twenty minutes later in Stacie's big blue truck. I hurried down my stairs and hopped in. Thomas and Stacie both smiled welcoming at me and moved over to give me room. I was so glad to get the window. It was going to be a long day.

"Why are we picking up stuff from so far away? Couldn't they have just shipped it?" I questioned. Stacie swung a glare over at me.

"The original theatre we were getting them from sent them to the wrong theatre. We got scripts and costumes for 'The Three Musketeers'. They got ours. We didn't find out until last night. With auditions tonight and rehearsals starting next week we kind of need this stuff like now," she practically growled.

Thomas turned to me.

"Isn't she just a treat?"

I burst out laughing and the tension in the truck eased. We made a quick coffee and snacks run and then got onto the freeway. Thankfully Stacie's truck had a newer stereo system, so we were able to plug our phones into it. We turned it all the way and for four hours we sang musicals and 90's tunes terribly. We jammed out and pretended we were professionals. When there was a slight pause in the songs Thomas spoke.

"Is this what it's like when you're with your husband and the band?" I frowned.

"Not really. They are huge goofballs, but they take their music seriously. Ethan and Cleo are obnoxious with the singing though. They are always looking for opportunities to belt out a song," I chuckled. In their defense, their instruments were always with them. I'm positive if Mark or the other two could bring theirs along everywhere, they'd play them constantly too. Actually, Mark kind of does. He never stood still. He was always tapping something.

"She's the singer, right? And that's her husband, the guy who Duchess wrote that book about?" He asked. I cringed. It didn't even involve me in the slightest, but I still felt bad for them.

"Yep, that's him. You know that book was total bull crap. She lied about 90 percent of whatever was in it," I defended. He raised his eyebrows, clearly amused by my reaction.

"Yeah, I remember seeing something about it. They pulled her book off the shelves before they even made it onto them. Did you watch the video of her attacking that guy at the signing?"

I smiled. "Yeah, that was my husband. His back was tore up for weeks after that." Both of my friends' mouths fell open.

"That was him? Oh my God. Did she recognize him? Is that why she attacked him?" Stacie asked.

"Didn't she get arrested for running someone over too? Was it your husband?"

I shook my head, trying to answer before they could ask another question. I held up my hand.

"Mark was not involved in the hit and run. Their bassist

and the guitarist's husband were the ones she hit. And at the signing my husband was there with Adrian, the guitarist. She did recognize them. I guess the room was divided between people loving her and people wanting to call her out for the lies. A few people had already been escorted out. She was crazy before that though. She was harassing Ethan for months."

"I got that scorned lover vibe. That was what the book was about right?" Thomas asked. I nodded.

"When she ran over your friends, was she trying to hit Ethan?" Stacie asked.

"No. Ethan wasn't there. I don't know what she was doing then. It's been horrible. Both Ethan and Cleo still get lots of crap from fans who think that he should be with Duchess. People need to get a life. They are real people." The truck grew quiet for a moment before Thomas switched the music back on.

Finally, after four long, long hours Stacie pulled into the small theatre. I hopped out and began stretching my legs. It felt so good to be on solid ground again. It brought memories of traveling when I was younger to the surface. I hated it then, I hate it now. Glancing at Thomas who was also stretching, I remembered why I did it for so long.

He saw me staring and smiled wide. I looked away quickly and when Stacie called for us to hurry up, I turned and joined her. Inside the members of this particular theatre were more than happy to help.

"Sorry we couldn't meet you any closer. We were the only people available at the last minute to come open up the place," a little old lady said, motioning to an even older man.

"It's okay," Stacie threw her arm over Thomas' shoulder. "I brought a strapping young buck to carry everything for us." The old woman giggled and I watched her eyes start from his head and slowly move down Thomas' body. I could hardly contain a giggle of my own when I saw that his face was turning red. He nudged me to stop but that only made me laugh harder.

"Okay enough chit chat," Thomas cut us off. "Where is all this stuff we came for?"

The old couple took him to the back and Stacie and I went back to her truck to grab the boxes of stuff for them.

When we returned Thomas was carrying a wooden bed frame to the truck. It looked heavy. I was glad he came. Me and Stacie would have struggled to get that together. We traded boxes of puffy musketeer costumes for boxes with old money clothes.

"They even included the Jackie-O costume. I'm sure you could tailor it to fit whoever needs it," the old woman told us. Stacie took it out of the box and lifted it up.

She eyed me and then the costume, then me again. She folded it back up and put it back.

"I think it will be perfect. Thanks again Mr. and Mrs. Horowitz. We appreciate the help on such sudden notice."

When we were back in the truck and on the road, I scolded her.

"You can't cast before auditions Stacie. That's not fair."

She rolled her eyes.

"Fine, but promise me if you don't get the part that you'll be the stage manager or my assistant. Something. I don't want you to leave us again. We just got you back," she pouted.

"I promise. Scout's honor."

By the time we got back and put everything in the back of the theatre we had time to grab a bite to eat before people would start showing for auditions. I called Mark to see if he wanted to meet up, but they had ordered pizza and were eating in the studio.

"I'm sorry baby, Saturday I'll make sure it's just me and you. We'll kick Derek out for the weekend."

I heard Derek swear at him in the background.

"I think we should buy a small trailer to put in the back-yard for him. Maybe build a small outhouse. He would never have to come in ever again," he said loudly, baiting Derek. I sighed and got back in Stacie's truck.

"Okay, Saturday sounds great. Auditions are in a few hours," I reminded him.

"Oh, damn it. I totally forgot. Sorry babe, break a leg okay? I know you're gonna get the part. I gotta go. Pizza just got here. We're only taking a small break. Sam came over with a list of green lighted music to sample. It's been crazy today. I love you," he said.

"I love you too," I said before he hung up. I sighed deeply. I understood, but it was still crappy sometimes.

"Well we are excited to be eating dinner with you too," Thomas said, bringing me back to my surroundings. I forced a smile and apologized.

"Sorry, I just haven't seen him much this last week or so."

We stopped at a little sub shop and ordered to go so we could eat at the theater. Stacie and Thomas ordered first and before I could tell the person behind the counter what I wanted Thomas interrupted me.

"Let me see if I can still remember what you'll order." I smirked and crossed my arms over my chest.

"You really think you know me that well?"

"I used to. Let's see," he looked at the menu and the ingre-dients behind the glass. "She's going to take the classic club on plain white bread. Toasted, with tomatoes, lettuce, mayo, tons of provolone and black pepper. Oh, and onions. White, not red," he told the cook proudly. I scowled.

"That's not fair. My order is easy," I whined and nodded to the cook to make that exact sub. Thomas and Stacie laughed at me when I took my sandwich and paid grudgingly.

By the time we got to the theater we had just enough time to scarf down our food before people started arriving. Erin had made it a little early so she could help Stacie stay organized. Surprisingly, by the time Stacie stood up to do her introduction there were about twenty people here.

"Hello everyone. Lots of old faces, a few new. Glad to have everyone here. My name is Stacie and I am the director. We are hosting auditions for the black comedy "The House of Yes". There are five speaking parts. Two male, three female. Obviously, we won't be able to cast everyone here. However, after I announce the cast, I encourage anyone who still wants to be a part of this production to come see me or my assistant. We will need help with all sorts of things. There are plenty of behind the scenes roles to go around." She walked back to her seat and produced the box of scripts.

"We have seven scripts. So, we will have to share for tonight. Everyone come up and form five lines. One for each part. I'll pass the scripts out once we are a little more organized."

Everyone leapt up and with excited chatter they scurried down and made five lines like Stacie had asked. I waited until it was a little less crowded before standing up. To my surprise, Thomas, who had been sitting next to me also stood up.

"You're auditioning?" I whispered harshly. He gave me a coy smile and winked.

"Sure, why not? I'm already here," he said before heading straight to the line where all the hopeful 'Marty's' were. I followed him onto the stage but went to the Jackie-O line. I gulped. If we both got these parts, we'd be playing the leads. Lovers and twin siblings.

Despite it being quite known of Stacie's preference to have me cast as Jackie-O, there were still six other women auditioning. That made me feel guilty. I hated to toot my own horn, but I was pretty much promised the part. These women were auditioning for nothing. It wasn't fair.

While I waited for my turn to read for the part, I counted

the other lines. Five men came out for Anthony, the other brother. Two middle aged women read for Mrs. Pascal, the mother. There were eight girls here for Lesly, Marty's fiancé, and surprisingly only three men were here to read for the part of Marty.

The scene Stacie had us read was one that included all five parts in some way. Due to the large amount of Lesly's and Jackie-O's, the other three lines had to read several times to give us all a chance. With the order of the lines, I ended up reading with Thomas.

Having seen the movie, I knew how to play the character. I lowered my script to set my eyes on Thomas. I flirted with him, while he awkwardly tried to move away from my advances. I saw his Adam's apple bob as he gulped and said his own lines. He was good. Much better than the other two that had auditioned. When our quick scene was done Stacie had us stand there for a moment. She had been writing things down furiously on her notepad.

Turning to Erin, the two of them discussed things while we stood there awkwardly on the stage. I was looking out into the empty audience when I felt a hand reaching for my own. I whipped around to see Thomas. He squeezed my hand and let go quickly.

"You were really good!" He whispered excitedly. I smiled.

"Thanks, you too!"

Our talking first broke the tension around us. Everyone began whispering around us, chatting excitedly. A few moments later Erin and Stacie started changing up the order of things. They wanted this person to read with this person, or they wanted a Lesly to read for Jackie-O or Marty move to Anthony's line. We spent the next hour being scrambled all over, eventually I ended up reading for all three female parts.

Finally, both of the women in the audience stood up and began clapping.

"Everyone give yourselves a round of applause. You all were so good! I do have a list of people I'd like to come back tomorrow to read again. Erin has a list of people that she'd like to talk to before you leave. Thank you all for coming out, and I can't wait to get this show started!" She set us free.

Everyone scrambled to see the lists they handed to the people the closest to the head of the stage. I stood back with Thomas while everyone went through the list. I saw some faces fall and others light up. When the papers were free, we both reached for one. Despite already knowing, it was still exciting to see that I had gotten a call back. Thomas had as well. I would be up against two other women, while Thomas had only one to audition with.

Erin had a long line of people that hadn't made the call back list, but she was going to try to recruit for painting, props, costumes, and other various backstage jobs. Some looked eager to help, while others were sulking. Sorry guys, it was part of the theatre. Everyone had to do it at some point. I think I had done more offstage work than onstage roles. Sometimes those were the more fun parts.

I saw some girls clumped together murmuring something low while giving me the stink eye. I wanted to roll my eyes, but I understood their frustration. I was once in their place. I felt Thomas' strong hand on the small of my back. I looked up and he was smiling down at me.

"I'm gonna take off, see you tomorrow," he said. I told him goodbye and hurried back to Stacie.

The room was fading out now. Soon the only ones left were me, Stacie, and Erin. Stacie finished making notes and stood up.

"Anyone want to go for drinks?"

"I've actually got to let my dogs out, but we can have some drinks at my place if you're interested," I offered.

"Actually," Stacie started; her face had that 'I've got an idea' look on it. "What if we have a movie night? We can watch 'The house Of Yes', with Parker Posey and Tori Spelling. Beer, popcorn, late night pizza?" Erin perked right up and they both started getting excited about the idea. I was hesitant. I looked at the time on my phone. It was only eight. Mark hadn't been coming home until after midnight.

"I do have some time. But I really need to let the dogs out. How about I drive over to your place when I'm ready?"

"Or we can wait the five minutes and just take you? I don't mind giving you a ride home. Or, just have your husband swing by when he's off work," Erin suggested. That wasn't a bad idea. That way I didn't miss him.

"I'll call him. That will work out great actually."

By the time we had reached my house our small plans for a movie night had turned into a party at Stacie's.

"Lizzie, Michelle, and Thomas are coming. Erin is picking up Justin now. It's just like old times!" She squealed as we walked into my place. Beau and Bonnie came running to the door excitedly. I was starting to feel a little bad. Lately I hadn't been around as much as they needed. Maybe we should hire a full-time housekeeper. We had only been using temporary ones for vacations.

"Wow, you really are loaded now. Far cry from the Reynolds van you were living in when we met," she said. I smiled and leaned against the side of the house.

"Yeah, I'm lucky. Mark is amazing. He didn't have this house when I met him. He was sharing this dump of an apartment with his friend," I chuckled. Way back when Derek did understand the concept of paying rent.

"Well is his friend still single? I'd love to get me a house like this," she laughed. I thought about it for a moment. Was he? Derek had been acting really weird lately when it came to girls. He wasn't bringing strangers over anymore and he didn't even have a date to prom. It was odd for him to be like that. I would have to remember to ask Mark about it.

As soon as the dogs were in, we fed them and left again. I swore to myself that I would spend more time with them. I did remember to turn the TV on for them this time. Maybe they'd enjoy a movie while we were gone.

By the time we got to Stacie's place Erin and Justin were already inside. Lizzie and Michelle followed shortly after us, and Thomas showed up about a half hour later with a woman on his arm. I didn't recognize her.

"Hey Tommy! I'm glad you could make it to our first unofficial cast party. Who's your friend?" Stacie called from the spot next to me. I knew I wore my confusion on my face, but I quickly forced it away with a smile. The only seats left were right next to me. I would have to sit with the two of them.

"Howdy folks! This is Cassandra. Cassandra, this is everyone. Did you start the movie yet?" He asked, moving further inside. Stacie leapt up to take their coats. I looked over at the pretty girl looking nervously around the room.

She was shorter and slim. Her hair was mousy brown and her eyes were a bright blue. She had a nose ring and bright red lips. She looked like someone had done her makeup professionally. I was instantly self-conscious. I was dressed for comfort, while she looked like she was going dancing.

Questioning her fashion choice, my eyes swung to her date. He too looked more dressed up than before. He had showered, and now was in a slick black suit. Did they skip out on a date for this?

"We're gonna start the movie once everyone has a drink and the pizza comes. They should be here any minute. Here, let's get you both a beer," Stacie led them into the kitchen.

"I didn't know Thomas was dating someone," I whispered to Erin. She shrugged her shoulders, eyebrows raised.

"Me either. The more the merrier I guess." The three of

them returned and just as she was about to sit down the door-bell rang and she jumped back up to get the pizza.

Thomas offered Cassandra a seat on the couch next to me. She smiled politely at me and I smiled back.

"Actually, I have to use the restroom. Can you take my drink?" She handed him a glass of wine and he directed her to the bathroom with a quick motion of his arm.

"Sure thing. It's that way, first door on the right." He looked around the room awkwardly. I was just about to move over when Stacie returned and insisted on taking her spot back. Leaving me to sit either next to Thomas or Cassandra. Great.

Thomas saw my dilemma as well and decided to bite the bullet and sit next to me. His date returned a moment later and took the end of the couch. He handed her back her glass.

"Okay, pizza's here, everyone has a drink. Now, while we were waiting, Erin and I came up with a little game," Stacie eyed the redhead on her other side conspiratorially. She pulled out a folded piece of paper out of her shirt and we all groaned. Stacie was notorious for awful drinking games.

"Take a sip every time someone insults Lesly, someone says a non-English word, and when someone talks about someone else's clothing," she paused for effect. "Take a full drink when someone mentions dinner, Anthony says something awkward, and when they talk about Jackie's meds. And finally," she took a breath and everyone groaned. "Chug your drink when there is any reference to incest. Okay, okay. I'm done. I'm pushing play."

We barely made it five minutes into the movie before Stacie was shouting at us to take a sip. I turned to give an eye roll to Thomas but found him looking at his date instead. She had asked him who he auditioned to play. He pointed to Marty on the screen. She nodded, but her face still showed confusion. He then took his sip and looked back at the screen.

When the pair sat at the piano and began their little banter, she asked about it again.

"Who is going to play Jackie?" Thomas smiled and patted my thigh. I jerked away, but still leaned over and waved to her. She frowned, but quickly covered it up with a smile. I extended my hand to her.

"I'm Renee. It's nice to meet you Cassandra," I said politely. She took my hand and shook it.

"Same here. You all are so close, it's kind of hard to get a word in," she laughed. I shrugged.

"We get that a lot."

Thomas shushed me and pushed me gently back to my side. I pushed him back and he smirked at me. We looked at each other for a beat longer than necessary. He winked at me and I quickly looked away.

I felt so uncomfortable sitting next to him. He had his hand on her thigh the entire time. I wished there were more places to sit. When everyone had depleted their first beers, I volunteered to get us all another.

I stuck my head in the fridge, grabbed a six pack, and when I popped back up, I jumped when I saw Cassandra only a few feet away from me. She jumped as well.

"Sorry, I didn't mean to scare you. I was just refilling my glass. I've never played a drinking game before."

"Oh, it's alright. I just hadn't expected to see you there." I grabbed one extra beer for the seven of us. She poured her glass, took a sip and then leaned against the counter. I stood there for a moment. I could tell she wanted to say something. I figured I'd help her out.

"Count yourself lucky. Stacie has made us play way too many dumb movie drinking games over the years." When she didn't say anything, I changed subjects.

"So how long have you been seeing Thomas?" I asked

politely. Her big eyes swung over to me. Gosh she was stunning.

"It's our third date. We were supposed to go dancing. We were actually on our way when he got the invite. He didn't want to miss out on everyone hanging out," she frowned. Oh, I understood her disappointment. Why would he want to bring her to something so uneventful, when he could be out scoring some major points with the pretty girl?

"That's the life of a theatre nerd. We're like family. Do you act?" I said hopefully. Maybe she could be a part of the production. She shook her head.

"No, I sell makeup. Door to door. That's actually how we met," she giggled. I smiled warmly, but I was not interested in listening to her story. Thankfully Thomas interrupted us. He came into the kitchen and looked from her to me.

"The crowd is getting rowdy, we need beer. You two coming?" He said. I nodded and left the room first. Plopping back down I continued playing Stacie's game and let someone else get the next round of drinks. By the time Jackie-O shoots Marty we were all falling over each other in laughter and tears. Someone turned the lights on and suggested another movie.

"I've actually got to go," Cassandra said first. She looked like she wanted to run. I noticed that she hadn't been drinking when the rest of us did. Thomas laughed and stood up but stumbled.

"I can call us a tab, I mean a cab," he laughed. His date didn't look amused.

"That's okay, I got it." She pulled out her cell phone and quickly made a phone call. I swung my head over to Stacie. I leaned against her.

"I gotta go too. Hopefully Mark is done working." I sat up and texted him. He said he'd be there in half an hour. He was already on the road. Thomas told us he was going to see Cassandra out.

"I'm gonna wait with her outside for her ride. I'll be back, go ahead and start whatever without me." They left quickly and I sat back and relaxed with everyone else.

About twenty minutes later Mark called me and told me he was less than ten minutes away. I said goodbye to everyone, grabbed my jacket and left the house. I stopped short when I saw that Thomas was still standing outside, but he was now alone.

"Cassandra already leave?" I asked. He turned his head towards me. Guilt covered his face.

"Yeah, I have a feeling there won't be a fourth date," he murmured. "Your ride on the way?"

I nodded. "Yeah, my husband got off early." There was a long silence afterwards. I crossed my arms over my chest. "You should have just taken her dancing."

He snorted.

"I realize that now. I really didn't think it'd be a big deal. I thought she'd like to meet my friends. I guess not."

"I don't think it was that. It was probably because she was all dressed up and she felt out of place. You know you most likely missed your chance of getting laid, right?" I teased. He rolled his eyes.

"When's your hubby getting here again? You can take your sass somewhere else. Lord knows I'm going to be getting enough of it over the next six weeks."

I looked up from the ground.

"Did she really already pick the cast?"

Thomas gave me a bored look.

"No, but you saw who I was up against. I'm going to get it. So are you." Before I could comment I saw Mark's car in the distance. I stood up straighter and took a few steps forward. Thomas saw and took a few steps back.

"I'll see you tomorrow. Don't leave me hanging Jackie-O,"

he winked right as Mark pulled up. I laughed and waved goodbye.

"Anything for you Marty dear," I said as I opened my door. Mark kissed me as soon as I was buckled in.

"Hey you, long time no see," he joked.

"Ugh, let's go home. I want to get into my pajamas," I sighed. Today had been exhausting.

"Is that pink nightie an option? It looked pretty comfy to me."

I only half laughed at his joke. I was too busy looking at the side mirror. Thomas stood there for a moment as we drove off before heading back into the party. I knew his date didn't go well, but why did he look that sad? It was only their third date. But more importantly, why did I feel so guilty?

Chapter Six

THE CURSE OF CURVES

SATURDAY after the auditions we went to the Andrews' for Lunch. Cleo was excited about the new backyard furniture they had bought and wanted to use it.

"Ethan surprised me with it Thursday. I think he's been feeling bad about how he reacted at first to the surrogate thing," she told me cheerfully as we started setting the large glass table.

"It is a really nice set. He must have been feeling pretty awful."

She rolled her eyes and chuckled.

"Yeah, it's just weird how his apology came the same week the doctor cleared me for sex again."

We both paused for a moment and then burst into laughter. Just then the men came out and gave us questioning looks.

"What's so funny?" Ethan asked. He was holding Blue, so after setting him down in his highchair he walked over to Cleo and planted a kiss on her cheek. Her and I exchanged a look and started giggling again. Ethan frowned.

"Just you," she told him and set the rest of the plates down. "How's lunch coming?"

"It's all ready to go. You want me to bring it out?" She nodded and reached up on her tiptoes to kiss him.

"Yes please. Renee, want to help with the drinks?" I smiled and followed them inside to get the food. While I grabbed the pitcher of lemonade, Cleo and Ethan grabbed the chicken and salads they had made earlier. As soon as all the food was placed on the table and we took our seats all the men started diving in.

I glanced over at Cleo before grabbing my own skewer of chicken, peppers, and onions. She smiled tightly at me but refrained from grabbing anything. She took a sip of her ice water and focused on feeding Blue some fruit. I frowned.

"Cleo, is your stomach not doing okay? Have you started morning sickness yet?" I asked innocently. The eating and conversation dropped, and all eyes swung to her. She turned red and then rolled her eyes.

"I'm fine. I'm not throwing up, but I have been nauseous a lot this week. I'm just not hungry right now. It'll pass," she assured us. I glanced at Mark. His brow was furrowed.

"You want me to bring some crackers or something over?" I reached for his hand and squeezed it under the table. He squeezed it back gently. Cleo shook her head.

"I'm fine guys, really. If I need something, I'll say something," she shut the conversation down sharply. Hesitantly, everyone returned to their lunch.

"How's the album going?" Ethan asked. That ignited a reaction at the table and the men began discussing equipment and other things that were beyond me. I was almost sure Cleo and I sighed at the exact same time. She turned to me, adjusting her body in her seat, bringing her short legs up under her.

"We should have lunch like once a week or something. That way I can get away from all of this," she motioned with her arms at the excited men. "And we can get to know each other better. It always feels like we're too busy to socialize."

"I'd love that. Some girl talk will do you some good I'm sure. Plus, you can keep me updated on everything," I looked down at her flat stomach. "And I won't have to ask Mark every day." I said cheerfully.

"Perfect!"

"Speaking of plays and musicals, Renee, how did your thing go?" Chase shouted across the table. A smile quickly spread on my face.

"I got the part. We start rehearsals Monday." The table let out small cheers and woo's.

"Well that calls for a toast. Cleo, Ethan, you got any-" Derek stopped short, realizing what he was asking. He shut his mouth quick and reached for his glass of lemonade. "A toast, to Renee. May the play go well enough that they are throwing roses, but not well enough to where we have to go see new shows every other month." Everyone chuckled and we toasted to it with our lemonades. When Mark put his glass down, he snickered.

"If you're still crashing on my couch, you'll go to every single show she's in."

Derek glared at him but said nothing. He opted to give him the finger instead.

"Derek, what are you going to do when the baby comes? You don't think they'll want their private time?" Cleo scolded.

"You're not living here," Ethan added.

"Jesus, why is everyone on my back about this? I'll worry about it when it happens. When is the little tater tot due anyways?"

"August. Consider it your eviction notice," Mark quipped. Derek scowled and turned back to Ethan to discuss music. That conversation led to them excusing themselves to go into the studio. I asked about it and Mark explained why they were the only ones to leave.

"We want Derek to sing with Cleo on some tracks. Our

West Side Story song is going to be the first single and the heart and soul of the album. We're going to start every show with it. Since Derek played Tony way back in the day it's only right he sings it again. Ethan's offered to help him train his voice. It's been years since he's really sang."

"Don't him and Adrian already sing?" I asked, glancing at Adrian. He was shoving another piece of chicken in his mouth. He did not look happy.

"Yeah, but that's different. Those are just backup vocals. Anyways, he's nervous about it." Cleo yawned loudly.

"I am so sick of shop talk! Can we talk about anything besides work? Chase, how's the baby? Renee, what about the play; do you know the other people in the cast?"

"He's good. We only woke up once last night. Oh! He laughed the other day. It was so cute," Chase said. Adrian snorted.

"We were watching Clue, that old movie with Tim Curry. He was giggling through the whole movie." Cleo and I both sighed deeply over how cute the three of them were. She then turned to me expectantly.

"The play is going to be great. My two oldest friends are the director and assistant director. The cast is small, but I do know the guy who is playing my twin brother," my eyes shifted to Mark. I wondered for a moment if he had ever even seen the movie. If he had, I really thought he'd have some kind of reaction.

"Wait, isn't that play like the movie? Where the brother and sister get it on and they are all rich and weird?" Adrian called out suddenly. Cleo and Mark's mouths fell open a bit and they looked from him to me. I could feel the heat rushing to my face.

"That's the one. I'm playing Jackie-O."

Adrian's eyebrows lifted in surprise and then he nodded. "Nice."

"Like Jackie Onassis?" Cleo asked, her interest piqued. "Are they going to make you dye your hair?"

I shook my head. "The characters are obsessed with the Kennedy's. But no, I'll be wearing a wig. It was my one condition," I chuckled. I glanced at Mark again and he didn't look happy. His face was blank. I reached for his hand and it brought him back down to earth. He looked over at me and forced a smile.

"Good. Because I'll be damned if they take away the purple. I can't imagine you any other way." He leaned over and kissed my cheek.

"How long have you had your hair like that?" Cleo asked.

"I think I was about seventeen. When I first left home. I can't even remember what I look like without it," I laughed.

"Are you a natural blonde?" She smiled and rubbed her stomach. "I'm just trying to imagine what the little - tater tot is going to look like."

"Is that what we're calling it now? Did Derek start a thing?" Mark yawned. Cleo shrugged.

"Why not? What do you think Renee?"

"I love it, and yes, Mark and I both have naturally blonde hair, so I assume they will too."

"You never know. I have brown hair and brown eyes, but all three of mine have jet black and beautiful blue eyes. Genes are funny that way," she mused.

"Speaking of names, have you thought of any good ones yet?" Adrian asked. Cleo's eyes lit up excitedly. She leaned forward and put her hands flat on the table.

"What do you guys think of Pubert, for a boy of course."

"What if it's a girl?" Adrian asked.

"How do you guys feel about Hannibelle?"

We decided on Wednesday lunches. It marked Cleo's next week in her pregnancy and after two full days with the guys, I think it helped to get a mini break. It was my turn to pick restaurants, and today I was feeling Italian. Both of us were so hungry we ordered quickly and started on the endless breadsticks.

"So, how is week nine?" I asked cheerfully. She beamed with a mouthful of bread. Swallowing she quickly answered.

"Tater tot is now the size of a green olive. Still no vomiting, but my stomach is going crazy. Either I can't eat all day, or I can't eat enough. Today, for instance," she giggled, grabbing another breadstick.

"How's rehearsal going?"

"Great. It's been a lot of fun so far. We have three more weeks left so we are going to start kicking it up a notch. Rehearsal 5 days a week, plus on weekends we'll be finishing building the set and then painting everything. Ugh, I'm tired already."

"I bet. I know these long days in the studio are kicking my ass," she grumbled and then rolled her eyes when she saw my look of concern.

"It's not because of Tot. Just because I'm human. I think it's wearing on all of us a little. Adrian and Derek's hands are all sorts of wrapped up, I'm downing hot tea and lozenges like candy."

"I know. Mark's shoulder is starting to ache. I don't know how you guys do it. You sure are dedicated." She smiled through her bite of bread.

"Well we aren't touring until Tot comes, and I don't know how I'm going to be in a few months. I might start to lose steam with the kids and the music. We're just trying to cram as much work in as we can right now. Just in case."

"Did you get put on bed rest with the twins at all?" I asked. She shook her head.

"No, but I was as big as a house. With all the stress Christopher used to cause I probably should have been in bed. Pregnancy with Blue was like heaven compared to the twins."

I chuckled. "I'm sure the birth was much better too. Considering you only had to do one."

She laughed.

"Yeah, that was nice. Having Ethan and everyone else there was nice too." She sat back and placed her hands on her belly. She smiled softly at me.

"God I can't wait. You are going to be an amazing mom."

My eyes started to water, but I held them in place. She sat up straight and reached for another breadstick.

"Plus, now we have enough for a full band! We have Jimmy on drums, Dallas on guitar, and Blue, Tot, and Rocky can fight for vocals, bass, and another guitar. They are gonna top the charts before they finish high school." She laughed.

"Technically so did all of you," I teased. She scowled.

"Yeah, but they aren't going to be dumbasses and quit like we did."

"I got mine on the road. Home schooled my last year. Got the diploma in the mail."

She eyed me curiously.

"You left home to travel in a theatre troupe? What prompted that? Were your parents mad?" I took a sip of my lemon water.

"I left when I was seventeen. I had met a boy. The whole young, dumb, and in love thing. My parents were pretty pissed when they found out, but figured since I was almost eighteen they wouldn't bother trying to force me to come back." She raised an eyebrow.

"A boy? Obviously it didn't work out, but how long did it last? Did you regret it?" She quickly asked and then apologized. "Sorry, I don't mean to give you an interrogation. It's just-we've never really talked. Or when we do talk it's about me, Mark, or the band. It's not fair."

I chuckled.

"You're fine. Let me think, the boy? His name was Thomas. We dated for about four years. We just kind of fizzled out. The break-up was pretty mutual. We both stayed with the troupe. It was all we knew. I dated casually for a few years after that, until I met Mark. He scooped me up and wouldn't let go." I smiled, thinking about the first time we met. He was so cute.

"Wait, Thomas. Is that the Thomas that is playing your brother in the play? Does Mark know?" She pointed a breadstick at me and furrowed her brows. A chill of guilt ran through me. I coughed.

"Yes, it is the same guy. Mark does know about my previous relationship. If he has a problem with it, he hasn't said anything to me."

She frowned.

"Me either. I guess that's a good thing. If he was upset about it, we wouldn't have heard the end of it." Relief came and took some of the guilt away. She switched gears soon after.

"My belly is getting hard now, even though I'm not showing. You want to feel it?"

Eagerly I reached out and felt her stomach. Sure enough, it felt rock hard.

"That is so cool. Thanks for sharing that with me," I said, now I was going to start crying. She reached out and hugged me.

"Of course! I want to share everything I can with both of you guys. Just because I'm the oven doesn't mean you shouldn't get to experience fun pre-mom stuff."

"Like what?" I asked, wiping the tears off my cheeks.

"Gender reveals, maternity photos, talking to Tot, feeling him or her kick. I want you to experience all of those things."

"I'd like that," I told her.

"I can't wait, but at the same time I know it's going to fly by so fast. I'm dreading the weeks when I start getting huge and can't move around easily anymore. I want to have fun before that." She pouted.

"Maybe we should take a mini vacation or something," I suggested. Her eyes lit up and she put down her breadstick.

"Let's do it! Right after your show is done. Go somewhere fun."

"Where? We spent most of last year going all over the country. What's left?"

"I want to do something different," she put her finger to her lips and tapped while thinking. "Do you like camping?" She asked.

I grinned.

"Heck yes! Before I met Mark, I pretty much slept in a tent for eight years. I'd love to do that. I know how to cook and start a fire. We can fish and hike, make smore's and tell ghost stories to the kids. Oh, I'm already excited!" I clapped my hands together excitedly.

"Alright, alright. Calm down, it's not happening this weekend," she laughed. "I'll get with everyone back at the house and we'll start planning it. And the timing works out great because I should be getting over my nausea and I'm not huge yet."

The waiter finally came with our food. He set a large bowl of fettuccine alfredo in front of me, and shells stuffed with marinara and and ricotta in front of Cleo.

"Perfect."

We ate in silence. We were both starving at this point. I had only eaten one breadstick, while Cleo had finished off the basket. When Cleo came up for air she asked again about the play.

"You have to kiss this guy, right? He's your brother and lover?"

"Yeah, we haven't gotten to that yet. I think we've both been avoiding it. You know, with our history."

"Does he have a girlfriend?" I tilted my head back and forth, wishy washy like.

"He did a few weeks ago. He brought her to a party we had. They ended up fighting though, so I don't know if they worked it out or not."

"How does Mark feel about it? Thomas being possibly single and an old flame."

"He hasn't really said much about it. He wanted to watch the movie, so we did. He said it was gross. I asked him if he was okay with it and he said he kind of had to be."

Cleo sighed. A small smile on her face. I didn't know if it was because of the food or something else.

"He's too sweet. He's changed so much since he met you. Back in the day he would have had a conniption over his girlfriend kissing someone else on stage. You two are so perfect."

Comfortable silence fell over the table as we ate our food. I ate my food at what I felt was a regular pace, while Cleo seemed to think that someone was about to steal her plate if she paused for even a second. When she was finished, she looked over at me and blushed.

"Wow, Tot really has me starving today. He's gonna go from an olive to a peach by tomorrow at this rate." She rubbed her stomach lovingly. "Can we go to a rehearsal sometime? I'd love to see it in action."

"Sure, whenever you want to come just let me know. It's open to the public, well kind of. Friends and family can come check it out. You all should come sometime," I suggested. She smirked.

"You really think Mark wants to see you practicing kissing?" I shook my head.

The waiter brought our check and doggy bags for both of us. As we were standing up, I chuckled.

"No, probably not, but I think it would help him to know that we haven't actually kissed yet. Even so, he wouldn't make a scene. Mark likes to put up a tough front." Cleo put her arm in mine and we walked out of the restaurant side by side.

"He acts like a big tough guy, but he's really a soft teddy bear." We laughed.

"Okay, tonight we are blocking the Kennedy re-enactment. Marty, Jackie, Lesly, and Mrs. Pascal we need you down here," Stacie ordered from the front row. Thomas and I turned our heads towards each other. He gave me a reassuring smile and I forced one in response. This was the scene I had been dreading. Gabby, who was playing Lesly was in the row ahead of us. She jumped up excitedly and hurried down.

"You ready?" Thomas asked as he stood up.

"I don't think we have a choice," I replied and followed him down to the stage. The set was built but only half painted and decorated. We had built a second story, where a bedroom sat. Underneath the bedroom was the living room, where most of the play would be performed. Gabby hurried up the stairs to the bedroom with Joyce, who played our mother. Stacie ordered Thomas to take a few steps onto the stairs and freeze.

"Okay now Renee, the box is under the couch. Go ahead and grab it, open it and pull out the pillbox hat."

I did as told, eyeing the hat in fake wonder. "Now you put it on your head and turn to face him. All the while, you start back down the stairs to her."

As we did so we said our lines. I had them memorized already, as did he. "Okay, then you step out of your dress and put it on. Not today though. Jackie needs help. Marty walk over and shakily help her zip it up."

Thomas came up behind me. I knew I was nervous, but I

discovered he was too. His mouth was only inches away from my neck. His hot breath came ragged. I nearly jumped when his fingers started on my lower back and slowly danced upward. When they reached my neck, he pulled his entire body away from mine.

"Finish putting on the coat and at the bottom of the box is the gun. Reach for it and pull it out."

Since the outfit was still in the box I pretended to do so, pointing my fingers like a gun. I glanced at the director and she nodded approvingly.

"Thomas take the gun and begin walking around the room. Okay, say your lines." Thomas stayed looking at the gun and asked me, Jackie-O, if I remembered the day we did this years ago. I took a few steps towards him and began describing it to him. In her mind, it had been only yesterday.

"Give her back the gun."

I take it and suggest we pretend again, like we did that day the Pascal's father left. Thomas sat down on the couch and began that slow, presidential wave. The room was completely silent. Even Stacie didn't dare speak. I lifted my hand and aimed my gun at him and shot. My hand jumping up like it would with a real weapon. Thomas fell forward and I hurried over to him, putting my body over his. This was it. My heart was racing. We really had to do this.

Thomas sat up and I pulled away a few inches. We looked into each other's eyes. He was just as nervous as I was. He gulped. Neither of us dared move any closer. Suddenly he closed his eyes and moved forward. I did the same and instead of our lips touching his lips went to my ear and he whispered into it. "I like wearing women's underwear."

Immediately I bust out laughing and slap his chest. He starts laughing too and suddenly the tension of the scene was gone. The other ten people in the room chuckled.

"You know you will have to kiss eventually right?" Stacie said annoyed.

"Yeah, yeah. We will. Don't start freaking out on us. We've got this," Thomas played it off. I was thankful to him so much for this.

"Your first kiss cannot be on opening night. I'm serious Thomas. You too Renee," she scolded. The two of us held up our hands.

"Fine. How about we take some private time and rehearse this stuff tonight when everyone goes. I think that could help make it a little less uncomfortable," Thomas suggested, turning to me. I thought about it for a minute. He was right. All these people staring wasn't making it any easier. I nodded and Stacie returned to barking direction at us.

"Okay, after the kiss you two start making out. Thomas your hands will be all over her, Renee start unbuttoning his shirt." We return to the couch but do none of those things. Stacie glared but said nothing.

"As you guys start furiously removing clothing and kissing the lights will dim and then shut off completely. Now, Gabby. While the lights are off you come down the stairs and stand at the foot of the couch. Look shocked when the spotlight turns on you and you are looking at them in the throws."

Gabby hurried down and did as she was told. She was a nice girl. New to the theatre, but eager to learn and friendly.

"Okay, now back away and the lights will shut back off. Thomas and Renee, lay on the couch, embraced in each other's arms. Like you fell asleep afterwards." I did that. The couch was small, so Thomas put his upper body on top of mine, making sure to position just right to not put his weight on me.

"Gabby you will be sobbing softly this entire time and then when you are cued you run up the stairs, face in your hands."

I started to tune out the rest of the direction. The rest of this scene was just Lesly and Mrs. Pascal on the top floor. Mrs.

Pascal confronted Lesly about sleeping with our brother Anthony and was shipping her off. I had heard them go through this several times already and was bored with it. Thomas shifted his body over mine and I instantly stiffened.

"Sorry," he whispered. "I can't hold myself for that long like that."

"It's okay," I whispered back. His head rested on mine. I heard him inhale deeply and a tiny sigh. Did he just smell my hair? We stayed quiet for the rest of the scene and finally when it ended, he leapt off me as if I were on fire. I glanced at him, but he wouldn't look at me. There was a pause, then Stacie told us good job and to run the scene again.

We did the scene two more times before she called it quits. I was so ready to go home. I hoped that Thomas was tired too and didn't want to do some more rehearsing. I stepped off the stage and chatted with Stacie and Erin while everyone packed up.

"You and Thomas are gonna stay here and practice? Or are you guys going somewhere else?" Thomas walked up to the group and asked what we were talking about. She repeated herself and he looked at me, raising an eyebrow and pursing his lips.

"Uh, I guess that's up to you Renee," he said. I smirked. What were my options? Stay here or go to one of our houses. I really didn't think Mark would like to see me making out with someone on our couch.

"We'll stay here. That way we can practice blocking too." Stacie nodded and handed me the keys.

"We're turning off all the special lights. Just use the switch over there. Don't forget to turn everything off and lock up. I'm serious. I'll kill both of you." She grabbed her purse and left with Erin and the rest of the cast. Moments later it was only me and Thomas in the entire building.

He coughed awkwardly and shoved his hands in his pockets.

"I guess I'm ready when you are." I sighed deeply and grabbed my script from the chair I had left it on earlier. He reached for his and trudged up the stairs. I stared at the antique red velvet couch. It was too quiet in here; it was making everything seem more extreme than it had to be. Thomas must have been thinking the same thing, because he pulled out his cell phone.

"We need music." He scrolled through his phone and then walked over to the speakers that were kept backstage. Turning them on, I watched him plug his phone on and suddenly Dion's voice erupted from all around the large room. It took me a moment to recognize it, but after a few lines I realized it was 'Life Is But A Dream'.

Thomas returned to the stage and shrugged, with a slight grin.

"I didn't know what to put on. There's no real good way to go about this," he sighed. I agreed with him. He paced the floor slowly, keeping his eyes turned away from me.

"You know, it wouldn't be so bad if we were strangers. I've done this a million times. It's easy. Hell, some women weren't even attractive. You just pretend they're someone else. But how do you pretend it's someone else when-" he stopped short and stared up at me, like he was just noticing that I was in the room. I crossed my arms.

"When what?" I asked. He gulped and shook his head.

"Nothing. Let's just start the scene." He went to the stairs and we began acting. I wasn't Renee Lacey, I was Jackie-O Pascal, and he was my twin brother and lover, Marty. I pulled out the box with my costume in it while Dion stopped singing and The Paris Sisters started serenaded us. He moved behind me and I gasped when his lips trailed lightly on my neck when he zipped up my dress. It sent a jolt of excitement and terror up my spine.

Memories of Thomas kissing me when we were teenagers flooded over me. Pushing them away I reached for the gun and moved away from him. The music was booming in our ears, so we mouthed our lines, instead of trying to be heard above the speakers.

He took his seat on the couch and began the smile and wave. I lifted my arm and aimed the gun at him. "I hear a symphony" came on and I pulled the trigger. The gun let out a pop and Marty fell over. I ran to him. Pulling him to my chest I began rocking him. After a moment he pulled his head up and we looked at each other. Without another thought, Thomas kissed me. It was hard and needy.

My lips parted and his tongue slipped in. I kissed him back, just as eager as he was. His hand slipped down to my thigh and started climbing towards my skirt. I reached for his shirt and began unbuttoning it quickly. All the while our mouths never left each other's.

I sat up straighter to remove my coat and he quickly unzipped my dress. He pushed me down into the couch and I heard him groan. I could feel his hardness pressed against my thigh. My hands reached for his belt and began undoing it. I didn't go any further. The lights would go down at this point. I pulled my face away from his and tried to catch my breath. Both of us were gasping for breath. I looked up at him and his eyes were filled with confusion and pain. Suddenly he said. "End scene."

My eyes fell down to his mouth and I licked my lips. This was it. We were no longer Marty and Jackie. I had a choice to make. Before I could think any more about it, my phone began ringing on the coffee table. It snapped both of us out of this thick trance the scene had put us under.

He sat up and blew air out of his nose and mouth. I

reached for my phone and saw that it was Cleo. I asked Thomas to shut the music off. He shot me a glare but moved to do so. I answered it once I could hear her properly.

"Hello?"

"Renee? I know you're at rehearsal, but we need you to come to the hospital." I gasped and jumped up. Oh no.

"Are you okay? Is it-" My heart had stopped completely. I couldn't breathe.

"No, no. I'm fine. Tot's fine. It's Mark."

Chapter Seven

YESTERDAY'S FEELINGS

I LEFT Thomas at the theater to lock up by himself. Cleo explained that they were about to sedate him so if I didn't get there quickly, I wouldn't get to talk to him.

I pulled off the pink dress and shoved it roughly into the box. The gun and pillbox hat was tossed on top and slid under the couch.

"I've got to go. My husband is in the hospital. I'll see you later," I said and ran out the back door and leapt into my car.

I sped towards the hospital and was quickly directed to the proper floor. He was no longer in the ER. They had admitted him. Stepping into his room I found the band sitting around his bed chatting lightly. They all turned to me when I came in.

I looked at the bed where my husband slept. My heart fell. I had missed him. Cleo saw my face and stood up to hug me.

"He was in a lot of pain, so they just went for it."

"What happened?" I asked, moving to his side. Adrian and Derek moved to let me through. His right shoulder was all sorts of wrapped up. I raised my hand to his forehead and brushed his light hair back. He looked peaceful.

"He tore his rotator cuff. He's going for surgery first thing in the morning." Adrian told me. My gaze was ripped away from Mark. I gasped.

"Oh no. It's that bad?"

"It's hard to say. The doctor said he thinks it's been torn for a while. Which would make sense. I guess the tear is pretty big. He said after surgery and proper recovery he'll be 100% and ready to play. We've all been pushing ourselves a little too hard these last few weeks. It was a matter of time before one of us finally cracked."

"How was he? When he was awake?"

Derek snorted and crossed his arms over his chest.

"Whiny mostly. Woe is me. I'll never play again. It hurts so much. Blah blah blah. The doc said he'll be fine; he's just freaking out." I whipped my head around. I could punch him right now. Derek saw the look in my eyes and backed off. Cleo yawned.

"Okay, well he's asleep now. Renee, do you want us to stay or do you want to be alone with him? Are you staying the night?"

I nodded.

"I'll stay with him. Can someone go let the dogs out for us?"

Derek raised his hand. "I got it." I rolled my eyes. I wasn't in the mood for him right now.

"Do you want some clothes for both of you?" Cleo asked.

"Yes please. Just go into our room and you'll see the closet. We're not picky, thanks Cleo."

"Sure, anytime," she told me, rubbing my shoulders. They left and Adrian returned an hour later with a bag of things for us.

"Cleo packed it, but she wanted to get the kids settled for bed. Do you want company or would you rather I leave?"

"You can go. Your family needs you more than we do tonight. Come back tomorrow. Thanks for the clothes. I'm going to go to sleep soon. The nurses brought me a blanket." He nodded and took his exit.

I dimmed the lights and reclined in the chair provided in each room. I put a pillow under my head and reached for the extra blanket. Mark was fast asleep. He tried to turn but instantly winced. I sat back up but noticed that his eyes never opened. They must have really doped him up. The nurses stopped in twice throughout the night to make sure his IV was working still.

When he woke up, he was thirsty. I went to get him ice water and when I returned, the doctor was talking to him.

"Okay Mark, we are going to get a nurse in here to make sure you're prepped. They'll take you shortly to the operating room. I've done this surgery hundreds of times. Your tear is pretty big, but still fixable. By the looks of it, it's been torn for a while, but you finally tipped it over the edge." He eyed my husband like a father expecting his son to fess up the truth over something. Mark looked away guiltily.

"It's been hurting awhile. I'm a drummer. I get sore," he confessed. The doctor shook his head.

"If you had come in when it first flared up, we probably wouldn't be here prepping you for surgery. Next time know your limits, take a break if you are starting to get sore. I think you'll heal okay this time, but the more it happens the less likely you'll be going back to your drumming." Mark gulped and then nodded, understanding what the doctor said, but not wanting to hear it. The doctor cleared his throat and continued.

"It is outpatient, so you get to go home and rest comfortably instead of here, so that's a plus. Do you have any questions?" Mark's eyes trailed to me and when I shook my head that I didn't he told him no.

I was just about to give him the water when the doctor saw me and quickly told me to stop.

"He can't have any food or liquids until after the surgery."

"Oh duh. I knew that. I'm sorry, lack of sleep," I mumbled and put the cup down. Shortly after the doctor left the nurses came in and took him away. I squeezed his hand one last time and told him I loved him. He blew me a kiss with his good arm as they wheeled him out of the room and down the hall.

The surgery lasted almost three hours. By the time he got out I had already had breakfast with Cleo and Derek and changed into my other clothes. Adrian showed up shortly before they wheeled my husband back into the room. We stayed for another hour until the anesthesia wore off and a nurse returned with release papers. The nurses then put him in a wheelchair, and we followed behind them as they went to the elevator. He was in a sling and drowsy. I ran ahead of them and pulled my car up. With the help of the guys, we got him into the car and strapped in. They told me they'd meet me at the house.

Before I went home, I stopped to get his prescriptions. Thankfully they were all ready for me to pick up right when I got there. I picked up some snacks he liked as well before I headed to the counter.

When I got back into the car, he was whining that I left him alone. The heavy meds they had him on made him loopy.

"I got you some pudding cups," I said cheerfully. He looked at me mournfully.

"How am I supposed to eat them with no arm?"

I sighed. "You have an arm. But I can help you."

"Did you get chocolate?"

"I did."

"I knew there was a reason I made you my best girl," he grinned. I chuckled. He was high from the meds they gave him, but it was still nice to hear a compliment.

The band was already at our house when we returned home. Despite having just seen them a little over an hour ago, they jumped up when we came into the room, their faces filled with worry.

"How you feeling?" Adrian asked. Mark glared at him and tried plopping onto the couch. He winced, having bumped his shoulder falling down.

I swore and hurried over to him.

"Mark, you need to be more careful. If you don't follow the doctor's orders you won't fully heal," I reminded him. He was still pouting, so I stood back up and crossed my arms. I turned to his bandmates.

"He's probably going to be sulking or sleeping the rest of the day. You can probably take off. Enjoy the break."

They looked at each other and slowly nodded. I noticed it was hard for all three of them to leave their best friend when he was hurting. Guilt seeped into me. They were just as much his family as I was.

"But, maybe staying will cheer him up some. I don't think I can take his mood today. Stay." They all seemed so relieved and quickly joined him on the couch.

I went into the kitchen and my eyes settled on the empty coffee pot. Suddenly I was exhausted. A night in a hospital recliner doesn't exactly equal a great night's sleep. I wanted to nap. I heard light footsteps and turned.

Cleo came into the room. She smiled warmly.

"Hey you," I greeted.

"Hey. I wanted to make sure it really was okay we stayed. I know we all have trouble with boundaries sometimes. If you want some time alone, I can totally make the guys leave with me."

I shook my head and waved her off.

"No, it's fine. Really. I was actually thinking of taking a nap. Having you all here is great. You can keep him company. I'm more tired than I thought."

"Sure, go right ahead." I smiled and started to leave the kitchen when she called to me.

"Hey before you go, do you have something I can eat? Tot is telling me I missed lunch." Heading back into the kitchen I opened the fridge and listed some possibilities for her.

"Ooh, mac and cheese sounds amazing right now."

Nodding, I went to the cupboards and started searching for a pan. Cleo walked over to me and put her hand on mine.

"I can make it Renee. You go nap. I'll see if the guys are hungry too. I'll even clean up afterwards." I stood up straight.

"You sure?"

She rolled her eyes.

"Yes. I can boil some water and pour in the noodles. I know I've never been a culinary great, but I can do some stuff." I laughed.

"That's not what Ethan says." She reached out and lightly punched my shoulder.

"Go before I put you to sleep." She held up her tiny fist at me. Hugging her quickly I ran up the stairs before the dogs could hear me and follow. Once I was in my room I quickly undressed and hopped in the shower.

I turned the heat up and let my body soak up the warmth. I started thinking about the last few hours. It was crazy how much had changed. I was at rehearsal and then dropped everything and ran to Mark. Suddenly I felt dirty, thinking about what I had been doing when he hurt himself. I took the loofah and started scrubbing yesterday off of me.

Once I was out of the shower, I put lotion on and slipped on some pjs. Feeling relaxed, I fell asleep almost instantly.

I woke up naturally about four hours later, feeling refreshed and ready to deal with my husband. Grabbing some jeans and a shirt out of the closet I headed downstairs and was immediately met with hushed shouting from the kitchen.

"Do you even know what you're doing?"

"No! I've never made pudding on the stove. Is that what it's supposed to look like?"

"I don't think so. It smells gross. Dude, Renee's gonna kill you."

Reaching the ground floor, the smell of burning chocolate hit me like a wall. I ran into the kitchen and my jaw dropped.

Cleo and Derek spun around quickly, both looking extremely guilty. The room was a mess. I didn't know where to look first. Why was it so hot in here? I rushed over to the stove and pushed past the two kitchen idiots and turned the burner off quickly, removing the disastrous mess from the hot spot. Turning back to them I slowly looked around.

The table had a casserole pan in the center with some chicken breasts in it. Someone had opened a can of cream of something and poured it on top of the meat. Only they didn't spread it, so it sat wiggling like some weird yellow gelatin on top. I noticed a bag of stuffing next to the pan. It had been opened, no, ripped open. Bread crumbs were everywhere. The table, the floor, some did land in the pan.

The floor was covered in what looked like chocolate powder. The counters were covered with every ingredient these two felt like they needed to do whatever the hell they were thinking. The sink was filled with pans and plates, like they had fed a dozen people. I didn't know how to react. I blinked a few times, took a few long, deep, breaths, and then looked back at the two guilty parties.

"What happened?" I said as calmly as I could.

"We were hungry and Cleo said not to wake you up," Derek pointed at his partner in crime. She shot him a nasty glare.

"It's almost dinner time. Derek didn't want me to cook so he was in charge of the main dish. That was all him," she motioned to the table.

"Yeah, well she was in charge of the dessert and look how that turned out."

I put my fingers to my temples and rubbed them, closing my eyes. I really didn't know how to talk to these two right now.

"Have you ever cooked food in your life Derek?"

"No, not really. Mark was the one who told me what to make. He said it was easy. Chicken, a can of soup, stuffing."

"Have you ever opened a bag like a normal human being?" I shouted. He flinched.

"It was an accident. I was excited. I'll clean it up. I can fix my mess. You'll probably have to throw out the pudding pan," he looked back at Cleo. I sighed deeply, trying to calm myself. I was not used to this kind of mess in my kitchen.

"Why were you making pudding?"

"Mark wanted some. He said you bought some and that's all I could find. I must have not added enough milk or something. I'll buy you a new pan. I promise," she said, her big brown eyes turning to mournful puppy dog eyes. I gulped, nodded, and then went to the kitchen table. Looking at the casserole dish, I decided that this was still able to be fixed.

"Okay, both of you start cleaning. I'll work on dinner." Grabbing some green beans from the crisper in the fridge I set to work making dinner. Both of them apologized repeatedly, but I stayed focused on the task at hand.

I heard the front door open and after putting the casserole in the oven I went out to see who was there. Adrian was walking in with Rocky on his hip. Behind him Ethan came in with Blue as the twins followed behind. They saw me and lit up. The stress from the kitchen melted off me and I smiled genuinely for the first time since I woke up.

"Hey twins, what's going on?" They hurried over to me.

"We're here for dinner. My Dad said Uncle Mark is hurt, so we gotta be quiet and leave him alone," Dallas said.

"Yeah, Uncle Adrian said he can't play the drums for a long time. I brought him my favorite bear," she reached behind her and pulled out a cute brown bear out of the backpack I hadn't realized she'd been wearing. She was adorable.

"I bet he's still in the living room if you want to go give it to him. Just remember, be careful. Don't plop on the couch and don't touch his shoulder, okay?" They both nodded in synchronization and then hurried towards the living room. I looked back at Adrian and Ethan.

"Is dinner done? It smells - weird." Adrian made a disgusted face and walked into the kitchen. "What the hell." I heard him say.

"Yeah, that's why I help with the cooking at home. If it's not chicken nuggets or pancakes she's kind of lost," Ethan chuckled. He was teasing, but his eyes revealed nothing but love.

I reached for the baby and took him from Ethan. Giving him a big kiss on his chubby cheeks, I took him to the living room to see Mark. He was sitting on the couch, looking miserable. He was looking at the TV, but his eyes were glazed over. Jimmy's bear sat next to him, keeping him company.

"He's probably a little gone right now. He was scheduled for his meds about half an hour ago." Adrian came up behind me and explained.

"How was he when I was sleeping?" I asked. Ethan stepped past me and grabbed the playpen we kept packed up in the corner. He unfolded it and clicked it into place. I brought Blue over and set him inside as his dad grabbed his little box of toys and tossed them inside the playpen. Standing up straight I turned back to Adrian.

"You'd have to ask the two chefs in there," he glanced towards the kitchen. I started steaming again, just thinking about them. Adrian chuckled.

"I had to go get the baby so Chase could go to radiation.

But when I was here, he was mostly just angry. He wants to get back to work. You know how he is."

I nodded, going to sit with my husband. He turned his head towards me and gave me a half smile.

"Hey baby. I can't feel a thing." I laughed and kissed his good shoulder.

"Well that's good."

"Can I have some pudding now?" He asked. Despite not wanting to go into the kitchen I stood up to go get the prepackaged cups I had bought earlier. Sure enough, they were in the fridge. I pulled them out and gave both Derek and Cleo a pointed look. They saw me and both looked away quickly.

"The mop is in that cupboard," I told them as I grabbed a spoon. Derek shot a glare at me, but I didn't back down. He sighed and told Cleo to go grab it.

Sitting back down with Mark I opened the packs and helped him figure out how to use his left hand. Of course, him being high off his rocker didn't help the situation. He ended up a mess with chocolate everywhere.

Slowly everyone poured into the room and while we waited for dinner to cook, we watched TV. I was content in spending my evening like this when my phone rang and reminded me of my other obligations. I pulled my phone from my back pocket and swore. It was a text from Thomas.

EVERYTHING OKAY? YOU STILL COMING TO REHEARSAL?

"What's wrong?" Cleo asked, her brows furrowed with worry.

"I forgot about rehearsal."

"Oh, we can hold down the fort for you. Go." I shot her a look and she held her hands up.

"I won't step a foot in the kitchen. I swear. Seriously. We all understand the importance of rehearsal," she said and everyone more or less agreed.

"Plus, I really don't think Mark even realizes you're sitting next to him right now, so I doubt he'll notice if you leave for a while," Adrian joked. Everyone chuckled and even I could agree with that. Looking up at him, I saw he was slowly closing his eyes.

"I'll have dinner with you guys and get him settled and then go," I decided.

Despite Derek's first attempt at dinner, I was able to salvage it and dinner wasn't half bad. Of course, he took credit for it. I didn't feel like arguing about it. My stomach was turning, making me not up for much conversation.

Guilt was slowly seeping into my stomach as I finished cleaning up and getting Mark comfortable on the couch. I grabbed a blanket and laid him down. Taking another dose of his meds after eating made him drowsy. It didn't feel right leaving him to go have fun with my friends- with Thomas.

Before he drifted off to sleep Jimmy handed him her bear and he clutched it tightly in his good arm. The twins went up to the playroom while the adults relaxed with Mark. I thanked them again and grabbed my keys.

Heading to the theater I couldn't shake the nagging feeling that I shouldn't be going. My husband needed me. I mean, he didn't, but he did. Everyone else could handle helping him and his meds, but I was supposed to be his moral support.

When I got there, everyone was waiting for me. I apologized and explained what had happened. Everyone nodded and seemed sympathetic and understanding. When I glanced at Thomas, even though he was smiling politely, I could see that it didn't reach his eyes. His eyes looked sad.

Stacie wanted to go over last night's scene.

"Did you guys get a little more comfortable with each other

last night?" She asked us. I glanced at Thomas and he smirked. I blushed.

"Yeah, I think so. You wanna go for it tonight?"

My stomach was in knots. Did I? Last night, right before my phone rang, was I? I felt like his question was more than just rehearsal. I didn't know how to answer him. I didn't know the answer. Mark kept popping in my head, pushing all thoughts of Thomas away.

"Okay, let's just start the scene. Remember, tomorrow is your last day for books. Monday everyone is off-script."

We climbed onto the stage and started the scene. I was shaking when he came behind me and zipped me up. He kissed me again on my neck and I shivered. It was as if I was ice and his lips were fire. When he kissed me, I forced myself to become Jackie-O.

We played out the assassination and I ran to him. I swear he could hear my heart beating furiously. He sat up and we looked at each other for a moment. I watched his eyes dart to my lips and then he went for it. His lips were eager and demanding. I closed my eyes and forgot our audience. I pressed my breasts into his chest, and he groaned. His fingers felt familiar in a disgusting way as he moved them down. It took everything in me not to shove him away.

When his hands reached my knees, they started moving back up my thigh and suddenly I felt the heat of the lights disappear. My eyes went open and I saw that someone was working with the lighting today.

"We can still see you, the scene is just focusing on Lesly and Mrs. Pascal," Stacie explained. Thomas pulled his face away from mine but kept his arms around me.

"What are we supposed to do? You want us to freeze or keep going?"

Stacie turned to Erin to discuss. They looked at us but

covered up their mouths with Stacie's clipboard. It irritated me. Finally, they lowered it.

"Keep going, just lower her to the couch and from time to time wiggle around. Give the illusion of a passionate affair. After Lesly finds you, we are going to see her run upstairs and talk with Anthony. The audience will still see you, but you'll be in the dark. We don't want to take focus off of the two upstairs, but we don't want you two completely frozen either. Okay, take it from the start of the kissing and then we'll start blocking Lesly and Anthony's scene."

Thomas turned back to me, but in the dark I couldn't see his facial reactions. Instead he pulled me closer and put his lips on mine. Initially it felt wrong, but I quickly moved past it and kissed him back. He pushed me gently onto the sofa and he climbed on top of me. We continued kissing, but it wasn't as heavy as when the spotlight was on us. His hands explored my legs and waist but didn't go much further. I remembered the line that signaled we were supposed to go to sleep. When we heard it, he pulled away and we pretended to drift off to sleep. Thomas wrapped his arms around me, and his fingers grazed my breast.

If he hadn't been able to hear it, he could certainly feel my heart racing in this position. I sure could feel something of his pulse. It felt like forever, but finally the lights turned back on and our mother was waking us up. I was confident enough to be off script, so I blocked this scene hands free. The rest felt easy. It was as if a weight had been lifted once I moved from the couch.

We finished the blocking and of course we ran it two more times. I was more rigid when we were kissing the second time around and when the lights went out, he whispered to me.

"I'm sorry, it was involuntary." I nodded and kissed him again, pulling him down, not wanting to break the scene and get yelled at.

The third time around I was more relaxed but still visibly stiff. Stacie called me out on it. "Renee, what happened? I know you're having a rough day. Should we call it?" I shook my head.

"No, sorry. I'm good. Let's keep going." We finished the third go around and she finally announced that she was satisfied.

"Alright, everyone. Let's get out of here and regroup tomorrow. You're all looking great up there."

I leapt off the stage and quickly gathered my things.

"Renee, wait." I glanced over my shoulder at Thomas. He was jumping down and moving towards me. I didn't want to talk to him right now.

"I should really get going," I said lamely and put my jacket on.

"I'll walk out with you, hold up." I sighed and slowed for him to catch up with me.

"Hey, you know it didn't mean anything."

I said nothing. After what happened last night, I knew that was a lie. When we were outside, I looked and saw that our cars were the only ones left. How did everyone leave so quick? I stopped moving and turned to him.

"Thomas, I'm married," I said, deciding to just be blunt. I needed to stop this before I couldn't anymore. It was my responsibility, not his. He shook his head and shrugged.

"And I'm dating Cassandra. I'm going over to her place now. We don't have to make this awkward. So, I got a little hard. It happens when a guy is pressed against a gorgeous woman," he pressed his lips together. He used to do that whenever he was holding something back. I knew him way too well. That was the problem. Our history.

"Okay. You're all good. We are all good. Now go see your girlfriend, I have to get home to my husband."

His face fell, but reluctantly he nodded.

"See you tomorrow."

I walked over to my car and as I climbed in told him goodbye. I practically sped home. I needed another shower. As soon as I stepped up to the door, I was greeted by Derek ripping the door open. I jumped.

"Jesus, you scared me," he chuckled, closing it.

"Where are you going?"

He shook his head and pulled out a pack of cigarettes.

"I just wanted a smoke." He sniffled and then gave me an odd look. I paused with my hand on the door handle.

"What?"

"You reek of men's cologne." His eyes widened and he began wiggling his eyebrows. "Was tonight the night?"

I rolled my eyes.

"What are you talking about?"

"Oh, you know." He made kissing noises in between puffs. "You might want to shower. Mark is going to smell that."

"He knows I have to kiss someone," I defended but Derek shook his head.

"Yeah, but you smelling like him, that's like tossing it in his face. How is it, by the way? Is it weird?" I crossed my arms.

"It is," I confessed.

"Just don't do what Cleo did." He pointed his cigarette at me and looked at me sternly. I smiled, but it fell when his expression didn't change.

"What did she do?" He gave me a blank look.

"We did the song with Cruel Distraction and they hooked up in real life while pretending they were just doing it for the show. I mean, do what you want, I guess. It worked out in the end for them. But that was different. Ignore all that, I'm starting to confuse myself." He finished his cigarette and flicked it out of his hand and onto the ground, stomping it out with his shoe. Looking up at me he shook his head.

"Just don't cheat on my man. You two are good together,

and you shouldn't let some old boyfriend get in the way of that. Some people aren't meant to have that second chance. You got it right with Mark. Mark's crazy over you."

I felt my lips start to tremble. My eyes began to water. Derek could see it from the porch light and his hard expression softened.

"Aw, don't start that," he said, pulling me into a hug. "You know we are all crazy over you too. I can't lose you just as much as Mark can't." I sniffled and he squeezed me a little tighter. Finally, he pulled away and when I looked at him, he grabbed the door handle and tilted his head.

"We should probably go in before they start thinking I'm the one you've been sucking face with," he teased. I gave him a half smile as I wiped my face.

As soon as I got in the house, I stopped in the living room. Mark was up, as was everyone else. Mark turned and his face lit up.

"Hey babe, how was rehearsal?" I was hesitant but chose to go sit with him for a moment. I gave him a gentle, awkward hug, avoiding his shoulder. He went to kiss me and scrunched up his nose. He looked at me and then the realization hit him.

"Can I go shower?" I asked meekly. He didn't say anything for a moment and then his face broke into a smile. He leaned forward to plant a quick kiss on my lips.

"Please." I laughed and thanked him. I excused myself and as I was heading up the stairs I smiled when I heard him yelling at me.

"You wanna brush your teeth and use some mouthwash too?"

Chapter Eight

READY FOR THE FLOOR

"All I can think about is all the times I didn't use my shoulder. I should have played more baseball, been an air traffic controller. Hell, I even want to do yoga. Renee, you have no idea how badly I need to stretch," he moaned. I peeked my head out of the shower to glance at my miserable husband.

"I know baby. Well when you finish healing, I'm sure we can find a way to live out your fantasy of being an air traffic controller. How's Cleo doing, by the way?"

He grimaced. "Every time she sits down at the set I cringe."

"Is she getting any better?" I did a final rinse and turned the water off. Grabbing a towel, I wrapped myself up and stepped out onto the pink padded mat. He tilted his head back and forth.

"Yeah, she's really trying. I just don't like the idea of her getting too comfy. Drums are my thing. Singing is for the birds."

I chuckled. "I thought you liked the idea." He rolled his eyes.

"I did at first, but we can't agree on a song to sample. We

are going with Hedwig and the Angry Inch, though. It's progress."

I reached for my lotion and as I rubbed the moisturizer on my calves, I noticed that Mark's eyes followed my hands. He gulped.

"Well that's something. I love that musical."

Mark's resting at home lasted about a week. He has never been able to just sit still, so finally he said they needed to figure out a way to make it work. They had the idea of Cleo jumping on drums and Mark would take her microphone and sing a song. There were two things problematic with that idea. Cleo couldn't play drums, and Mark can't carry a tune.

Over the last three weeks, Cleo has been spending her time working on learning the new instrument, while Mark has been working with Derek and Ethan to train his voice. All the while trying to find a good song to write. Since they would have two guys on vocals, they wanted to do something fun that Cleo wouldn't be able to do. Ethan suggested they sample 'Hedwig and the Angry Inch'. Naturally we had to rewatch it that night.

"I can agree to the musical, but I will not sing "Angry Inch"," Mark said. It wasn't the song that bothered him, it was the performance that would go with it.

"I'm having to get used to the idea of being front and center, performing something crazy like that is too much for my first time. I want something more focused on my voice," he reasoned. Everyone thought that was fair and have been trying to find a song in the musical to sample.

"I still like 'Origin of Love'," I commented as he followed me into the bedroom where I opened the closet and dropped my towel. He whistled.

"Baby, if you come over here with that hot body, I'll sing you whatever you want," he said. I reached for a bra and pressed it against my chest as I turned around. He pouted.

"Oh, come on."

"Sorry, we need to get you over there." He groaned and sat down on the bed.

"They are going to make me sing 'Sugar Daddy'. To Derek."

I snorted and my hands went to my face to try to stop the laughter. The bra dropped to the floor and Mark grew excited.

"Sweet! Is that what does it for you? Whatever works, come here. I miss you," he whined.

I waved my finger at him and reached down to grab my bra. Slipping it on I hurried to pick out my other clothes.

"You're not the only one with things to do. I've got to be at the theatre. The show is tomorrow so it's crunch time."

"What can you possibly have left to do?" He asked, following me down the stairs.

"As far as the show itself goes, just one more dress rehearsal. But we have to prep the theater for patrons. We do a lot of baking for intermission and the after party. Lots of cookies and brownies." Mark thought about it for a moment and then patted my shoulder.

"Just bring me back something good. Maybe a lemon square?" His big eyes pleaded. I kissed him quickly.

"I will bring you a whole plate of lemon squares if you will just get your shoes on. We need to go."

I dropped him off at the Andrew's and the band quickly went to the studio. Looking at my phone I saw I had some time to spare. I popped my head in and saw that Jimmy was seated at the drums, her mother watching her with curiosity.

"Maybe we should have Jimmy join us on tour and take over for this song," Derek teased. Mark shot him a look that told him he'd kill him. He was having some hardcore replacement issues. Jimmy beamed.

"My mom isn't too bad. But her big belly is gonna get in the way," she giggled and poked her mom with a tiny finger. Cleo gasped and looked down at her stomach. She was just starting to show. She looked like she had eaten a lot at breakfast.

"Here, Mom you can sit down. I'm gonna go find Dallas." Jimmy jumped up and said goodbye to everyone before quickly running off. I stepped further into the room and watched them get into position.

Mark grabbed his microphone begrudgingly and waited for Adrian and Derek to start playing their instruments. They warmed up with some fun songs from their old albums. It was hilarious and kind of cute hearing Mark try to sing them. He looked miserable the entire time.

I figured the next week would be rough. They took him off the painkillers. Even he admitted that the pain wasn't nearly as bad as it once was. He was going to start physical therapy on Monday, and I did not envy his future therapist. Mark was already a hothead, so now he was extra moody.

I stuck around until I had to leave. I blew him a kiss and took my exit, not wanting to disrupt their work. When I arrived, Erin, Stacie, and Gabby were already inside and mixing things in bowls. They all brightened when I stepped into the kitchen.

"Yay, you're here. You can make the margaritas."

By the time dress rehearsal rolled around I had drank at least five strong drinks. I had made about seven batches. Stumbling into the dressing room I could barely pin my hair back to put the Jackie-O wig on. Thomas, who had shown up only minutes ago came in and helped me. Gabby giggled as she struggled with her own costume.

"It smells like a bar in here. Have you guys been drinking?" He asked which set us into a fit of giggles. He groaned.

"Are you serious? I really don't want to play this game." He gave me a pointed look, but I didn't really care. I stifled my laughs and slipped my black cocktail dress on.

"Well then catch up. Drinks in the kitchen," I murmured as I set to work on my makeup. With a giant sigh he left the dressing room. He returned just as I was finishing my lipstick. He had a tall red drink in his hand. I giggled and he smiled, taking a long drink.

"If you can't beat 'em, join 'em."

We performed the entire show drunk or buzzed. It was a stumbling mess, but we got through it without a single person missing a line. It was the ultimate test. When we were teenagers, we used to play this game. The only difference was back then we did it in the woods in the middle of the night where no one was going to catch us. It was something completely different being on the actual performance stage. Stacie and Erin made us swear never to tell any of the higher ups what we did. They'd never let them direct again.

When it came to the scene where Marty and Jackie-O finally give in to their desires my scene partner was rather bold. He didn't hesitate to use his tongue. I pulled away and he reigned in his excitement. When the lights went out, his hands went further than they ever had. I felt him harden against me. I adjusted my body away from him as we continued to kiss. His hand tried going under my dress, and even drunk I knew to push him away. He groaned but didn't try again.

Once we had all sobered up and had a light dinner together, he apologized in private.

"I know no means no, and even drunk I backed off. I'm sorry if I took it too far."

I gave him a quick hug and apologized as well.

"I was drunk too, but it's okay. We were kissing. It's hard not to get riled up when you've been drinking. Let's just have a bang out show tomorrow." We all stayed until we were all sober. Finally, I started back to Cleo and Ethan's. Looking at my car's radio I saw that it was just after eight.

I popped in and was greeted by Tabatha leaving. I walked through the house, peaking in doorways to find my husband and his friends. I paused when I saw Jimmy in the kitchen alone. She was sitting at the island, eating some red jello. I went into the kitchen and joined her.

"Hey girly, shouldn't you be in bed?" She shook her head. Her jet black piggy tales bounced.

"We have half a day at school tomorrow. Daddy says we don't have to go to half days if we don't want to." I pondered that for a moment as I watched her eat her late night snack. I guess I understood. Back when I was in school half days were a joke. We just came in and played games or watched a movie until they released us. It was pointless.

"Where's your brother?" I asked and she gave me a irritated look.

"I don't know. We do stuff without each other you know," she snipped.

"Oh. I'm sorry. Do you like doing stuff by yourself?" Her face relaxed and she shrugged.

"Sometimes. Dallas won't play dolls with me, so I have to do that alone. Or he won't play tea party with me."

"Does he do stuff that you don't like to do?" I asked her and she had to think for a minute. After a moment she nodded.

"He likes scary movies. Him and Daddy watch movies without me all the time." She sounded jealous.

"Maybe we should do a movie night. Me, you, and your mom. We could make it a real girls' night." She lit up.

"Can we? I'm going to go ask my mom right now!" she said and leapt off her chair to go find her. She returned quickly, pulling Cleo along. Cleo was laughing.

"What's this I hear about a girl's night?"

"She said Dallas watches movies with his dad all the time, so I said we should watch girl movies. Have popcorn and root beer floats."

"Can we, can we, can we? Please please please!" Jimmy begged, pulling on Cleo's arm as she bounced up and down. Cleo pondered it for a moment and then nodded.

"That sounds like so much fun. Jimmy, why don't you go grab your pillow while we figure this out."

"Wait, are we doing this tonight?" I asked. Cleo shrugged.

"I'm not doing anything. Why not? I think she could definitely use some girl time. She's been kind of bummed since Dallas started becoming a little more independent."

"Are we having a slumber party? If so, we should probably do it at my house. I need to be there for Mark."

"Oh crap. Yeah. Let me go see if Ethan is okay with the baby or if he wants me to take him. I'll be back," she said and quickly turned. Moments later I was joined by my husband and his friends. He came over and although his face was sour, planted a kiss on my lips.

"Jesus, that guy really needs to wear less cologne."

I reminded him I loved him, and he told me the same.

"What's the plan for tonight?" He asked me.

"Slumber party. Just the girls."

Jimmy ran into the room with a backpack on and her red pillow in hand.

"Dallas is mad because he doesn't get to have a slumber party like the girls do," she told us, beaming. Cleo returned soon after wearing her own pajamas and with no baby.

"He's already sleeping, so Ethan said he can stay here with him. Are we ready?" Without much else holding us back we all piled in my car and drove over to our place. Derek and Adrian had to stop over at his apartment to let Chester out, but were back at my house with the dog in tow an hour later. I didn't really mind, their dog played well with both of ours.

Originally the girls and I were going to take over the living room, but after Mark and the boys whined over having nowhere to go, we went upstairs and took my bedroom. Jimmy went berserk over my bathroom, and then screamed when she saw the closet.

"You have so many pretty clothes!"

Cleo chuckled. "I don't go shopping enough apparently." I was kind of embarrassed. Cleo and Ethan had much more money than us, but yet she lived much simpler than me. Did they think I was spending all of my husband's money? He was the one who bought most of this stuff. I just wore it. Cleo must have read my mind because she put her hand on my shoulder and I turned.

"Mark spoils you, doesn't he?" I giggled.

"He really does."

"You know how I could tell?"

"How?"

"All of those heels are six inches plus and the dresses are shorter than I am."

"You got him. I did pick out the jeans."

Once Jimmy tried on a dozen dresses, sampled three different shoes, and went wild with my costume jewelry she came out satisfied and climbed into bed with us. I had picked out the girliest movie I could find on cable to watch and we relaxed, ate snacks, and giggled when the girl fell into the water trying to impress the guy or all the other various staples for a great romantic comedy. The movie ended with the girl surprising her now husband with a pregnancy announcement, teasing the inevitable sequel. While I was looking for something else Jimmy sat up and looked at her mother, then me.

"When mom has the baby, she's going to give it to you? Why don't you just give her Blue?" Cleo and I didn't say anything for a moment before we burst into laughter. Jimmy was not amused.

"What? Then you wouldn't have to make another one."

"It doesn't work like that. Blue is your brother. He is mine and Daddy's baby. Tot is Uncle Mark and Aunt Renee's baby. He's going to look like them, not you guys."

Jimmy grimaced with confusion.

"I couldn't hold the baby in my belly. So, your mommy said she would do it. The baby needs a place to grow and her belly was the only place they could go," I tried to explain. Jimmy pushed her little tummy out and rubbed it.

"I would have done it. My friends at school have dolls that look like real babies and they say that they are the baby's moms. I want a doll like that."

I chuckled. "Okay, maybe next time we'll let you do it."

"Can I get a baby like the girls in my class have Mom?" She pleaded with Cleo. Cleo frowned.

"Why don't you wait and ask your daddy? Maybe for your birthday," she offered and then shushed her so we can start the next movie. This one wasn't as entertaining as the first one, and we all eventually grew bored. Jimmy declared her boredom halfway through, so I started trying to think of things we could do.

"We could make brownies, do makeovers, or maybe prank phone calls," I said, wiggling my eyebrows.

"What is a prank phone call?" She asked excitedly. I giggled and reached for my phone and dialed *67 to hide my number, then dialed Mark's cell number. I whispered to them who I called while it was ringing. I pushed the button to put it on speaker, so they could hear. Jimmy started giggling and Cleo was trying to conceal her own smile with a pillow over half her face. He answered after the fourth ring.

"Hello?"

I lowered my voice as low as it could go. "Hello, is Mr. Wall there?"

"Uh, no? Who is this?" He demanded.

"Well is there a Mrs. Wall? Or maybe another Wall?" I insisted. We heard Derek in the background complain about hanging up the phone.

"Dude come on, unpause the game."

"There are no Walls here!" Mark snarled and I drove the joke home.

"Then how does your roof stay up?" I shouted and quickly hung up. The three of us erupted into giggles and fell over holding onto our guts. We heard Mark swear from downstairs which only made us laugh harder.

"I want to try!" Jimmy exclaimed. I looked over at her mom who nodded her approval.

"Who should we call?" I asked. Cleo burst into laughter again and when she could breathe, she spoke.

"Derek."

Perfect. I dialed the number, pushed the speaker button, then handed the phone to the little girl who was bouncing with excitement. It took him a moment before he answered.

"Yo," he said smoothly. Jimmy's eyes went wide with panic. I motioned with my hand for her to speak. She gulped and then asked if Mr. Wall was there.

"What? No! What is with the Walls? There are no Walls here!" He shouted so loud we could hear it from the phone and downstairs.

"Well then how does the roof stay up?" Jimmy squealed and started laughing before she hung up. A moment later we heard pounding on the stairs. They were coming up. We all looked at each other in panic. I leapt off the bed and put my body against the door. It jostled and then there was a deep sigh. I recognized my husband's voice.

"Girls only. What's the password?" I asked innocently. Looking back at the two Andrews' girls, they looked like they were having a blast. I realized that this sleepover was a first for both of them. There was a pause and then Mark responded.

"Is it wall?" The three of us on this side giggled and I pulled away from the door to open it a crack and peek out.

"Yes?" I looked at him blankly. Him and Derek stood there, arms crossed, not amused.

"Having fun in there?"

I nodded and winked at him. He softened and rolled his eyes.

"Can't you do some other sleepover activity? Maybe some makeovers or make some brownies or something?" He suggested.

"Pillow fights!" Derek added excitedly. Mark turned and shot a glare at him.

"Dude, that's my wife."

Derek apologized.

"I could go for some brownies," he tagged on. I turned to look at my girlfriends. Jimmy hopped off the bed and reached for her mom's arm.

"Alright, we'll stop. Now go away!" I said again and shut the door quickly. Turning back to the girls I suggested we all get into our pajamas.

"Jimmy you can take off all the things you found in my closet and put them in that basket. Let's get into comfy clothes." She pouted but did as she was told.

I went into my closet and found a lilac pajama shorts and tank top set. I slipped on my robe and slippers. Walking back into the room I saw Jimmy had put on a black nightgown that went down to her feet. Where did you even get a nightgown like that in that small a size? She looked like a goth princess with her black robe and slippers to go with it. I commented on it on the way downstairs and Cleo laughed.

"You're not the only one who gets spoiled rotten. She has her Daddy wrapped around her finger. If he takes her along to do errands, she always comes back with clothes. I don't even want to know how much they cost."

"She's going to break hearts when she's older."

"Don't I know it. Dallas too. He looks so much like Ethan it's crazy."

Once we were in the kitchen, I told Cleo to sit down and relax. She frowned but I wasn't throwing out any more of my pots or pans. I told her that teasingly, but sternly.

"Fine. Maybe I'll get some music going. Where's your stereo?" I pointed towards the far side of the room and while she did that, I got out everything to make brownies for the boys and cupcakes for us.

Jimmy loved helping me. Her and her brother used to help me all the time while I was their nanny.

"Who taught you how to cook so good Aunt Renee?" She asked once the brownies were in the oven and the cupcake batter was prepped and in the liners. We sat down with her mother, who looked up curiously.

"Yeah, didn't you say you left home when you were young?" I nodded. Realizing that we were just twiddling our thumbs I stood back up and grabbed three wine glasses.

"I did. My old boyfriend's mom taught me a lot. She was like my own mom on the road. She loved to cook and was usually in charge of cooking for the troupe. Once I had my own kitchen, I started teaching myself more things." I went to the fridge and pulled out a bottle of wine and then realized that I was the only one able to drink it. I put it back and grabbed juice for Jimmy and asked Cleo what she wanted.

"Juice is fine. It's like wine," she said cheerfully. I smiled and brought it back to the table and poured three glasses. Jimmy reached for hers first and put her pinky out to drink.

"Do I get to do the toast?" She asked.

"Sure, what are we toasting?" She thought for a minute and then raised her glass.

"To the best sleepover ever!" We clinked glasses and drank our juice.

I checked the timer and saw we still had almost half an hour for the brownies to be done. I looked back at the girls who were realizing the same thing. I thought about other fun things we could do while we waited.

"Do you guys want to paint your nails?" I asked and Jimmy's hand shot up.

Chuckling I left them at the table to go get my nail cover case from the bathroom closet downstairs. When I got back, I opened it and began unloading the case. While I was traveling with the theatre, I had a slight addiction to nail polish. Most of these were old, but I'm sure they'd still work. I counted as I set them down and stopped at 45 bottles.

I let the girls pick out their colors before selecting mine. Jimmy immediately reached for a black. I looked over at Cleo to see if she approved. She bit her lip as she glanced at her daughter.

"What about a different color?" She suggested, plucking the black bottle out of her tiny hand. Jimmy scowled, but after a moment began looking through the colors. I was starting to pick out my own color when I remembered the show in two days.

"Oh shoot. I can't color mine. The director would kill me. Eh, that's okay. I'll just paint yours for you." Jimmy looked up from the three colors she was choosing from to stare at me curiously.

"You're in a show? Like when I did Peter Pan?" I nodded.

"Yep. Just like that. I get to play a crazy woman." Cleo grabbed a deep red and handed it to me. I shook it and when she laid her hand down on the table, began applying the polish to her fingernails.

"I want to go see it," Jimmy whined. I shook my head, glancing at the timer on the brownies.

"Not this time. It's an adult only show. You can come to a different show," I promised. She crossed her arms and sat back.

Cleo sighed but said nothing. I looked up at her and she smiled, rolling her eyes.

"I hope Tot is a boy, for your sake," she joked. I smiled but said nothing. Jimmy finally picked a bright green and when I finished Cleo's first coat, I started on hers.

"What do you want Tot to be Aunt Renee?" She asked me.

"Mmm… it's hard to decide. Girls are fun to dress up and have sleepovers with," I reached over and pinched her little cheek. She giggled. "But on the other hand, I would love to have a little boy that looks just like Uncle Mark."

"My mom said Tot is gonna learn music too so he can play with us. Rocky too." She made a grimace and then looked me dead in the eye. "I really hope Tot is a girl. There's too many boys." I burst into laughter by the suddenness and seriousness of her statement. The timer went off on the oven.

I hurried over and quickly took the pan out and threw the cupcake pan in. I went back to the table and started a second coat on Cleo.

"What names are on the table this week?" I asked. She sighed.

"Hmm…I don't know. Anaconda for a girl, Bug for a boy."

"Just Bug?" I asked, she shrugged.

"Yeah, no middle name. Bug Lacey. Has a nice ring to it I thought."

I stopped painting and looked up at her. She tried desperately not to smile but she finally cracked.

"Stop worrying about it. We've got plenty of time. Six months in fact."

When I finished both sets of nails I cleaned up and put the box away. While they let their hands dry, I started looking for the can of frosting I had bought the last time I was at the grocery store. It was strawberry flavor, full of sugar, and perfect for a slumber party. Taking the cupcakes out I checked the brownies, and seeing that they were cool enough, cut them and put them on a small platter.

"You guys want some before I take them to the boys?" I asked. They both nodded and I pulled three squares off the plate for us. I took the plate to the living room. Setting it down on the coffee table I looked up at the two men still playing video games.

"Hey you, brownies are done." I reached over and planted a kiss on my reluctant husband's cheek.

"Aw thanks, baby. Sorry, I'm in the middle of a fight," he said, not looking away from the TV.

"Yeah thanks baby," Derek smirked, and Mark clenched his teeth.

"Watch it Turtle," he snarled and then snuck a very quick glance at me.

"How's girls night going?"

I looked back at the kitchen and sat down next to him.

"Great actually. We're having a lot of fun. We did our nails, watched girly movies, made cupcakes, did some prank phone calls," I added and kissed him quickly again. He smirked.

"That's great baby. Hey if you get the chance can you bring me down a blanket and pillow? I'm going to sleep down here. You guys can take the room."

"Are you sure? With your shoulder?" He nodded.

"I'll be fine. I'm almost healed. One night won't kill me. You go have fun. Thanks again for the brownies baby, you're the best." He puckered his lips and leaned over for me to kiss him. His eyes not looking my way. I sighed and gave him his kiss quickly before heading back into the kitchen.

I pulled the cupcakes out of the pan and while they cooled a little more, I grabbed sprinkles out of the cabinet and a spatula for the frosting. When they were ready Cleo and Jimmy helped me decorate them.

"You wanna take these upstairs, start a movie, and relax?" I suggested and we all hurried up to my room. I brought Mark his pillow and a spare blanket and returned to Cleo starting another Rom-com.

Within a half hour Jimmy had fallen asleep in between us. I took the cupcake plate and set it on my side table. Cleo reached over and covered her up. She looked up at me and smiled.

"Are you nervous about your thing?"

"About what? The baby? Not really. Well kind of. Just because it's something new."

"Oh, no. Sorry, I was talking about your play. I should have clarified, my bad," she chuckled.

"Oh, that. Yes and no. I've got the actual performance down, but Mark…" I trailed off.

"He seems like he's in a good place with it. The guys tease him about it a lot, but he just shrugs it off. How does your scene partner's girlfriend feel about it?"

"I don't know. He doesn't really say much about it. I'm assuming she's dealing with it. I've met her before. I assured her that it was just acting and there's nothing there."

"I used to say that about Ethan," Cleo muttered, her voice barely above a whisper. I turned to look her in the eyes.

"Yes, but my history with Thomas is nothing like yours with Ethan. Don't compare the two." She blanched away from me and quickly apologized.

"I'm sorry. I just- Mark's my best friend. I don't want-" I relaxed and smiled softly at her.

"It's okay. I understand. I know how it may seem to someone on the outside, but me and Thomas are not like that. Mark and I have an amazing marriage and no one is breaking that. Hell, we are about to have a baby. No amount of good looking men can pull me away from him," I said with confidence. I reached for my water on the stand.

She smiled wide and then raised an eyebrow.

"So, you confirm that he is good looking, this Thomas?" I was taking a drink and choked when she said it. I looked over at her and she was holding her stomach laughing. I rolled my eyes and joined her in laughing.

"Well, he is an ex, and you've seen Mark. It can't be denied I have great taste in men."

Chapter Nine

LIKE IT'S HER BIRTHDAY

THE TWO LEFT in the morning with Derek and Mark after a breakfast of french toast, bacon, and orange juice. Before they got into Mark's car, Jimmy hugged me and told me she wants to do it again. I promised we would and then helped her get buckled in. Cleo hugged me as well. It was nice that we were becoming closer, but it still took me by surprise every time she went out of her way to give me attention.

After the crew left, Adrian came and dropped off Rocky to me. He looked extra exhausted today.

"You alright? You want some coffee or something?" I asked him and he shook his head.

"No, I'll be fine. It was Chase's night for Rocky duty, but he was fighting sleep all night, so neither of us got any sleep either."

"Have you tried taking him for a car ride? I've heard that can put a baby to sleep quick," I suggested. He looked at me blankly for a moment.

"I'll have to try that tonight. What time do I need to pick him again?"

"I have to be at the theatre at five. I know this week got a little confusing, sorry."

He scoffed.

"You're fine. You have been a savior these last few weeks. Actually, everyone has been a great help with everything," he chuckled and then rubbed his hair. "It's crazy. One moment I was thinking Chase was gonna die and I would be completely alone forever and the next I have a baby and Chase is sticking around for the long haul."

I looked down at the sleeping baby in the car seat.

"It's crazy how things change so quickly," I said. He grinned and patted me on the shoulder.

"Oh man, I can't wait until you guys have your baby. Mark's gonna flip," he laughed. I agreed with him and then he realized the time and left quickly.

The rest of my day was spent doing some light cleaning and getting showered and ready for rehearsal. Adrian came to pick up a still sleeping Rocky right on time.

"I tried to wake him, but he only stayed up long enough to eat and poop. Sorry. If he ever gets too much during the night just call one of us. Me or Cleo will come over."

He thanked me and left.

I drove to rehearsal confidently and overanxious to get this over and done with. We had done this so many times I just wanted to get to opening night. I stepped into the dressing room and slipped on my wig and dress. As I was finishing up my makeup Thomas came in. He greeted us all and quickly slipped out of his jeans and t-shirt and into his suit.

I could see him from the mirror but forced myself not to look. He really kept himself in good shape. When he was pulling off his t-shirt his undershirt raised a little and I saw his abs.

"Cassandra is a lucky girl," Gabby muttered under her breathe. I looked over at her and saw her ogling him in the mirror, not bothering to try hiding it. I chuckled and hurried to finish up.

Stepping out of the dressing room I stood in the darkly lit backstage area alone. It felt weird just standing here, but I couldn't keep trying to look away from him anymore. The dressing room door opened and of course, Thomas was the one to come out.

"Hey! Just the girl I was looking for," he greeted me.

I forced a smile and waved awkwardly.

"What's up?" I asked.

"I was wondering if you had plans for after rehearsal tonight. I thought maybe we could do a little double dinner date. Me and Cassandra, you and your husband?" He gave me an uneasy smile. I thought about it for a minute. I couldn't decide how to feel about it.

"Sure. That sounds great. I like Cassandra," he let out a breath I hadn't realized he'd been holding.

"Sweet. I'm going to be honest here for a minute. This is mostly for her. I thought maybe if she sees you two together that she'll be a little more comfortable with us tomorrow. Give her a little bit of ease knowing that we are both on the same page- just friends."

That made sense. I was sure Mark could appreciate that as well.

"I'll call him now to tell him. Do you have any place in mind?" We discussed some restaurants and afterwards I called Mark and told him about the double date.

"I know you guys are crazy busy, but could you call around and see if we can get reservations for somewhere nice? Oh, and I want you to shower and put on a suit." He groaned loudly into the phone.

"I guess, but you're putting out tonight," he said in his stern, teasing voice that I recognized instantly. I could picture his smile now. His eyebrows would be furrowed, and he'd be crossing his arms, but his lips would be wavering, struggling not to smile.

I giggled.

"You got it. Okay I gotta go, text me with the reservation info, love ya," I said and quickly hung up.

Stacie did her quick speech for the cast and we launched into rehearsal. Everything went smoothly and the time just flew by. Next thing I knew, I was getting dressed back into my street clothes and sending Thomas the details for dinner tonight.

"It's a new French restaurant called Chérir," I told him. He was looking at his phone. He nodded and then looked up at me, he looked embarrassed.

"Cassandra wants to know what you'll be wearing," he said tentatively. I chuckled.

"A cocktail dress of some sort and Mark will be in a suit in tie. Nothing too fancy, just like a normal date. She really shouldn't worry so much."

"I tell her that all the time. Hopefully this dinner will help." He reached out and hugged me, taking me off guard.

"I really appreciate you doing this for me." He said. I told him that it was nothing and that it would be fun before we left the theater.

I called Mark on the way home and was surprised to find that he was already home and had showered.

"Adrian was practically falling asleep standing up, so we just called it an early one. I don't know what suit you want me to wear so I'm just going to wait here for you- naked," he teased. I laughed.

"Okay, I get it. I owe you one. I'll be home soon." By the time I walked through the doors Mark was sitting on the couch in his boxers and an undershirt. He gave me a fake glare.

"The dogs needed to go out. You missed out on some crazy naked man action."

I nodded and hurried over to kiss him.

"Sorry sweetie. Okay, I gotta get showered and dressed. Come up in a bit and I'll pick you out a suit."

He grumbled but did as I asked. By the time I was out of the shower he was in the closet, picking out dresses.

"How about this one, or this?" He held up a very short, very tight, maroon dress in one hand, while in the other he had a similar dress in navy. I shook my head.

"I'm thinking something a little longer, like this," I pulled out a powder blue, knee length dress. It was off the shoulder and formed tightly to my body. Sexy, but covered everything. He frowned and put the other dresses away.

"Okay, now what do I wear?" I pulled out a few suits from his side of the closet and settled for a simple black on black. We finished getting ready separately, and by the time I was done with my hair and makeup, he was downstairs waiting for me.

When I started down the stairs, he came out of the living room. He looked up and his face burst into a huge grin. It made me feel amazing. When I reached the landing, he leaned over and kissed me hard. I felt his arm twitch, and instead of picking me up he opted for a light hug.

"You look stunning. Everyone is going to be so jealous of me when we get there," he told me on the way to the restaurant.

We arrived first, so we had time to get a drink and relax at the bar.

"White Russian for me," Mark ordered, and the bartender looked at me.

"Cosmo please," I told her. She made our drinks and we quickly paid her and turned to watch for our dinner mates. Ten minutes later I noticed Cassandra enter, followed by Thomas.

"They're here. Why don't we go meet them?" I suggested, getting off my stool.

We took our drinks and went to the front of the restaurant where they were talking to the maitre d, Thomas saw us first and gave us a small wave. He looked at me first, and then I watched his eyes go to Mark. His face hardened ever so slightly as he took him in. I wondered if Mark was doing the same thing. I assumed so because he suddenly put his good arm around me.

My attention turned to the woman beside my co-star. I gave her a smile and pulled away from Mark to hug her. She looked surprised but accepted the hug.

"Cassandra, it's so nice to see you again." She gave a similar response, but I could see that her smile and nice words were very forced.

I turned to the two men who were awkwardly shaking hands.

"Thomas, this is my husband Mark Lacey, Mark this is my costar and old friend Thomas Reynolds." The two nodded at each other. They were formal, but neither particularly friendly.

"I knew I recognized you!" Cassandra suddenly gasped, her eyes growing wide staring at my husband. My mood fell slightly. Please don't let this be a weird dinner now. Mark wrapped his arm around my waist again and pulled me closer. I looked up at him and he forced a smile.

"You do?" He said in such a fake, sarcastic enthusiasm I tightened my lips so as not to giggle.

"Yes! You're the drummer from Maria Maria. I've been to three of your shows. No way. I had no idea you were married," she gushed. Thomas cleared his throat and she flushed pink with embarrassment.

"Sorry, I've never met a celebrity before."

My husband chuckled and then excused himself to go see about our table. When he was out of earshot Thomas asked her if she was alright.

"Am I going to be the jealous one tonight?" He teased, but I could see that he wasn't amused. She shot a glare at him.

"I'm fine. It just surprised me is all. Renee, I apologize. I didn't mean to ogle your man," she joked. I gave her a quick smile.

"It's okay. We get it a lot. Well I do. I'm not the famous one. I'm the behind the scenes unofficial band family member." Her eyes went wide.

"Oh my God. That means you know Ethan Andrews too! Oh, and Adrian and the one with the Mohawk!" I nodded, realizing that this evening was not going to be pleasant.

"Yep. Derek. They are all nice people." I took a gulp of the drink in my hand. I glanced up at Thomas who looked mortified. Mark returned and told us to follow the maitre d. We did and thankfully were given a table in a corner. I was sure Mark probably requested it. Once we were seated Mark and I ordered another round of drinks and Thomas got himself an old fashioned and Cassandra some red wine. Silence fell over the table.

"I love your dress," I said to her. I made sure to sit across from her, so that she didn't spend the night making googly eyes at Mark.

"Thanks! I bought it for tonight. I like yours too." I thanked her as well. Her dress was pretty, but I noticed once she took off her coat that it was way skimpier than mine. She had chosen a midnight blue strapless dress that went barely to her knees. I noticed that she had a tiny butterfly tattoo on her collarbone.

"Cute tattoo," I offered, starting to feel repetitive. Someone else needed to start a conversation quickly. I couldn't keep offering compliments. Her hands reached up to touch it.

"Thanks, me and a few of my friends all went and got them together right after high school. I'm not much of a rebel. I've only got two." Her eyes were sliding over my inked skin. I had a little more than two. My shoulders and upper chest were covered with tattoos, as well as most of my back. Out of my group of friends I'd say I had the least amount.

"Most of mine were done when I was much younger too." Thomas chuckled.

"I remember taking you to go get your first tattoo. You were such a chicken," he accused.

I rolled my eyes.

"You weren't much better, I swear I saw tears when he started on your back," I added and he shrugged and laughed it off. There was another awkward pause so when we got our drinks and each had the chance to get a sip in, Thomas clapped his hands and looked at Mark.

"So, elephant in the room. I'm the old boyfriend and the guy who's been making out with your wife for the last few weeks." He smiled awkwardly at Mark. My eyes shot to my darling husband. He was notorious for his temper. Oh God, this wasn't going to be good. He gulped, clenched his jaw, then visibly relaxed. He started chuckling, and that turned into a full-on belly laugh.

"Well nice to meet you man, I'm the guy who gets to watch it tomorrow." It was like the tension was finally lifted off the table and we were all able to relax. We opened our menus and began looking for our meals. I had never been to a strictly french restaurant, so I didn't recognize most of the food. I mentioned it to Mark and he chuckled. Leaning over to gaze at my menu he pointed to a few things.

"This isn't bad. Or this one, I bet you'd like the beef bourguignon. Order that," he suggested. I looked at him in confusion. He gave me a shoulder lift.

"I've been to France before."

"When?" I accused. I don't think the band had ever played outside of the country.

"Me and Derek went once for a weekend. Right after the band went on the hiatus. Just for fun. We were young, dumb, and had a bunch of cash. It was fun. We should go sometime."

Hmm. I learned something new about him everyday. I loved how spontaneous he was.

When the waiter returned, I ordered the beef bourguignon like he recommended. The rest of the evening went better than the first half hour. We talked about movies, laughed when Thomas' dish was found to be covered in garlic, and for the first time in a long time, didn't discuss music. Well, for the most part. Cassandra did try to interject once or twice and ask about the band. Mark skillfully shot the conversation down quickly. He was more used to crazy fans than I was.

I did start to feel a little guilty. I noticed that as the night went on the more she started disconnecting from the table. She drank more and merely pretended to listen. In his defense, her boyfriend did attempt several times to bring her into the conversation, but she didn't really have much to contribute. She didn't seem to have any mutual interests in any of us. When our plates had been removed and we were merely relaxing I put my elbows up onto the table and put my head in my hands and looked at her.

"We've spent the evening talking about all of us, let's get to know you Cassandra. What do you do for fun?"

She looked around the table with wide doe eyes. "I don't know. I like to bake." Thomas reached for her hand. She lit up for the first time in an hour.

"Cassandra makes the best cakes. They look so cool. She could be on one of those baking shows," he bragged. She was blushing but beamed at the attention.

"I'm making a cake for the afterparty tomorrow."

"It's awesome. The top is a pillbox hat and she made fake macaroni and ketchup to put on the bottom tier. You're gonna love it."

"I can't wait. I actually enjoy cooking too. I'm not a great baker but maybe you can show me some of your tricks sometime."

After that she seemed drawn back into the conversation. When we finally decided to call this evening to a close, I felt like the four of us were all in a great place. It felt like all the tension and paranoia had disappeared. We paid the bill and walked out together after gathering our coats. "This was a great night. I'm glad we did this," I said.

"I agree, I think we were all a little nervous about the play and this helped. What do you think Sweet Pea?" Thomas asked Cassandra. Her eyes went wide, she looked uncomfortable, but finally smiled. I could tell that it was very forced.

"Yes. I think the show is going to be great and you two are going to shine up there," she told us, but her words felt rehearsed. I thanked her and gave her one last hug before we turned to our separate vehicles. Once we were alone, I asked Mark how he thought the night went.

"I thought it went good. She hates you, you know," he told me, clearly amused. I sighed.

"Yeah, I know."

The next day despite having rehearsed for weeks and this not being my first time on stage, I was wracked with nerves. I got ready way too early, so was left twiddling my thumbs for hours. Mark was amused, but he had work so he couldn't entertain me.

"We are only doing a half day. I promise I'll be showered, dressed, and in the front row right on time," he promised as he walked out the door.

After an hour of wandering around the house I finally decided to just go to the theatre and see if anyone needed help with any last-minute things. I called Stacie and Erin on the way and they were already there.

When I stepped inside, they put me right to work helping them bake cookies for intermission.

"Thomas is on his way with the cake his girlfriend made and we sent Gabby for coffee and juice. Come get this chocolate chip dough made," Erin directed.

I lost track of time as we baked and drank beer. We were having a blast. It reminded me so much of my younger years. I wanted to do this more often. A few hours later there was a knock on the kitchen door. Stacie went to open it and found Thomas on the other side. He glanced behind her at the rest of us. I noticed that he avoided looking at me.

"We have the cake. It's going to take both of us to get it in here, so we need someone to keep the door and fridge open." Stacie was already there, so she kept it open for them to get the cake in.

I gasped when I saw the cake. She really was good at baking. It looked awesome. They only paused for a moment to let us look at it before placing it in the refrigerator. It was a three-tiered cake, with a pillbox hat as the top layer. The second layer was covered in pearls like the ones I'd be wearing, and the bottom cake was pink and covered in the fake macaroni and ketchup, just like my costume. She had also made some cookies that she placed around the cake that were so detailed they looked professionally done. There was a gun, a few wine glasses with red wine in them, and some candles.

Everyone showered her with compliments, but she was very curt and left quickly. Thomas gave us all a tight smile and followed her out. Stacie, being the gossip queen quickly left the kitchen to go find a window. Gabby and Erin followed, but I hesitated and ultimately decided against snooping.

"They're fighting! Right in the parking lot!" Stacie called out to me.

"Stop watching then!" I called back, but they ignored me. I went back to putting frosting on the sugar cookies. Five minutes later the three of them came running back into the kitchen with guilty looks on their faces. I was just about to ask when there was a loud banging on the door. Stacie went to it and took a deep breath before opening it. Thomas came storming in.

He stalked past all of us and went somewhere into the theatre. All of us girls looked at each other, waiting for someone to talk, but no one said a word. I continued frosting my cookies and they went back to their various baking duties. Once I was done, I left to go find him.

I found him smoking a cigarette in the dressing room. He didn't look my way when I came into the room.

"Hey, are you okay?" I stepped further into the room, closing the door.

"I'll be alright. Just had a long night."

"She still has a problem with the show?" He scoffed.

"Yeah, something like that. I told her she can either come to the show or not. But if she doesn't come, then she doesn't need to call me ever again." He finished his cigarette and put it out in a small glass I hadn't noticed before sitting next to him. He stood up and gave me a smile.

"You guys need any help in the kitchen?"

I looked at the clock on the wall. "Well we have an hour before the rest of the crew and ushers get here, so we can probably get the lobby prepped." I was right, Joyce and Bill, the guy playing Anthony were already setting up tables. I reached for the tablecloths and Thomas went to see if the ticket box was ready.

Once the ushers and the stage crew showed up the five of us actors excused ourselves to get dressed and ready for the show. I took the opportunity to call Mark and he assured me that he and everyone else were ready and about to leave.

"We're going to be the first ones in line, I swear. Break a leg, I love you."

Hearing his voice helped me relax a little.

"I love you too," I told him before hanging up. I hurried back to the dressing room and slid my dress and wig on. When I was satisfied with my appearance I held back and chatted with the other four. Once Thomas came out of the dressing room before he seemed to leave his relationship problems behind him, for now. He had been in a great mood like he always was. Erin came in and announced that they would be opening the doors in ten minutes, so Stacie wanted us all out on stage.

Everyone involved in the show gathered together. Stacie stood in the middle and thanked everyone for all the hard work and gave us a quick pep talk. "Okay, now let's make a circle and all put our hands in. On the count of three we shout "Yes!" You know, because of the title of the show," We rolled our eyes, but did it anyways. The huddle was customary, but Stacie was a goofball.

When we were done, we rushed off stage and into our places. The doors were opened and we could hear people coming in. Genie, the stage manager came over to Joyce and I and whispered that we had sold out.

"All weekend. And next weekend is filling up quickly already. They are talking about adding shows." Joyce reached over and squeezed my hand, we both had to keep ourselves from screaming out of excitement.

The lights began flashing and Stacie stepped onto the stage to introduce the show. I took the opportunity to sneak a peak at the audience. Sure enough, my amazing husband was front and center. He was smiling wide, looking handsome in his navy suit. My heart melted when I saw he was holding a bouquet of red roses in his lap. I glanced over and saw the rest of the band and their spouses. Stacie ended her speech and excited the stage. The lights lowered and the curtains went up, starting the show.

The moment I stepped onto the stage I was Jackie-O. I didn't miss a single step or screw up a line. I was in the zone. Everything was going perfect. When I excited the scenes, I would let out the breath I had been holding on stage. I would relax and regain composure for the next scene. Thomas came up behind me right before the shooting re-enactment. He leaned down and whispered directly into my ear.

"You ready for this?" I gulped and nodded. He squeezed my hand quickly and let go.

I hadn't realized that I was so nervous, but when he moved away, I realized my palms were clammy. I could do this, I reminded myself. Mark told me just last night that he was comfortable now with it. With one last long, deep, breath I stepped back onto the stage and seduced my brother.

There were gasps from the audience. I could feel Thomas trying not to smile as we kissed. I closed my eyes and let myself be in the moment. I wasn't Renee Lacey, I was Jackie-O Pascal, and I was about to make love to my brother Marty. When the lights started dimming on the two of us, he pushed me down onto the couch and threw his shirt into the crowd. Someone let out a hoot as they presumably caught it.

My heart was racing furiously. As we lay together in the dark, Marty lazily ran his hands up and down my body and planted kisses on my mouth, neck, and shoulders. I could feel myself starting to sweat. I moved my hands along his chest and felt his abs hiding under his undershirt.

When the lights came up on us and we were confronted I felt a sense of relief as Marty moved away from me. I pulled my dress back on and began to run my fingers through my hair, acting as if nothing dirty had happened. Despite that scene always being so painstakingly long, the rest of the play flew by and what felt like mere moments later I was holding hands with Thomas and Gabby to bow.

Once the curtains were closed and then raised again to

greet the audience my husband was the first one to the stage. He jumped up in one giant leap and picked me up. He squeezed me tight and twirled me around. I swatted him on the chest to let me down.

"Mark, your shoulder!" I exclaimed. He laughed and kissed me quickly.

"You were amazing baby! That was so good!" He told me. Quickly we were surrounded by the other patrons congratulating the cast. My friends surrounded me with hugs and bouquets.

"You really liked it?" I asked my husband and he rolled his eyes.

"Well, watching you practically screw someone right in front of me wasn't the greatest, but the rest of the show was great. You really were a different person. I almost didn't recognize you with the hair."

I hugged him tightly and looked around. Thomas was surrounded by people just like the rest of us. I excused myself and hurried over to him. He saw me and waved. When I reached him, we hugged and I grabbed his hand and pulled him over to my group. He chuckled and greeted everyone. Mark was the first one to congratulate him.

He slapped him on the back, then extended his hand to him. Thomas looked down at it for a moment, and then shook it.

"You're a good actor. I really thought I was watching a brother and sister up there."

Thomas burst into laughter and thanked him.

Once the volume started to die down and guests started to leave Stacie announced that the small reception was to start in the lobby. I gave my bouquets to Mark and told my friends that I had to change. I quickly hurried backstage and got into my street clothes. Just as I was grabbing my bag to head back, I noticed Thomas with Cassandra.

I paused for only a moment. She had her back towards me, so only he could see me. He glanced up and I shot him a thumbs up, but he didn't respond. He looked back at his girlfriend and then she turned slightly. She had tears running down her face. Seeing that, I hurried off to leave them to it.

I went into the lobby to find Mark waiting for me with a giant smile on his face. Seeing him smile made everything better. I leaned over and kissed him again.

"I sent everyone away. They are going to drop off all of your flowers at the house. We'll need to get like ten vases," he chuckled and reached for my hand.

I motioned to the food that had been set out.

"You want to get something to eat? Or maybe some punch. I think they are going to cut the cake. Did you see it?"

"I'm good on the sandwiches, but I do want to try the cake. I don't want to rush you, but how long are we staying?" I looked at him curiously.

"Probably another half hour or so. Why?" He didn't answer me, but instead pulled me towards the center of the room where everyone was admiring Cassandra's cake.

"Wow, she really is good," he commented. Suddenly the doors from the theatre burst open. Everyone turned and stared at the two storming in. Cassandra came in first, followed by Thomas, still in costume.

She was furious. He looked frantic.

"Cassandra, don't do this. I think it's time to go."

She whipped around to glare at him.

"No, not until I've had my say," she turned back to the room and scanned everyone until she zeroed in on me.

"You." She pointed and pushed through the people to reach me, her heels clicking on the tile.

She pointed her finger at my chest.

"You. From the moment you returned everyone has been fawning over the prodigal daughter. You were the one that got away. I've had to hear it from all of his friends. Every time we went out or I tried to help, the conversation returned back to you. Everyone here thinks you are God's gift to this play but you're not. You just loved the idea of making out with Thomas. I bet you couldn't wait to take his clothes off. You get your kicks kissing him in front of your husband, don't you?" She screamed at me. I took a step back, not sure of how to handle this. Where was all of this coming from?

"He won't admit it, but I know he still loves you. I can see it whenever he talks about you or when you're in the same room." She took a step closer to me. Backing another step away I bumped into the cake table. Thomas came up behind her and began furiously apologizing. I held my hands up but that must have made her angrier.

She turned to Thomas, her eyes blazing fury.

"What are you apologizing to her for? You should be apologizing to me for wasting my time-" Her voice was cut off by the sudden small push my dear husband gave her, straight into her own cake.

The silent room let out a collective gasp as her entire face crashed into the center of the beautifully crafted dessert. The pillbox top fell to the floor and pearls from the middle went everywhere. Mark moved away quickly, but everyone saw him do it. He reached for me and I embraced him. Unsure of how to feel. I wanted desperately to laugh, but at the same time, I felt bad for Thomas.

Silence reigned down on the room again as she finally stood back up. Her face was covered in pink buttercream and chocolate cake crumbles. Her head swung around the room, looking at us all in shock and confusion. Finally, her face settled on Thomas'. He was looking at her with such pity I began to feel sorry for her. Her lips trembled, and then choked on a sob.

"You pushed me," she accused. Thomas smirked and shook his head, but before he could deny it Mark spoke up.

"No, I did."

She turned quickly, cake and frosting flying off her face. People grimaced as it hit them.

"This was my wife's and everyone else's special night in the spotlight. They worked hard to get here, and you tried ruining it with your tantrum. So, I stopped it. You should probably go now so everyone who deserves the attention can enjoy the rest of the night."

There was a slight pause and then slowly people began clapping and agreeing with him.

With one last scream of frustration she spun around and stormed out of the building. Thomas took a few steps and then decided not to follow her. People patted him on the back and told him to relax and get some food. Nodding he went over and poured himself some coffee.

I turned back to my husband. He was trying so hard not to smile. I rolled my eyes.

"Well, we were waiting for cake, now what do you want to do?" He cracked a grin.

"I've got an idea. Go ahead and make your rounds with your friends. When you're ready I've got another place to take you." I raised an eyebrow and he winked. A tap on the shoulder made me turn. It was Thomas.

"I really am sorry about all that. The woman is clearly insane."

I lifted my hand to fist bump his.

"It's all good. She really should have auditioned. She'd make one hell of a crazy Jackie-O," I joked. He nodded and then turned and apologized to Mark. Mark accepted it and they moved into light conversation after that. I excused myself and began saying my goodbyes. When I returned back to the two men, I was ready to leave.

Once we were out in the parking lot Mark insisted on blindfolding me. I protested but he pleaded. We drove for about twenty minutes and then when he was buzzed into the Andrew's house I burst into laughter.

"Really?" He chuckled and reached over to push the blindfold back down.

"Hush, it's a surprise. You don't know for sure that's where we're at."

I smirked but let him take me up their stairs, into the house and to Ethan's man cave. When he untied the blindfold, everyone screamed.

"Surprise!"

I turned to my husband who was beaming. I embraced him and rested my head on his warm chest.

"I am so proud of you baby," he murmured into my hair.

"I love you," I raised my head to look up at him. "Now do I get to tell them what happened or are you going to?" I asked. He pulled away from me and shot me dirty look. Rubbing his hands together he moved towards his friends.

"You guys won't believe what just happened." He glanced back at me and winked.

"You had your moment in the spotlight, now its my time to shine."

Chapter Ten

MAKING IT UP

"I STILL CAN'T BELIEVE Mark did that," Cleo gasped. We had just sat down for our weekly girls only lunch. Well, we made only one exception. I had Rocky with me every other week. He was getting so big so fast. He sat up in the chair the restaurant provided and played with his pacifier.

"I mean, I can. That sounds exactly like something he would do, but it's still hilarious." I looked up from my menu to chuckle.

"Yeah, I'm kind of glad this weekend is the final shows. I need a break." It had been a long couple of months.

She nodded in understanding.

"Same here. I can not wait until Friday. Mark can take the drums back. I'm done." I laughed.

"I think we are all ready for him to get cleared by the doctor. He's been in such a good mood this week. Best he's been since the accident. The drums are his life."

"I hate sitting down so much. That and my arms are so sore! It's a workout for sure." I took a sip of my tea and picked up the toy that Rocky had tossed off the table.

"How are you feeling otherwise? With Tot?" We had our

doctor's appointment Monday morning. We got to hear his heartbeat. It was amazing. I cried. I think even Mark teared up a little. The doctor said everything was looking great. Cleo reached for her water.

"Could be better, could be worse. My jeans are getting tight. I'm going to start pulling out some of my old clothes I wore when I was pregnant with Blue."

"Do you want some new things? I can take you shopping," I offered and she rolled her eyes.

"Nah, I've got clothes. Use that to get Tot some fun clothes. You know I'm almost convinced it's a boy. I keep saying he."

"Me too! I can't help it. It's just a feeling I get."

She lifted her fist up to bump mine.

"That's mother's intuition there."

After lunch we walked to our separate cars and said our goodbyes. It was strange. This was the first time we took our own cars.

"I've got some errands to run before I head back to the guys. Rocky could probably go for a nap too," she said, giving him a quick kiss before rushing to her car.

I shrugged off my uneasiness with my favorite playlist. As I drove through town, I slowed down to admire the shops. Maybe Cleo was right. It couldn't hurt to get Tot one or two cute onesies. I found a spot to park and pulled out the stroller and got Rocky out.

We walked up and down the strip of boutiques. Some we went in, others we simply looked at their window display. I found a new cologne for Mark, and some chocolates for the twins. I stopped at the baby boutique I had been purposely saving for last. It was a dangerous place.

I didn't know if I could show the restraint needed to not buy everything in sight. I stared at the window displays. On one side was a pink and black Parisian themed nursery, while the other side was a green music themed set up. That had me sold. I pushed Rocky in and went straight to the boys' side of the store.

I picked up a black onesie that said Future Rockstar. It was cheesy, but I didn't really care. There were so many cute clothes I made myself choose only two outfits. A sales associate approached me while I was tending to Rocky.

"Hi, is there anything I can help you with today?" She asked.

I stood back up and turned her way. I brushed my messy hair away from my face.

"I'm just kind of looking right now. Thank you," I told her. She gave me a giant smile and looked down at Rocky.

"He's a doll. Well, if you need any help my name is Becky. I'm around." She told me and walked away. I had to stop myself from screaming from across the room to ask how much the entire music bedroom set was. Boy or girl, I knew Mark would love it. I'd have to bring him back here to help pick out some things once we found out what Tot was. We had four more weeks of guessing.

I picked out some striped black and white mittens to go with the black onesies and went to the counter. Becky asked me if I wanted to open up an account with them.

"Every purchase adds up to points and you can get tons of free stuff. It's totally free," she enticed. The word "free" had me sold. She finished ringing me up and I quickly left before I could buy more things.

Today was a lovely day. There was a nice breeze. Rocky was in a great mood, so I decided to keep walking and browsing. I had nothing else going on today, so might as well. I was rounding the corner to the next block when I saw something that made me stop dead in my tracks.

Cleo was sitting outside a cafe with a man. I knew it was her. I had just seen her, and she was wearing the same clothes from lunch. Her posture was tense, and she was sitting as far away as she could from the man across from her. I didn't blame her, considering who it was. There was no denying it. That man was Christopher Thomas, her ex-husband.

Before she married Ethan, she was married to Chris for about five years. During that time, he cheated on her, abused her mentally and physically, and at the end of their relationship almost killed her. He was a monster. He went to prison for what he did.

Last year he got out and immediately jumped back into the public eye. Before being arrested, he was running for a senator position in Michigan where they lived. Needless to say, the campaign was derailed with scandal upon scandal.

Once my mind wrapped around what I was seeing I pulled back and moved behind a small food truck. I could see them clearly, but I doubted Cleo would spot us.

They were talking. He was smiling, but she wasn't. She looked upset. He reached for her hand across the table, but she shook her head furiously. He didn't like that. I watched as they seemed to bicker about something. I wondered if Ethan knew about this. Of course he didn't. He would have never let her see him, let alone go alone. What was she thinking?

Chris leaned down and pulled something out of a laptop bag I hadn't noticed before. It was a book. He slid it across the table to her. She looked down at it but didn't reach for it. He spoke, his mouth turning up in a smile that made him look like a cat with a mouse. Finally, she picked it up and examined it.

She turned it around and read the back, then opened it and began scanning it. After a few minutes she threw it at him. He ducked, then reached down to grab it off the cement. He crossed his arms on the table and she then stood up. She yelled something that I couldn't hear from this distance, and then stormed off.

I watched him for a few more minutes. If he chased after

her, I was calling the police, and then Ethan. Then probably Mark, just for good measure. You couldn't be too safe when it came to that monster. I had seen what he could do.

He didn't move from the table though. Instead he put the book back in his bag and picked up his phone to make a call. When I was satisfied that he was going to leave her alone I continued my walk.

I thought long and hard about whether to say something to anyone about what I saw, but decided to wait until next Wednesday, when I could talk to her alone. I wanted to get to the bottom of it before it got blown up into something major for no reason. It was killing me though.

That night at dinner I fought with myself about whether or not to tell Mark. The constant going back and forth made me lose my appetite. When he asked about my day, I almost spilled everything. Instead I chose to talk about the baby clothes I had bought for Tot.

"She's convinced it's a boy. I kind of think so too," I told him. He chuckled and took a drink of his beer.

"Yeah, she's mentioned it once or twice. Did she tell you her new name for him?"

"No, what is it this week?"

"Kermit. We'd call him Kermie for short."

"Oh joy," I sighed.

"Saturday night is the cast party. Are you coming?" I asked.

"Sure. Sounds like fun," he said. I gave him a look and he smirked.

"Okay, it doesn't, but I'll still go with you. You support me with my things, I can support you too." I reached for his hand. I don't know how I got so lucky.

Friday morning Mark woke me up and insisted I hurry up and shower. "Come on, come on, come on. It's time!" I groaned and put a pillow over my head.

"What time is it?"

"Time to get up to get me to the doctor. I need my drums, they miss me," he whined. I sighed and groggily made my way to the shower.

Much to Mark's dismay, although he was able to take his arm out of the sling, he couldn't play the drums until he went through physical therapy. He was fairly confident that he would be able to play again.

"Know your limits. Otherwise next time you might not be so lucky."

He let out a giant "Woo!" When he got outside. I rolled my eyes.

"You still have to do physical therapy. You're not playing until you're cleared," I reminded him, but he ignored me as he whistled on his way to the car.

When we got home I asked him if he was hungry, but he laughed. "Hell no baby. I just got my arm back. I need to bang something."

I assumed he was talking about his drums but the moment we closed the front door he was ripping off his shirt and pressing his lips to mine. My eyes went wide with surprise, but I embraced the moment quickly.

"You have no idea how much I have been wanting to get you upstairs and show you I still got it," he murmured as he pulled away and quickly scooped me up in his arms.

I squealed as he turned and ran to the stairs. He sped up them as I giggled. I wanted to scold him for pushing his shoulder, but his adorable grin made me temporarily forget. He tossed me on the bed lightly and looked down at me, biting his lip. I sat up on my elbows and raised an eyebrow.

"You gonna show me or what?" I asked and he practically pounced on me.

He held himself over me as he placed kisses all over my body. He began inching lower and when he got to my jeans, he took the buttons in his teeth and began pulling on them. I took my pants off and he helped me with my panties. He stripped down to nothing and climbed back on the bed. Reaching over he lifted my shirt off and began playing with my breasts.

I moved to take my bra off, but he grabbed my hands and lifted them up and pressed them to the headboard. I gasped lightly and he raised an eyebrow as he lowered his head, pushing the bra away to kiss my nipples.

He continued to hold my hands in place with his freshly healed arm. With his other hand he began moving past my breasts to my sex. He teased me with his skilled fingers. I squirmed and begged him to take me.

With one swift motion he positioned himself between my legs and pushed gently inside me, quickly getting into a rhythm. I tried to pull my hands out of his grip, but he shook his head.

"Uh uh. Not this time," he said, biting my neck gently. I gasped with pleasure, my orgasm quickly rising. He groaned and taking his quick moment of weakness I ripped my hands away and forced him to roll over, letting me on top.

"That's not fair!" He exclaimed, but quickly got back in sync with me. I leaned down and nibbled on his ear. It took his breath away for a second. His hands moved from my shoulders to my lower back and began moving lower. He gently spanked me, and it bounced me in just the right way that my body responded with an explosion of my nerves. I screamed out in surprise and arched my back. He swore and only a few thrusts later he joined me in ecstasy.

I moved off him and he wrapped his arm around me. When our breathing relaxed, he leaned over and kissed my hair.

"It feels amazing to be able to stretch like that again."

I laughed and snuggled in closer to him. I couldn't agree more.

I tried to take a light doze, but he was too excited about the things he could do again to sleep. He apologized but I understood and told him I needed to get showered for the show tonight. He murmured something about going downstairs to his kit and I stopped him mid sentence.

"Mark, you can not play yet. I know you're eager now that you don't have the sling, but if you go full force then you risk screwing your shoulder up worse than before."

He glared at me for a long moment before turning and grumbling about how stupid physical therapy was. Satisfied that he would listen to the doctor I hurried up and got ready.

The second to last show went well, although I did notice that Thomas's hands wandered a little more than normal. I thought about mentioning it, but we only had one more show, why start an argument.

As we closed up, everyone wanted to go out for drinks. I called Mark to tell him and left with everyone else. We had a big group, and I sat next to Thomas and Stacie. We had all had more than a few drinks. I knew I'd have to get a ride home.

Of course, someone wanted to do karaoke. I got up there with Stacie and Erin and we sang "Our Lips Are Sealed" very badly and loudly. When we stumbled off the stage, we were greeted by Gabby's phone snapping pictures. I fell back into my seat and accidentally bumped into Thomas. He turned from where he was talking to someone.

He shot me a dirty look at first, but then smiled when he realized who it was.

"You alright over there?" I sighed and leaned my head on his shoulder.

"I think I should probably get home. I'm a little drunk," I admitted.

"A little? I can take you home," he offered. Some internal alert sounded. I sat up and shook my head.

"It's okay, I'm going to call my husband." I stepped outside for some fresh air and called. Of course, Derek was there, so they'd both come and Derek would take my car home. I went back inside and paid my tab. I told everyone goodbye and by the time I made it back outside they were pulling up. I hadn't realized I had taken that long to say goodbye.

I was dozing off by the time we got home. I felt Mark lift me out of the car and take me inside. I lifted my head and told him to set me down in the living room. He kissed me and did as I asked.

"Thank you for coming to get me. Thomas offered to take me home, but I wanted to see you," I looked over at him. He winked at me.

"Anything for you baby. Do you need some aspirin? You're gonna have a headache tomorrow."

I closed my eyes and nodded. When he put them in my hand, I took them quickly and followed them with a swig of his beer. I heard him tell Derek to put a movie on. Mark came to sit with me, wrapping a blanket around me. Derek put on a comedy I had already seen, and I fell asleep barely halfway through.

I woke up that next morning to the smell of coffee right under my nose. I rose and ground the sleep out of my eyes. I looked up to see my dear husband smiling down at me with coffee and toast. I thanked him and scarfed down the toast. I sipped on my coffee while he told me about his plans for the day.

"I'm heading over to Cleo's for a bit, then head to your show and we can go to the party right after that."

"You're coming tonight?" I asked.

"Of course. I saw it open. I should see it close."

"We have to do the breakdown right after, so it's going to be later than usual."

"Alright, no problem."

I took a peek out into the audience while Stacie did her speech and I found my husband with another bouquet in the front row. He was alone this time, but he was here, and that was what mattered most.

Everything was going perfect until the lights went out on Thomas and I. Instead of backing up he pressed himself harder onto me and began sucking on my neck. I froze. I didn't want to ruin the scene, but I didn't have much room to pull away. I sat there in silence while he continued to kiss me. Finally, when I regained thought I pinched him hard on his shoulder. He ripped his arm away quickly and got the hint.

I wanted to murder him in real life. When the show ended and I got the chance to get out of costume I hurried to a mirror, and sure enough there was a giant hickey on my neck. He came in shortly after and I spun around. He saw me giving him the death glare and he held up his hands.

"It was a joke. A parting gift," I shook my head and finished packing up.

"It's not funny Thomas."

I hurried out to start helping break down the set. Everyone here was skilled and had done this so many times it barely took twenty minutes. Stacie reminded everyone that the party was at her house and we shut the theater down and all left.

I was still fuming from Thomas' not funny joke. I wanted to vent, but I knew Mark would flip a lid and I didn't want to start a fight between the two. He was in such a great mood; it would be a shame to ruin it over something that was over and done with. I could cover it up with makeup easily.

Stacie's house was overflowing by the time we arrived. The music was blaring and beer and food covered every available surface. I grabbed a beer and forced myself to relax and enjoy the company. This was the last time this specific group of people would be together.

Someone had set up the live taping of the show on her TV, so we went to the living room and watched a bit of it. It was kind of crazy to see myself on the screen. I had never had a show taped before. We were a traveling troupe with little money. We used to rely on local theatres for costumes, scripts, and whatever sets they had that we could borrow. Hiring a cameraman was never in the budget.

"You look great up there," someone I didn't recognize told me. I thanked them. Mark squeezed my shoulder and excused himself to find a bathroom. Moments later his empty space was replaced with Thomas' presence. I rolled my eyes and sighed deeply.

"I'm not in the mood right now Thomas," I told him, but he reached out to touch my shoulder.

"I need to apologize. I don't know why I thought it would be funny, but obviously it wasn't. I don't want you to think of me as some scumbag. I swear I'll be good. Friends?" He offered his hand out for me to shake. I was hesitant, but finally shook his hand.

Suddenly the music lowered and we turned to see Stacie holding up two rather large bottles of vodka.

"Who wants to play a game?" She shouted. The room let out a collective groan. Feeling bad that no one wanted to play with her I raised my hand.

"Are you crazy?" Thomas asked me and I shrugged.

"I guess. Come with us," I said. He glared at me but followed me. Mark was coming out of the bathroom just as we were heading outside with Stacie and a few others. I grabbed his hand and pulled him forward.

We sat at her patio table and she gave us all shot glasses, pouring vodka in each of them. Mark sat on one side of me, while I insisted Gabby sit on my other side. I saw Thomas frown but quickly sit on the other side of the table opposite me.

"Can we get some chasers?" I asked and she hurried back inside, returning with cans of coke. She set them on the table for us to grab.

"Okay, we are playing name that line. I am going to say a line. The first person to shout out whose line it was gets to tell someone to drink. If you guess wrong, you have to drink. Okay, first line. *Were you poor? Did you eat chicken pot pies?*"

The table erupted but the first person to get their hand up was Gabby. Stacie motioned to her.

"That would be miss Jackie-O herself," she leaned over and squeezed my shoulder. Everyone cheered and Gabby looked around the table for her victim.

"Stacie, you drink."

Stacie blinked rapidly for a moment. I think she was confused about what had just happened. "What?"

Gabby repeated herself and after a long moment Stacie took her shot. I looked at Gabby and she winked at me, and then turned to give everyone a look. The table quickly understood and everyone who guessed a line correctly chose Stacie to take the shot. After the fifth shot she called the game off and slumped in her seat.

"When this kicks in I'm going to throw up. I hate you all," she murmured. Everyone laughed and Thomas offered to grab everyone beers.

We spent the rest of the evening shooting the breeze with the cast. We laughed about the show in which my wig slipped to the side so much it was very obvious, and the audience started laughing.

"Yeah, but what about the time you tripped on the stairs and almost landed on your face?" I teased Gabby.

"I almost peed myself I was so freaked out for a split second!" She exclaimed.

Eventually the party started thinning and I let out a yawn. Mark, who had been a trooper the entire time asked me if I wanted to leave. I looked over at him. He was so handsome. I told him so and played with his jacket. He kissed my cheek and stood up.

"I'm going to go grab the car." He waved to everyone. "It was nice meeting all of you. Maybe I'll audition for the next show, get to make some inside jokes with all of you." He gave them one last smile and left.

Stacie made a choking noise that made us all jump up from the table. Thomas hurried to stand her up and help her onto the grass so she could throw up. Gabby went over and held her hair, while I went inside to get her some water.

I returned with the water to see Gabby having taken over the care of our director, and Thomas standing off to the side away from the vomit.

"I guess this is goodbye, for now." I said, giving him a half-hearted smile. He forced one as well and nodded.

"I guess it is." He shoved his hands in his pockets and rocked on his feet for a moment. "It was nice catching up. You know, when we broke up, I always thought that someday we'd make our way back to each other."

I didn't know how to respond. How did he want me to respond?

"I kind of thought that maybe taking this role that we'd reconnect. That maybe kissing each other for a month would spark some old memories or something. It was stupid. I'm sorry Renee, for everything. I was a jerk back then. I lost out on something great."

I reached out and hugged him. Pulling away I gave him a genuine smile, but it was out of pity.

"We were young and dumb. I'm glad we got to see each other again, but I'm not sad for breaking up. Mark is my everything. We were meant for each other. Me and you- we weren't."

"How can you be so sure? You guys are total opposites. You have no common interests. Why do you stay with him?"

I crossed my arms and took a step away.

"Because he makes me happy, and -"

"Were about to have a baby." Mark's voice behind me interrupted my thoughts.

"What?" Thomas looked down at my flat stomach and then up at my face and then to Mark. "You're pregnant?"

I shook my head and could feel the heat rushing to my face. God, I just wanted to leave. I wrapped my arms around Mark, and he pulled me close.

"Our surrogate is 14 weeks pregnant. I think it's best that you don't see my wife anymore Tom," Mark said firmly.

We all turned when Gabby and Stacie stood up and stumbled over to us.

"You're having a baby?" Gabby asked me, wide eyed. I nodded.

"We didn't want to say anything until after the first trimester," I explained. I turned back to look at the two men staring each other down. We had to leave soon. Mark was a ticking time bomb. He could only be courteous for so long. I squeezed on his hand and gently pulled him towards the house. He stood firmly, not looking away from Thomas.

Suddenly Thomas' cool demeanor changed into anger.

"Wow, so you get married to a rockstar and decide to pay someone to have your kid. Why? So you don't lose your figure? Are you that vain Renee? We've all seen it. Your clothes, your nails and hair. Is that why you chose him over me? You're a little rich bitch now?"

I stared at him and could feel my eyes watering up. My chin began to tremble, but before I could open my mouth to speak

Mark reacted. He swung his arm over, and his fist connected with Thomas' jaw. He fell to the ground and Mark moved to stand over him, arm pulled back ready to punch him again.

Gabby and Stacie screamed. I ran to Mark and put my hands on his back.

"Baby, it's not worth hurting your shoulder. Let's go."

Mark didn't move, so I began rubbing his back, trying to calm him down.

"That's not why you did it, is it?" Gabby asked from behind us.

"We have never said any of that stuff Renee. I don't know where he's getting that from, I swear. We love you," Stacie added.

I turned away from the two men to look at my friends.

"I know that. And no, I didn't hire anyone, and it certainly wasn't to keep my figure." I looked back at Thomas who was trying to get up. He glared up at me.

"Since you think you know more about me than my husband, you should know that I can't get pregnant. So, go ahead and share it with all of your friends who apparently talk about me. I'm sure you'll meet someone who's perfect for you in that mix. We're done. Thank you for reminding me why we broke up," I finished and pulled on Mark.

"Let's go."

Mark gave him one last look before letting me pull him along. When we got into the car, I noticed he was gripping the steering wheel so tight his knuckles were white.

"Baby, I'm so sorry. He was a jerk, and you know I never felt the same way for him as he did for me during the show-" I rushed, trying to calm him but he shook his head.

"No, I'm sorry. You shouldn't have to hear those things. You're not any of those things he called you."

A tear slid down my cheek. I hadn't realized I was crying.

Halfway home he reached for my hand and when we climbed into bed that night, we talked about everything.

He had calmed down enough to where we could begin to laugh about it.

"I wish I had punched him," I told him.

"That look when I came up behind you was priceless. Like what did he expect would happen? He'd whisk you away and you'd get married and live happily ever?" I laid down on his bare chest. I kissed him quickly and looked up at him.

"Is that such a crazy fantasy? After all, that's what you did when we met."

Chapter Eleven

SUPERHERO HEART

I sat across the small cafe table, watching Cleo butter a roll, looking as relaxed as usual. I had spent most of the morning trying to figure out how to bring up what I had seen between her and Christopher last week but had come up blank.

"Are you sad or relieved that your show is over?" Cleo asked me. I blinked a few times and finally registered what she had said.

"Kind of both. It's always sad when its over, but it's nice to have the free time again." There was more long pauses of silence than usual today. Normally the conversation flowed, and it was a pleasant break from everything. Today it didn't feel right. I felt guilty, when I felt that she should be the one feeling sick to her stomach about it.

I chewed on my lip some and then had an idea.

"I took your advice last week and bought a few things for Tot."

Her face brightened as she took a giant bite of the bread.

"Really? You'll have to show me. He's gonna be such a stylish little guy. I can not wait. Where'd you go?"

I paused, looking her dead in the eye.

"You know that little group of shops with the chocolate shop? It's French, um.. Délice prometteur? It has all sorts of shops over there. Me and Rocky took a long walk in the afternoon, taking advantage of the nice weather."

She rolled her eyes.

"It's California, it's always nice weather here."

I chuckled. She had a point.

"We got a few things for Tot, some chocolate for the twins, and I was going to get some coffee but that cafe on the other side of the plaza was full," I said, making direct eye contact. Her face paled and her mouth fell open slightly. Suddenly the waitress brought our lunch.

"Is there anything else I can get for you right now?" She asked us and I shook my head, not taking my eyes off of Cleo. She gulped and looked up at the woman.

"No thanks, I think we're good here," she croaked. Once she left her eyes narrowed and she leaned in to speak to me.

"I don't know what you saw, but it's not what you think."

I reached for my fork to stab at my salad.

"Then explain it. Does Ethan know?"

She shook her head furiously.

"No, and please don't tell him. I need time to - to figure this out without him. Christopher is threatening to sue me. For lying about the twins."

"Sue you for what? Is that even possible?"

She shrugged, sighed and then rubbed her face.

"I guess. He wants a lot of money. Damages. He lost everything when he went to prison, so now he's coming after everything I have."

"What was that book he gave you?"

"It was a book similar to the one Duchess wrote. His own tell all, how an educated, wealthy man with a promising future was led astray by a wild woman who destroyed his political career, his ability to trust, and then how he rose from the ashes and is using that to help the people by changing some of his political opinions. Pure garbage. He was the one who cheated first, and then continued to cheat on me for the rest of our marriage."

"Is he blackmailing you? Give him the money or he'll release the book?" She shook her head.

"No, he was bragging. He's signed a deal. The book is going to be published. People eat up that political crap. He wanted to meet me in person to tell me he's suing for mental distress. Him and Holly both have went through so much at the hands of my fans." She held up her hands making air quotes.

"What are you going to do? Will he win?"

Seeming to relax, she finally picked up her sandwich and took a bite.

"No, well I'm not sure but I called his brother last week and he said the lawsuit was laughable. He recommended some lawyers, but Ethan has a lawyer he has on retainer, so I was considering using him. I just don't want Ethan to know. Not yet. He's going to be furious that I met with him at all."

"Why did you?" I asked, feeling like it was a very stupid question. She looked down at her lap and grew quiet.

"I don't know. I don't even know how he got my phone number. He called me and asked if we could talk. I told him no at first, but then he promised he'd be civil, and we could be in a public place. I kind of thought maybe we could get some closure."

I said nothing. I understood the need for closure. At one time, I had wanted it with Thomas. Now I had it, but it wasn't very satisfying. He was the same man I had broken up with. I was sure that Christopher hadn't changed either.

"I think you have to accept that you might not get the closure you expect. He's not well. He travelled across the country just to sue you. You are putting yourself and everyone around you in danger with keeping in contact with him."

She bit her lip.

"I never understood what it was about him that drew me in. He told me to jump and I'd say how high. I guess I still feel guilty that I hid the truth from him for so long. From both of them."

"You should really tell Ethan. He could help," I urged. She hesitated, but finally nodded.

"I wasn't planning on seeing Chris again, unless it's in a courtroom. I'll tell Ethan. Just let me do it please." She placed one hand on the table and the other on her growing belly. Smiling, she wiggled her hand for me to take it. It still didn't feel right. Was she using the baby to make me promise not to tell anyone her secret? I reached over and she squeezed my hand tightly. I made a silent prayer that this wasn't the biggest mistake of my life. Something about it felt like it was.

Adrian was taking Rocky from my arms to take him home for the evening.

"Hey, do you guys have plans this weekend? Chase wanted to go out for a mini celebration for Rocky. We missed his six month, but he's seven months old on Saturday." I gave him a confused look and he chuckled.

"Do they do that now? Celebrate the months?"

"I guess. I don't know. Half the time I'm just along for the ride. This is just as much new to me as it is to you. Well him too, but he likes to make a big deal out of every little thing he learns. You know, the whole almost dying thing really changes a person's appreciation for the little things," he explained. I reached out to squeeze Rocky's tiny cheek. He smiled at me and my heart melted.

"We'll be there. Just let us know the time and place." He lit up told me he'd be in touch.

When Mark came home that night, I told him about dinner and he rolled his eyes.

"We are not doing that for Tot. Don't get me wrong, Rocky is a cute little man, but I am not throwing a party every time the baby poops."

When Saturday came, we were told to dress nice, so I put on a plum colored cocktail dress. The restaurant they picked wasn't exactly kid friendly. I made a comment to Adrian about it and he explained that they had reserved a private room.

"Do we need to get a gift?" Mark moaned. I realized that I didn't know. What was the proper etiquette for things like this?

"Well it's a little late now. Let's just go. I need a drink," I said. It had been a long day. I finally decided it was time to call my parents and tell them the good news.

Overall the phone call went well. They were happy for me, although confused about the medical side of it. I didn't come home often, or call often for that matter, so when I did contact them the phone calls typically lasted a few hours. Today was no exception.

My mother had told me every piece of gossip she had from her church quilting group and Dad talked about the shows he was watching. They were sweet and their intentions were good, but I just couldn't handle living the small town life they enjoyed so much. If I hadn't met Thomas I would have stayed and become a carbon copy of my mother. I guess that was the only good thing I could take away from that relationship.

I told Mark about my day while we drove to the restaurant and he laughed.

"Oh fun. Can you make that call for me tomorrow to my folks? Be sure to explain that we are still not moving back to Michigan."

"I offered to buy them tickets to come out after he's born

and they didn't take them," I murmured. Despite their love for me, they refused to leave their small world.

He reached for my hand across the seat.

"I'm sorry baby. Don't take it personally. You know how they are," he rubbed his thumb over my knuckles, soothing me. He was right, it was to be expected. We were quickly escorted to the party room when we arrived. Silver and blue balloons were placed around the room. The rest of the decor matched the balloons. It appeared that we were the last ones to arrive. We quickly took our seats across from the Andrews'.

"You're not the last ones. Derek is still missing," Chase said from the head of the table. Adrian was on his right, with Rocky on his left in a highchair.

"Where is he?" I asked, but no one seemed to know. He showed up about ten minutes later, dressed in a maroon suit and looking more than a little frazzled.

"Sorry, got a little caught up with some stuff. Did you guys cut the cake? Where is the not really birthday boy?"

Once everyone had arrived a waiter came and took our orders and poured us wine.

"We actually kind of lied. We aren't here to celebrate Rocky," Adrian said, after clinking a fork on his glass to quiet us. We all stared down at him curiously.

"He did turn seven months old, but you all can rest assured we aren't going to do this every month," Chase chuckled. He was all smiles tonight. He was usually a pretty chipper person, but tonight he was just beaming.

"Okay, so why are we here then?" Derek snapped, his brow furrowing. Why did he care? If we weren't here, he would most likely be sitting on my couch playing video games all night. My attention turned back to the head of the table. Chase looked at Adrian and they reached for each other's hands.

"Do you want to tell them, or should I?" Adrian said low to

his husband. They were so adorable together. Chase tightened his lips and his eyes went glossy.

"Maybe you should," he said, his voice raising slightly. Adrian smiled and stood up.

"As of this Thursday, Chase is tumor free. The radiation worked."

The room fell completely silent for only a split second before erupting in cheers and applause.

Cleo jumped up and ran to hug Chase from behind. She squeezed him tightly. When she let him go the rest of the table stood up and he accepted hugs and pats on the backs from everyone.

"This is seriously the best thing we could be celebrating!" Cleo exclaimed when we returned to our seats.

"Yeah, no offense but we all thought you were being obnoxious having us come out for a seven-month-old party," Ethan added, glancing at his own baby sitting next to him. Both Wilson men laughed.

"We know. We just needed a reason to get you all together for something nice. We knew if we just said who wants to go out, half of you wouldn't show," Adrian explained. We all more or less muttered agreements. After the day I had today, there's a chance I would have canceled to spend the evening soaking in a hot bath and relaxing in bed.

The food, wine, and company made for a great evening.

"Does this mean that I no longer get to watch Rocky?" I asked.

Chase thought for a moment and then answered.

"I'm not sure yet. The good news is still pretty fresh, so we haven't made any definite plans yet. I was hoping to go back to work eventually. But I kind of want to wait until Rocky's at least a year. We'll discuss it and get back to you soon," he promised.

When the twins and the two babies started to yawn and

close their eyes, we decided to pay the bill and have a little afterparty at the Andrews' house.

"Since this is a special night for you guys, let us take care of the bill," Ethan said.

"Oh wow, thanks Ethan," Chase said, and Adrian and Derek agreed. Ethan shot Derek and then Mark and I looks.

"I meant, let me pay for those two. You," staring hard at Derek, "Can pay for your food and drinks." Derek frowned but said nothing back. Cleo grabbed Blue and asked if someone could help with the twins. Before I could offer my help, Adrian told her he would.

I turned to Mark as everyone was standing to leave.

"I have to use the restroom before we leave. Wait for me?"

He kissed my forehead quickly as I left out of the room. Knowing we were probably the only ones left I didn't doddle.

Stepping out, I started looking for my husband. I scanned the dining area and found him standing with Derek, mouth hanging open and staring hard at something. My eyes followed his look and my heart stopped. Ethan was standing toe to toe with Christopher.

Breaking my stare, I hurried over to Mark and grabbed his hand. His fingers curled over mine and squeezed a little tighter than comfortable. I let out a yelp and that seemed to break the spell. He looked over at me and apologized.

"Sorry, I just need to stay and see how this plays out. You can go to the car if you want."

I shook my head and stayed with him and watched.

Ethan's fists were clenched and even though we could only see the back of him, you could see how angry he was. Christopher on the other hand looked amused. He was talking to him, a happy glint in his eye. He looked relaxed, joyful even, that he happened to see Cleo's new husband.

"Hey what's the hold up? Adrian's waiting in my car and they are ready to go." Cleo's voice made me jump from behind me. I turned quickly and opened my mouth to say something but came up blank. She came forward and gasped.

"Oh my God." She pushed past us and hurried over to her husband and ex-husband. She tugged on Ethan's sleeve, but he didn't budge. Christopher looked down at her and flashed a gorgeous smile. By the way his lips move I knew he had just greeted her.

Seeing him from a distance I understood why she fell for him quickly when she was younger. He was very handsome, and exhumed confidence. A woman suddenly appeared next to him. I recognized her as Holly, the woman he had been having an affair with for years before marrying her in prison. They had a daughter together now. She had gotten pregnant while Cleo was still married to him.

Holly came up smiling, and then her face fell when she realized who he had been talking to. She glared at Cleo and grabbed Christopher possessively. Looking quite satisfied, she said something and that made Ethan step back and turn to leave. Christopher laughed as he came towards us and stormed out. Cleo ran after him, and we followed her.

He got into their car and slammed the door.

"Is it a good idea for him to drive right now? He's got the kids in the car," I mentioned.

"Good point. I'm gonna go say something," Mark said and ran towards their car before they left. He knocked on Ethan's window and after a long moment of him ignoring him he rolled it down and spoke to him. Ethan's anger started to subside and finally nodded. He got out of the car and traded places with his wife.

We asked if we were still going to their house, and Cleo said to come over. Derek jumped in our car and we left the restaurant.

"Holy shit guys," Derek leaned forward in the back to be eye level with the two of us in front. "What do you think he said to Ethan?" I looked out the window, afraid that I would give anything away.

"Who knows. I want to know why he's here in Los Angeles. Shouldn't he have a tether or something?" Mark said. I chose not to speak for the duration of the car ride while the guys discussed various theories to Chris' sudden reappearance.

We arrived at their house and Derek jumped out and practically sprinted inside. Mark and I took our time getting inside. We went straight into Ethan's den, where our parties almost always were. Cleo and Ethan were noticeably absent.

Chase was behind the bar pouring scotch into two tumblers.

"Tabatha took the kids to bed and they went straight into his office."

Mark went over to the stereo system and turned it on. Having something other than silence surrounding us helped to relax us. I joined Chase at the bar and reached down into the cabinet for my bottle of rum. I mixed it with a can of ginger ale and went to the card table where Adrian was starting to shuffle a deck.

"I think we can all appreciate Ethan for letting us keep alcohol here now," he chuckled. I nodded enthusiastically. For the first two years of Ethan's recovery their house was kept dry. We were allowed to bring alcohol, but we had to take it home. Somewhere down the line Ethan must have decided he was in a good place with his addiction and agreed to let us keep a very small shelf in his bar. The only rule was that it was to be locked and only Mark, Derek, and Adrian have keys that they kept on their persons.

"I have no problem seeing the bottles anymore or watching you drink, but you never can be too safe," he explained when he told us.

We started a game of poker, playing for pennies. After a long twenty minutes the couple of the house came out of the office and joined the party. No one said anything for a moment, we only stared at them. Ethan rolled his eyes and went to the fridge to grab some water. Cleo looked like she was in shock but chose to head to the table with us.

Ethan joined her a moment later with two lemon waters. Adrian dealt them in and we started a new game. "Can we ask questions now?" Derek asked excitedly. I groaned inwardly. Why was he so obnoxious? Ethan's eyes shot up and glared at him, but Cleo put her hand on his, relaxing him.

"Apparently they are here to do some daytime talk show."

"What did he say to piss you off?" Mark added, seeing as how Derek broke the seal of awkwardness.

"He asked how the twins were doing. He wanted to know if Jimmy missed her 'Daddy'," Cleo did air quotes at that last word.

"Even when I lived with him, he wasn't ever there. She didn't miss him then, she doesn't miss him now. He was just trying to irritate him. That's what Chris does."

There was a small lull after that, so finally Ethan forced a smile and asked if we wanted to make the game a little more interesting.

"How so?"

"Are we stripping? Cause hell yeah. Wait, there's only two girls…" Derek said. Everyone shot him down quickly.

"Nice try," Mark told him.

"What, it's not like we haven't seen almost all of each other naked anyways. Granted most of the time it wasn't by choice, but some of it is ingrained in my brain!" He groaned and pulled on his face dramatically. I looked over at Mark, who turned away quickly. Had he seen Cleo naked?

"Hold up, has everyone seen everyone in the buff?" I asked.

Everyone burst into laughter. Derek held up his hand and then lowered it.

"I have- wait no. Only my bandmates. Cleo you probably have."

She shook her head and gave him a disgusted look.

"No!" She paused and then blushed. "Not Chase or Renee," she mumbled. I was slightly bothered by her confession, but I understood that their careers didn't have much room for modesty. Plus, she knew him way longer than I did. Across the table Adrian raised his hand smugly.

"I've seen everyone." I shot him a glare.

"Uh, when have you seen me?" I pointed to my chest.

He winked at me and I felt my face grow red hot.

"Not in person."

I whipped my head to look at my husband, who was conveniently looking at the cards in his hands very intensely.

"I'll explain later," he mumbled, but I was already piecing it together. I knew exactly what pictures he had seen.

"You haven't seen me," Ethan added. Adrian smirked and gave him a skeptical look.

"Haven't I? Might as well have."

Ethan's eyes bulged and he flipped him off. Cleo burst into laughter, she held on to her stomach, trying to catch her breath.

"That's not funny."

"What's not? Tell us, tell us now!" Derek banged on the table excitedly. The three of them looked at each other. Cleo and Adrian were sharing a look that said go for it, while Ethan was going to kick their asses. Adrian coughed.

"I may not have seen Ethan, but I have seen someone's bare ass that looked EXACTLY like him." He raised his eyebrows suggestively. I swear all the sound in the room disappeared for a split moment before the room erupted.

"I hate you both," Ethan said, which only made everyone laugh harder.

"You and Evan? When?" Mark asked him. Cleo leaned over and punched Adrian's shoulder.

"While we were dating," she said. This story was just getting better and better.

"Alright, alright," Ethan said after the whole story was revealed. "Can we just get back to cards? Adrian wins- he's the group slut," he teased. We laughed and Derek insisted we get him a crown. Adrian chuckled but shook his head.

"Sadly, I can't wear that crown anymore. I will have to pass that down to you Derek." He reached over to squeeze Chase's hand. They shared a look and my heart warmed. Derek didn't look too happy.

"You don't know. Maybe monogamy is something I could do."

"Have you ever had a long-term relationship?" I asked, genuinely curious. He glared at me but said nothing.

"You ever hear the song 'The Wanderer' by Dion? That's me." He smirked and took a swig of his beer. Returning to the card game I began humming the song and slowly the rest of the table started singing the song. Soon we were all shouting the words and rocking back and forth.

I had been worried that the entire evening was going to be ruined by Chris' sudden appearance. Despite that, this was turning into a great night.

"Why don't we bargain something other than money?" Derek suggested.

"Like what?" I asked him, knowing it was probably something ridiculous.

"I don't know, perhaps we could ask someone to put something in. If you can't think of anything specific it will just be a truth or dare situation to the loser."

We agreed to try it. The first game had Ethan against Chase.

"What do you want me to add to the pot?" Chase asked him. Ethan thought for a moment.

"Plan the prom for this year." Chase thought it over and then nodded.

"I can do that. I want you to shave your head," he said quickly. His eyes had a glint of evil that I had never seen. It was amusing. Ethan's mouth fell open.

"That's not fair. I picked something nice."

Chase shrugged his shoulders innocently.

"Derek didn't give us any guidelines."

We all mumbled agreements, and Ethan shook on it, but he didn't look happy. They quickly revealed their cards and Ethan leapt up excitedly.

"Ha! Alright all bets are off. Anything goes," he said and the game suddenly got interesting. Cleo left to grab a notebook to keep track of all of the wagers. By the end of the night Derek was getting Adrian's name tattooed on his ass, Mark was singing 'Sugar Daddy' on the album, and Ethan had shove Derek's sock in his mouth. Ethan was getting royally boned with this game.

I swear when Derek took off his shoe, we all let out a tear for him. Ethan gulped and shut his eyes. He shoved it in his mouth and started gagging right away. Derek counted a full sixty seconds and when he was allowed to spit it out Ethan reached out and punched him hard on the shoulder.

We finally called the last game of the night and it was down to Derek and I. It was a rather delicious moment, because I had great cards.

"What do you want?" He asked, raising an eyebrow to me. He was grinning ear to ear.

"You have to paint the nursery," I decided. It was the least he could do since he was living with me. He scrunched up his nose but shrugged.

"Okay. I can do that. I'll even do a good job, how's that?"

He said sarcastically. I was starting to feel uneasy. My smile faded quickly. Why was he giving in so easily?

"What do you want from me?" I asked nervously. His smile grew wider, and his eyes blazed with excitement.

"I want to see those pictures of you Adrian was talking about."

Everyone stopped talking. I glanced at Mark, who's face was completely blank. I think it was shock, but also a little guilt for letting it slip. I gulped, but finally agreed.

We laid down our cards and the whole moment felt like it was going in slow motion. We looked at each other's hands, then back up at each other. My mouth fell open as he leapt up from the table and let out a loud cheer. Oh. My. God.

Chapter Twelve

THE PROMISE

"It's going to be so nice to get out of the city for awhile. I can't wait." Cleo sighed deeply. "One full week of no work, no stress, and fresh air." She reached across her kitchen counter to grab a strawberry. She had mentioned that she was craving strawberry shortcake so I made some fresh for her this morning.

"And when we get home, we get to see what Tot is. This is going to be the best week ever." I agreed with her. I had spent the last month planning our family vacation. Once we decided on a location, I went to work gathering everything we would need.

We decided to rent a few small pop up campers. Nothing fancy, but considering I had spent years camping in tents, I knew that we would enjoy the experience way more if we could sleep well.

We were lucky that the only one who really needed to get their work in order was Ethan. One of his bandmates, Christian, was taking over while he was gone. It also just happened that the week before our big ultrasound appointment was also the twins spring break from school. This was the perfect time to go.

When we got to the Andrews, Mark and Derek went straight into the studio. Despite Mark being upset over having to do the song from Hedwig and the Angry Inch that he didn't want to do, a bet was a bet. If I had to show Derek the pictures I had gotten done for a Valentine's Day the first year we were married, then he could do this. He'd been rehearsing it and was now working on the actual performance.

"It's going to be so much fun. This is the first time ever we are going to wear actual costumes. The label already has someone working on ideas," Cleo went on excitedly about their future plans. Her cell phone started ringing and she jumped up.

"Oh! I have an errand to run really quick. I've got to go. Why don't you go check out the guys for a bit."

I gave her a look, but she ignored it. She grabbed her keys off the counter and practically ran out of the house.

I did as she recommended. It was so cute watching my husband trying to dance. Despite being a drummer, he didn't have great rhythm. For dancing anyways. He saw me sneak in and blew me a kiss. They paused their rough recording of their song and he put his hand on his hip.

"I'm not wearing heels. That's gonna be a bitch to change in and out of. We need quick transitions. I'll wear red shoes, but that's it," he told Derek. Derek gave him a face but turned the music back on to start back on the dance moves.

I had to admit, what I had heard from their work in progress album was pretty damn good. It was going to be successful. I was so proud of all of them. It was interesting to watch their process. I didn't get to see it often, but when I did, I enjoyed it. Well some of it, I guess. The technical stuff was beyond my knowledge, but when they discussed costumes and lines, they wanted to borrow from the musicals I liked to sit in.

Soon Adrian joined them in the room and they decided to work on another song. Even though Cleo was gone, they could still work on their parts. I had fun trying to guess what songs they had taken pieces from. I recognized West Side Story, Hedwig, and a few others.

After awhile I stepped out to use the restroom and when I was on my way back, I heard Ethan call my name.

"Renee, hold up." I turned to see him leaning against his office door.

"What's up?" I asked, taking a few steps his way.

"Can we talk? In private?" He asked, moving from the door to let me inside. I went in tentatively, and he shut the door quickly. Sitting in one of his chairs, he sat behind his desk and leaned forward.

"Do you think Cleo has been acting weird lately?" *Yes*.

I shook my head.

"No, not that I have noticed," I lied. He frowned.

"I feel like I'm paranoid but the last few weeks she's been-off. We saw her ex at that restaurant and things have been different. I don't know, I just got a weird vibe from him. Like he knew something about her I didn't."

I started twisting my hands together. I didn't like where this was going.

"Have you tried talking to her about it?"

He shook his head.

"No. She gets so defensive when I bring him up. Like I'm throwing it in her face again. We've gotten past all of that, so I don't want to keep bringing it up. I just thought maybe she had said something to you at one of your lunches." His eyes were pleading for me to give him some shred of information. I wanted to confess everything. He deserved to know. I couldn't believe she still hadn't told him she had talked to him. I sighed deeply and lied again.

"She hasn't mentioned anything to me. I don't think you have anything to worry about. Maybe her hormones are going out of whack with the pregnancy," I offered, but the guilt of using Tot to lie made my stomach turn. I had to get out of this room. He chewed on his lip some and finally nodded.

"You're probably right. I'm sorry for putting you on the spot. I just-" he paused and looked away. Turning back to me I saw his eyes were shiny. "It took so long to finally get her. I don't want to lose her."

I gave him a halfhearted smile and tried to assure him it would be alright. He thanked me and I practically ran from the room. The next time I spoke to him we were putting the final bags in our vehicles to leave for our vacation.

"Does Cleo need anything to snack on for the drive?" I asked.

"I don't think so. She grabbed some crackers. We should be good. Is everyone else ready?" He looked around at the group of us standing in his driveway.

The pop ups had arrived this morning, and luckily we all had vehicles we could hitch them too.

"Who am I bunking with?" Derek bounced down the house steps with one last bag over his shoulder. No one spoke up. I walked over to him and smiled wide.

"I got you a tent."

He swore and looked desperately around the group for help.

"Oh, come on, not cool. Why do I have to sleep in a tent?"

Adrian crossed his arms.

"You don't have a car, you didn't pay for a camper like the rest of us did. What was your plan?"

Derek's face grew slightly pink.

"I don't know. I thought there'd be room in one of yours."

"Not in ours. We're at full capacity," Ethan said, shutting the back of his Escalade.

"Fine. I'll pay for half of someone's camper," he said, pouting.

I looked over at Mark who was giving me the look that said, 'Don't you dare'. I gave him my best apologetic smile, and he frowned.

"You can stay with us," I sighed. He brightened and ran over to our vehicle.

"But I will not hesitate to make you sleep in that tent if you can't behave!" I shouted after him.

Cleo was the last one to exit the house. She gave us all a thumbs up.

"Alright, we're all ready to go. Tabatha's gonna cat sit for Kitty and Big D. Let's get a move on." We piled into our cars and started the six-hour trip to the Anthony Chabot Campground.

When scouting for a place to visit, the thing we had all agreed on was that we preferred something not so local. I think we all wanted to just get away from Los Angeles for a bit. I spent an entire afternoon searching for campgrounds that let us have pop ups, dogs, and were kid friendly. Finally, I settled on this place. I was excited. I had never been here before.

Derek talked our ears off the entire ride. He seemed more excited than the twins were. I almost wished we had offered to take them instead. I made a note to see if they'd trade them for Derek on the way back.

Once they started talking video game stuff, I closed my eyes and put my pillow against the window to take a nap. By the time I woke up we were less than a half hour away.

The Andrews' were at the head of our little parade, so Ethan got out and talked to the gate people. They waved their hands, directing him to our spots I assumed. He climbed back in the car and when we got up the guy told us to just follow Ethan. We were good to go.

I managed to rent three lots in the same area. The Andrews' and the Wilson's were side by side, and our camper was across the small dirt path not even thirty feet away.

Once we were parked, I quickly found that I was the only one with pop up experience. I had to help everyone get their campers set up. By the time we were unloaded and starting to settle in it was time for dinner. Thankfully I wasn't the only one who knew how to start a fire.

Our lot had no neighbors on one side, so we brought all of the chairs and tables over to our side and had hot dogs and burgers in the cool shade. Once dinner had been consumed, we moved our chairs over to the fire pit to enjoy the warmth while the sun set.

Beau and Bonnie didn't seem to like the change of scenery. I laid out a blanket for them near the camper and they hadn't strayed much from it. Ozzy, Dallas' dog, and Chester, Chase and Adrian's dog on the other hand were going crazy with the extra space. They had spent most of the evening playing and chasing each other around. Now they had settled near their owners.

As soon as the sun was fully set Derek ran into the camper and returned with the ingredients to make s'mores. The twins and Cleo squealed and hurried to grab the sticks we had used for hot dogs earlier.

Derek filled the twins up with marshmallows until they were falling asleep on each other. When Ethan had to pull a half-eaten marshmallow out of Dallas' mouth he called it a night for them and took them to bed. Soon after the rest of us were yawning and we put the fire out so we could get a good night's sleep.

In the morning we found Derek was already gone. Setting

things up for breakfast we discovered that no one knew where he had gone off to.

"He went to sleep when we did." Mark told the group, but he was just as mystified as the rest of us.

I was beginning to get worried when noon rolled around and we still hadn't heard from him. I was telling Mark that maybe we should go look for him when suddenly Derek appeared walking down the road towards our lot, holding a fishing pole.

When he reached us, he saw the confused look we were all giving him, and he gave us a dirty look.

"What? Why are you all looking at me like that?"

"Where were you?" I asked. He waved his fishing pole at me like I was an idiot.

"I went fishing. Catch and release. What? I like fishing. I used to go with my dad all the time," he said defensively. Mark just shook his head and chuckled.

"Alright, don't get all worked up. Just tell someone when you leave next time."

He put his pole against the camper and came to join us in relaxing with some good beer and good music. Chase offered to go with him tomorrow morning and he was hesitant.

"I'm not trying to teach someone. Do you know how to fish?" Chase rolled his eyes.

"I'm from Louisiana, of course I know how to fish."

We had some time before dinner, so I offered to take the twins over to the beach to swim for a bit. I asked Mark if he wanted to join us, but he declined. He was cooking dinner tonight, and he wanted to prep.

"I'm making hobo packets. Potatoes, onions, sausage, all smothered in cheese," he bragged. I kissed him quickly and hurried off to catch up with the twins.

"Sounds delicious. Have fun," I shouted back at him.

The twins had a blast playing in the lake. I don't think they had ever been to a lake, or if they had they had been too young to remember. They got a kick out of seeing people pass by on their boats and wave at them. I relaxed on a blanket and soaked up the sun.

After a few hours the kids started complaining that they were getting cold, so we packed up headed back to the campsite. I looked around for Mark when we returned and stopped in my tracks. My stomach did a complete flip.

He was standing with Cleo, her back to me. His hands were on her stomach and his face was lit up like he had won the lottery. I was stuck in place, frozen to the spot. Finally, Cleo turned and saw me. She hurried over excitedly and grabbed my hands. She put them on her belly and looked up at me, her eyes wide and smile even wider.

"Tot's moving! This is the first time I'm feeling it."

Mark came up behind me and put his hands next to mine on her hard, round belly.

It took an excruciatingly long minute but finally I felt a little something bump against my palm. I felt three more small but definite movements before it stopped.

"That was amazing. I am so glad you guys were both here to feel it," she exclaimed and then threw her arms around me, squeezing me tight. I forced a chuckle, but it still didn't feel great. I think Cleo could tell I wasn't as excited as her and Mark. She pointed to her belly and rubbed it.

"That's your baby in there! Little Icarus Lesley."

"Icarus?" I asked and she nodded enthusiastically.

"Yeah and we can call him Icky for short!" Realizing that she really was trying to cheer me up I hugged her again and thanked her. I shouldn't ruin a good moment with my insecurities. However, I must have still been acting weird because that night when we went to bed Mark asked me if I was okay.

"You've been acting weird ever since you got back from the lake. Do you want to talk about it?" He reached for me in bed and I snuggled closer to him. It was comforting being wrapped up in his warmth.

"I don't know. I just felt like I missed it. Tot's first kicks, and I walked up to you and her sharing that beautiful moment together. I just wish I had been there." *I wished it could have been me sharing those feelings with him.*

He reached up to run his fingers through my hair.

"Oh baby, I'm sorry. You know it wasn't like you were left out. She just got excited. You literally walked up a moment after he started kicking."

I turned my body to face his. His eyes were filled with unnecessary guilt.

"I know. It's just weird. I'll get over it. I just wish things could have been different." He leaned in to kiss me tenderly.

"I know baby. I wish that too. But just think, in five months we'll get to hold little baby Icky in our arms and he'll be 100% ours," he chuckled lightly. I rolled my eyes.

"If that is the boy name she has her heart set on then I really, really hope it's a girl," I joked as I closed my eyes for sleep.

The next morning Cleo pulled me aside and asked me if I was okay. She also explained that I was just a moment late, and I didn't miss anything.

"I know that. I was a little sad, but I'm okay now. I'm just excited I got to feel him at all. I can't wait til he's here." We hugged it out and went back to making oatmeal for the group.

The rest of the trip went fantastic. It was the break from reality that we all desperately needed. We all tried our hardest to stay off of our phones, but I think we all broke down a little at least once a day. I caught Derek video chatting with a very bored looking Big D.

That last full day I covered my head in a white bandana while getting dressed for the day. Seeing my roots growing, even I was ready to get back home. Once everyone gathered for a hobo breakfast I was teased for not being able to 'fully rough it'. I think I was on my phone the least amount of anyone here, but I didn't feel like arguing that one.

"Are you trying to tell us that your hair is not naturally purple?" Cleo gasped dramatically. I smirked but said nothing.

"You've been part of our group for how long now? You can reveal your true colors to us, we won't tell," Adrian winked.

"I can assure you, that she is in fact, not naturally purple." Derek closed his eyes and sighed deeply. He turned to me and gave me a grin that made me want to shower. "I remember her natural look to be-"

"Derek!" Cleo shouted, shutting him up. I chose not to respond to his comments. I remembered those photos well, and I knew for a fact that he didn't see a single hair that wasn't on my head.

After breakfast we decided to go for a hike. Well everyone but Cleo, Blue, and Rocky.

"There's no way I'm doing any hiking with Tot wiggling around like he is. The three of us can take a nap."

We packed our backpacks full of water, snacks and a first aid kit and started out. With the twins with the group we decided to not be too adventurous and just stick to the path in the woods.

Derek lead the way with a large walking stick and an oddly large knowledge for plant life. He was like a giant Boy Scout. I'd say troop leader, but it was Derek after all. The twins followed him closely as he pointed out the various trees, flowers, and mushrooms.

We stopped for lunch and I asked him about it.

"You fish, you make s'mores, and are like a walking encyclopedia with trees and flowers. Where has this version of Derek been hiding?" Derek looked up from his bologna sandwich and stared at me blankly.

"My dad liked to camp. This was our summer vacations

growing up. So what?" He said sharply. I shook my head and dropped it. It was obvious he wasn't interested in discussing it further.

After we cleaned up our picnic, we made our way back to the campsite. Everyone more or less went their separate ways to relax for a bit before dinner. I went into our camper and promptly fell asleep. Mark gently rocked me awake.

"Hey you, we're about to start dinner if you want to come out." I thanked him and got out of bed. Readjusting my bandanna, I followed him out.

Everyone was relaxing around the campfire chatting. I joined them quickly.

"You want a beer Renee?" Chase offered me from the cooler he was standing in front of. Nodding he grabbed an extra and brought it to me when he sat back down.

I had just taken a sip of my drink when Dallas ran up excitedly.

"Aunt Renee did you see it yet?" I gave him a confused look and glanced around the circle. A few had small smiles on their faces, but Derek was beaming.

"See what?" I asked and he reached for my hand, pulling me up and out of the circle. We only took a few steps before I saw what had gotten him so excited. The tent had been erected.

"Are you sleeping in there tonight?"

He nodded enthusiastically and dropped my hand. The tent unzipped and his sister's dark head popped out.

"Did you get the pillows?" She screamed at her brother. Seeing as his hands were empty, I assumed that no he hadn't. He spun back around and quickly went to his family's camper to grab them.

Sitting back down Derek explained that instead of napping he decided to set the tent up.

"I thought they'd get a kick out of one night of real camping."

I raised an eyebrow.

"And you're the one sleeping in there with them?" I asked him skeptically.

"Nah, it only fits the two of them. I'm gonna sleep outside the tent. I have an air mattress."

Ethan and Cleo got up to start dinner. It was their turn. They were making grilled chicken for the adults and hot dogs for the kids. We had a lot of hot dogs this week.

Despite Cleo being a part of the equation dinner was pretty good. Everyone teased her and she crossed her arms in a pout. Ethan kissed her temple and told her he'd eat her burnt food for the rest of his life if that meant she was there everyday to cook it.

When the sun started setting Derek pulled out his acoustic guitar and began playing some cheesy songs that everyone could sing along to. He really was in his element here. He was almost pleasant. I was going to miss this version of him. I made a note to consider making this an annual thing. Maybe it would help tolerate him the rest of the year.

Taking a break from entertaining he went to blow up his bed and grab his blankets. He returned with more marshmallows. I swear he had brought an entire suitcase of them, and another with cookies, crackers, and various chocolates to go with them.

Ethan took the opportunity to grab the guitar from his seat and reach for his wife's hand. She looked up at him with such admiration. He excused them and they started walking down the road towards the woods. I looked around and saw Adrian waving the baby monitor.

"He mentioned something earlier. We've got both babies in our camper."

I ate my final s'more for the week and leaned back in my

chair. I felt so bloated, I was sure that I was going to look like I had a baby bump for a week or so.

When Derek returned to the group he looked around for his guitar and swore when he heard what happened.

"Damn Andrews and his romantic gestures," he mumbled. He slumped for a minute and then shot up excitedly. He looked over at the twins who were waiting for him to do something else fun. He was definitely winning lots of best uncle points this week.

"Do you guys want to hear a ghost story?" He whispered to them. His eyes wide and smile even wider. He looked like a psychopath. The kids nodded excitedly and sat up straighter in their seats.

"Derek," I started but he waved me away.

"Calm down, they'll be fine." He jumped back up and hurried into the camper, returning with a flashlight. He flicked it on and put it under his chin.

"Yeah, we'll be fine Aunt Renee. We're old enough," Jimmy defended. I sighed and said nothing else.

"Okay, this story is about some campers just like yourselves many years ago. In this very campsite, on this very evening. A group of boys and girls much like yourself were staying overnight in tents scattered all around the ground." He waved his arms around. Their eyes grew wide, all of their attention on him.

"There was only one adult to watch over all of them, and it became hard to keep track of everyone. When night fell, he decided to do roll call. He called out everyone's name and they'd come forward. He called out for Harry, Donna, Penny, Carl, Randy, Lloyd, and finally Tony." He stopped and let the words settle in with the kids. They gasped and reached for the others hand.

My heart melted a little. They spent so much time fighting with each other, when they needed it the most they reached out for their twin. A cold breeze ran through the camp and I shivered.

"Are you cold? You want me to grab your sweater?" Mark asked me. I nodded and he stood up to get it.

"Aw you're gonna miss the rest of the story," Derek whined. The twins whipped their heads around in sync and shot identical nasty glares at him. Mark shot his hands up in innocence.

"I'll be right back, just go on without me."

They turned back to Derek and told him to keep going. With a big sigh he started back up.

"Tony was the only one that hadn't answered roll call. So, he asked all the children to start looking around the area for him. Everyone started calling his name. "Tony!" But he didn't call back.

Starting to worry, the counselor decided to take roll call again and found that Lloyd and Randy were missing now too. Everyone began to get frightened. They had just seen them. Where did they go?

The counselor decided to call the police, but it was too late. They'd be there first thing in the morning. When he turned back around Carl, Penny, and Donna were all gone too!

He looked down at the only boy left. Little Harry. He asked him where they went and he said Tony took them. He asked Harry where and he pointed to the forest."

Derek stopped to take a breath and pointed to the forest we had gone into that afternoon. The twins were so entranced I wasn't sure they were breathing. With a large inhale he picked up the story again.

"He took little Harry's hand and went into the dark forest to look for all the missing children." Derek leaned forward to whisper to them. "The next morning when the police came, they found all of the children, including Tony, but no counselor. They were crying and holding on to each other. They couldn't explain how they got back to the campsite, but they all said that they could hear the counselor screaming in the woods all night, still looking for Tony. They say if little kids are back where Tony went missing, the counselor will come back for them and take them into the woods with him. If you hear him screaming, you know it's too late."

As if on cue we heard a loud earsplitting screech come from the woods.

"Tony! Tony!"

The twins screamed bloody murder and reached for each other. My mouth fell open in horror as Derek burst into laughter as Mark continued to scream for the lost boy. Adrian and Chase were slapping their thighs and holding their stomachs laughing and I reached out to smack both of them.

Mark walked out of the woods with a huge grin on his face. The twins screamed again, not recognizing him right away. They leapt out of their seats and ran to me. I held them tightly and told them it wasn't real.

"Shh… it's just Uncle Mark. Uncle Derek was just telling a spooky story. It was fake." I repeated over and over until they stopped shaking.

When Mark tried to plop down next to me, I kicked his shin. He yelped and I shot a death glare at him.

"What? Oh come on, you know that was a good one," he defended. I lifted my head to demand Derek tell them it was fake, but he had gotten up to smoke a cigarette.

"You are all terrible." I told them.

Cleo and Ethan reappeared a few moments later.

"Did you guys hear that guy screaming?" Ethan asked, amused, and apparently not in the loop. The twins, hearing their father's voice ran to him, wrapping their arms around him. He looked at the adults in confusion and then realizing who was gone his eyes turned hard.

"What'd he do?"

"Scary story," I explained. Relaxing, he chuckled and shook his head.

"I'm glad he's the one sleeping outside with them tonight. Have fun listening to that all night," he said as Derek returned to the party. Derek frowned, realizing the mistake he had made. They would most likely be up all night terrified, and they were.

The next morning we packed everything up and cleaned the area for the next guests. Derek looked exhausted, while the twins couldn't stop gabbing about how scary and fun last night was.

Once everyone was good to go Cleo pulled me aside and squeezed my hand.

"Are you ready?" She asked excitedly. I nodded, although I wasn't quite sure if I was. We were leaving early because our appointment was this afternoon. We'd be figuring out in just a few short hours if the baby was a boy or girl.

"Just think, by tonight you'll have a little Phigaro or Lusitania," she said dreamily."

"I would almost rather we just name him Tot," I laughed. She rolled her eyes and reached up to put her hand on my shoulder.

"This kid is going to be just as awesome and unique as his parents. He has to have a name to match, and I'm going to make sure it's the best most kick-ass name I can think of. This kid is gonna be a fuckin' legend."

Chapter Thirteen

WALK THROUGH HELL

CLEO REACHED for both mine and Mark's hands while the technician moved the wand all over her belly. I stared at the monitor, trying to figure out what was what. I saw the head, and an arm, I thought.

"Here's a good one of its face," the woman stopped her wand and pointed to the screen, explaining where the baby's eyes, nose, and tiny mouth was. "Okay, so I've looked at everything I had to. I'm going to look now and see if we can get a good look in between the legs. Do you guys want to know?"

"Yes."

"Yes."

"No."

The three of us looked down at the woman on the table in the paper gown. She looked up at me, then Mark, then back at me.

"I want to surprise you two. Would you guys be okay waiting just a few more days? I want to do a gender reveal party for you." Her brown eyes were wide with hope.

I looked over to my husband who looked a little disappointed.

"Please, if you let me do this, I swear I'll make it worth it," she pleaded. Mark seemed to soften, looking back up at me. We locked eyes and tried to silently communicate.

"What do you think, baby? I don't think a week could hurt," I said. Hesitantly he nodded and told the tech not to tell us. She smiled at us and nodded.

"I'll write it down and stick it in an envelope for you to read whenever you want." When she was finished Cleo sat up and took the envelope triumphantly.

"You won't regret this," she said.

That evening as we finished unpacking, I asked Mark how he felt about it. He shrugged and climbed into bed. "I don't know. I was really excited. I'm sure I'll be excited for the party too."

We were woken in the early morning hours to people shouting and loud thumping downstairs. Groaning I pulled on my robe and went downstairs to see who was causing all the racket.

I was greeted by Derek and Adrian lifting a very large box, with Cleo directing them to take it upstairs. I ground the sleep from my eyes.

"What are you guys doing here?"

"What room is going to be the baby's room?" She asked me instead of answering.

"The one right next to ours on the right. Why?"

She looked over at the guys and they nodded, lifting the box higher, and began climbing the stairs.

"What is in the box?"

"Can't tell you that. Sorry. Just a heads up, we'll be in and out of here most of the week. We'll be working mostly in the baby's room and you're not allowed to come in." A hand went around my waist and I turned to see Mark standing next to me.

"What are you doing now?" He asked, clearly just as exhausted as I was.

"Don't worry about it. We'll be practically non-existent."

Adrian and Derek came back down the stairs and with a look towards us, headed out the front door, returning with another large box. I crossed my arms as they took it upstairs.

"If we can't be involved, what are we supposed to do?"

Cleo looked at my hair and I quickly covered the top of my head with my hands.

"Why don't you go get your hair done? Maybe go have a couple's date. The more time you leave us to do what we have to do, the quicker we'll be out of your hair." Sighing, I turned to Mark. He was amused. He looked back at me.

"What do you say, baby?"

"I do need to get my hair done."

Cleo squealed and rested her hand on her bump.

"Thank you. Now go get dressed to go," she demanded.

Heading back to my bedroom I tried to sneak a peek at the room next door, but Adrian and Chase were still inside. When I went to open the door Adrian caught it, peaked his face out and then shook his head.

"No can do," he said, shutting the door in my face.

I called my beautician once I was in my room and got my appointment scheduled for an hour from now. To save time Mark hopped in on my shower. Once we were out, I saw how much time we had, so I rushed him to get dressed and I threw on only a little mascara.

"You still look gorgeous," he commented as I frowned at my roots in the tiny visor mirror in his car.

I told him he didn't have to wait for me, but he insisted he'd stay while she touched up my roots and freshened the color. He went through the magazines and they changed the TV in the corner to a sitcom for him.

Walking out of the salon I felt refreshed and more like

myself again. We stopped for lunch at a small cafe. "What would you like to drink?" The waitress asked us.

"Coffee." We answered at the same time. We locked eyes and burst into laughter. She giggled and when she returned with our cups she sighed.

"You two are so adorable," she commented as she poured our drinks.

We took a walk after lunch, not going anywhere particular, just enjoying each other's company. Finally, he decided to call Cleo and ask if we could come home. I couldn't hear her on the other line, but Mark didn't look too happy. He hung up and looked at me, giving me an uneasy smile.

"You up for a movie?"

We finished up our day out with a nice, intimate dinner at a taco truck.

"You know we rarely have dinner with just the two of us?" He chuckled, putting his paper tray in the trash.

"We should do this more often," I said, finishing up my own food. He reached for my hand and we walked back to our car.

"They've had enough time," he decided.

When we got home, we were greeted not only by his three bandmates, but their spouses and children. We stepped into the house just as they were coming down the stairs from the baby's room.

"Hey! We are actually heading out now. We'll be back tomorrow," she said before they all left.

Naturally the curiosity got the best of me and as soon as they left, I rushed upstairs only to find that someone had installed a padlock on the door. "Mark!" I protested, but when he saw the lock he started laughing.

"She knows you too well," he said. The rest of the week Mark's bandmates were here bright and early.

"Shouldn't you guys be practicing or something?" I asked

after the fourth day, but they all agreed that they were enjoying the break.

"We're running out of things to do," I protested.

"Why don't you go to the beach?" Adrian suggested.

"Or check out a museum," Derek added. Sighing, I took Mark by the hand and we left to go wander the city. Despite hating not being in the loop, I loved having Mark all to myself for just a little bit. It was almost like a small, second honeymoon.

We hadn't had much time like this since our first year of marriage. Back then the band was on hiatus. Cleo was in Michigan while the others were here, so they couldn't really do much. Once she decided to move out here, the band returned to their formal glory full force and this had been my life ever since. Small moments in between band stuff.

I didn't mind usually. They treated me like family and I always had fun when they were around, but it was nice to have these moments too. I realized while we were taking a celebrity homes tour that this was probably the last moments we would have with just the two of us for the next eighteen years.

"You realize that, right? From now on even when the band isn't around, we'll never be alone. They'll be an extra member to tag along," I commented, looking out at some late-night talk show hosts grand mansion.

"I know, isn't that awesome. I can't wait," he told me.

"We need to cherish these moments while they're here."

He leaned over and kissed my nose.

"I cherish you," he smiled.

After day six I was totally over it. I wanted them out of my house. I needed space. I couldn't keep going with this. They needed to leave. When we returned that evening from a day of paintball, bowling, and pizza I stormed in ready to snap. I tossed the front door open prepared to scream at the first person in sight. However, the house was quiet.

Looking around I saw no one. This was suspicious. I called out and heard a rough, yet distinctly feminine voice.

"Up here."

I paused, glancing at Mark. He was just as confused as I was. We took the stairs together and stopped when we saw tiny little Cleo standing in front of the baby's door, arms behind her back.

She had a small smile on her face but didn't move. I glanced past her and saw the lock was still firmly on the door. She brought an arm around and revealed a plain white envelope. Reaching forward I grabbed it and opened it slowly, almost nervous about what was in it.

Reading the thick card stock paper, I let out a breath of relief and then a small chuckle. It was an invitation.

"You are formally invited to the gender reveal of little Tot Lesley, tomorrow afternoon. Lunch will be served after the news. BYOB," she tagged on the end joking. I quickly embraced her.

"Thank you. I can't wait."

"Me either! I'm having Ethan record your reactions," she said as we walked her downstairs. Giving us both one final hug she left.

That night I had a hard time falling asleep. Mark was watching a movie while I tried to close my eyes, but finally I sat back up.

"What do you think it is. Like really?"

He looked over and thought for a moment.

"I don't know, girl?"

"Why, is it a feeling or did you see something?"

He rolled his eyes.

"More like I didn't see anything. You were looking at the same screen I was. I couldn't tell his hands from his lips. It was all a bunch of squiggles."

I got out of bed and went to the book where I had placed the pictures we had been given last week.

"Let's look again. Maybe we can figure it out." He sighed but reached for one of the pictures.

"Well this one is clearly his face," he said. "I think it has your nose," he reached over and pinched the tip of my face. I sighed, realizing that we really wouldn't know for a few more hours.

"I can't wait. Mark, I need to know. Call her and tell her the party is off," I pouted.

"I love you, but I am not doing that. If you just go to sleep, we will know in no time."

I don't remember falling asleep, but I was able to finally manage getting a few hours in. I woke up to the twins' distinct screams of joy. I leapt up and practically ran to the shower. Remembering that I would be photographed I took care to curl my short locks and get my makeup right. I had plenty of time, I might as well take advantage of it and look nice. Mark waited patiently with me while I got ready for the day.

"Wear that light purple dress. It goes good with the dark purple hair." I thanked him for his suggestion and slipped the sundress on. When I was finally ready mentally and physically, we stepped out together.

We stopped short at our door. Everyone was waiting at the staircase, looking at us. A camera snapped loudly, and I looked to see Ethan holding a large black camera up at us.

"Are you ready?" Cleo asked. My eyes went to the smallest adult in the center of the group.

Squeezing Mark's hand, I looked up at him for reassurance. He looked down at me and then nodded.

"I think so." Cleo stepped forward, producing a small key from behind her back. She winked at me as she went to the door right next to ours and unlocked it. She stepped back and looked at us.

"Go in when you're ready."

Mark and I took matching steps to the door and stood right in front of it.

"Want to open it together?" I asked. He took the hand that was holding mine and twisted the door knob quickly, then pulled away. The door clicked open but didn't move more than a few centimeters.

"On the count of three we push it open," he said, and we reached our hands down and before we could start counting our friends behind us started counting for us.

"Three! Two! One!" They called out and we pushed the door open. My mouth fell open and my hands went to my face. My eyes grew wet instantly and despite trying to stop them, they started moving down my face. The room was purple.

Regaining movement and speech I reached for Mark and pulled him into the room. His feet had been nailed to the floor; he was in shock. They let us explore the room alone, while they watched us from the door. Mark stood in the middle of the room and put his hands up. He tugged at his hair as tears slowly made their way down.

"A girl? We're having a girl?" He asked, his voice cracking.

As if planned ahead of time, everyone nodded together and then poured into the room. Adrian and Derek went to Mark and hugged him, congratulating him. Cleo came right over to me and wrapped her arms around me.

"I am so happy for you guys! She's going to be beautiful," she exclaimed. I looked around the room again. It was a work of art.

"This is too much. I love it, but you didn't have to do this."

The room was gorgeous. They had painted the walls a lavender, with hand painted cherry blossom trees in various spots around the room. They had even managed to get carpet placed in here in the small time frame.

The boxes they had been carrying up had to have been the crib, dressers, rocking chair, changing table, and toy box. Everything was either a shade of purple, pink, or white. It was everything I could have dreamed. It was perfect for a little girl.

"It's my gift to you," she said, waving her hand nonchalantly. I laughed and wiped another set of tears from my face.

"I would have thought you'd done enough," I said. The twins entered the room and gazed around in wonder.

"Aunt Renee, are you having a baby girl?" Dallas asked me. I nodded and pressed my lips together. *A baby girl. Girl.*

"Okay, now that the big news has been revealed, anyone in the mood for some chicken salad sandwiches?" Chase called out, waving for us all to follow him down. I almost didn't want to leave. It was so beautiful in here. Ethan put his hand on my shoulder.

"Take your time, come down when you're ready."

I thanked him and soon it was just me and my husband. I ran to him and he pulled me into his tight embrace.

"A girl baby, a girl," he whispered.

"I know. Can you believe it?" There was a long silence, so I looked up at him. He was looking at the wall, not blinking.

"I don't think I can handle a daughter."

When we pulled apart, we followed the crew downstairs and had lunch with everyone. Sitting out in the yard, a nice spring breeze swept around us lazily. It was the perfect day.

"Who painted the trees?" I asked, when we started talking about the work they had put in this past week. Adrian raised his hand.

"That'd be me. But, before someone rats on me I did have a stencil and the internet to help me."

"Well you can't even tell. They look amazing," I told him. Chase called for a toast and we all lifted our glasses.

"To baby girl Lesley!" He said and we all repeated him while clinking our glasses together.

"Now that you know what she is, have you started narrowing down on some names?" Adrian asked Cleo. She scrunched up her face and then shrugged.

"No not really. Balboa- you know, to go with Rocky. I thought of that one last night. It's not an easy task."

"How did you come up with your own kids' names?" Chase asked.

"Jimmy was named after Adrian. Dallas was named after the character in the book 'The Outsiders'," Cleo started but Ethan started choking on his drink. We all turned towards him to see him laughing and choking at the same time. Cleo blushed furiously and slapped his shoulder.

"What? What's so funny?" Derek demanded. When Ethan regained composure, he looked over at his wife and smiled at her conspiratorially.

"That's not why she named him Dallas."

"Yes it is! I swear. That's just a coincidence."

"What is?" Half the table shouted at them. They turned to us and Ethan laughed again.

"Dallas, Texas is where the twins- happened."

The table fell quiet for a moment and then erupted in laughter. Cleo was furious. She crossed her arms and looked down, pouting. Once we all calmed down, she spoke again.

"As I was saying, that's just a coincidence. I liked the name; and we named Blue after his eyes. He opened his eyes right when he was born and you could see those beautiful blue's for miles," she said dreamily, rubbing her belly.

"I can't wait to see what little Selkie is going to look like."

"Please don't name their baby that," Adrian smirked.

"If anything, go back to Balboa," Derek grimaced. I said another silent prayer that she kept looking for names.

The rest of the afternoon we spent relaxing, sipping on beer and eating snacks they had brought. Thankfully they had gotten a caterer to do the cooking and baking.

At some point we ran out of beer and vodka for the drink I had been making all day. Someone commented about going out to get more.

"Renee, you want to come with me? Ethan, babe, you can watch the baby while we make a beer run?"

Ethan shrugged and went back to his conversation with Adrian.

Derek stood up. "I'll go with you. I don't want you guys to pick up the wrong stuff. Chick beer." I gave him the finger.

"I drink the same beer you do." He gave me the finger right back.

"Fine, I want to stretch my legs. Shut it, I'm coming." He followed us out and sat in the back. Cleo being the only one sober enough to drive, drove us to the nearest liquor store and we hopped out. Grabbing a cart Derek began loading cases of beer in it.

"Why are you grabbing so much?"

"For the next week or so. I don't want to run out in the middle of the night or something," he answered. I stopped moving the cart.

"Derek, you don't live at my house."

He sighed deeply.

"Come on, not today. Not on your baby's gender day," he whined. I rolled my eyes and continued on down the aisle. We picked up some more of the vodka I liked and some pear juice.

Suddenly we were stopped by a young man with a lumberjack beard and thick, ironic glasses.

"Cleo De La Rosa?"

We stopped laughing with each other to stare at the young man. Cleo forced a smile and nodded.

"Yeah, that's me. Hi." There was that brief uncomfortable silence as Cleo tried to move.

"Hey I'm the guitarist. Do you want my autograph?" Derek said rather loudly. The guy shook his head.

"No thanks, this is for you." He pulled out a Manila envelope out of the bag I had missed before. "You've been served." He tipped his paperboy hat and quickly disappeared.

Cleo turned back to us, mouth agape. All of the buzz I had left dissipated immediately.

"What the hell. Open it," Derek demanded. With trembling fingers, she pulled up the flap and looked inside. She pulled out a packet of papers and quickly scanned the front page. She slammed the papers down into the cart and cursed.

"Christopher! He's suing me for damages. He's claiming mental distress over not knowing the truth about the twins."

"Jesus. What are you going to do?" She pushed her hair out of her face.

"I don't know. Shit. I don't know, I don't know," she kept repeating. I suggested we pay and get out of the store. We did just that and practically ran to the car.

"You gotta tell Ethan," Derek said, his voice rising in a panic. "We know he's here, and apparently still mad. What if he comes after you?" She shook her head and gripped the steering wheel tighter.

"He's not- it's fine. I'll deal with it. This doesn't have to be a big deal. Calm down."

"If you don't tell him I will." We were suddenly jerked forward by Cleo slamming on the breaks. The seatbelt jutted into my chest; it burned the bare skin. She whipped around to look at him in the backseat.

"If you tell anyone I'll tell everyone your secret," she said in a voice that I had never heard from her before. Derek shrunk in his seat and closed his mouth. The rest of the trip home was pure, icy, silence.

Derek and I practically fled the car. Mark took one look at me and asked what was wrong.

"Nothing," I told him and took my vodka and pear juice to

the kitchen. I began mixing my drink when I heard Cleo ask Ethan to come inside.

"Can we have the kitchen?" Cleo came in and asked, her voice weak. I reached for Mark and pulled him back outside. Derek was sitting with Adrian and Chase silently.

Moments later we heard shouting. I sighed deeply and put my hands on my face and leaned on the table. Right as the shouting started it abruptly stopped. Derek and I looked at each other. He stood up.

"I'm going to go check on them."

He returned a few minutes later, not any more relaxed.

"She told him," he told me. Looking around at his friends he explained the situation.

"Is that even legal? They were married."

"Technically you can sue for anything. Whether it will hold up in court is another thing," Chase said. The police officer in him coming out. "I've seen lots of weird cases. It's hard to say."

After a long, hour they both came out. Cleo had been crying and Ethan immediately lit a cigarette. After he took a long drag, he looked over at us.

"My lawyer is on it. He thinks he's just trying to wrack up her money in legal fees."

Wiping her face, she sat down with us. Laughing she spoke.

"He said he's so traumatized by finding out the truth that he has a hard time loving his wife and actual daughter." Her laugh was cold and emotionless.

"He had a hard time loving his first wife too, I wasn't the cause of that."

"What exactly does he want?"

"A couple million dollars. He says because of me he can't find a job. His career was ruined. Holly can't work either because she's so ashamed of the whole scandal."

"What a crack of -" Cleo held up her hand to stop Mark.

"I know. I swear when things are really good one of our

exes gets bored and decides to start trouble. God, maybe we should introduce them to each other. They can make each other miserable."

Ethan came to sit with us and reached for his wife's hand. He lifted it and kissed it.

"Thank you for telling me right away," he told her. Cleo's eyes flickered to mine and I looked away.

The party started to fizzle after that. They wanted to leave to see their lawyer, and Adrian and Chase wanted to get Rocky to bed. Derek had something he had to do, so he left as well. Once everyone had left and the dogs had come in for the night we went back into the nursery.

Mark decided to test the rocking chair and called for me to join him.

"It won't break, it feels pretty sturdy." I sat on his lap and he hugged me. "This whole week has been kind of crazy." He nuzzled his face against my neck.

"It really has. I feel like our lives changed overnight. We've still got a long way to go, but it feels just a little more real."

"A girl. I still can't believe it. I'm going to have to buy dresses, and sit and have tea parties," he chuckled.

"Yeah, but you'll also get to do the whole protective dad thing when she grows up, and the daddy daughter dances. Jimmy and Ethan were adorable last year."

"That could be fun."

We rocked quietly for a bit, enjoying each other's company.

"I hope she looks like you," he said.

"I think she'll look like you more. Your features are more dominant."

"She. We can officially say that now. She. Ha, and we kept calling her he this whole time. Go figure."

"I don't care what she looks like I guess, as long as she loves rock music." I turned my head to gaze at my handsome husband.

"How can she not? She's going to grow up with a family of musicians. Not just the adults, she's got two extremely talented cousins to look up to. Who knows, maybe even three if they get Rocky a guitar."

"True. It'd be fun to have another drummer in the family. I could really get into that."

I yawned and decided it was time for bed. Sitting up I stopped the chair and pulled him up. We did one more walk around the room, tracing the crib and dressers with my fingers. "They really made this room perfect. It's fit for a princess," I commented as we left the room.

"Princess, maybe that's what I'll call her." I laughed and headed into our room.

"You just might have to. Princess is better than Balboa."

Chapter Fourteen

CLASSIFIEDS

ONCE OUR NOT SO LITTLE two-week vacation was over the band went right back to work on their album.

"I think we are going to start recording a few tracks, while Cleo still has the lung power," Mark told me over breakfast one morning. "What are your plans for today?"

I reached for one of the books I had bought yesterday, "Babies first year". He raised an eyebrow.

"Sounds fun."

"I've got some other stuff too. One on baby proofing and another on basic first aid. What to do with fevers, what medicines for what symptom. Lots of handy things to know," I defended. He stood up from the table and leaned over to kiss my forehead.

"True. Well, get all educated and you can tell me the highlights tonight at dinner."

Once he left, I dove into the books. They were interesting. After the gender reveal party, the reality of our upcoming addition to the family really hit me. I spent the next two months buying clothes and boxes upon boxes of diapers. I got a baby bath and all the lotions and powders. The nursery was quickly filling up.

While the nursery was filling up, Cleo's stomach was filling out. She was 28 weeks now and looked it. She had started to waddle and had taken to wearing mostly skirts and dresses. With her small size, her big belly was almost comically adorable.

We all were invited to Evan's Place's second annual Prom and there was plenty of jokes made at her expense about being pregnant on prom night. Despite her size, she still looked gorgeous. She opted for a long, black dress that covered her growing midsection. She explained that she didn't want paparazzi to start assuming things and starting rumors. She carried a fake fur with her to cover herself outside of the building just in case.

Overall the second time around was just as fun as the first, but slightly less dramatic. Last year Chase surprised Adrian with an impromptu wedding. We had all been in on the secret, and it had gone off without a hitch. It was so romantic, and seeing them both here together, when we all thought Chase wouldn't be here, was something amazing. I swear, they didn't take their eyes off each other the entire night.

Once prom passed Cleo was forced to deal with reality again. Christopher seemed to be a thorn she couldn't get out of her side. Despite her recent troubles with her ex she still kept a cheery disposition. Christopher's lawyer contacted theirs and requested an outlandish amount of money to stay out of court. Ethan of course shot it down and they set a date for almost six months from now. They'd see what a judge had to say about the ridiculous civil suit.

The baby was now kicking all the time. Whenever I'd stop over, she'd make me feel her belly. Mark was so excited.

"She's gonna be great at using the pedal!" He would joke.

He now had his heart fully set on her being a drummer like her daddy.

After a long, rather relaxing day of reading, Mark finally came home. I tossed a frozen pizza in the oven and sat down with him.

"Thanks for not eating without me. I like having dinner with you."

I smiled and looked around.

"No Derek?"

He shook his head.

"Nah, said he had plans. Beats me. Maybe he's got a date. Don't know, don't care. Just enjoy it," he laughed.

Once we finished our pizza, we went to the bedroom to relax.

"Oh, I almost forgot, Cleo wants to catch us on a day off and do something. She didn't say what so don't ask. Talk to her about it." He said before drifting off to sleep.

Luckily, I didn't have to wait long, because the next day was our weekly lunch. If I had tried to call her she would have made me wait until I saw her in person, so I learned to stop expecting phone calls could solve my curiosities.

"Mark said you wanted to do something this weekend?" I asked, reaching for my tea. She nodded and sipped on her own water.

"Yes! I have something really fun I want to do with you guys. Both of you need to be free, so Derek will need a different gaming friend for the afternoon. What day works better for you two?"

I thought about it and decided Saturday would be fine.

"Do I get to know what it is?"

She brightened and smacked her forehead lightly.

"Sorry, baby brain. I've been getting a little more spacey lately. She's a wiggler. I hired a photographer to do maternity pictures."

I gave her a confused look and she waved her hand at me.

"I told her the situation and she was really excited. She said she'd do something really fun. Do you still have those shirts you guys got for Christmas?"

Her energetic mood got me excited about it. We talked outfits and makeup and locations.

"She's got a studio, so we could go there. Or if we wanted to do some outside photos we could always use one of our backyards. There's tons of great spots for pictures." We both left lunch excited for the weekend.

I headed straight to my closet when I got home and began searching for the perfect dress. My hair was on the lighter side of purple this time around, more like a lavender color. It looked gorgeous with a mint green dress I had. I sent Cleo a picture of the dress and told me she'd find something to match. She called back later to tell me she found a light pink dress.

"Great, I'll put Mark in a Navy shirt and he'll look good with both of us.

I was right. When we stepped into the photographer's studio, we saw that he looked good paired with either of us. Cleo had driven herself here ahead of us, so when she saw us come in she waddled over and hugged us.

"Are you excited? These are going to be so freaking cute!"

The photographer came over and introduced herself. "Hello, my name is Jackie. I've got some great ideas for you today. This is the highlight of my week. You want to come with me, and I can show you where you'll be?" We introduced ourselves and then the three of us followed her to the other side of the rather large studio. We passed about a dozen different backdrops, but she stopped us at a blank white one.

"You guys are so beautiful, you don't need anything fancy to make the pictures stand out," she explained. She told us to relax and settle in. Jackie stepped away and went over to her tablet on her desk. She clicked some things and the room erupted with music.

Some fun rock music surrounded us. I looked around and saw that she had speakers hung up all over the room. She returned to us bobbing her head and smiling wide. Reaching for a white stool she put it in the middle of our area.

"Okay, Cleo sit down, hands on your belly. Renee, stand behind her and put your hands on her forearms. Mark, you stand behind your wife and hug her. Oh! And ladies, take these," she ordered. She reached down into a box by her feet and produced two pretty flower wreaths for our heads. "They'll look beautiful with your curls." Cleo must have told her our color plans, because I was handed a mint one that perfectly matched my dress, while Cleo had a pink one to match hers. After setting them on our head we got into the pose she wanted. It felt awkward but after a few snaps of her camera we began relaxing.

We took hundreds of photos it felt like. Every pose, every combination of the three of us. She took some of me and Cleo first. After a few of us hugging I leaned down and kissed her forehead. She gasped and started giggling. Jackie exclaimed that those would be beautiful later.

Then her and Mark got a few taken. Those were funny too, although I insisted they get a few more serious ones. Finally, Jackie insisted that Mark and I get some of just the two of us.

"You guys look gorgeous together. I love it," she murmured more than once.

Later we changed into our mom and dad to be shirts, while Cleo slipped on hers that said, "just babysitting". This shoot was pure fun. Jackie brought out pink paint and pink powder.

"You guys do whatever you want with this. I'm just an observer. Have fun." There was a moment where the three of us stood looking at the props in front of us, but Mark broke the hesitance by reaching into the bucket of powder. He grabbed a fistful and threw it at Cleo's belly. She let out a small squeal and grabbed some for herself and threw some at him. Before I could even think to begin to feel left out my loving husband grabbed a paintbrush and ran it across my cheek! Game on.

I understand why Jackie insisted on the blank backdrop. It looked awesome after our pink on pink fight. I had powder in my hair and Mark's shirt was completely covered in paint. At some point the three of us had placed our bare hands in the paint and placed them flat on her belly. Then when we pulled them away I promptly slapped Mark on the cheek. He got me back by rubbing the powder all over my arms. By the time Jackie called it a wrap the three of us were filthy.

"We should do one of these shoots with the whole group," Cleo suggested as we took washcloths to ourselves. "We could each get a color. My family blue, you guys purple, Wilson's could do green, you get the jist. That would be a blast."

"We could do that when Tot is born. When the whole family is finally here," I agreed with her. Jackie overhearing us gave me her card.

"I would absolutely love to shoot your baby girl. Please, call me when she's born. I'll make time for you." Thanking her, she told us our pictures would be ready in two days.

"I'm going to start working on them right now. I can't wait for you guys to see them. Are you guys thinking of selling them to someone?"

I didn't understand what she meant so I asked her to explain.

"Some celebrities will sell their big moment pictures to magazines. You can get a real nice chunk of money for going exclusive with someone. I have a few that I work with that would buy them if you were interested. Many people use that money for their children's college funds or others do charities."

I bit my lip. This all felt a little weird. Before I could protest Mark piped up excitedly.

"We could donate to Evan's place."

"That would be amazing!" Cleo exclaimed. Jackie raised her eyebrows but turned to look at me directly.

"Mom? Do you want me to make some calls? No offense, but I think ultimately she has the last say," she chuckled. I felt a pit in my stomach but seeing my husband and Cleo so excited about the idea made me nod.

"Go ahead. Let us know if you get any takers. Do you need their agent's info? He usually deals with stuff like that." Mark gave her Sam's phone number and email and we left.

Stopping home to shower and let the dogs out we slipped over to the Andrews' to have dinner. Derek and the Wilson trio were already there, enjoying beers and some appetizers.

"How'd the shoot go? Cleo's still showering," Ethan said as we came to join them in the den.

"Great. It was surprisingly kind of fun. We're going to sell the photos and donate the money to Evan's place," Mark told him. Ethan perked up. He was genuinely surprised. Reaching across the table he shook his hand.

"Thanks man. I'll stop giving you shit for knocking up my wife. Consider it even."

When Cleo came down, she was dressed in pajamas. Adrian commented on it and she glared at him.

"I've got a bowling ball sitting on my bladder, my stomach is itchy, and I just want to be comfy for a little bit, is that alright with you?" She practically snarled.

"Alrighty then," he said and shut up.

Cleo plopped down next to me and leaned towards me.

"I hate you and your devils spawn," she sighed.

"Has she been moving a lot today?"

"Just since we left the photography studio. I think she's trying to push herself out via my belly button. I'm so over it today." The rest of the evening she was much quieter than usual. After dinner the guys wanted to throw darts. I wasn't any good, so I sat with her and Chase, who had also opted out.

"The baby has been up a lot the last few days. I'm whooped." Cleo turned on the TV for the three of us and turned it to a music channel. The show on was one that Mark enjoyed at home too. It was just music videos by one single artist for half an hour. The band featured in this episode was one everyone recognized, Accepted Perversion.

"Hey!" Chase flipped around to look for his husband. "I forgot to tell you, Cotton called me the other day. Emile is down there with her now."

Adrian paused in mid throw to look over.

"Really? So, is it going good then?" Chase shrugged his shoulders.

"She didn't say. My folks had told her about my good news, so she just wanted to congratulate me. She was purposely vague about him. I don't know why she brought him up at all."

"Probably because I was the one who mentioned to him to go see her. You could tell she was still into him."

Cleo's and I's interest was piqued. We sat up slightly and joined in on the conversation.

"Who's Cotton?"

"She's the owner of that tattoo shop we went to. She lives in my hometown now. While we were staying there with my folks, we got to know her. She did our wedding photos."

"Yeah, I guess her and Emile Dahl have been head over heels for each other for years. She was miserable and he always looks miserable. I happened to see him at a show and told him to go see her. Sounds like he finally did. Good."

Our attention turned back to the TV, where his gorgeous face was singing passionately about heartbreak. I wondered if the song was about her. I could see how someone would fall for him. The man not only had a great voice, he played like ten instruments, and he was drop dead sexy. I loved my husband dearly, but it was fun to look.

After their block of videos Chase and I stole the remote and put on a comedy we both liked. Cleo ended up falling asleep leaning against Chase.

Jackie kept true to her word and gave us our photos two days later. They really were amazing. I was impressed. We would definitely be calling her for more photos when the baby was born.

I went to work putting them in an album and framing our favorites. Not even a day later Sam called Mark and told us that we had a buyer for the photos.

"Reality Now wants to do a small interview with the three of you. What day works for you?" He said over the speaker. I looked at Mark. I had nothing but free time.

"Let's do Wednesday."

Instead of our normal private lunch we had lunch with Mark, Sam, and Lindsey, the woman who would be doing the interview. She was nice and cheery, but it felt completely fake. I didn't like her. She made a point to ask Mark and Cleo questions, but only looked at me when one of them mentioned me.

"So how is it having a celebrity husband?"

I chuckled. He was a normal person. I didn't really consider his "status" to be anything to note.

"It's alright. He's just like you and me. I met him before they were more known, so it doesn't really effect me much."

"How long have you two known each other?"

I reached for Mark's hand.

"Four years? We got married pretty quickly after we met."

She already seemed bored. She moved her tape recorder to Cleo without giving me a second glance.

"And how long have you two known each other? You guys

go way back I bet," she winked at her. Cleo's mouth fell open and she looked at me apologetically.

"The entire band has been best friends since we were ten. That's why when Mark and Renee asked for me to help them out, I was more than happy to do so. They are so perfect for each other, and they'll make great parents."

"Are you going to help out when she comes?"

"Maybe some, but I'm sure Renee won't need much help. She was my twin's nanny while we went on tour. She's gonna do just fine."

"Your band has always been known for being goofballs at shows and in real life. What kind of jokes have you made about this situation?" She directed the question at Mark. I gritted my teeth. Why was I even here at this point? She was clearly not interested in the entire story.

"Oh, we don't make too many jokes. We appreciate what Cleo has done for us and don't take that lightly. Ethan, her husband sometimes makes jokes though. Since she's having my baby, I'm technically the one on call for her midnight cravings." Lindsey laughed so obnoxiously it made me nauseous.

"Oh, that is hilarious! Speaking of cravings, have you had any crazy ones?"

The entire interview went like that. I finished my chef's salad quietly while I listened to her go on and on. After what felt like an eternity the meal ended and we all stood up.

"Thank you all so much for letting me in to a little bit of your lives for a moment. I'm going to start working on the article when I get back to the office, and hopefully it will run in about two weeks."

As soon as she was out of sight Cleo turned to me and quickly apologized.

"I kept trying to direct her attention to you I swear," her eyes were desperate for me to believe her. I forced a smile and blinked away the tears that had started forming.

"I know. No worries. I'm just glad the money we're getting is going to a good cause. How much was it?" We all turned to Sam. He started beaming, looking very smug.

"Well, thanks to Ethan's celebrity status and the band's very successful last album, we were able to snag a very cool $200,000. Not bad for pictures without the kid."

My jaw dropped.

"Is that the standard?"

"For maternity yes. Weddings and actual babies can go for up to two million. So, if you guys want to do this again in a few months…"

I shook my head. This lunch had been mortifying. I don't want to go through it again. Mark took my hand.

"We'll talk about it when it happens. Thanks for the help Sam. Just sign the check over to Evan's Place."

I tried to put the upcoming article out of mind over the next two weeks, but it felt like I was waiting for the next bomb to drop. Mark spent as much time as he could reassuring me that whatever was printed was ridiculous and I had nothing to worry about. In my heart I knew that, but when I finally had the magazine in hand it nearly broke it.

Cleo called us at 7am the day it was released.

"It's horrible. They took everything completely out of context!" She cried. My stomach rolled. I hadn't even seen it yet, but I knew it had to be bad.

Getting showered and dressed we headed over to her place and went to the kitchen where the rest of the band and Ethan were standing leaning over the island looking at something. It had to be the magazine. They all turned when they heard us, and instant looks of pity were thrown at me. I gulped and moved forward, my heart beating out of my chest.

"Let me see it."

No one moved for a long moment, but finally Cleo reached for it and shut it. Handing it to me, I looked down and my heart stopped. We had made the front cover. Well, I didn't. Cleo and Mark did. His hands were wrapped around her stomach and they were both laughing. The headline said "She's Having My Baby!" Scrolling down I saw Lindsey did give me a tiny shout out in the subtitle. "See how singer Cleo De La Rosa gave her bandmate Mark Lesley and his wife the ultimate gift."

I practically tore the magazine open and hurried to the article. Again, another picture of the two of them. At least this one was one where she had her "just babysitting" shirt on. No one spoke while I read the article. It was just as ridiculous as the live interview had been. It focused on their friendship and unbreakable bond that was now just a little bit stronger. I actually let out a laugh when I was mentioned.

It was only to say that I didn't seem jealous and based on the lunch seemed to prefer a more subtle role in Mark's life. "While Cleo is no stranger to the spotlight, Renee Lesley seemed to enjoy listening to her husband and best friend share stories of their lives pre-domestication."

At the very, very, end of the article a small picture of the three of us was placed in the bottom right corner. Mark, who had been reading the article over my shoulder swore and pulled it out of my hands. He ripped it in half and then again. He stormed over to the trash and threw it in the bin with a ferocity that made even me calm down.

I reached out to him, moving to put my hand on his shoulder.

"Baby, it's not that bad. So what? This doesn't change anything. We knew the article was going to be bad," I tried to comfort him.

"We should sue. Can we do that?" He demanded. Ethan shook his head.

"I mean, you can. But they have the right to print whatever they want. It would just lose you money in the end. You know how much crap they've printed about me over the years? I stopped looking."

By the time noon came around the band's phones were ringing constantly. After a while everyone just put them on silent and decided to go rehearse. Must be nice, I thought. At least they had a way to release their emotions. What could I do other than stew over how awful this was?

I sat in the studio with them for a bit until Ethan came in and sat down next to me. He leaned over and cupped his hands over his mouth and shouted at me over the music.

"You want to get out of here for a bit?" Oddly enough, I did.

I followed him out and got in his car.

"Where are we going?" He looked over and gave me a sly smile.

"Just this little club I know about. You'll like it. Trust Me." Despite never really being alone with Ethan, I decided to do as he said, trust him. We drove for almost an hour. We didn't talk much. He asked me what I wanted to listen to.

"Can we listen to some 90's music? Like pop?"

He laughed and changed it to the station I had requested.

"Does your rockstar husband know you like this stuff?" He asked me as I moved my shoulders to "Groove Is In The Heart". I shook my head furiously and looked at him with fake horror.

"No! And you can never tell him."

He laughed and made a cross on his chest.

"Cross my heart."

Finally, he pulled into a large parking lot with a small building in the center of it. The building looked very out of place. The parking lot looked brand new, while the club looked ancient. Stepping out I saw a small sign hanging above the door. Sam's Bar. Despite the small size, there were about twenty cars here. I looked at my watch. It was barely five.

"What is this?" He didn't answer me.

"Come on, see for yourself." I followed him and looked around.

The room was dark, my eyes had to adjust. Inside the room was about 20 small circle tables. In the far back was a small stage, while on the far right was the bar. The room was quickly filling up with patrons. Ethan turned to me and smiled.

"Go pick a table. I'm going to sign us up. Do you want something to drink? You might need it."

I hesitated but finally asked for a vodka tonic.

I found a table in the middle of the room. There wasn't many options left. I looked around at the people around me. Everyone was excited, laughing and talking quickly. Light music was playing, helping the ambience. Ethan found me in the midst and hurried over with my drink and his water in hand.

"Drink up. I'm gonna go first, and you just wait for your name." I stared at him strangely, but he revealed nothing. About fifteen minutes later the lights began flashing and the room fell quiet.

"Miracle Moore," A voice called over the speakers. The crowd began cheering excitedly as a tiny redhead popped up out of her seat and headed to the stage. She looked around and reached for the microphone.

"Hello," she said nervously, looking around the room. People said hello back and they urged her to speak. She closed her eyes, opened her mouth, and exploded.

"My mom always told me that I was too skinny. I had my dad's nose. My hair was too course. No wonder boys didn't like me, I was too smart. I needed to stop reading so much and put on some lipstick.

She pushed me to get lip injections, and after I graduated, she gave me a gift certificate for breast implants. She had ingrained in the thoughts that I could never be loved the way I was.

I got pregnant at nineteen and she couldn't understand how it happened. "How could you do this to yourself? Is this what you want to teach your child?" She screamed at me. No. It wasn't," she paused and people clapped. Bringing the mic back up to her lips she was completely emotionless.

"I gave my baby up at twenty and removed the fake boobs. I gave the parents a letter to give to her, when she's older. In it I tell her that she has her father's nose, her hair is perfect, and that she'd always be loved, lipstick or not." She placed the mic back and stepped off the stage. The room went wild with cheers and applause. The bartender called for another person, who was just as passionate about what was upsetting them.

After the fifth person I realized that this was just a stage for people to vent without being judged. What an interesting concept. I looked over at Ethan who had been waiting for me to catch on.

"You want to try?"

I bit my lip, unsure. We listened to people talk about their cheating spouses, deaths that they were struggling with, drugs, their jobs. When the bartender called "Ol' Blue Eyes," Ethan stood up and hurried to the stage. I chuckled. That was the nickname Adrian had for him.

He took the mic and greeted everyone with that flirty smile he was known for and then started speaking.

"My wife is pregnant with someone else's baby." People boo'd and swore. He raised his hand. "She's doing it for a good cause. She's her best friend's surrogate. I know I should be okay with it, but I'm really not. I waited years to finally have her, and less than two years into our marriage I feel like I've taken the backseat and she's determined to help him.

She tries to keep me happy. Our sex life is great, if I can stop focusing on the baby kicking while we're doing it. Like she knows that this is wrong. I'm an outsider. I want to shout, "She's mine!" But I know that her friend could shout "She was mine first!" Because it's true. How do you compete with people who have been inseparable since they were ten years old? You don't.

Her friends say jump, she says 'how high'. The feeling is mutual. They'd lay their lives down for her, but I still struggle to find my place in her life. Where do I fit in? In what order does she place her priorities?

I can't wait until this baby is born. I can't wait to have my wife back. To enjoy just a brief moment with only her. She's my life, and I can't even tell her how I feel. How do you tell someone you hate how perfect they are?"

He stopped, his chest heaving. He put the mic back and quickly left the stage. There was a pause and then another eruption of cheers. When he sat back in his chair, I saw that he was sweating. I clapped for him and he smirked.

"I haven't wanted a drink in forever, but man I could really take one." I gave him a sharp look and he assured me it would pass.

"Pretty in Purple," the bartender announced, and Ethan nudged me.

"Is that me?" I asked incredulously. He shrugged. "He picked it out. I pointed and he wrote that name down. Go," he urged. I stood up and slowly made my way to the stage. My hands were shaking. Was I going to do this?

I reached for the microphone and saw the people staring at me, waiting. I could barely get it out of the stand but managed to pull it down and hold it tightly.

"Hi. Umm.." I froze up, but once my eyes found Ethan I relaxed. He motioned for me to keep talking. I closed my eyes, took a deep breath and started.

"I didn't want to do it. I told my husband that I was okay

with it. I could be the best aunt and dog mom ever, but he wasn't okay with it. I did it for him.

We took my egg and his sperm and put it in his closest friend. She was the right person for the job, but I hate knowing that I don't get that. I don't get to feel her kick, or pee all the time, or throw up because I smelled barbecue chips.

I was gone when the baby kicked for the first time. You know who was there? My husband. He got to feel our child's first kicks with another woman. They got to share that moment, while I was left to catch the next batch of movement.

She tries constantly to include me and make me excited about the baby, but the more she tries the more distant I feel about it. I can't wait to be a mother, but I hate people thinking that my husband and her are more important than me. I'm important too!" I paused and people started agreeing with me.

"Amen!" Someone shouted.

"People have a way of taking beautiful moments and turning them ugly. I deserve those beautiful moments just as much as they do, and I really wish fans would see that." I finished. I left the stage and began wiping my face. I don't remember when I started crying. As I walked back to my table people patted me on the back and said kind words while they clapped.

When I returned to my seat Ethan was waiting for me with a napkin to clean my face up.

"How'd it feel?" He asked as the next person took the stage. I relaxed in my seat and thought about it. Smiling, I turned to him and laughed.

"So damn good."

Chapter Fifteen

GIRL, YOU SHOULDA BEEN A DRUMMER

ON THE WAY home Ethan and I had a long talk about what we had said on stage.

"I know it's completely irrational, but sometimes I wonder if he has deeper feelings for her," I revealed. Ethan nodded.

"Despite her choosing to marry me I still have insecurities with the band. Adrian slept with her and and I have been on tour with them. Before they began settling down all four of them had no boundaries. It sucked seeing her cuddle with one of them, even if it was strictly platonic."

I gulped.

"I don't mean to upset you. I just don't get to talk to anyone about it, it's nice to know someone understands. You know they aren't like that anymore. Mark would never touch another woman."

"Don't tell him, or her, about what I said," I whispered. He chuckled lightly.

"I figured that went without saying. Same here. I love her, but sometimes she makes it really hard to get on board with her crazy ideas."

We relaxed and the mood turned from somber to a much

lighter mood. He turned back on my music and even sang along to a few songs. Realizing that I had an opportunity, I thought I'd take it.

"Since we are being truthful, does she have a name picked out?" Ethan shot a glance at me and clicked his tongue.

"Nice try." Damn, I was so close.

Cleo hit thirty weeks and we celebrated with ice cream cake. Her pick, naturally. I invited everyone over for dinner and when everyone else left the twins remained. We were having a sleepover, and in the morning, we were taking them to play mini golf.

I tried to set them up in the living room to sleep but Derek returned from wherever he had gone and thrown a fit.

"Where am I supposed to sleep?"

"I don't care, go to Adrian's."

He glared at me.

"I can't. The baby cries too much."

"What are you going to do when our baby is here?" I demanded. He stared at me blankly for a moment before asking if I'd put them in one of the spare rooms. Sighing, I grabbed their pillows and blankets and moved them.

Once I was in my own bed I turned to Mark and said something to him. "Derek can't keep staying here. There is no reason he can't find his own apartment or even buy a house. We all know he has the money. Or a car for that matter. It took Adrian forever to get one too. Why are you guys so hesitant with getting basic things?"

"Roots. Houses and cars say that this is where we are staying."

"So? Does Derek really think he's going somewhere?"

He sighed and set his book aside.

"Baby I do not know. I'll talk to him. He already knows he has to find something when the baby comes, why rush him?"

"Because he's driving me insane!" I exclaimed.

"Okay, okay. I'll bring it up again. Or at the very least tell him to leave you alone."

Mark did talk to him the next day, but I had a strong feeling it was only to tell him to knock off his attitude, and not so much to find a new place to live. When we returned from mini golf, he had cleaned up the living room and had bought a cheesecake as a peace offering he told me. I didn't really like cheesecake.

The band was officially stepping into the studio to record their album. I decided to start baby proofing the house. With their long hours some nights I went to bed before they came home.

I had forgotten to mention that I had done all of the bathrooms the day before and was awoken in the middle of the night to a drunk Derek yelling from the downstairs bathroom. I pushed Mark, trying to wake him up but he just grunted and rolled over. Finally, I pulled on my robe and went to see why he was being so loud.

Following the sound I found him in the bathroom off the kitchen, pants unbuttoned and struggling to open the toilet. "What the hell. Help! I pissed everywhere!" He shouted. His words jolted me out of the sleepy haze I had walked down in. I looked around the bathroom and saw that he had indeed urinated all over my bathroom floor.

I was speechless. I didn't know where to start with this. It was three in the morning, he was drunk, and I couldn't take a step into the room without stepping in pee. Sighing I went back to the kitchen and opened my cleaning supply cupboard. I pulled out a mop and floor cleaner.

I set them down in the bathroom and told him to clean it up.

"You better not leave this house tomorrow without having this taken care of," I said to him. He waved me away and I left him to it.

In the morning when we came back down, we found him in the bathroom still. He had managed to get the toilet seat up, but only to throw up in it. Mark kicked his foot to wake him up. Derek jumped and looked around, his eyes settling on us.

"Get this cleaned up. All of it," Mark demanded.

The smell of vomit and urine was stuck inside the kitchen, so we decided to go out for breakfast. By the time we returned, thankfully, he had gotten up and cleaned up the mess he had made last night. He started pouting when he discovered that we had gone out.

"Oh, come on, you didn't bring me anything?"

I had to leave the room, afraid of what I'd do if he said one more word to me.

After that Mark told him to stay somewhere else for awhile, and he did. He left for four glorious days and upon his return he promised not to make such a mess. I'd believe it when I saw it.

One morning while I was in the shower Mark came into the bathroom.

"Have you checked your phone this morning? Someone wrote an article about us and it's getting a lot of attention." Sighing, I closed my eyes and rinsed my hair. I thought this crap was over. I didn't feel like hearing more about how awesome my husband and Cleo were.

"No, I think I'll pass this time," I said, opening the shower and stepping out to grab my towel. "I've had enough nonsense journalism for a lifetime." I glanced over at him, but he was shaking his head.

"No, it's not like that. Someone wrote a rebuttal to the magazine article. It's freaking awesome," he said handing me his phone. I scrolled to the top and the read the headline. "The

Bullsh*t Truth About Being A Celebrity's Wife" I smiled and continued on.

Whoever wrote this got it just right. She talked about how we were always in the background despite hungry fans and that despite celebrity's often times being flirty, they were pretty loyal to the ones sitting at home.

She then addressed the magazine that did the article.

"What happened here is clearly the person doing the interview decided that the MOTHER of this future child is not as important as the best friend. What a joke. Renee Lesley was mentioned twice, TWICE, in the entire article that was about HER baby."

She finished her rant with a hashtags #Rockstarwivesrock and #ReneeandMark. I gave the phone back to him and finished drying myself.

"That's pretty awesome. She hit the nail right on the head."

"Oh no, you don't even know the half of it. Those hashtags are trending. Baby, people are loving you. They've created fan pages and are posting pictures of us. It's insane. Look," he went through his phone again and pulled up a profile. OFFICIAL #MARKANDRENEE FAN PAGE, it said. I went through and saw they had pinned the article and then hundreds of people were commenting and sharing their opinions and pictures from shows or my own social media page.

I didn't see a single mean comment in the hundreds I scanned through. Everyone was supportive and thought it was awesome how close we all were.

I spent the rest of the morning going through as many of the posts as I could. When Mark announced he was leaving for work he wrapped his arms around me from behind and kissed my cheek.

"Have fun, Love. See, I told you she was insane. Now you're not so behind the scenes," he teased. I rolled my eyes and kissed him back. I had to admit it was nice seeing people acknowledging my role in the my husband's life.

After lots of thought I decided to address it on my page. I thanked everyone for the support and appreciated the acknowledgments, adding the hashtag of the day #Rockstarwivesrock to the end.

Naturally that started another flood of responses, but I finally gave up trying to read them all. I got up off the couch and began going through my everyday routine. When I had a few lulls I would go back and look again. One post caught my eye. A girl asked if we had a P.O. Box for fan-mail. Did we?

I called Mark and asked.

"The band does, and Cleo you have one right?" I heard her answer him faintly in the background.

"Yeah, I'll have Sam text you the info. Why?"

"People are asking for it."

"Oh, cool. Maybe we'll get some fun letters to put in a book or something for Scooby."

"Scooby?"

"Name of the day, thank God she's got nine more week to go through names," he chuckled.

Five minutes after we hung up Sam sent me the P.O. Box information. I then shared it with the band's fans. With that last post I decided that I needed to be done for the day otherwise it would consume me. It was so easy to become addicted to reading the comments.

Not even three days later the post office called and asked that someone come pick up the mail. Since the band was pretty busy Mark asked me to go get it. I stopped over and grabbed the key from Cleo.

"If I have any do you mind grabbing mine too? It comes in spurts usually."

When I got there, it was revealed that I had five totes of

packages and envelopes to take home. It took me three trips to get them all in the car. I went right over to Cleo's and started unloading them. Ethan was coming home right as I was opening my trunk, so he grabbed three totes to take into the house.

Setting them down in the living room I popped into the studio and asked if they had time to take a break. Cleo nodded and promptly sat down on the stool she had next to her. She was getting tired more quickly now.

"I actually have the mail out here, if you guys want to check it out," I suggested. She shot me a small 'How dare you ask me to move' glare but got up and joined us in leaving the room.

When they saw all the mail they swore and let out excited murmurs. Making a small circle Adrian reached out first and started separating the mail.

"Mark, Renee, Renee, Renee, Cleo, Mark," he sang as he pushed envelopes and boxes over to us.

"Aw man, is there any for us?" Derek whined. He shook his head.

"Not that I see, oh wait. This one's for me," he lifted the large Manila envelope.

"This is from a mister Frederick Arizona." He opened it and looked inside, pulling out a large poster. He stared at it and then shoved it right back into the envelope. "So unsolicited dick pics still go through snail mail. Nice," he chuckled and tossed it aside.

I opened the first envelope with my name on it. It was a baby shower card, with a small handwritten note inside. Oh, how cute. I pressed it to my chest. I wanted to squeal. Mark handed me a handful more of them and I started carefully digging in. I wanted to save the envelopes.

Most of them were congratulations on the baby cards. Some were handmade, others had drawings or little things inside for her. Someone had put tiny socks in hers, while another had some mittens. It was all so adorable.

Since I had taken charge of the cards Mark opened the boxes. Most of them contained various baby things. Lots of clothes. We received a handmade blanket, and someone had knitted a hat and boots. All of it was a little overwhelming, I had to sit back for a moment.

I watched Mark reach for a box and open it. He pulled out a black shirt and when he unfolded it he laughed.

"Hell yeah, baby look at this." He flipped it around to show me. It said #Rockstarwivesrock.

"Oh, how cool! I'm gonna have to wear that and get a picture."

It took an hour but finally we opened the last card. Cleo and I were surrounded by boxes, while Adrian had a handful of cards and Derek had one.

"Can we start a new hashtag #guitaristslivesmatter?" He pouted.

"Maybe #Derekneedslove," Cleo giggled. Mark sat up excitedly.

"Can we do that? Maybe sign him up for some dating sights. How about it man?"

Derek flipped him off and said nothing.

"I do just fine on my own, thanks."

"Do you? I haven't seen you with a chick in since before Cleo's wedding," Mark smirked.

"So what? That doesn't mean I'm not dating. That just means I don't want them around you," he said cooly. Silence followed for a moment before the subject was changed.

"Can we call it for today? Tot and me want a nap," Cleo yawned. Everyone agreed to be done rehearsing today.

"What's everyone doing for dinner tonight?" Adrian asked as we loaded up my car with all of our gifts.

"I don't know, why you guys wanna come chill?" Mark looked up at him and he shrugged.

"That boxing match is tonight. I figured we could watch it at your place, all come over, have some food and beer."

"Sounds great, I'll order it when I get home. Just stop over whenever."

Derek came out of the house and asked if we were watching the fight tonight. Mark told him the plans and he got excited.

"Hell yeah. I was hoping we'd get to watch it on your big screen. Let's go," he said, hopping into the backseat. I looked over at Mark who just shrugged. What could you do?

Mark immediately ordered the show on whatever premium channel it would be streaming on. Next, he went and brought a TV from his practice room and set it up next to the other TV. When I asked him what he was doing he explained that the second one would be for gaming.

"We can play the game while we watch the pre-fights and stuff. Plus, Derek and I are probably gonna play afterward. They just added some DLC last night."

I rolled my eyes but didn't complain. Derek helped him set it up and as soon as it was good to go, they both sat down and started up the game. I went to work in the kitchen, pulling out chips and beer. I brought them out for the guys to enjoy while they played.

"Hey, you should make those things, with the bacon. You know," Derek asked, not looking away from the screen.

"What, poppers?"

He nodded excitedly.

"Yeah those. That and the mushrooms. Make those."

I put my hand on my hip and didn't move.

"Please?" I said and I saw his jaw clench. Instead of answering he chose to ignore me. Mark, who wasn't looking away either asked if I would make the food.

"I love those mushrooms. You wanna order pizza too? I'll go get it if you call," he promised. I was skeptical but called anyways while I started on the appetizers. When there was a break in their game Mark came into the kitchen.

"Everyone just got here. How's cooking going?" I turned away from the counter.

"Why does he purposely try to irritate me?"

"Who, Derek? He does that to everyone. He just knows he can get under your skin easier. Ignore him and he'll go away." He came over to hug me. I relaxed into his warm, toned body.

"I'm this close to kicking him out. I don't know how much more I can take," I murmured.

"I know. I'll bring it up again tomorrow, and really push him to start looking," he assured me. Derek yelled from the other room for Mark to get back. He reached for a mushroom, popped it in his mouth and hurried out.

Realizing I still didn't want to be around him right now I decided to make a few more snacks. I made a dip for the chips and then brownies for later. When everyone began to arrive, I brought the food out. Setting the bowls and trays out on the coffee table, I had bent down. Suddenly I felt a light slap on my bottom.

I jerked upright and turned around. Derek had been the one to smack my ass. He gave me a wink and reached for a popper.

"Thanks doll, keep up the good work." I stared at him in shock and anger. I balled my hands up in fists.

"You do that again and you won't have a hand to smack with," Mark growled. Taking a deep breath, I left the room. This was too much, I needed a break. He could not stay here anymore. The timer in the kitchen went off, telling me that it was time to get the pizza. I returned to the living room and told my husband.

He groaned but handed the controller to Adrian.

"Alright, Derek come on." Derek shook his head.

"Nah, make someone else go with you. I'm on a kill streak." Mark looked around for takers and finally Ethan volunteered to go. Mark reached for a kiss, but I just wasn't feeling it right then. He frowned.

"Oh, come on. Don't be mad at me for his mouth. That's not fair," he pouted. I kissed him quickly and hurried into the kitchen. I poured myself a glass of wine and stared at it. Was I making a big deal out of nothing? No one else seemed to be as bothered by it as I was. Why was that?

Cleo entered the kitchen and asked me if I was alright. I shrugged. "I guess, just- am I being crazy about Derek? He's driving me nuts. He eats my food, sleeps on my couch, throws up in my bathroom. He's annoying and rude and I don't know how much more I can take of it!"

Cleo stared at me for a moment before cracking a smile and then chuckling.

"You're not nuts. He has been pretty bad lately. Worse than usual. I think it's because Mark's his last buddy. Adrian and I are more focused on the kids and our husband's. Mark's freedom is coming to a close. Well, you know what I mean. No more late nights playing video games and binge drinking. He misses that and is holding on to Mark for dear life."

When she explained it to me like that, I started to feel guilty. It made sense. He was the only one still unchanged by the years. He was still living that total rockstar life. She came over and reached for my shoulder.

"Try not to take it so personally. He's just upset that you're taking his bff away from him. He'll get over it."

I nodded and left the wine in the kitchen. Returning to the living room I went to sit down on the couch. However, I was stopped by Derek opening his mouth.

"Hey, go get me another beer."

"Excuse me? Go get it yourself," I snapped back.

"Why are you being such a bitch lately? It's just a beer," he smirked. That was it. I had finally had it. I stormed over to him and snatched the controller out of his hand.

"What the hell!"

"No, we're done. You can't stay here anymore. Get out of my house."

He opened and shut his mouth quickly. Seeing my face, he didn't know how to properly respond. He looked around the room for support, but everyone was either looking away or not giving him the reaction he wanted.

"Is this a joke? You can't do that. This isn't your place. Mark's my brother, he won't let you just kick me out." He crossed his arms triumphantly. I put my hand on my hip and burst out laughing.

"This isn't my place? I was the one who picked it out. We're married. We're partners. He doesn't have more say than me. Despite what you think we're equals, and I can't have you here anymore. I'm done."

"Done with what? Okay, I can get my own beer. Happy? Are you satisfied, making a big deal out of nothing?" He stood up and moved to stand toe to toe with me. I clenched my fist. I was seeing spots.

"Get the hell out of my way," he brushed past me and I pounced on him.

He fell to the floor and I pushed his head into the carpet. He yelled and started wiggling, trying to get me off his back. I put all my weight into keeping him down. Suddenly I heard a voice that made me look up and return back to earth.

"Jesus Renee, what are you doing?" Mark.

My brief confusion was all Derek needed to shove me off him and get on his feet.

"Your wife went crazy over a joke!" He shouted, adjusting his clothes. Mark sat down the pizzas and came into the room to help me up. We stood there, with him between us. Derek was shooting daggers at me, while I was trying hard not to punch him in the face.

"Renee, do you need to get some air?" He asked me. I ignored him. I swore if he took Derek's side in this, I was divorcing him. They could have each other. I was sick of it.

"Mark, Derek has been purposely trying to provoke her," Cleo said gently from her seat.

"It was a joke!" Derek shouted. "She's trying to kick me out man." He looked at Mark, pleading for him to do something.

"Dude, you can't keep doing this-" he started. I could tell in his tone that he was going to try to pacify both of us. Go figure, the hot head of the band was the one trying to keep us from going off.

"Play me." I said suddenly. They looked at me confused, so I decided to make a deal. "Play me in your game. You win, I'll drop it and you can stay here until the baby comes, like planned. I win and you leave with everyone else tonight and you never sleep here again."

Derek laughed, crossing his arms.

"You can't beat me. I've been playing this game since it came out. Sure, let's play. Then maybe you'll finally shut up."

Mark slugged his shoulder.

"Dude, watch it." I extended my hand and locked eyes with him. He shook my hand, squeezing it hard. I forced myself not to wince.

"This is better than the fight we actually came here for," Ethan murmured. Everyone turned to him and he looked down quickly. "My bad."

"No, it is. I didn't really pick a side for the boxing match, but I'm picking sides now," Chase laughed. Adrian nudged him and silently scolded him.

I went over and took the controller from him. He moved aside to let me take his spot.

"What are we playing?" He asked, grabbing the controller I

had ripped from his hands and sitting down next to me. It was a shooting game. You had enemy teams that you played against in different games. Nothing real original but they loved it.

"I think you should play the new mode that came with the pack we bought today. That way you both are on unfamiliar grounds."

"It doesn't matter, she's gonna be on unfamiliar grounds in whatever mode we play in."

"Not really, I play all the time." Derek turned his head quickly and Mark chuckled.

"She does. She plays with me when you're not here and when she's home alone and bored. She's actually pretty good." Dereks smirk slid off his face. There was a flash of worry that quickly was replaced with determination.

"Fine, let's play the new stuff. It's called Hide and Seek. It's hard. 50 against 50. Whoever can find and kill the other first wins. Sound fair?" I agreed to the terms and we picked our characters and weapons.

"Are we still watching the other fight? It's gonna start soon," Adrian asked. Everyone shushed him and he sighed deeply, grabbing the remote to find the channel.

"Fine. I'll watch it. This game isn't going to solve anything,"

"Shut it Crespo." Derek snarled as we pushed the start buttons on our controllers. The chatter stopped completely as the music from the game filled the room. My eyes focused on the screen and tried to get my bearings. They weren't kidding, this was hard.

This was the largest amount of players I'd ever played with. People were running everywhere. I had the top screen, while Derek played on the bottom. I focused on getting out of the clump that was my team. As people were dying, they'd spawn everywhere. It was frustrating trying to run when I'd hit a wall of someone returning to the game.

As I ran, I searched for his name, KISSMYBASS. I hid inside buildings and ran using the rooftops. Suddenly a bullet shot right past me. I ducked and rolled. Another shot and I heard Derek mumble, "Bingo,". I swore and army crawled to the edge of the roof.

Taking a risk, I jumped up and leapt down. Another bullet and he groaned loudly, frustrated that he was missing me. As soon as I was on the ground I sprinted away. Then, realizing he knew where I'd run decided to run back towards the building I had just been on top of. I snuck inside and started climbing the stairs, moving slow and cautiously.

There was a hatch open for the player to climb up onto the roof. I angled myself just right to look out without being seen right away. Moments later I saw a player jump onto the roof and begin whipping his gun around, looking for someone. It was Derek. My heart was racing, and my palms were so sweaty I could barely hold the controller. This was it. Finally.

I aimed my gun and pushed the trigger. He dropped to the ground, revealing that I had a managed a perfect head shot.

"NO!" He screamed. I bit my lip and sighed with such relief. Thank God. I laid back into the couch, satisfied and still in shock over what had just happened.

Turning to my right, I saw Derek pulling on his hair.

"This can't be happening. What the hell just happened. I lost. I lost!" Mark, being the best friend in the world patted him on the shoulder.

"It's no big deal man. I'm sure you can crash with someone else for the night and tomorrow I'll help you find a place."

Derek brushed his hand off him and stood up.

"You can stay with us tonight," Adrian offered but he shook his head.

"No, no, no, no. I can't," he mumbled, then turned his eyes on me. They were filled with fury.

"Fuck you Renee. You think you're so damn funny. You all

think this is a joke? Sure, make fun of me all you want. I don't need this." He turned abruptly and started out. Adrian jumped up and grabbed his shoulder stopping him.

"Dude, why are you making this into such a big deal? So what, you'll have to find a place of your own. Just come stay with me for a night or two."

Derek laughed. It came out hollow and cold.

"I think it's great that the only friend who actually has my back is the one I really betrayed."

Adrian frowned and took a step back.

"What?"

Derek laughed again and extended his arms, turning around slowly, as if revealing himself.

"You guys keep asking about who I've been seeing. Why do you think I've been so secretive since before Cleo's wedding?" He took a step towards Adrian and put his face two inches in front of his.

"Who do you think fucked Dita?"

Adrian swung his fist forward and Derek was knocked out completely cold before he could say another word.

Chapter Sixteen

THE NERVE

It all happened so fast. Adrian popped Derek square in the nose. The crunch of the impact was audible.

He hit the ground and didn't stir. Adrian was shaking mad. Without another word or look to any of us he walked out of the room calmly and left, slamming the front door so hard our rather large house rattled.

Everyone was too stunned to move for a moment. Finally, Ethan moved forward and lifted Derek off the ground with a grunt.

"Jesus, some help here?" He asked. Mark leapt to action and got him sitting up on the couch. Derek groaned but his eyes remained closed and his head flopped to the side.

Cleo left the room and returned with a damp cloth from the kitchen. She sat next to him and began wiping the blood off his face. After a few minutes he came to. Looking around, he was visibly confused and then his memory returned. He shot up and just like his former best friend, left the house; slamming the door behind him.

The rest of us sat there in silence. Did we go after them? Chase cleared his throat and stood up.

"I'm going to go find Adrian. Make sure he doesn't get into any trouble. Can you guys watch the baby?" I nodded and he left, a little quieter than the others.

The four of us were the only ones left. We looked at each other uncomfortably.

"Did anyone know? About Derek and-" Mark stopped short. I shook my head. There was no way I could have guessed. Derek was surprisingly good at secret keeping apparently. Ethan said that he also had no idea, and then our eyes fell on his wife. She looked down guiltily. My eyes widened with memory. The day she had been served. She told Derek that if he told Ethan, she'd tell his secret.

"How'd you find out?" I asked. She chewed on her lip and swallowed.

"At the hospital. When him and Chase had the accident. I stopped over one night alone, and she was there. It was obvious how close they were. She left and I made him tell me the truth." She shook her head and laughed coldly. "That's why he refuses to stay over at Adrian's apartment."

We stayed up until Chase returned for Rocky. He said that he had found Adrian but couldn't find Derek.

"I don't know where he went. Maybe he went to Dita's place?"

We didn't hear from him for a full month. No calls, no pictures of him surfaced from some tabloid. He didn't show up to rehearsals. Eventually they stopped all together. His bandmates were all too stressed out to practice without him.

Adrian was pissed. For about a full week you couldn't even bring Derek up without his jaw clenching and him growing deathly silent. However, once the second week came and no word from him, even Adrian started worrying. They tried Dita's phone and work, but her coworkers said she took a leave of absence. She had disappeared as well.

Then, one day Adrian got a phone call. We all happened to

be together when it came. It was Derek's mother's number. He answered it quickly, putting it on speaker. His three bandmates hurried across the room to hear the call.

"Hello? Derek? Have you heard from Derek Mrs. Turtle?" They all shouted questions at the phone. There was a pause and then Derek's voice came across from the other side.

"124 Middle St." Then there was another long pause before he hung up the phone. His friends looked up at each other, communicating without speaking. Adrian reached for the phone, shoving it deep into his pocket and sighing. He looked over at his husband.

"I'm leaving for home. Back to Michigan. You want to drive me to the airport?"

He took the first flight out and we waited. At first, we heard nothing for almost three days. Then on the fourth night Chase called Mark. We looked at each other before he answered. When he answered I could hear Chase laughing on the other end of the line. Mark put the phone on speaker so I could hear better.

"Adrian, Derek, and Dita will all be home by Friday. They have to wait for Derek to be released."

"From Jail? Shit. What happened?" Mark groaned. I rolled my eyes, not surprised. I can only imagine the fight those two had once Adrian showed up.

"No, not jail. I was actually sworn to secrecy. You'll see when they get here. Do you guys want to meet them at the airport?"

"Yeah, sure. So, are Dita and Adrian okay then? I'm confused," Mark shook his head. There was a deep pause on the other side.

"He made it sound like they were alright. Obviously he's not happy about how long they hid it. I guess him and Derek had a long talk and he's pretty serious with Dita. I was given a lecture about how if he can be okay with it then I have to be too." Chase didn't sound too eager about it but chuckled again.

"I think Derek is paying for it. Anyways, I'll see you guys when they come in. I just wanted to check in and let you know everyone is okay."

We thanked him and hung up, soaking in the information. If he wasn't in jail, where was he?

Our questions were answered when we met them at the airport. Adrian came out first, a wide smile on his face. He hurried over to his husband and son and embraced them. Next, Dita followed. She smiled and waved, but her face was red with embarrassment.

No one reacted for a moment, so I decided to make the first move. I smiled back and walked over to her, giving her a hug. She relaxed in my arms and squeezed me back.

"How have you been?" I asked. She giggled, tears shining in her eyes.

"Could be better."

I motioned for her to join the rest of us and she did with uneasy eyes. We watched the line of people exiting and still no Derek. Just as I was about to ask, we saw wheels and then Derek in the seat, his legs back in full casts.

Everyone gasped and then when he saw us and glared, we erupted in laughter. He flipped us off as he wheeled over to us.

"Fuck off," he grumbled.

"What happened?" Mark said, trying his hardest to stop laughing. Derek didn't answer him, but instead forced himself past everyone.

"He fell. We were both drunk and fighting. I didn't see the open window. I grabbed him and pulled him back in, but he shoved me away and then fell two stories. It was disgusting," Adrian grimaced. Cleo let out a small scream.

"It was an honest accident. I saw the whole thing," Dita

defended Adrian. He chuckled as we turned to start following Derek.

"First thing that came out of his mouth after he screamed was 'aw fuck'. You could see the bones coming out of both legs."

We had dinner at our house that night with everyone. Once Derek stopped pouting, he assured us that he didn't blame Adrian. If anything, he blamed Karma.

"I just got out of this chair. I just can't believe they both broke. Again. F- my life man. I hate these casts," he groaned. Eventually the jokes started in and everything seemed to go back to normal. As the evening got later someone asked Derek where he was staying tonight. He glanced at Dita, who had been quiet most of the evening. He cleared his throat.

"I just wanted to let everyone know that I am looking at houses, hopefully I pick up something soon. Also, after tonight, Dita will be joining us for things. I am making it official. We've been dating for awhile now, it's time we stop hiding it." There was a pause and we all clapped and congratulated him. If Adrian could be okay with it, so could we. We had to be.

"So where are you looking? Any particular neighborhoods?" Mark asked. Derek sipped his beer and smiled coyly.

"The realtor is showing me Emile Dahl's house next week. It's low-key on the market apparently. He doesn't want people to know he's selling it."

"Is he staying in Louisiana with Cotton then?" Adrian asked.

"I have no idea. I was just told that he wants it to be kept under wraps. Maybe he's thinking of going AWOL again," he said, referring to the time where the biggest rockstar of this generation disappeared for about three years and just popped back up one day.

"Well, either way. I'm glad you're back," I said, genuinely

meaning it. Derek lowered his eyes and after a moment softened.

"Thanks Renee. I'm sorry for being an ass. I think my secret was just really starting to get to me."

After that, things went back to normal. Well, with one addition to the group- Dita. At first it was extremely awkward, and you could tell she didn't want to be there, but after a few days she began to relax and turned back into the girl I had remembered from when she was dating Adrian. We invited her to our weekly lunches.

The first lunch we forced her to explain herself.

"How did it happen? When? Why did you keep it a secret for so long?" Cleo shot at her. Dita blushed and blew on her blonde bangs nervously.

"Um, the first time was shortly after your last tour. Derek made the first move, for the record. He kissed me and I didn't stop it. We were both drunk, not that it makes it okay," she was rambling. I ordered a mimosas for the two of us and she relaxed.

"After Adrian caught us and we broke up we didn't see each other for a few weeks, but then he called and we went out on a date. It was weird. For a long time we didn't want to pursue anything other than random hookups but after the car accident we decided to officially, secretly, date. I wanted to tell Adrian ages ago, but Derek was afraid it would break up the band." She finished explaining and then gulped down her drink.

Cleo grew quiet.

"It almost did," she said, her voice barely audible. After a long moment of silence Cleo lit back up and assured her that she was glad she was back in our lives.

"We missed you."

"I missed you too," Dita replied.

On Cleo's 34th week of pregnancy Cleo called and said she couldn't make it. She assured me that she was fine, but something came up. Just as I was about to call Dita, she too canceled. Frowning at my phone, I was just about to take the dogs out when Erin called me.

We had been in touch since the party. Not much, but her, Stacie, and I had gone to dinner once or twice. Her call was still unexpected. She asked if I'd come help with a set emergency.

"We need this backdrop finished for this weekend and all my help didn't bother to show. Can you please come help? I'll buy you dinner, lunch, whatever. Just come down here!" After she calmed down, I told her I was on my way.

I drove on down to the theatre, paint shirt in hands. However, when I pulled into the parking lot, I saw that there were about ten cars there. Did everyone end up showing up after all? I parked and went inside, figuring I was already there, might as well go help. Going through the doors I was met with total silence. That was odd.

"Hello?" I called but no one responded. I went through the theatre doors and jumped when I heard screams.

"Congratulations!" The women on stage yelled excitedly. A hand touched my shoulder and I spun around to see little- well big- Cleo. She was holding her belly and smiling wide.

"What is this?" I asked as she took my hand and pulled me down the aisle to the stage. I looked up and saw pink streamers, balloons, and a table with wrapped boxes and gift bags.

"A baby shower, silly," she said, pushing me gently up the stairs to my friends. I looked around at the group sitting at the small circle tables. All of my theatre friends, Dita and Cleo, Tabatha, and Jimmy. I turned to hug her tightly. She giggled and reached up to wipe the tears off my cheeks.

"Don't cry. This is a happy day," she said soothingly.

I lost it. I hugged her again and just let myself cry. She was seriously amazing. I couldn't have asked for a better person to carry my child. When I finally pulled away, I saw that my group of friends were also wiping away tears. I thanked them all for coming.

Stacie stood up and raised her glass of champagne. She took a fork to it, getting the room to quite down.

"Alright! Let's eat and then we can play some games!"

We had chicken salad croissants and fruit and vegetable trays. Nothing too fancy, but perfect for a light lunch. I walked around the stage and stopped when I found the cake. Holy smokes. It was a beautiful pink, three-tiered cake with a cute baby on top. She had a bow on her head and was clutching two drumsticks. I had to take pictures to show Mark later.

"Did Mark know about this?" I asked suddenly. Cleo nodded, rolling her eyes.

"I told him about it a few weeks ago and he got me in touch with your friends. They did a lot of the heavy lifting, food, cake, venue. I figured they'd know how to do it right."

After lunch Erin brought out four bowls of rice. One for each table.

"Okay, in the rice are safety pins. We are going to blindfold you and you'll take turns trying to get as many safety pins out of the bowl. Whoever has the most wins!"

She set the timers and we went to town. It was way harder than I thought it'd be. I had eight, while Dita plucked out fifteen.

However, she wasn't even close to the winner. Gabby from the play, somehow found thirty-two in two minutes time. She was awarded a small bag filled with candles and chocolates. Next, we played a more vulgar game that had Stacie's name all over it. I gave her a look and she erupted in giggles. The game was called 'Labor or Porn?' We looked at pictures of women's faces and had to guess what they were doing. It was hilarious, but so awful, but perfect.

After the games they announced it was time for me to open presents. It felt awkward, but I still sat in front of everyone and opened their gifts. I was never any good at receiving things like this.

Everything I was given was amazing. Joyce, who played the mother in the play had made a quilt; and Gabby had gotten me a beautiful baby book to put all of her first moments in. Finally, I made it to the bottom of the very full table. There was a single white envelope left. Picking it up I turned it over and frowned. There was no name on it. I asked if anyone wanted to claim it, but no one knew where it came from.

Opening it I pulled out the card and read it silently first. Quickly the tears came and slid down my face before I could force myself to stay strong. It was from Mark.

"Baby,

You are the most amazing thing in my life. I was never really complete until I found you. You are my rock, and you are going to be the best mom our daughter could ever ask for. I am so excited to share this next chapter of my life with you. You are the only person I want to do this with. I can't wait to see you hold her and take you both home with me for the rest of our lives.

Mark

P.S. Here is a three-person ticket to an all-inclusive spa. Take Dita and Cleo. Have one last relaxing day before all hell breaks loose when Tot comes. "

I covered my mouth when I started to laugh. Looking into the envelope I saw the tickets inside. My friends asked me who it was from and I told them my husband and nothing else.

Stacie and Erin helped me pack up my car while everyone else began cleaning up the stage. I hugged them both tightly and thanked them over and over.

"You're welcome. We're just happy that we got to see you happy. It was hard when you left the troupe, so it's nice to see you again. We should never let that happen again," Stacie warned me. I promised her I wouldn't ever lose touch again.

Surprisingly, when I got home, Mark was home. I saw his car and quickly parked mine. Leaping out of the vehicle I ran inside and hurried to his work room. Sure enough, he was behind his drums. The doctor had finally cleared him to play, although he start slow. He looked up in surprise when I came in and he tried to hide a smile. He knew the shower had been today.

I went to him and he moved to let me sit on his lap. I kissed him, hard and with as much passion as I could muster. He pulled away and gave me that cocky grin.

"Whoa, did you have a good day?"

I chuckled and stood up. I pulled his arm and started leading up the stairs to the bedroom.

"You have no idea."

I called and got our spa day scheduled for the weekend. Cleo wanted to do it before she got to the cranky end of her pregnancy.

"Towards the end all I'll want to do is get little Nicholson out of me. I want to enjoy this," she said.

Saturday morning Dita picked me up and we drove to get Cleo. Climbing into the car we sped off to our day of massages, face masks, and manicures. A woman in a crisp white suit called our trio and began getting our day scheduled. We decided to start with mud baths, then shower, get full body massages, and finish off the day with head massages, manicures, and pedicures for Dita and I. Cleo couldn't get her feet massaged, but they would paint them for her.

Relaxing in the mud room was heavenly. We sipped on lemon water and snacked on fruit and little cucumber sandwiches. I closed my eyes, sat back and enjoyed the soothing environment.

Showering, we headed into the massage rooms. They took us to private rooms. My masseuse had magic hands. I told her so and she chuckled.

"That's why I got into the business. I couldn't waste such a gift," she joked. I made sure to tip her well when I was finished and wrapped back in my mint colored robe.

When we all stepped out of our rooms, we all seemed very satisfied with how the day had gone so far.

"What's next again? I forgot," Dita asked, her voice sounding far off and almost dreamy. She was beyond relaxed.

The woman who had helped us with picking our activities found us and directed us to get facials. I was so relaxed I was pretty sure I was dozing off in the chair. When they peeled the mask off me my face felt so soft and looked like it was glowing. I couldn't stop touching my cheeks.

We stopped for a light lunch and then would finish with our nails. They had a small cafe off the lobby, where we got coffee and sandwiches.

"This has been the best day I've had in such a long time. Tot is even relaxing. She's not trying to kick her way out today. She must sense she's in good company," Cleo exclaimed. Dita agreed.

"Yes, oh my God. With all the mess I've been dealing with Derek and Adrian… it's nice to have a chance to de-stress."

"How is that, by the way?" I asked, sipping on my coffee. She shrugged.

"Adrian and I had a good talk and he's happy with Chase, so he's not jealous. He's just angry Derek and I lied to him for so long."

I could understand that. Adrian and Chase were perfect for

each other, so I'm glad him and Dita didn't work out; and oddly enough Derek and Dita kind of work.

Out of the corner of my eye I saw a flash of red hair that made me turn slightly and then my eyes bulged when I realized who I had spotted. Holly had just walked into the spa. I swung my head back to my friends, but they were both already looking past me and at her.

Dita and I quickly shared a look and then looked at Cleo simultaneously. The blood had ran from her face. She was no longer smiling. Her eyes were glued to the woman who had hurt her for so many years. My gaze returned to the counter where Holly stood proudly, having not noticed the three of us watching her from across the way.

"Hello, I was here just the other day. I filled out an application and wanted to turn it back in," she said sweetly to the receptionist, handing her a slip of paper I hadn't noticed before. The receptionist took it, thanked her, and went back to whatever she had been doing before hand. Holly didn't seem to appreciate that. Her sugary sweet face turned into a sneer. She slapped her hands down on the counter, making everyone in the area turn their heads.

"That's it? I was told when I turned it in, I would be given an interview time," she demanded. The woman apologized and shrank away, telling her that she would go get her manager. Holly crossed her arms and turned away, gazing around the room. Eventually she spotted us, and her irritation grew into anger.

Seeming to calm herself she sauntered over to our table, hips shaking, fire-red hair tossed behind her back.

"Of course I'd see you here," she smirked, looking at Cleo. Cleo shrank in her seat. I could see the tension she had just let go of return back to her mind and body in an instant. I cleared my throat and looked back to the former mistress, current wife, of Cleo's ex-husband.

"Hello Holly. You're looking for work? I didn't realize you two were staying in Cali. Why the sudden move?" I asked innocently. Her eyes turned into thin slits of rage as she gritted her teeth.

"Don't act like you don't know," she seethed. We glanced around the table with confused faces. We really didn't.

"What are you talking about?" Dita said sharply.

"Chris left me. He's with your husband's ex," she revealed, looking straight at Cleo.

Cleo pointed to herself.

"Mine? Wait, you're talking about Duchess? Chris is with Duchess? How? When did that happen?"

Holly huffed and stood up straighter.

"Don't know, don't really care. He took all of the money we had left and ditched me and our daughter. We have no money to go back home and everything is in his name so there is no home to really go back to. So, you'll be happy to know that I have sunken so low I have to go get a job like this while you sit up in your mansion with the singer."

Jealousy filled her eyes. Cleo looked at her blankly for a long moment, blinking rapidly before erupting into a grin.

The grin turned into a low chuckle and then erupted into a full-on belly laugh. Dita and I looked at each other, mouths slack, and eyes wide. Had she gone insane? She was holding her bulging belly, trying to stop herself but she continued grinning like a mad man.

Holly took a deep breathe and spun around, taking a step away from us. That made Cleo stop laughing and sit back up.

"It hurts, doesn't it? Don't worry. When he gets bored with her, he'll come home. He always did."

Holly turned to shoot daggers at her one last time before storming off. The receptionist had come back to the front desk with a post it note for her. Holly snatched it out of her hand and gave us one last glare before leaving.

Once she had left the building the three of us looked back at each other and then began rapidly talking over ourselves. Duchess, with Chris?

"She's obviously doing it on purpose. To get under your skin. Or maybe to get under Ethan's," I said. Cleo snorted.

"She can try all she wants but screwing around with him, of all people, would get under my skin if anyone's, but nope. I think it's hilarious and a little sad. Karma's a bitch. Holly, Chris, and Duchess will all get what they deserve."

"I still can't believe she got completely off," Dita commented. I rolled my eyes.

"Yeah, we all are still pretty pissed about it. She claimed momentary insanity brought on by the pressure of being a celebrity. They gave her probation and made her pay a fine. She could have killed one of them and she probably would have gotten off scot-free," I said.

The whole trial, if you could even call it that, was a joke. She walked in with her team of lawyers, all dressed up like an old porcelain doll, with a smirk planted firmly on her face. She knew she was getting off.

Everyone but Ethan and Cleo came to see it play out. I think seeing us walk in and realizing that her old boyfriend wasn't with us was the only thing that made her frown. Still, she thought he'd come back to her. She really was insane.

When we got back to Cleo's, she found Ethan and told him about our meeting with Holly. He was reading a book on the couch when we came in. He looked up, almost bored. He raised his eyebrows, but only chuckled.

"I hope they are very happy together," he smirked.

"Do you think we should go get a restraining order on them? Or Holly? God, I don't know. Is Tot making me crazy?" She plopped down next to him. He moved his legs and put his book down. Reaching over, he wrapped tattooed arms around his round wife. She leaned into him and he kissed her hair.

"You're not crazy. If you want to, we can ask my lawyer what he thinks. It would be just extending Duchess' and then adding Chris and Holly. I don't think it will be a big deal. Stop stressing about them. They are nothing. They don't matter," he soothed. Suddenly feeling like an intruder on an intimate moment, I nudge Dita and we left the room.

We went into the kitchen and found the twins sitting at the counter looking at each other with hardened faces. They seemed to be speaking to each other with just their eyes. Dallas looked up when we came in but said nothing.

"What's up guys?" I asked cheerfully, but they didn't respond. I frowned and went over to them. I put my elbows on the counter and leaned down.

"Is everything okay?"

They glanced at each other again.

"We saw our old Daddy the other day," Jimmy finally said, her lips trembling. I stood back up abruptly.

"Where?"

"At our school, outside."

Dallas glared at his sister.

"We didn't talk to him. He wanted us to come with him, but I told him no," he added.

"Are we in trouble?" Jimmy asked, her little eyebrows scrunching together. I shook my head.

"No, of course not. You did exactly what you were supposed to do. If you see him again, do the same thing."

I hurried back to their parents and told them what the twins had just told me. Ethan leapt up and went to find his kids. He demanded they tell him everything. Cleo started crying. I didn't know who to respond to. Turning to Dita, I told her to stay with the crying pregnant woman, and I would see to her screaming husband.

"Ethan, you're scaring them," I said, coming into the kitchen. Ethan's hands were slammed against the counter, he was leaning towards his son menacingly. Obviously, he wasn't-couldn't be angry at them. He just didn't know how to react and was taking it out on the wrong people.

I went over and put my hand on Ethan's shoulder. He glared up at me, saw my hardened face and relaxed. Standing straight he ran his fingers through his hair and swore.

"Dallas, I'm sorry, man. I didn't mean to get so angry at you. None of this is your or your sister's fault. It just scared me a little. Did you tell an adult he was there?"

Dallas shook his head quickly, his eyes were showing fear. I scowled. Ethan may have just done something irreversible. Dallas may be too afraid to ever tell anyone again. I looked towards Jimmy, who was silently crying.

"We knew he was bad. We told him to go away!" She said, hopping off her stool and running from the room. Ethan swore again and hurried after her. Dallas crossed his arms and shook his head.

"It's going to be okay. Your mom and dad are going to get it all sorted out. If you see him again though, tell an adult," I said gently, yet firmly.

By the end of the week Ethan and his family had been granted the restraining order. If Christopher violated it, he would be arrested. Hopefully that was enough to deter him. What was he thinking? I mentioned this to Cleo after lunch the next week and she just shook her head.

"He's not thinking. He's insane. I never understood it. He never really loved me, but now that I finally realize it, he can't leave me alone. He used to be gone for weeks a time. When he was home, he was abusive mentally and sometimes physically. Something's just-" she trailed off. "Not right."

After our regular scheduled lunch Cleo claimed Tot wanted ice cream. There was a great little parlor right down the street, so we decided to walk there. I noticed quickly that Cleo was now waddling more and more. It was adorable. By the time we made it to the shop she was out of breath.

"Ugh, I do not know if I can do two more months of this. She is ridiculous," she groaned as she put one hand on her belly, the other on her back.

Once she caught her breath we entered, and her big brown eyes grew even larger. I hadn't realized that was even possible.

"Mmm... mint chocolate chip," she mused as she waddled up to the counter. She gasped and turned back to me.

"I would kill for some blue moon!"

When I shook my head with confusion her jaw dropped.

"You have never had blue moon ice cream?"

"Sorry. I've never even heard of it. What is it?"

She turned and pressed her back to the glass, sighing deeply. Her eyes closed and she licked her lips.

"Pure Michigan deliciousness."

I laughed and suggested we get something else.

"Next time we are visiting we will all go out to get some. How about a banana split?"

She frowned but turned back to the man at the counter.

"Triple scoop of mint chocolate chip, smother it with chocolate syrup and put it in a waffle cone."

The man chuckled, looking from her to her bulging belly.

"Now that the baby has ordered would you like something miss?" He joked. She giggled like a little girl and moved to watch him make her sweet, cold, treat.

After he handed her the obnoxiously oversized cone, he looked over at me.

"And for you?"

I looked around and nothing really stuck out to me. I mentioned it and he asked if he could surprise me. I looked over at Cleo who was shoving her ice cream in her mouth.

"Do it!" She paused long enough to exclaim excitedly. I

gave him the go ahead and he told me to close my eyes. I turned around while he did his magic.

"Okay, here you go miss!" The man said. I turned around and started giggling myself. He handed me a black waffle cone, with two scoops of light pink ice cream. It was topped with lilac sprinkles and a single, pink, frosted animal cracker.

"I love it!"

Thanking him, I tipped him well and we sat down at one of the tables to enjoy our desserts. Despite the massive size of Cleo's cone, she finished hers before me. She sat back and patted her belly.

"I am going to have to actually go to the gym after Tot. This is the most I've eaten out of all of my pregnancies. Even the twins I wasn't this bad."

"I wonder if that means something? Like if you have heartburn the baby will have lots of hair. That sort of thing."

She thought about it for a moment then shrugged.

"Who knows, probably. All I know is that she's probably gonna be like fifteen pounds. She sure kicks like it."

Once I finished my cone, we stood up to leave and were startled when we heard a loud cling of something metallic falling to the floor. We turned and saw a flurry of red hair flying towards us.

Pink and brown liquid ice cream covered the floor next to the metal tray that the red head had been holding. Mine and Cleo's backs were splattered with the sticky shake. Holly reached us in seconds.

She grabbed onto Cleo's shoulders and held her in place.

"Why is it that no matter where I go, I can't get away from you?" She screeched. Cleo and I stared at her speechless and in shock. Looking at her better, I realized she was wearing a pink and white striped uniform. Her little hat to match had fallen to the floor. She worked here. I wanted to laugh, thinking about the spa. The interview must have not gone well.

"How were we to know you worked here?" I shot back, pulling her arms off Cleo. She stumbled back and glared at us. It was then that I noticed her giant black eye. Oh, no.

"Christopher isn't happy about the restraining order. Why do you have to take everything to the extreme? He thinks it's my fault. Can't you just leave us alone!" She screamed. Cleo shook her head and backed away.

"We are leaving now. Don't worry. Holly, you need to get help. You can't let him do this to you."

Holly spit at Cleo's feet.

"Don't act like we are one in the same. He loves me, he never loved you."

Cleo flinched. Gulping, she nodded.

"You're right. I hope it works out for you. Good luck Holly."

On the way out we could hear the rabid red head being fired. She started sobbing and in that moment, I felt only pity. It seemed like she would never be good enough for her husband, despite trying so hard to be what he wanted. I never wanted to live like that. Never being good enough.

My eyes turned from the road to glance at Cleo's belly. Would just one baby and me be enough for my husband? Could we be?

I drove quietly, letting the dark thoughts absorb and take over all the happiness I had felt lately. However, when we got back to the house Mark hurried over and wrapped me in a giant hug.

"I missed my favorite girl," he said, snuggling his face into my hair. I relaxed, realizing that I was worrying about nothing. I held him tighter and then he grimaced.

"Why are you so sticky and smell like strawberry syrup?"

Chapter Seventeen

KISS ME, KILL ME

AT HER NEXT doctor's appointment, the doctor decided that she was under too much stress and that she needed to really start taking it easy.

"You are 35 weeks, so close to the home stretch. Baby is sounding good, it feels like she's gotten into position. So, stay off your feet and relax. The longer she stays in there the better."

"Should we stop rehearsing?" Mark asked the doctor.

"If it is a high energy activity, then probably. I'm sure you can find things to do that will allow her to sit often and keep drinking water."

Cleo rolled her eyes at the doctor.

"I was performing up until the day I had my youngest son, I think I'll be fine."

There were some more directions on how to stay comfortable and let Tot grow. I think most of it went in one ear and out the other for Cleo. It was mildly frustrating. We needed a happy, on time, baby.

Mark decided to call it on the way back to Cleo's house.

"We are officially taking a break from recording and

rehearsing until the baby is born. We can work on other stuff. Promo, costumes, social media."

Cleo began to protest but Mark put his hand up.

"Everyone could use a break. A few weeks isn't going to kill us. We are already way ahead of schedule. Stop worrying about it and enjoy the rest of your time with Tot."

She crossed her arms under her giant chest and pouted.

"I'm naming her Tarantula," she threatened. Mark ignored her and continued driving.

"Lucy,"

Mark looked over at me and we shared a look that said that's the best she's said so far.

"Fer," she finished. And there it was.

The rest of the way home was spent listening to Cleo threaten her bandmate with horrible names for our child.

"Tequila, Jezebel, Jemima, Oprah!"

When we were able to drop her off and go home, I think we were both relieved to get her out of the car. Hoping for some intimate time, I was disappointed when Mark asked if he could hop on over to Adrian's.

"Just for a few hours. Then I'll get home and take you out. What do you want to do? Dinner, dancing?" He teased me, doing a quick cha cha slide type move. I rolled my eyes.

"You don't dance."

He laughed and kissed me quickly.

"Well, I have you here to teach me. I'll be back, just be ready."

"Ready for what?"

He grinned ear to ear and winked.

"I'll surprise you," he said, backing away towards the door and disappearing.

Deciding that maybe he really was going to take me dancing I bathed, curled my hair and did my makeup as perfect as I could. Stepping into my closet I searched until I found silver dress that he had bought for me a while back. It was silk and form-fitting. I looked great in it.

Slipping it on, I checked the time. It was almost eight o clock. Where was he? As if on cue, my phone started ringing.

"Hello?" I answered when his name popped up.

"Babe? I'm late. A semi tipped over on the highway and caused this huge pile up. All traffic is completely stopped. The police say it's gonna be a few hours."

"Oh my God. Are you okay?" I gasped, sitting down on the bed.

"Yeah we are all fine. Just wrong place at the wrong time. I was supposed to take you out dancing. I'm so sorry baby."

"It's okay. It's the thought that counts," I said. Disappointment fell over me, but the guilt from blaming him pushed it back. It wasn't his fault.

"Why don't you see what Cleo or Dita are doing? You can still go out. I'm sure you are looking way too hot to be sitting at home alone," he teased. I smiled, my heart skipping a beat.

"I'm in that silver dress you like," I murmured.

He hissed and groaned.

"Okay, you have to stop. I've got the guys in the car. I can't be popping a woody for the next few hours. Call one of the girls, go have fun. But, not too much fun. Save some for me," he chuckled.

"Will do. Love you. Call me with updates."

He told me he loved me too and I called Dita first. She squealed with excitement and told me she was getting ready now. We called Cleo but there was no answer. Dita picked me up and we decided to drive over there and invite her out personally.

"You really think she's wanting to dance right now? Or can, for that matter?" Dita asked.

"If the tables were reversed you know she'd be the first one to jump in the car to get either one of us. Whether she wants to go or not, we should extend the invite."

"That's true. You know, it's kind of crazy. Derek and Adrian both built Cleo up to seem like some kind of dragon gate-keeper. If she didn't approve, I was out. I was so afraid to meet her, I kept making Adrian make excuses for me. I liked him so much I was afraid that she'd end it for me."

"Then, no offense, why did you cheat on him?" I tried to chuckle but Dita shot me a glare that told me she didn't find it funny.

"It just kind of happened. It's hard to explain. Well, not really. It wasn't something either of us planned on happening. But- it feels right now. I know that despite how we got together, Derek is the one I'm meant to be with. Plus, Chase is so perfect for Adrian it's not even funny. Seeing them together makes it all feel kind of perfect."

I fell silent, taking in her words. I didn't really know what to say to that. I guess she was right. It all worked out in the end and that's all that mattered. Each couple was perfect.

"I don't think dancing will pan out tonight. It looks like it's about to start raining. I can feel the electricity in the air," she commented. I looked out the window. She was right. The sky was darkening and clouds moving furiously. By the time we got onto the Andrew's property it had started to drizzle.

Ethan's car was parked in the front, not in the garage as usual. Odd. Did he stop home really quick to grab something before leaving again? Maybe he had to pull it out of the garage because Cleo was in labor. Why didn't they call if something was wrong? Would they call, or just go and call at the hospital?

I leapt out of the car and despite my heels I ran towards the door. Was I panicking for nothing? Something in my gut told me I wasn't. Something felt off. I knocked, no, pounded on the door and when I received no answer tried the knob. It opened, making my nerves even worse. They always locked the door.

Dita came up behind me.

"Renee, what is up with you?"

"Something is off. I can feel it," I said, walking inside.

The house was silent. Too silent. I called out for someone.

"Hello? Ethan, Cleo, Tabatha?"

Silence. Dita walked in further and called as well. Finally, Ethan's office door opened and Cleo rushed out. She looked up at us in surprise and when her eyes fell to me, she glared and pushed past us. What the hell? I looked in to the office and saw Ethan sitting on the edge of his desk, arms crossed, head down.

"What's wrong?" I asked. Dita mumbled that she was going to see what was wrong with Cleo. Nodding to her, I went to talk to her husband.

He sighed when he looked up at me. Shaking his head, he rubbed his mouth and chuckled a dark, empty laugh came out.

"Someone leaked a video of us at the bar."

It took me a moment to understand and comprehend what he said. I stared at him blankly before his words sank in. My eyes grew wide with realization and my guilt came over me like a tsunami. I could tell Ethan had already been hit at well.

"How? I thought you weren't supposed to record," I said, crossing my arms. He stood up and went to the door, shutting it softly. It clicked into place, the quiet of the room making it echo.

"I called the owner and they've already found the culprit. A regular had brought their friend and now both of them have been banned. This has never happened before. They recorded the whole show and then somehow it got leaked and eventually sent to Cleo's email. Fuuuuck——" he groaned, stretching out the word.

"Who all has seen it? Did they just edit ours together or

something? How bad is it?" I shot at him and before he could answer me, my phone rang inside my purse.

It was like a bucket of ice had been dumped on me. Mark.

Ethan and I looked at my vibrating bag and then back at each other. Gulping I took it out and saw that, to my relief, it was Derek. Answering it, I tried to be chipper and not give away anything.

"Hello?"

"Renee? Mark's seen the video. We had just made it off the highway and then got stopped again. He got out of the car. He's walking. I have no idea where he's at or going."

"Well aren't you going to go after him?" I demanded. Panic and fear started moving in. Mark couldn't walk all the way home. There were too many crazy people out there. He didn't carry any sort of weapon. There was nothing to defend himself. That and the weather. It was raining. I doubted he had a coat. He'd freeze.

"I'm in a wheelchair, thank you very much. Adrian went but then came back after about five minutes. You know Mark, he's gonna do what he's gonna do."

Thanking him for calling, I calmed myself and hung up. I explained the situation to Ethan who gave me a look that said, 'what are we supposed to do about both of our spouses?'

Suddenly feeling drained I plopped down into one of his chairs and brushed my hair back.

"What did Cleo have to say about it?"

"She's hurt. She tries really hard for everyone to like her and it feels like a slap in the face."

"I have no idea what Mark is thinking right now. God," I groaned, closing my eyes. This was a disaster.

We heard a door slam and both of our eyes darted towards the closed office. Ethan leapt up and tore the door open, running out to see who had come or gone. I joined him and we bumped into Dita. She looked exasperated.

"Cleo left. I couldn't really stop her. I've never seen her this upset before."

Ethan pushed past her and sprinted to the front door. Opening it, he swore.

"She's gone. Dammit Dita!"

She flinched and apologized. I put my hand on her shoulder.

"It's our fault not yours. Come on,"

"Are we going to follow her? She peeled out pretty quick, she's probably already too far to find her."

Ethan joined us as we piled into her car.

"Maybe we'll get lucky and she'll find Mark. Two birds, one stone," she commented, starting the car and leaving the premises. I exchanged glances with Ethan.

"If we find them both together, it will be more like walking right into a war zone."

A war we started. I wish I could say unknowingly, but despite the club's rules, there was always a chance this could get out. At the time though, I didn't care. I needed that release. I glanced at Ethan again and he gave me a half-hearted, exhausted smile. I'm sure it was exhausting being married to Cleo. Well, either of them actually.

Ethan and Cleo were so alike it made sense that they'd be together. However, it constantly caused problems between the two. Both were so used to being in charge, being the frontmen of their bands. It was difficult for either of them to let the other take the reins. I gave Ethan a small, hopefully reassuring smile back, and returned my eyes to the road. We had to find one of them. I just couldn't decide which one I wanted to face first.

After an hour of driving around with no sign of either spouse Ethan growled with frustration. The rain had turned from a drizzle to a downpour. We could hear thunder from time to time. The thought of Mark or Cleo out there was making everyone in the car even more stressed.

"This is getting us nowhere. Dita, pull over. I'm getting out. I need to take a walk," Ethan said.

Before she could fully stop, he opened his door and hopped out. We called after him, but he ignored us. Dita asked me what I wanted to do. I thought for a moment and then told her to take us to Adrian's.

Sure enough, even though Adrian's vehicle was missing, hers was in the parking lot of the apartment complex. I got out and told Dita that she could take off and I'd get a ride from Cleo. She was hesitant, but eventually left. I pulled my spare key out and ran up the stairs to their place.

The apartment was quiet. I debated calling out, but something told me not to. I closed the front door as softly as I could and walked carefully to where I had a feeling she'd be.

Sure enough, she was huddled up in a ball on Adrian and Chase's bed. She was clutching a pillow and crying. It must be Adrian's side. I shifted and the floor creaked. She turned slightly.

"Adrian?"

Her voice was small and desperate. The guilt came back full force. I was the reason she was crying. I crossed my arms and walked into the room. She recognized me and struggled to sit up. She glared at me.

"What are you doing here? Shouldn't you be telling complete strangers how much you don't want the baby?" She spat at me. I flinched.

"That's not what I said," I murmured. She rolled her eyes as she tried to wipe the tears off her face.

"You might as well have. If you didn't want a baby, why did you ask for this?" She pointed to her belly angrily.

"Mark wanted it. He wanted a child. I told him over and over I was okay with it. He wouldn't listen. Cleo, that- speech wasn't about you. I was just really upset and needed someone who wasn't in our group to listen."

"So, you choose my husband?"

"He actually took me there. Cleo, I don't know how to explain to you-"

She cut me off.

"It's so humiliating. Once again, I'm the butt of the joke. I can never be enough for anybody. I give, give, give, but all you can think is about how inconvenient it all is. I just wanted you to finally like me, but even this isn't enough!" She burst into sobs again, falling back onto the bed.

I stopped trying to make excuses. She worried that I didn't like her? Of course I liked her. It was me that had to worry.

"Why do you think I don't like you?"

"Oh, come on. I know my relationship with the guys makes everyone upset. I've never had a girl not hate me. Even Chase didn't like me for a bit!"

"Not me. Well, not hate. Scared of you, sure. Never hate. Once I met you, I realized that Mark was being way over dramatic. Cleo, you have never done anything wrong. That video- those words- that was my issues. Not yours. I should have talked to Mark about them, I'll admit. I shouldn't have let them bottle up. It's hard though, when he is so excited about her and I'm not at that level yet."

"Then what level are you at?" Mark's voice made us turn towards the door. I stood up and froze. He was soaking wet. His long hair was plastered to his face. He was holding a sopping wet shirt in his hands. Beads of rainwater dripped from his hair to bare, tattooed chest. I gulped. He looked furious. Despite the freezing rain, he was still blazing with anger.

"Cleo, Ethan is downstairs. Go home."

I turned to help her up. We looked at each other and Cleo suddenly wrapped her arms around me.

"I'm sorry. I didn't know. We'll talk later, okay?" She whispered. I nodded and hugged her back. Mark moved aside to let her leave. He glared at me, unmoving, until we heard the click of the door shutting. I gulped. I was not ready for this argument. I didn't want this argument.

"Mark, let me explain-" I tried to start but he held up his empty hand.

"You didn't want Tot?" His voice cracking at our daughter's nickname. A tear came out of nowhere and slid down my face.

"It's not that I didn't want her, it's that I was okay without her. It felt like you were forcing me to do this. Kids don't make a family. We were a family before her," I defended. He scoffed.

"See, that's what I'm talking about. You couldn't get the idea out of your head. We needed a baby. YOU needed a baby. I told you I was fine!"

"I wanted to give you everything you deserved!" He cried. "This was all for you. Renee, when I convinced you to leave the troupe and marry me, I promised you I'd give you the world. How could I not give you something as simple as a kid? How do you not see that?" His bottom lip trembled.

I broke the gap between us and went to him, pressing my dry body against his soaking wet one. He tensed his entire body. I rested my head on his chest, right over his heart.

"I went with you for more than grand promises. I was madly in love with you without you having to try so hard."

His body softened ever so slightly.

"I just want to make you happy."

"You do make me happy. Just you. Not the house, the clothes, the cars. I didn't need all of this. I still don't. If you tell me tomorrow you're quitting music and want me to get a job, I will. If you want to pick up exotic art collecting you know sure as hell I'll pick up the bill. This doesn't have to be so one-sided. Let me take some of this off you."

I looked up at him and he gulped. Silent tears were streaming from his grey eyes. With only light from the other room behind him they almost looked silver.

"I am supposed to provide for you. That's my job," he whispered.

"I never asked for that. I only want you… and our daughter," I said. My voice was hesitant, yet I was never so sure of anything in my life.

I pulled away from him and his arms instantly shot out to pull me back to him.

"Are you sure? Because if you don't really want this then I suppose I can ride this parent thing solo you don't have to stay-" his words were rushed, panicked, and he was stumbling over them. I leaned up and crushed my lips to his. His lips matched my urgency.

"I promised to be here no matter what. I'm not going anywhere. She wasn't created for you, or for me. She was made for us."

His eyes shone with tears trying to stay put. He pressed his lips tightly and nodded. I kissed his cheek tenderly and he squeezed me tightly. Leaning down, he kissed my lips and then my neck. His hands slid down to my bottom and groaned.

"You look so Goddamn good in that dress," he murmured as he sucked lightly on my ear. I gasped and felt my body react. I needed his body on mine. He dropped the sopping wet shirt on the floor and I kicked it out of my way as he gently pushed me backwards onto his best friends bed.

I commented on it and he growled.

"They aren't here, who cares? I won't tell anyone," he whispered as he lifted my legs up and slipped off my panties. He kissed and sucked on my body as he got me completely naked. I closed my eyes and soaked in the attention. These times when it was only the two of us was rare and I needed to savor every second.

When I opened my eyes, I found him now also naked and climbing over me. I shifted to let him take me. He gave me a long, sweet kiss that told me he needed me as much as I needed him. All the tension left my body as he took me. I was unable to focus on anything but what his body was doing to mine.

Quickly we found our rhythm and all of the outside distractions disappeared as pleasure flooded through my body. I cried out as my passion overcame me and he gasped, releasing himself as well. I closed my eyes and let the ecstasy take over me. Just as my body was beginning to relax and Mark began moving off of me, we heard someone swearing.

"Not cool guys!" Adrian shouted.

Mark chuckled and I screamed, scrambling for something to cover up with. Mark reached down unashamedly and grabbed his wet clothes. Frowning he looked towards the open door.

"Hey, can I borrow some clothes?"

"Sure, you've already used my bed. Want my toothbrush too?"

"That'd be great, thanks."

I rolled my eyes at the friends teasing. He went to their closet as I slipped my dress back on. I couldn't find my underwear to save my life. I moaned to my husband as he slipped on grey sweats and black shirt.

"Eh, it'll be fine. I'm sure Chase will find it funny."

When we finally excited the bedroom, we were greeted by four people staring at us. Two looked amused, two very much did not. I noticed that Derek and Dita were dressed regularly and rather dry, while the Wilson's were still in damp suits.

"I cannot wait until the next time we are at your place. Oh, the dirty things we are gonna do," Adrian threatened.

"Believe me, this isn't the worst thing you could have walked in on." We sat down on the couch with them and looked around.

"Where's Andrews and Cleo?"

"They went home. Probably still fighting. I'm sure one of them will call soon," Adrian sighed.

Sure enough, his phone started ringing. Raising his eyebrows, he picked up his phone and answered the phone with an exaggerated greeting.

"Hello!"

A female voice spoke from the other side. He listened for a long moment, nodding, even though she couldn't see him.

"Alright, alright. Calm down. Someone will come get you. No big deal. See you soon."

He hung up and looked around the room. Everyone looked away from his stares.

"Seriously? No takers?"

There was a long pause before Derek spoke up.

"It's raining."

"Oh, a little rain never hurt anyone," he argued. Derek smirked.

"It never rains in Los Angeles. I'm not prepared for this!"

The room erupted in laughter and then I remembered that we had promised to talk after all of this. Despite wanting to stay close to my husband after what we had just done in the bedroom, I lifted my hand.

"I'll go. We should probably talk too," I said. Adrian shrugged and tossed me his keys.

"Don't take too long. We have to get Rocky by two," he told me. I looked around for a clock.

"What time is it now?"

"Around midnight," Chase said. Holy cow. Time flies. I promised him we wouldn't be long and left to go get her.

The storm was still raging outside. I braced myself and ran towards the car, stumbling slightly with the heels. I was grateful in that moment for the years of training in stage shoes.

I hopped into the car and tried my best to contain the wetness to as small an area as possible. Driving to their house took almost twice as long as usual. It was hard to see more than five feet in front of the car. Derek was right, I wasn't used to driving in this kind of weather. It had been a while.

I pulled up and before I could even get out Cleo was storming out of her house, slamming the door behind her. I unlocked the door and assisted her in climbing into the passenger seat. She crossed her arms in a pout and then let out what I could only describe as a wail.

I drove off the property and let her cry until they turned into merely sniffles.

"I don't even know why I'm crying anymore," she said. I glanced over at her. I had taken to just mindlessly driving. I glanced at the clock. We still had a solid hour before we were due back at Adrian's.

"Like your hormones or…" I trailed off, not really knowing what she was trying to explain. She shook her head.

"No, I mean, I don't know. It's so hard. Ethan. He's so amazing and he's constantly telling me I'm good and enough for him and all this other stuff but it's hard to believe him. Just look at him!" She choked a back a sob.

"He started a fuckin' charity! He's helped so many people and touched so many lives with his music. What have I done?"

I found a safe place to park in the weather and stopped the car. I unbuckled my seat and turned my body to look at her.

"Are you serious right now? You literally helped create a baby for someone else. You are doing all the work just to hand her off the day you have her. People are constantly coming up to Mark and the others telling them how much your songs affected them. He gets letters from suicide survivors, talking about how your voice stopped them. Your songs, your words. Cleo, you can't think like this. I don't know who is telling you otherwise, but you are an amazing woman. Who is telling you this stuff?"

She shook her head and began wiping the tears from her face.

"It was a part of the email I got this afternoon," she said. Seeing the confusion on my face she pulled out her cell phone and pulled up the email. Clicking on something she handed me the phone.

It was a video. I watched as someone had scanned around the bar, muffling the sound of the person on stage. They had over-layed their own voice, but had used a voice changer to make them unrecognizable.

"He's got it all. Gorgeous wife, beautiful children, millions of dollars, successful career. Yet, there's always something that isn't just right in that picture-perfect story. Why don't we see what, or rather who, is the problem?"

Then we see Ethan walk on stage and do his speech. I shook my head, stopping the video. She sniffled as she took her phone back.

"They keep going. It's horrible."

"I'm sure it's going to be leaked to the media soon," I muttered. I leaned over and hugged her tightly; repeating that she was enough.

I pulled away and started the car back up.

"We've got some time, anywhere you want to go before we head to give the car back?"

She thought for a moment and then giggled.

"You know how long it's been since I've been to a bar?" I gave her a side eye and she rolled her eyes, patting her tummy.

"Of course, I won't have any alcohol. But I can have a Shirley temple and enjoy the ambiance."

Sighing, I found the closest bar and pulled into the parking lot. Just as we were stepping out of the car, I noticed a familiar vehicle that made me stop short. A yellow jaguar was parked near the door. It couldn't be the same one. The odds of that were- I didn't even know. Before I could react or think three people stumbled out of the bar, giggling and screaming at each other.

I groaned, recognizing them all instantly. Confusion fell over me. Why would Holly be with Duchess and Christopher?

Cleo hadn't seen them yet, but when she looked up, she let out a yelp. The rain was finally slowing to a steady downpour. Either we went inside or got back in the car, I didn't care I just didn't enjoy being drenched. I turned to tell Cleo this when the trio started screaming louder.

"You can't just come to my work and harass me! You know how hard it was to get this job? And the bouncer kicking you out, Chris, you can't keep showing up like this, embarrassing me?"

"Oh, you are embarrassed by me?"

"Well when you show up completely drunk with your girl-friend, yes, you embarrass your wife!"

"Good God, is she always like this? Such a downer!" Duchess exclaimed. She seemed just as belligerent as Christopher was.

"I am so sick of everyone acting like they are so much better than me," Chris said, than motioned from himself to the pop diva.

"Me and you both. Who do they think they are?"

I knew suddenly that it was time to go. I grabbed Cleo's elbow and urged her back, but she was frozen to the spot. Chris looked around the parking lot and his eyes settled on us. He squinted, then his eyes grew big with recognition. He smiled wide and sauntered or rather, stumbled, over to us. I kept my hand on her arm.

"Well, well, well, look who it is. Can't get enough of me, eh? I knew it. I always knew you'd end up coming back." He looked down at her bulging belly and tipped an imaginary hat at her.

"Congrats, by the way. On being pregnant with another kid that's not your husband's. Old habits, huh?" He hiccuped then began laughing. Duchess stormed over, followed by a swearing Holly.

"Can't you just leave us alone?" She whined. Grabbing Chris, she tried to pull him towards her car. "Come on."

He ripped his arm away and moved closer to Cleo. I tried to pull her, but she was standing firm. Her eyes were wild with fear.

Holly crossed her arms from behind the drunk couple and smirked.

"How did you like the little video I sent you? It's a little hard seeing the guy that kisses the ground you walk on talk shit about you, huh?" She looked at her husband and her eyes grew shiny. "Hurts, don't it?" Her voice cracked.

Holly's revelation told me that this was not going to get any better. I told Cleo to get in the car, and finally she snapped out of her trance. I think it was just a moment too late.

Chapter Eighteen

MEMORIES

WE SCRAMBLED into the car and as soon as I saw she was buckled in, I pulled out. I looked back and saw Chris and Duchess howling with laughter. Holly tried to grab the keys from him, but he pushed her away.

Of course, we were stuck behind some people trying to leave as well. I sighed, fighting the urge to lay on the horn. My nerves were wrecked. I felt like my stomach was about to empty all over Adrian's car.

I tried my hardest not to watch the scene behind us, but the long wait made it hard not to. I saw that next to me Cleo was watching as well.

Duchess got into the passenger's seat. Holly and Chris continued to fight outside the car. He grabbed her wrist and she tried to pull away. He was stronger than her and with one swift movement, shoved her in the back seat. I hadn't even realized you could fit a person in the back. He spat something at her and hopped into the driver's seat, slamming the door. Oh my God.

"Did you just see that?" Cleo said, her voice worried. I nodded, gulping.

"He's too drunk! He can't drive like that. Can we follow him?" I stared at her incredulously.

"Why? We need to get away from here, from them, as fast as possible. Whatever they do is on them," I snapped and as soon as the traffic started moving, I floored it.

I got on the road and sped off, trying to get as much distance between us and the yellow jaguar. The damn rain was forcing me to slow my speed. Within five minutes I saw the sports car trailing us. My heart stopped. How fast was he going? Before I could voice my concerns, he was right behind us. Cleo squeaked and I tried to calm her. Between the slick roads and the drunk behind us, I couldn't spare any extra attention on her.

"It's alright. He's just being stupid. He'll get bored. I'm slowing down. He'll just pass us eventually," I said, trying to keep my voice steady. If I believed it, she would. But he didn't.

I got down to 30 miles an hour when he tapped us. We jostled. The entire car shook with the impact. Oh, fuck. Adrian was going to kill us. Cleo started whimpering.

"Call one of the guys. Tell them to meet us at Lai's. It's not too far from here," I told her. It was the only place that came to mind, and it was twenty minutes away. Shit, why didn't I say someplace closer? My mind was too scrambled to think straight.

He tapped us again, so I put my foot on the gas to try to get out of his space. That just spurred him on. With every tick I made on the speedometer he matched me. His movements were shaky, and he was all over the road. He was going to crash. I prayed silently that he didn't hit anyone. That he didn't hit us.

Cleo pushed the buttons and put her phone to her ear. Her voice was shaky. "Chris?" She said into the phone and I almost laid on the break. Why would she call him? He's drunk and driving. What would calling him solve? That would only make it worse.

There was female laughing on the other end of the line. Cleo's lips shook as she talked to Duchess.

"Just put it on speaker. I need to talk to him." There was a pause and then Duchess must have done so because Cleo started talking.

"Chris, I know we have a long history. I wasn't the greatest wife and I should have told you about the twins. But you need to let this go," her voice was desperate as she pleaded for him to stop.

"Please, stop all of this. Someone is going to get seriously hurt."

You could hear Chris shouting something and Cleo sighed deeply, realizing her final plea was getting us all nowhere.

"Goodbye Christopher." She hung up the phone and took a few deep breaths but that didn't stop her tears. I repeated as calmly as I could that she needed to call someone that could actually help us.

He crashed into us again, this time just a little harder. I let out a small scream and clamped my mouth shut. If I lost my composure, then we were all screwed. I felt a tear slide down my face, but I refused to react to it. Instead I tightened my grip on the wheel and focused on the road. Cleo held her phone up to her face again as she called someone else.

"E-E-Ethan? I don't know how it happened. Chris is drunk and following us. We can't stop. He's already hit us twice. Renee is going to get us to Lai's where we'll be safe. We need help," she started crying. It wasn't wails, or sobs. It was the crying you did when you were terrified of what was going to happen. Her cries made the panic in me worse. This was serious. I couldn't keep this speed up much longer. The rain had picked up again. I needed to make a decision and quick.

I saw a turn coming up, so I moved to take it. Chris must

have seen what I was doing because he sped up to cut me off and instead our cars completely collided.

Everything came crashing down- or in- or together. The jaguar hit us hard, pushing us off the road and into a guardrail. I slammed on the brakes, but the car was beyond my control now. The sound of glass shattering and metal crunching surrounded us. I closed my eyes when I realized the car was rolling.

It happened so fast. We returned back upright but everything felt tight and I knew the car was totaled. Cleo screamed as her head hit her side window. I watched in horror as the seatbelt locked and tightened on her chest. Her head and neck bounced back in a grotesque movement.

My head had hit the something as well and everything flashed white. I blinked, but the ringing in my ears made it hard to concentrate on what was going on around me. I had to get her out of the car.

My entire body felt like I had been punched over and over, but I managed to unlock both of our seatbelts. I glanced at the rear-view mirror but it was smashed into so many pieces. I couldn't really see out of it. All I could make out was bits and pieces of the totaled yellow car.

I could faintly hear sirens and I tried to open my door, but my arms didn't have the strength. I could feel my body draining and as I saw the lights of a police car, I shut my eyes. That's when I heard the screams.

I woke up to the sound of two men fighting. I struggled to open my eyes, only to find Ethan holding my husband up by the neck against the wall. Where was I?

I looked around, lifted my hands, and sat up. It was bright in here. Bright and white. I was in a hospital bed. I had an IV in my hand and was covered in a blanket and hospital gown. Suddenly, my last memories came flooding back and I set into panic. Cleo. Chris, Duchess, Holly. What had happened?

My eyes shot back to the two men in front of me. Mark looked exhausted, and as if he had been crying. Ethan looked furious, and his eyes were red as well. The veins in his neck were bulging as he held onto my husband.

Mark wasn't fighting the assault. If he did, he'd easily overpower Ethan. Ethan, although very toned, was slim. Mark was all muscle.

"This is all your fault. You just had to ask her. Knowing she'd do it. You knew the risks and yet you still had to ask for one last small favor. Now look!" He shouted in Mark's face. Mark gulped and closed his eyes. Ethan, disgusted, dropped him to the ground. I watched my husband crumple to the floor like a rumpled shirt.

Adrian and Derek ran into the room and grabbed Ethan before he went for Mark again. They restrained him as he fought their grasps. Eventually he gave up and let his body fall against theirs. I watched this all in silent horror. Why couldn't I speak?

Moving my head, I looked for some water. Thankfully there was a styrofoam cup nearby. I reached for it and all heads turned towards me. My eyes went big and I didn't know who to look at first. Mark was the first to move. He stood up and ran over to me, grabbing my hand.

"Renee, oh my God." His eyes filled with tears and he let them fall freely. I reached up to touch his cheek. My hand, my entire body, felt heavy and sore. I dropped my hand to the blanket and smiled as strongly as I could, but I knew it looked weak. He frowned.

"Aw, the happy couple is reunited," Ethan snarled. All heads turned to him. He was still almost rabid with anger.

Mark stood back up and went to him. He pushed him, making Ethan fall back like he weighed nothing.

"You think I wanted this? I had no idea seven months ago that this would happen? How could I, they are your crazy exes. Why am I getting the blame for this?" He shouted. Ethan's eyes flashed with pain.

"If she wasn't pregnant, she could have defended herself," he argued. Mark scoffed, crossing his arms.

"Like she did all the years she was married to him? Don't put this on me. This is no one's fault other than theirs."

"Eric just got on a flight," Adrian interjected. The fighting men looked over in confusion.

"Chris's brother. He called me. Asking if I had any information. He's coming for the little girl…" his voice trailed off. The room fell deathly silent. I took in his words and tried to understand. Realizing that they all knew something I didn't I was forced to ask.

"What exactly happened?"

Adrian, Mark, and Ethan all looked away guiltily, not saying a word. I looked from one man to the next and when my eyes settled on the man in the wheelchair. He sighed and wheeled himself over to the bed.

He threw a glare back at his friends but then patted my thigh. I grimaced with pain and he apologized.

"Shit, sorry. Uh, well, there was a car accident. Chris plowed right into you guys. You should remember, you were there," he smiled, teasingly. I nodded.

"Yeah, but I passed out soon after the collision. Where is Cleo? What about the other car?"

Derek's eyes started watering and he moved away, shaking his head.

"Nope. I can't do this. Someone else tell her."

Adrian leaned down and wrapped his arms around his shoulder.

"Come on, I gotta go check on Chase and Rocky."

They left the room, leaving Ethan and my husband. Mark rubbed his face roughly. He looked so tired. He hadn't shaved, and his face was looking older.

"Everyone in the other car died." He said finally. It felt like all the air in the room was gone. I couldn't breathe. I had just seen them. They had been laughing, and talking, and- drunk. Except Holly. She had been an unwilling participant in Christopher's games.

"All of them?" I squeaked and he nodded.

"Yeah. Duchess and Chris died on impact. Holly made it to the hospital, but she died about half an hour ago."

I gulped, glancing over at Ethan.

"And Cleo?"

Ethan looked at the floor and then walked out of the room. His boots clicked on the tile with an echoing silence that was almost haunting. Mark bit his lip, trying to figure out how to say it. He came back over to me and sat next to my bed, once again reaching for my hand.

"Remember that fight we had, right before you left to go get her? About you not really wanting the baby, but doing it for me?" His eyes were desperate and watering again. Mine began to match his. The stretching out of what he was trying to explain was making this all so much worse.

"Do you regret it? The baby?" I looked at him and thought about it for a long moment.

"Does it matter?"

Tears began sliding down his face and he squeezed my hand. My face dropped. What happened? He gulped, wetting his lips with his tongue.

"Cleo was rushed into an emergency c-section. She's not doing good. There's a chance we are going to lose them both."

My silent tears turned into full on sobs. I covered my face with my hands, and I heard Mark break down as well. I leaned over to him and he embraced me, holding me as we cried for everything we had lost in the matter of a few hours.

Eventually our sobs turned into short, softer cries. I kept my eyes closed and rested on my husband.

There was a frantic knock on the open door. It was Adrian. We looked up at him and his face was grim.

"You better decide whether you're ready to do this," he said. His voice hard and tight. His hands were shoved into his pockets. Mark sat up straight and wiped his face, looking hopeful.

"Any news?"

"Yeah," Adrian nodded and then his hard face finally cracked. He let a small smile through.

"You have a daughter, and we still have our girl."

They made me use a wheelchair to leave the room. Mark and I moved as fast as we could to meet everyone in the hallway. We were met with the whole gang. Even Tabatha and their three children were here. I looked up at Mark who was just as confused as I was.

"Ethan called and had us get up here just in case they had to say goodbye. Looks like she pulled through," Tabatha smiled. You could tell she and everyone else in the small room had been crying as well. Ethan looked downright broken.

His hair was a complete mess, his face was puffy and tearstained. His body looked like it was slowly deflating. Wait, why was he still here?

"Her and the baby are in recovery. Cleo lost a lot of blood."

"Will she be alright?" I asked quickly.

Chase came over with a babbling Rocky. I smiled and stuck my tongue out at him, causing him to giggle.

"The doctor says it will take time, but they think she'll

make a full recovery. They'll be wheeling them back to her room."

Them.

I looked up at my husband quickly. He understood my sudden look and then burst into laughter. It seemed as if we all had a well of never-ending tears tonight. His sparkled in his eyes.

"It's a girl? We really have a daughter?" He asked to no one in particular. Everyone nodded to him, smiling widely.

"Ten fingers, ten toes, and absolutely no hint of a pen-" Derek started but Dita slapped her hand over his mouth. We all chuckled and got the message.

"When can we see her?" I asked. Chase told us that he was going to go ask. He returned moments later, informing us that Cleo was asleep and the baby was on Oxygen. We couldn't hold her until her oxygen levels were okay. However, before Cleo passed out, she insisted that I got to be the first one to hold her. Me? I wasn't sure if I wanted to see the baby without Cleo there. She was just as much a part of this as we were. I mentioned that to Mark. He leaned down and kissed my forehead.

"I'm sure she doesn't mind. She'll understand. We can see her through the window though," he said pointing up the hall. His reassurance comforted me and my excitement and nervousness returned. We waited eagerly with the rest of the group. Our somber mood turning into one of excitement. Despite the numerous losses that had happened tonight, we decided to look at the positive.

We hurried up the hall and pressed our faces to the window. There were about half a dozen pink and blue bundles in clear tubs. Everyone began reading off the names on the bins in search for ours. Finally, in the very back, hooked up to machines I couldn't fully see, was Baby Lacey.

My heart stopped.

I couldn't see her very well. They had her swaddled and the machines blocked most of her, but there she was. Our baby. Our daughter. Mark squeezed my hand and I looked up to see him staring hard at the tiny box.

The nurses let us stay there for almost half an hour before asking us to move to the family waiting room. I didn't want to go. She hadn't moved, but still, I wanted to watch her forever.

The doctors came and told us that neither Cleo or Baby Lacey would be up for visitation until morning. Everyone looked around the room and I was reminded that I need to go back to my own room to rest. Everyone else minus Ethan decided to leave and return in the morning.

While I slept, Mark stayed by my side. My body was sore. I needed to rest so I could properly take care of my daughter, the nurses reminded me. As soon as I woke up, I asked about her and they said that her oxygen had dipped a little during the night but as long as it stayed where it was now, we could see her at noon.

Slowly everyone began reappearing shortly before lunch. I got out of bed and back in the wheelchair. I felt more sore than I did the night before.

With everyone gathered in my room the conversation moved to Cleo and the accident. Eventually the other victims came up. A somber mood fell over the group once again.

"I feel terrible about them," I said. Mark squeezed my hand and nodded.

"Chris was destined to go out like that. It was a shame he was able to drag others down with him. Maybe they'll all finally find peace."

The memory of Holly fighting him, not wanting to get in the car made me almost cry again. She could have lived. She didn't have to die. I wanted to tell them all, but then a nurse came into the family room and told us that Cleo and baby were ready for guests. I asked them to bring the baby to

Cleo's room so we could all visit together. She nodded and left us.

Ethan shot up and cleared his throat.

"Uh, guys, before we go... Cleo doesn't know about anything. I didn't get the chance to see her when she got here and told them to not tell her if she asked. I don't want to stress her mind or body out more than it is already. Give it a day or so and I will tell her about Chris and the others."

Everyone nodded and murmured various agreements. He had a good point. Mark wheeled me out first and the others followed us out. We piled into the hallway and paused at her door. I giggled, hearing Cleo's voice. It was hoarse, but still uniquely and beautifully hers.

"No, no, no. Leave her there. I want her mom to be the first one to hold her."

Mark and I exchanged a look before he knocked and wheeled me in.

Cleo's face lit up, although her body didn't move.

"How are you feeling? No one would tell me anything," she frowned. As she spoke you could see the exhaustion in her face. She had a cut on her cheek and her lower lip had been stitched up. I shook my head. Even in her state she was still worried about everyone else.

People exchanged glances but said nothing. I forced a smile.

"I'm okay. Super sore, and I've got a concussion, but nothing major. How are you feeling?"

She rolled her eyes. "Well, I've felt better," she said. Everyone chuckled.

"They said my scar is gonna be pretty gnarly. I'm kind of curious," she joked, looking down at her slightly deflated stomach.

"How was it? Were you awake?" Chase asked from where he sat with his family. She shook her head.

"No, I was losing too much blood. I can only imagine how everyone else is looking right now. Are they arresting anyone? Have you seen the cars?" Her voiced cracked and Ethan touched her shoulder, urging her to lay back down. He gave us a desperate look. She was getting too worked up already.

"Yeah, my car's totaled. Thanks. I just got that thing," Adrian let out an exaggerated groan. I noted how he side stepped her questions about the passengers in the other car. Before anyone could avoid any more questions there was a small cry on the other side of her.

My heart stopped. My stomach rolled. Everything froze. That was- her. Our baby. I let out a cry myself and Mark reached for me quickly. I squeezed him tightly, my eyes not leaving the little basket she was in. I couldn't see her from this level, but her fussing was making all the attention in the room go to her.

Cleo smiled weakly.

"She knows you're here." Her words seemed to take everything out of her. She leaned back and let out a deep sigh of pure exhaustion.

I looked up at the tiny woman who created the baby in the bed. She was beautiful. She had just gone through hell. Her hair was a mess, she had scratches all over her face and her makeup had run down her face from hours of crying, but she was beautiful. She gave us the greatest gift anyone could give us.

Mark nudged me. I looked up and he wiggled his eyebrows.

"What do you say? You want to meet her together?"

I squeezed my lips tightly and then nodded quickly. Yeah, yeah I did.

Mark wheeled me over to her little plastic bed. I leaned forward and fell in love.

She was amazing. She was the cutest thing I had ever seen.

She was struggling against the pink blanket wrapped tightly around her. Mark leaned down and kissed my hair.

"She's beautiful," he whispered.

I couldn't stop staring at her to respond to him. I only nodded. He asked me if I was ready for her. I nodded again and he moved to pull her out of her bed.

Instantly she stopped fussing. My tough, buff, and never emotional husband choked as he laughed. He bounced her ever so slightly, cooing at her.

"Hey you, it's nice to meet you. You're a little early but that's alright. We'll take you."

I giggled and realized that my eyes were watering. He looked away and almost begrudgingly leaned down to hand her to me. I moved my arms so he could lay her on me easily.

She fit into my arms perfectly. As if she were meant to be there. I stared down at the miracle child. Our miracle child.

I was suddenly blinded by a deafening snap of a camera. Looking around I saw Derek holding a large camera. He was snapping photos of all of us. I glared at him and he shrugged his shoulders innocently.

"What? Cleo asked me to capture the moment."

Cleo smiled down at Mark and I and closed her eyes.

"She didn't tell you to go buy the most obnoxious camera you could find," Chase teased.

"It's not mine, it's Dita's. Thank you very much," he shot back, clicking and blinding us all more.

The child in my hands started fussing and I looked back down. I reached my hand over and pressed it to her tiny lips. She opened them instinctively and I giggled again. She must be hungry. I voiced my thoughts and Ethan pushed a button, alerting the nurses.

One came and brought me a tiny disposable bottle of formula. Mark took it from her and handed it to me, his hands shaky. I chuckled and commented on it. He smiled down at us and shrugged.

"I don't know, it's all kind of surreal. Sorry, I'll catch up."

I looked back at the tiny, squirming bundle in my hand and as I pressed the nipple to her lips, she opened her mouth wide and began trying her hardest to get it in her mouth.

I watched her eat in awe of her. This little person was a part of me and a part of Mark. I looked back up to Mark and found him staring down at us. His grey eyes showed nothing but love. All remnants of our fight from last night completely gone. None of it mattered anymore.

"You'll get to take her home tomorrow. I've got to stay a few more days, but she can leave sooner," Cleo murmured, keeping her eyes closed.

I searched for any signs that she was upset over this news, but nothing showed on her face. I couldn't imagine carrying a baby for this long and not getting to keep it. This was a big thing, and I didn't want to leave before she was ready.

"Are you sure? We could stay until you are ready to go," I suggested but she shook her head.

"No. I'm fine. Really. I am ready for some relaxing time to myself for a few days. Plus, I'll have tons of time for cuddles when you guys come over. I knew what I was signing up for," she promised, popping one eye open to glance at the baby in my arms.

"Mom, can I see the baby? Is it really a girl?" Jimmy popped up from her nanny's side. Cleo looked towards me for an answer.

"How about once she's done eating, she can be lightly passed around. You can be first if you want," I told her. She beamed and went back to her seat to wait patiently.

When she stopped eating, I positioned her to burp. It was almost instant and the room chuckled. Mark took her from me and coo'd at her as he took her to the eager little girl. She'd been waiting for so long for another little girl in the family. Dallas, Blue, and Rocky looked curiously at the two girls, but otherwise seemed uninterested.

"She's trying to open her eyes!" Jimmy exclaimed from across the room. Attention swung their way.

"She's probably wondering who is who. She's spent the last few months listening to all of us," Adrian mused.

Soon Jimmy was asked to pass her on and once everyone had a quick chance to snuggle with our newest family member the nurse came in and announced that she needed to take her to get her hearing test.

"Mom, Dad, do you want to come?" She looked around the room, unsure of who exactly we were. Mark raised his hand awkwardly and started pushing me out of the room after them. As we were leaving, I heard Cleo ask again about Christopher and Duchess.

Ethan cleared his throat and when I looked back, I saw everyone leaving the room. He was going to tell her. I couldn't even imagine having to do that. Despite being madly, head over heels in love with Ethan, I could still tell that she felt something for Christopher, right until the end. If I could see that, then Ethan had to know that too.

The room in which they were doing the test was small, so Mark went in while I watched from the window. They had to unswaddle her and she started wiggling her arms and legs furiously. She was so pink!

Mark started playing with her feet and the nurse gently but firmly scolded him. He pulled his hand away and looked at me with wide eyes. He lifted his shoulders as if to say, 'this is all new to me'. He was so damn adorable I giggled.

When they were all done, they wrapped her back up and we went back to Cleo's room. Passing by the family waiting room we saw our crew and they followed us back in. One look at Cleo told us that she didn't take the news too well.

The tired woman we had left was now a tiny little girl. She had been silently crying when we walked in. All the while her husband sitting next to her, holding her hand.

She wiped her tears from her face and tried to smile but failed. A few of us went and hugged her or patted her legs. She laughed and sniffled.

"The last words I ever said to him were 'Goodbye'. I knew when I said them that it was the last thing I'd ever say to him. I just didn't realize why that would be-" she choked again and let one last tear slip down her beautiful bruised face.

There was a long moment of silence in respect for Cleo. Finally, she sighed deeply, wiped her tears and straightened.

"Can I hold her now?"

I looked at her blankly. Had she really not had the chance yet? How did we miss her?

"Of course you can!" I exclaimed and looked towards my darling husband, who had been rocking our daughter back and forth in the rocking chair in the corner. He stopped and stood up to bring her over.

Cleo took her carefully and stared down at her.

"She's got your eyes," she said, looking at my husband. "And all that hair. Is it a wig?" She giggled, moving to brush it lightly away from her tender forehead.

"I know, right?" Mark exclaimed.

"That's all Renee." He walked over and embraced me from behind.

"She got the best of both of us."

"We need to get her out of these pink blankets and into some purple ones," Cleo commented. I agreed.

"Purple is much more her color."

She leaned down and kissed her small cheek.

"You are such an amazing miracle little one," she whispered.

Eventually a nurse from my own floor came and scolded

me for staying away so long. Seeing the scene in front of her she softened a bit. Cleo suggested that we take her upstairs with us, since she was all ready to go now. I looked at Mark to see his thoughts and his face lit up excitedly.

"If that's okay with everyone else. Hell yeah!" I thanked Cleo and her lips tightened. This was hard for her, despite her tough front. I asked if she wanted to hold her one more time before we left, and she eagerly took her back into her arms.

Everyone stood and started making excuses to call it a night. Suddenly a nurse came in with a clipboard shaking her head.

"We forgot one major thing. I don't know how that happened. The chaos of everything, I guess. I apologize for that. We need to get the birth certificate finished. Do we have a name?"

The nurse looked over at Mark and I, but we shook our heads and pointed. All of our heads swung towards the woman holding the baby tenderly. She had a look of 'Oops!'

Cleo nodded and gave our daughter another kiss and then positioned her so we could all get a good look of her tiny, round, face.

"Everyone, meet Lovelace."

Everyone in the room grew quiet, taking in the name.

"There's a long explanation but it basically translates to 'outlaw'. How cool is that?" Cleo explained.

"I like it," Derek said from the other side of the room. Everyone else agreed excitedly. I considered it and the more and more I said it in my head the more I started to fall in love with it. It was beautiful, just like her.

"We'll call her Lola for short." Mark smiled at Cleo, then looked down and winked at me. I raised my hands for him to hand me our daughter. He gave me her and I looked down at our newly named child. Lovelace Lacey.

"It's perfect."

Epilogue

ALL THE SMALL THINGS

Three Months Later

I laid in bed with my gorgeous husband after a long day with Lola. He had just climbed into bed and was already snoring. I pinched his nose and covered his mouth for just a moment, jolting him awake.

"What?" He whined.

"Thank you, for taking Lola last night," I kissed him playfully. He smiled and pulled me close to him.

"Of course. Fifty fifty, remember. She's just as much mine as yours."

"That's up for debate. Other than my hair that girl looks and acts just like her daddy," I chuckled.

"Can't really deny that."

Once Lola began to open her eyes more and grow out of her newborn face, we discovered that she almost a clone of Mark. Only much, much, cuter. She had his eyes, his nose, and face structure. Oh, and she liked to make noise. Beau and Bonnie were not fans of that at first, but she grew on them.

Yeah, all babies liked to play. This wasn't new to any of us, but Lola was different. She had to have music, a movie, or some kind of noise playing at all times. She watched her father intensely and soon began mimicking his movements. Now she's constantly banging on every surface she touches. Mark finds it adorable. Everyone else, not so much.

A whole lot happened once we took her home and Cleo was released from the hospital.

Eric, Christopher's brother came and took his daughter back to Michigan. He was her only family left. There was a funeral for the couple, but it was in their home state. Ethan offered to fly Cleo there, but she declined. She had said goodbye that night and was making peace with it.

Duchess' funeral was much more elaborate and, much like the woman, obnoxious. It was a three-day affair, and open to the public. There was a private service for a whopping 3,000 people, but after that she was displayed on a pedestal for an extra day for fans to come pay their respects from a distance.

She was buried in a giant tomb that was then covered from top to bottom with flowers, candles, and other gifts. Ethan was given an invitation to the private service. Cleo stood by his side and fully supported him if he wanted to go. He didn't want to go, but I think guilt over how he treated her over the years drew him to the service.

I think Ethan attending eased his conscience. Especially when it was discovered that all of her money had been designated to go towards his charity. In the will she had written a letter of apology that sounded like a real person. It was beautifully tragic. This was the Duchess that the world never got the chance to meet. Hollywood had created this image of her and in the end, it was her demise.

Cleo admitted to me in private that Ethan cried privately after receiving the letter. He told her this was the Duchess he knew. The one he had once cared for.

"Besides," Mark added, pulling me from my musings.

"That means that I get to sleep uninterrupted tonight completely guilt free. Have fun," he teased, kissing me on the tip of my nose.

As if on cue, the baby monitor lit up and her cry rang out from it. I looked at him and he shook his head. I stuck out my lip in a pout and he shook his head again.

"No!" I gave him one last look and sighing, he sat up and told me to come along. Jumping up, I followed on his tail like an eager puppy. He went into the nursery where our darling daughter fussed. She had already been fed, changed, and put to bed. She must have sensed that her dad was home and hadn't come to see her like he normally did.

"Sorry I missed ya kiddo," he said as he lifted her wiggling body out of her crib. The fussing immediately ceased as she snuggled her head into his shoulder. He took her to the rocking chair. I think the chair was bought originally for me to use, but those two were sitting there way more often than I was. She was a daddy's girl right from the start. It was adorable.

I crossed my arms and leaned against the crib, watching them. He closed his tired eyes and rocked her. He began to sing one of his band's slower songs. It was a sad one. One of my favorites. Mark was never meant to be a vocalist. But when he sang to our daughter, it was the most amazing sound I had ever heard. I think Lola agreed with me, because it only took a few minutes before she fell back asleep.

As we went to our own room, I went to our bathroom and examined the fresh tattoo on my lower abdomen. Earlier that week Cleo and I had gone to Wicked Little Tats and had some new ink added to our bodies.

I looked at the red roses on my hips. The heart in the middle, right above my mound had a banner over it that simply said "Lacey". Behind it were two large drumsticks. Diagonally, Moira, my artist, had placed two sparrows as well. One on the top left of the design, and the other on the bottom right. One for Mark, the other for Lola. It was perfect.

Cleo's tattoo blew mine out of the water. The detail Toddy put into it was amazing. It was a magnificent piece. I was thoroughly impressed. It was perfect for Cleo. She covered her c-section scar with a blue dragon, looking fierce and peaceful all at the same time. Its body was wrapped around a light purple egg.

"Just because the scar is covered doesn't mean I want to forget what I did. Lola's story is part of mine," she explained.

Mark came up behind me and offered to lotion the area. He wiggled his eyebrows suggestively, given the location of the tattoo. He kissed my cheek and left me to do it myself.

"Those pictures finally came in. I went and got frames for them if you want to hang them up tonight," Mark said from the bedroom.

"The maternity ones or the ones from the hospital?" I returned to our room to find him already in bed with his laptop open. I climbed back in with him and turned to look at him.

"Both," he said, looking guiltily away.

"I forgot to send them in to get printed. I only did it about a week ago," he revealed. I rolled my eyes but chuckled.

"I wondered why we still hadn't come in. That sounds great. Let's do it now,"

I glanced at his computer screen and saw that he was searching for kid's drum kits. I rolled my eyes and chuckled.

"She can barely hold a stick," I teased, and he grinned excitedly.

"I know. I just want to have them here for when she's ready. She's gonna be a natural."

"Her and Jimmy are going to be amazing."

"I can't wait. All of our kids following in our footsteps. It's every parent's dream."

I smiled, but my mood kind of sank. Would Lola get anything from me?

"She cried every time you left the room today," he mentioned, closing the laptop. Oddly enough, that perked me up some.

"Really?" He nodded.

"Yep. Definitely a momma's girl. She was not happy when you left. I tried everything but the only time she really calmed down was when she napped, ate, or you came back."

I hadn't even noticed. Guilt over being jealous of their bond washed over me. I pushed those thoughts away and smiled.

"Come on, let's get the photos up." I climbed out of bed and extended my hand and he took it, following me out of the room and to the nursery.

I glanced over at the crib, thankful that Lola was a heavy sleeper.

Mark went to work putting them on the walls. We had a dozen pictures hung in less than ten minutes. I held the last one in my hands and had him set it right above her crib.

Only when the last photo was hung did she finally begin to fuss. I glanced at the clock and saw it was about time for a bottle. I went down to the kitchen and when I returned, I found Mark rocking her slowly, trying to keep her calm.

He handed her to me and I took her to the chair to eat. He sat by my feet and waited quietly for her to finish her late night meal. She fussed a little after her burp, but eventually she went back to sleep. Mark wanted to stay in her room for a bit just to make sure she was down for the count.

He was so different, now that he was a father. He was still the adorably hot goof I had married, but now- now he was a protector. His goals were less band oriented and more family geared. He still wanted to tour and make music, but now he wanted to make sure we could join him whenever possible and that we had proper security when he was gone.

I hadn't decided if I was going to bring Lola to any shows this tour, but we'd definitely catch him post show for dinner or a night at a hotel. I would miss him just as much as he missed us.

He sat in the rocking chair and patted his thigh. I came and joined him, snuggling close.

"It's kind of amazing, isn't it?"

I turned my head to look at him. He had a soft smile on his face.

"What's that?"

"I was a dumb kid with friends who were just as dumb as me. We had no money, no education, just a dream. Of course, we all wanted to get big, but to actually make it happen," he whistled ever so softly.

"If we didn't make it as musicians, or if I didn't have great friends, we wouldn't have her," he said looking at the crib.

"That's a lot of if's," I said, running my hands through his hair.

"I'd like to think I'd still have you though," he grinned, kissing me.

"I was never interested in any of those if's and you still got me."

His face darkened for a moment, and I realized what I said. How he took it.

"I didn't mean it like that."

"Do you ever miss when it was just me and you?" He asked, after a long pause.

"Yes. But I also know that this is always how we were meant to be. A family of three. It wouldn't have been right without her."

"I was terrified. The day she was born," he said. I stared blankly at him until he explained.

"I got a phone call from Ethan and then we got to the hospital and were told that there were two dead, three unresponsive, and they couldn't tell us who was who. It felt like in quick sentence I had just lost everyone I've ever loved. I was looking forward to going on this journey with you and Lola, and then for a moment, you were both gone."

I hugged him tighter and he nestled his head against my cheek.

"It made me see all those little moments I wasted not being here with you. I was always so focused on everything else, and when that was all I had left, I realized that none of it was worth it without you. I sat in that chair, thinking about all the moments I missed out on. I don't want to ever feel like that again. I cherish every moment I have with you now," he finished.

I said nothing but kissed him again. My eyes filled with tears that didn't need to fall. We had both cried enough these last few months for a lifetime.

"You are a beautiful mess," I chuckled.

"Only for you, baby."

He groaned and lifted me up. I swatted for him to set me down. I took his hands as we went to the crib one last time. We looked at our sleeping daughter. She looked so peaceful, yet, you could see the storm brewing inside of her. That was her daddy's gift hiding, just waiting to be set free.

He bumped my shoulder with his and motioned to the picture that hung above her on the wall.

"Are you sure that's the photo you want there?"

I looked up. Inside the simple pink frame held a black and white photo of me and Cleo holding her bulging belly. I nodded.

"Yeah. It's important to me," I told him. We walked out of her room and as I closed her door softly, I turned to him.

"We will cherish all moments in this house, especially the ones that brought us together."

Acknowledgments

As always, Kristen Downer, my editor and open ear when I need to complain. You always know how to calm me down and help me to stop stressing over things that don't matter. My cover artist, Frinaart. Seriously, the kindest, most patient soul I swear. My formatter Caroline Andrus, thank you thank you thank you. Seth McClain bought was my final sale that allowed me to publish this book, so here is your shoutout. Whoo! Finally, last but not least, my reader group. Dolls, you rock. Your kind words are what motivates me to keep going. Without you, I probably would have given up a while ago. Thank you.

About the Author

With her dark eyeliner, My Chemical Romance tattoo, and the Twilight series still proudly displayed on her bookshelf, Tylor Paige is punk rock kid. A sucker for a good love triangle and second chances, she knew the wonderful world of romance writing was where she was meant to be.

When she's not writing, Tylor enjoys watching cult films, procrastinating on twitter, and searching for the next book to add to her ever growing collection. She writes for the readers who love, obsess, and collect, like her. Her ultimate dream is for people to write fanfiction about her stories and characters. Perhaps she'll inspire someone to write their own book boyfriend.

Find me on:
Tylorpaigebooks.com

Twitter: @TylorPaige
Instagram: @tylorpaige
Facebook: Author Tylor Paige

And join my reader group!
www.facebook.com/groups/376190999768893

facebook.com/tylorpaigeauthor

twitter.com/TylorPaige